D0528572

Also by Natalya Lowndes

CHEKAGO

Angel in the Su

Angel in the Sun

NATALYA LOWNDES

And I saw an angel standing in the sun; and he cried with a loud voice, saying to all the fowls that fly in the midst of heaven, Come and gather yourselves together unto the supper of the great God;

That ye may eat the flesh of kings, and the flesh of captains, and the flesh of mighty men, and the flesh of horses, and of them that sit on them, and the flesh of all men, both free and bond, both small and great.

Revelation xix:17–18

Hodder & Stoughton

LONDON SYDNEY AUCKLAND TORONTO

British Library Cataloguing in Publication Data

Lowndes, Natalya
  Angel in the sun.
  I. Title
823'.914[F]

ISBN 0-340-50697-0

First published in Great Britain 1989

Published by Hodder and Stoughton,
a division of Hodder and Stoughton Ltd,
Mill Road, Dunton Green, Sevenoaks, Kent TN13 2YA
Editorial Office: 47 Bedford Square, London WC1B 3DP

Photoset by Rowland Phototypesetting Ltd,
Bury St Edmunds, Suffolk

Printed in Great Britain by St Edmundsbury Press Ltd,
Bury St Edmunds, Suffolk

СЫН МОЙ
О КТО ДАЛ БЫ МНЕ УМЕРЕТЬ ВМЕСТО ТЕБЯ
СЫН МОЙ СЫН МОЙ

CONTENTS

LIST OF CHARACTERS

IMPERIAL ARMY: Last Postings South-Western Front, 1917

The young man: Valerian Isayevich (surname unknown)
    Gunner, 92nd Forward Battery, II Guards Corps, Seventh Army

The huntsman: Vladimir Ivanovich Belyakov (Vlady)
    Same rank and unit

The husband: Konstantin Maksimovich, Graf Alekseyev (Kostya)
    Major, Izmailovskii Guards; attached HQ Staff, Seventh Army

The lover: Martin Aleksandrovich Kabalyevskii
    Major, Cavalry Regt (Empress Marya Fyodorovna's Own); attached
    Fifth Army

The lieutenants:
  Schmidt (Hermann)
    5th Finnish Rifle Division, XXII Corps, Eleventh Army
  Titus
    2nd Siberian Rifle Division, Tenth Army
  Solomon
    607th Mlynovskii Regt, VI Grenadier Division, Eleventh Army
  Makar
    2nd Caucasus Grenadier Division, Tenth Army
  Osip
    3rd Grenadier Division, XXV Corps, Eleventh Army
  Vissarion
    12th Siberian Rifle Division, Seventh Army

The turncoat: Anton Ivanovich (surname unknown), a Slovene who tries
to betray Valerian
    QM sergeant, 210th Infantry Regt, XVI Corps, Third Army

RED ARMY

The captain: Aleksei (other names unknown)
    formerly Pavlovskii Guards on attachment to Brigade HQ, I Guards
    Corps, Eleventh Army

The corporal: Pavel Aleksandrovich Myelnikov
    formerly Moskovskii Regt, I Guards Corps, Eleventh Army

The sergeant: Filip Semyonovich Volkov
    formerly 707th Nezhavskii Regt, XXXI Corps, Special Army
The mulemaster: Viktor
    formerly NCO Mikhailovskii Mountain Battery
The Cossack: Igor
    formerly 5th Caucasian Cossack Horse Artillery
The Kalmuk: Hadzhii
    formerly 1st Turkestan Division, Special Army
The fuseboy: Mischa
    formerly of Volkov's Company

CIVILIANS
The countess: Natalya Igoryevna, Grafinya Alekseyeva
    (known to her family and close friends as Loulou), wife of Kostya
The dwarf: Yakob Pavlovich Rubin
    (Yasha), son of Jewish factor on Alekseyev estate
Dushan: Czech hanger-on, abortionist and pimp; old friend of Loulou's
    father
The family:
    Prince Dmitri and Princess Laskorin (Mimi)
    Apollonya Dmitryevna Laskorina (Polly)
    Her sisters Millie and Lola, and brother Petya
The nurse: Frossya
The gipsy: Pelagya, originally from Alekseyev estate
The women: Peasants from Laskorin estate villages:
    Matryona
    Masha, her daughter
    Old Marya
    Dunya
    Katya
    Asya
The girls: Debbie and Becky, sisters befriended by Valerian
The boys and old men:
    Fedya
    Yefim
    Gerasim, an old servant of Laskorin's
    Georgii Ivanov, lame brother of Makar

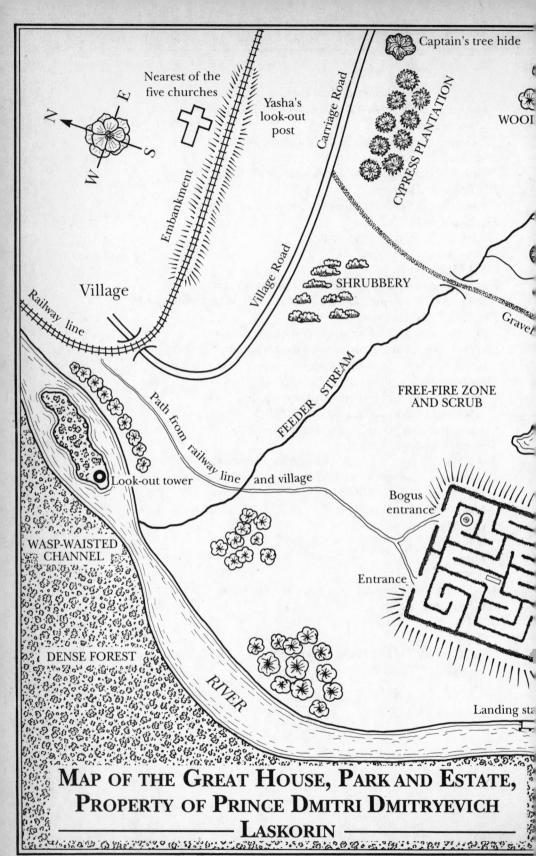

Captain's tree hide

Nearest of the five churches

Yasha's look-out post

Carriage Road

CYPRESS PLANTATION

WOO...

N E S W

Embankment

Village Road

SHRUBBERY

Railway line

Village

FEEDER STREAM

FREE-FIRE ZONE AND SCRUB

Grave...

Path from railway line and village

Look-out tower

Bogus entrance

WASP-WAISTED CHANNEL

Entrance

DENSE FOREST

RIVER

Landing sta...

MAP OF THE GREAT HOUSE, PARK AND ESTATE, PROPERTY OF PRINCE DMITRI DMITRYEVICH LASKORIN

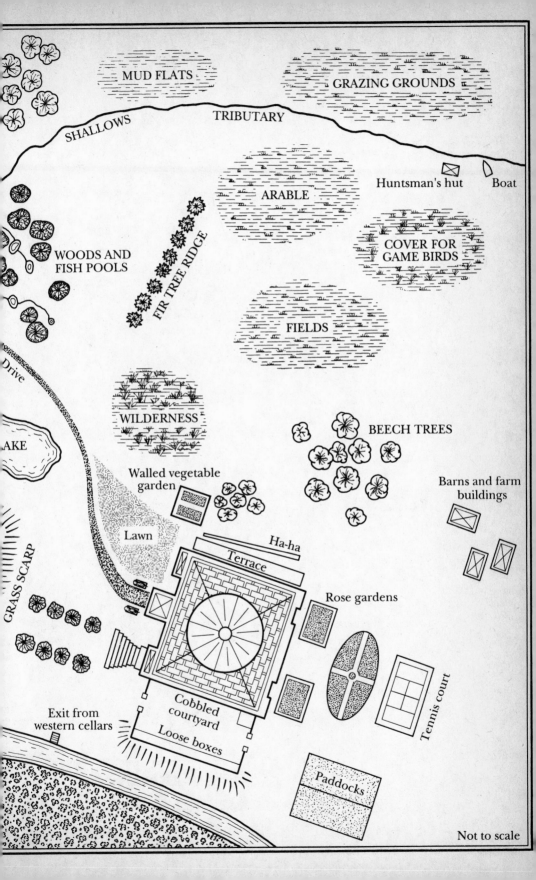

Background Note

Before the 1917 Revolution the Russian Orthodox Church was bedevilled by heretical sects: Filippovtsi burned themselves alive for the love of God; Byeguny rejected legal marriage; Molchal'niki vowed lifelong silence; Skoptsi castrated themselves out of purity and amputated the breasts of their women. But the strangest were the Khlysty (Russian *khlyst* – whip), a flagellant sect notorious for promiscuous immorality, founded in the seventeenth century by Daniel Filippov, a peasant claiming to be God the Father descended to earth on the Vladimir Government (Province) in a chariot of fire, who chose a fellow-peasant, Ivan Suslov, as his Christ-son. Ivan was subsequently flayed once and crucified twice, each time apparently rising from the dead. Under Filippov's dispensation an "angel" or prophet whose word was law presided over the community with a prophetess helpmeet. At prayer meetings believers indulged in wild abandoned dances to hymn tunes before foaming at the mouth and prophesying in ecstatic trance.

In the nineteenth century an offshoot of the German Baptists, the Stundists, took strong hold in the Southern Ukraine (Little Russia) and the North Black Sea coast (Kherson Government) where their primitive religious communism and refusal to perform military service had great appeal for the peasantry.

The fashion for things German originated in the Russia of Peter the Great (Soviet bureaucracy persisting as one of its latest manifestations) and the Russian aristocracy (Loulou, the captain) were almost as familiar with the language as with French. Hermann Schmidt comes from the eighteenth-century German settlements along the Volga uprooted by Stalin after World War II.

Following the chaos which succeeded the collapse of the Russian war effort in 1917, the peace treaty of Brest-Litovsk (early 1918) severely curtailed the authority of the new Bolshevik Government. In the capital anarchist communities flourished uncontrolled in the palaces of the dispossessed, and it was natural that Russia's outlying provinces should fall under the sway of bandits, adventurers and warlords. In the Soviet struggle to hold together this disintegrating inheritance the military was vital and, in preparation for Civil War, Reds and Whites absorbed into their ranks the flower of the old Russian Imperial Army, the names of whose regiments and corps, extinguished after the Red victory, are memorialised here.

N.L.

I

YAKOB

End of May 1917

1

The first thing the peasants did was to cut down the trees in the park.

Men came up the drive carrying long two-handled saws plundered from the foresters' sawpits near the chalk diggings. Some wore bits of uniform: Guards' forage caps, gauntlets taken from a dispatch rider, spurred cavalry boots. One or two were in sheepskins because the early mornings were still cold.

Loulou Alekseyeva watched through the ballroom window, the glass steaming up under her breath. For three months there had been no heating in the house but the trees were unfelled.

Panelling, floorboards, furniture, anything. But not the trees, darling. Promise? No pet name, no Loulou, but darling, darling, darling. *Promise?*

She had promised, overcome by Kostya's principles: the trees were not hers, or his; they belonged to this — and he had gestured, a shade drunk, at the skyline. So for most of one winter Loulou had frozen expressly on principle, only to awaken one morning and find that the same peasants who had refused to cut timber for her stoves were now felling her one-hundred-year-old beeches and limes. Evidently also on principle; what good was green wood to them?

"That's some nerve they've got, lady," came a voice at her back. She continued to watch.

Before blade was put to trunk an old woman in a pink hat made the sign of the cross over the sawyers. Loulou recognised the hat. It had come from a shop in the Rue de la Paix and there were velvet sloe berries round the brim. She had never worn it.

"Do not use those expressions, Yasha. You know how they grate on my nerves."

Yasha's father had been manager to a rich corn chandler in Lodz. When the merchant went bankrupt just before the war the boy left Poland for Russia with his parents and two suitcases. Loulou's husband had taken on the father out of pity and, to her mind, a quixotic regard for race: Kostya's great-grandmother had been a Jewish heiress to a leather-works fortune. She had brought the money

3

which, since then, the Alekseyevs had known only how to spend.

"In any case, you shouldn't be here." She put out a hand and pulled Yasha's thick black fringe.

He stood beside her. "You can say that again."

"*Ach Yakob, sei ruhig.* Yasha, Yashichka, my head aches from those words of yours."

What could you expect? The boy had some education but not much. Back home he had been left to fend for himself and lived off a cultural hash of cowboy stories and murder mysteries sent from abroad. Besides Polish he could read anything in German, Yiddish and Russian, yet adventures and detectives were all he wanted to study, and he hardly ever spoke except in gangster language.

His voice was unnaturally husky but that went with the talk. Apparently one had to hunch one's shoulders and stick out one's jaw. Idiotic.

"I've got a place to hide, lady. Come on."

Loulou turned. "Oh God, Yasha, you're quite mad. And stop calling me 'lady'. Next minute it will be 'Countess Alekseyeva'. I have told you before, Natalya Igoryevna is quite sufficient."

She looked down at him. Lovely eyes, the darkest blue she had ever seen. A shame he wasn't a child.

"Where's your father? He should have stopped this, you know. It's his job. How can I control them without . . . without a man?"

"He's not a man." Yasha's father had hated him, so why stick up for him now? He had hated Yasha for not growing, as if it were his fault for stopping at four foot six. Dear old Pa had told him he was touched, too, not just a freak but soft in the head, and not even a circus would buy him.

"Anyway, he's past it."

This was said with such forceful implication that Loulou shivered. Having long since learned to interpret the ambivalence of hints dropped by her domestics, she enquired no further.

"Not that any number of *men*," went on Yasha, "could control that lot now. You got them mixed up with your horses. You thought they were broken but all they were ever on was a lunging rein."

The clack of axes sounded jerkily over the park. Loulou rapped on the window. Outside no one thought to take notice. Why should they listen to her? reckoned Yasha. No one had listened to them. Or to him. Not even when he was there and saw it all begin.

Driven out by his father's taunts Yasha had taken to night-time trekking round the estate. He had built dens, hiked, rested up, imagined he was being tracked, trailed a suspect and wished all the

4

time that he were back in the narrow streets of a big city. He grew punier but more observant, lonelier but better informed.

Five days earlier he had lain beside the railway tracks waiting for the moon to light him on an expedition over the reed beds where he had planned a camp but there had been no need for natural light.

A huge bonfire of furniture looted from the co-operative at Kresti straddled the down line, forming a beacon visible for twenty miles across the flats. A grey saddle-tank locomotive had trundled past and halted a hundred yards from him and Yasha recognised every man in the party which dropped to the lines from the brake van and began to prise up the rails behind the train. The colour sergeant and half a dozen farriers had all been recalled to the reserve from the same village on exactly the same day. As if the smell of newly-mown hay from the verges were scenting them home, several left off work to strip away the last of their regimentals. They left behind a trail of cap-badges, regulation belts and greatcoats.

One trooper had unslung his carbine and fired twice over the heads of the figures hopping along the sharp chipstone metalling of the permanent way. "*Bastards*," he shouted. "It'll be a different story when they catch up with us. Going to stick together we were, remember?"

"Forget them," the sergeant said. "Pigswill they are, pigswill they were. You saw what they did to Major Graf Kabalyevskii. Give us an arm under this."

With the fire shovel and clinker rake from the engine cab they loosened the bolts from the sleepers and slewed the rails across the parallel line.

The next morning Yasha went to the great house and tried to tell Loulou.

She had screamed: "Deserters! Deserters! How dare you speak of disloyalty when you have all conspired to abandon me?"

Well, that was unfair, but she was in a state. After Easter her lady's maid had gone to the station in her English mackintosh with a trunk full of pilfered clothes. Then, one by one, the indoor domestics had begun to disappear. The cook, however, remained, setting up house in her quarters with the head gardener, gradually relinquishing her duties at his instance until, in the end, she stopped preparing meals for the mistress and took instead to selling off the silver and china.

Now, in the park, there were these dark men. Yasha tried to edge the countess away from the window. She flattened her hands against the glass and looked down at him imploringly. "The elder came to me bareheaded a year ago and I gave him the whole coppice in Nikolskoye and the spruce plantation even though it was immature. Why this? Why the park? It's taken hundreds of years. Why, Yasha? It's desecration."

"That's right," he said. "That's what it is."

She spat at the ringleader, Parfuta, and her spittle bubbled down the pane. "Just you dare, you lout!"

"He's past daring," said Yasha as Parfuta sank the rip-saw at chest height into the soft trunk of a lime. "He's onto the doing."

His flat tone seemed to quiet her. "What more will they do?" she murmured, not taking her eyes from the men levelling the saw in the cut.

Make a sacking kitty-bag for us and drop us over the edge of the quarry, was the closest he could guess at present. No point in saying so, not yet, not with a woman of breeding. She'd never seen them on the loose, the big people in boots, dispersed and uncontrolled. The "boys".

Loulou suddenly took off a shoe and banged on the window with the heel.

Yasha held his breath. Up to now they had been night-runners, this mob in the park, doing a bit of filching, settling a few old scores. Now they were getting defiant. Proprietorial. A line had been crossed. They were waiting for a challenge. They wanted to put their feet up on milady's table or in milady's bed. He knew Parfuta. To get that, Parfuta would kill.

Outside, the sawyers grinned and stepped back from the tree, bowing but leaving the saw in place.

"There!" shouted Loulou triumphantly. "I knew it all along! They haven't lost all vestige of honesty."

Yasha said nothing but remained at the window watching Parfuta.

The two sawyers were facing the mob, backs to the house. Women crowded up laughing and throwing their neckerchiefs up to their faces. The one in the toque fell to her knees and began to pluck daisies from the long grass, passing the flowers to the next in line. The laughter became hysterical as the men were pushed round to face the house.

Parfuta and his mate were holding their caps straight to their bodies at arm's length, and smiling.

The grins broadened. Loulou smiled back joyously. Parfuta gave a huzza and threw his cap into the air. His companion did likewise and the women squealed.

Loulou's expression was slow to change.

The men's clothing was disarranged. White petals twined in black, curling hair. To her, to their protectress, their mistress, these men, these smiling strong men, were displaying themselves.

Yasha wrenched her away. "Got the picture now? They're going to do things nice people don't talk about. They're giving you notice."

Loulou tried to pull her arm free. "Stop it, you're hurting me."

"Not as much as the lads with the daisy-chains will, if they climb in here. You got a place to go?"

Long ago he had made plans against just such an eventuality.

"This is my home. I won't be driven out. I'll die here."

A fusillade of stones crashed at the window-panes.

"You bet you will," said Yasha. "But they'll bury you first."

Loulou beat at her temple with her free hand. "I can't think . . . I can't think . . . All the men are at the Front, all the real men . . . The Laskorins . . . What about the Laskorins? They might, they might take me in . . ."

Yasha had not bargained for this. The Laskorin estate was near — only forty miles to the west. "We could risk it, I suppose. I had something else up my sleeve, but if . . ."

A rock the size of a dinner-plate shattered the great window. The crowd set up a jeering howl.

Loulou began to scream. "Take me away, they're going to kill me!"

Yasha pulled. He was very strong. His rolling, uneven stride made her sway as he dragged her across the dusty floor. He pulled her along the colonnade of the library, through the double doors of the music room, through the assembly room in the south wing, rooms in which she had not set foot for months. The tapestries had gone, the pictures lining the staircases, even the lustres from the electroliers.

One night she had crept from her room to find the cook and her man packing an immense *jardinière* with porcelain.

"Ten roubles apiece those with the flowers," said the gardener. "Get a move on. They've brought up the cart."

The long Venetian mirrors lining the walls were smashed.

"Poor soul," mumbled the toothless cook stuffing handfuls of straw between the cups. "It's like stories of those poor princesses drove out into the world."

Yasha pulled her down the back stairs. The carpet had been taken up. Where it had lain the treads were dry as cigar-box wood, edges worn down and naked. For the past months Loulou had listened for feet on these uncarpeted stairs and prayed swiftly and silently in front of the ikons, miming the half-forgotten gestures from childhood, waiting for the outburst but feeding on the excitement, trembling but eager as she had been as a little girl during nocturnal parties when she broke her mother's rules and peeped down at the flowers massed along the two grand pianos and waited for the singers to begin.

He pulled her past the billiard room with its lights still blazing. His palm sweated into hers but she held on tight, remembering how Kostya's laugh used to ring out above the crack of his cue and the voice of the deferential steward whispering: "As you wish, your honour, as you wish," while the girl he had brought in from the hooded sleigh waited in the shadow, flicking back the blue fringes of her shawl. This was where Kostya had taken them, flat-nosed village girls with blood and milk complexions, bundled them out of furs and pelerines reeking of camphor, to have them fish-flopping on their backs and ripping the baize with their nails when, in final spasm, they arched their thick waists up from the slate-bed screaming enough to bristle the hair of the borzois under the table.

At the last turning of the stair he pulled so hard that Loulou banged her elbow on the brass fixings of the handrail and gave a loud yelp.

Yasha turned his disproportionately large face on her like an exasperated Pekingese. "D'you want to turn someone out of bed to tread on your neck?"

Facing them, slightly ajar, was the door of the gun-room. Yasha pushed her behind him, crouched low and butted the door gently open with his brow.

Once the room had pleased Loulou by its orderly maleness. Now the red mahogany cases for rifles and shotguns serried on the far wall were empty and the wired glazing smashed and twisted.

All the full-bore rifled weapons and side-arms had been commandeered during mobilisation, but the shotguns, the pride of her father's life – four English pairs which had been fitted to him like bespoke shirtings – left in concession to his rank, were nowhere to be seen.

"There's only one way out on this side," whispered Yasha.

This was true. Entrance and egress one and the same. Out went the hounds and the master accoutred for forest and marsh; in came the night-women to spread their thighs on the green: ball of heel in the right pocket, ball of heel in the left. *Our male preserve, our gentlemen's club, our patrimony.*

Towards the lake the house displayed its public side, the chill columns rising steeply from the early-morning mist, as sharp and clear as in a steel engraving. The pre-dawn breeze had dropped and there was no sound now, apart from the honk and wheeple of marshbirds.

A guest in one of the cavernous rooms on this sunless west front, gazing out from the windows of the vast *piano nobile*, would have been surprised to see such an odd pair: a lady, the hem of her morning-gown raised high, the lace of her underskirts frothing in a ring round her knees, a lady trying to run through the grasses which bent up the slope to meet her, sodden with dew. She swayed among the wet stalks, pausing now and again, to shout at a boy who zig-zagged under the feathery tops in a crab-wise gait, flipper-like arms spinning to keep him in balance.

By the ice-house Yasha waited. Chaff from the bearded grass seeded the air and made him sneeze. Loulou caught up, panting, her stockings drenched.

"Watch your step, lady," he said tersely.

"If I've told you once, I've told you a thousand times . . ."

"Aaaargh!" Yasha sneezed three times in succession. "As if we didn't have enough to cope with."

Loulou flurried her skirts to shake off moisture and skipped round him. "I shall simply ignore you if you persist in that common way of talking."

Yasha waved her away. "Don't say I never warned you." Caught by a further bout of sneezing, he fell to his knees in the grass.

Loulou flounced up to the entrance of the ice-house. Once, two men had been needed to open the doors but since the family ceased to entertain after the defeats in 1916 and the furniture in the west wing was sheeted, the ice-house had been bolted against the risk that drunken gipsies might take the place for a shelter and freeze to death overnight. But now the bolts were drawn and the iron doors stood open.

The air smelled of fungus. Beneath Loulou's step leaf-mould crackled like paper. Her feet were soaked. A few yards from the ice-house doors she took off her shoes and waved them above her head, hitting out at the droning blow-flies.

Yasha's voice followed her. He was yelling now: "Don't . . . Don't look up . . ."

Only when he came crashing through the last of the tall grass and was nearly upon her did she do exactly what he had told her not to.

There was nothing extraordinary, not at first. Only branches of vine creaking on their training wires, the jittering leaves, and insects congregating on infant trusses before taking to the air.

Yasha seized her arm and pulled her away. "God and all His saints, I don't need this, this I could do without."

Suddenly her eye caught a movement on the gable. Some black and glossy thing was poking from the leaves and swinging from side to side with a gentle rustle.

Unalarmed, Loulou narrowed her eyes.

A pair of boots, soft leather boots, buttoned at the side; she laughed out loud and slapped away Yasha's hand. Stepping carefully over the squashy vine leaves she stopped at the place where the doors stood ajar and stared up.

The soles were flesh-brown and unmarked.

A gust of wind from the head of the valley swept down the lake. Before petering out against the foot of the slope the breeze was sufficient to ripple the ice-house greenery which parted like hair.

The boots were not empty. Nor, above them, were the striped flannel trousers or the frock-coat.

Recognising the dandified clothes, Loulou forgot to cry out. If this was *him*, the only thing that could be guaranteed to have remained empty to the end was his head.

The body twirled gracefully. At an unnatural angle to the points of a perfectly-laundered collar lolled the goatee chin.

"Dushan," she whispered, and crossed herself, unmoved.

"A pal of yours?" Yasha was aghast at her nerve.

"We were not close," said Loulou.

Tell us about the Jews, Dushan. And in a twinkling Dushan would be overwrought, striding to and fro, swinging his pocket watch by its chain. *The Chews is a people with which I have had much dealings* . . .

"My husband found him amusing."

Yasha had scrambled up one of the vines and made his way along to the top of the doors where he now perched directly under Dushan's feet.

"He wasn't the only one," he said, fingering the uppers of the boots. "Must have nearly killed themselves laughing, the ones who did this."

"How do you know that anyone is responsible? He might have done it himself."

Tired of his obsessions perhaps, he decided to get in first before they came for him, his *Chews*, out of the bolshevised Armageddon he swore they had plotted.

"Oh yes," said Yasha. "Some kind of athlete was he? Take a look up here."

Balanced precariously on the door he snatched at a bell-rope, the end of which was slung round a hook driven into the brick ten feet above his head.

"That's the blacksmith's forging, that hook, that's Semyon from round our way. He always hammers over the end."

Loulou recognised the bell-pull. A week before it had disappeared from the library. "They've been breaking in again!"

Yasha groaned. "Look, lady, you want to file a claim for your lost property, you call down the local council office." He checked the sway of Dushan's legs against his cheek. "Me, I want to keep inside my skin a bit longer. If that Semyon's screws get loosened when he claps eyes on a gent, God knows what he'd do to a Hebrew page-boy with a live countess in tow."

"Shouldn't we *do* something? Make it decent . . . bury him?"

Yasha stretched the full length of his body down the door before releasing his grip. He hit the ground with a thud and doubled up so that Loulou rushed over, thinking him hurt, but he was on his feet quickly, brushing flakes of rust from between his fingers.

"We can't hang about for that," he said. "Decency's what they rely on from your type. Decent people waiting around to do the decent thing, then getting jumped." His face flushed. "Know what they did?"

"How can *you* know? One minute it's 'one', next it's 'them' . . ."

"There's clues up there." Yasha was diffident now. "Now I can put two and two together. Trained myself up to it, detection. Been practising for years."

Loulou found a dry patch and sat down with her shoes, cleaning their insides with the soiled lace of her petticoats.

Yasha jumped up and down. "You're out of your mind," he shouted. "We can't sit round here – they could pop up any minute, armed to the teeth!"

Loulou was still unconvinced that Dushan had not done away with himself. "With bell-pulls?"

"That's what I'm trying to tell you, lady!" squealed Yasha. "He was dead when they strung him up!"

Loulou put on her shoes. "How can you tell?" Her tone was respectful.

From the breast of his shirt, Yasha drew out a pair of shears so fashioned that they could be worked with one hand. "Mild steel – see?" He held them towards her, snipping the air. Three parts of their length were stained black. Loulou got up and looked round wildly. "Your Mr Thing," hissed Yasha. "They cut his throat, they *bled* him first. Get it? Real *kosher*."

They sat in a hollow away from the ice-house where rhododendrons flourished out of control. Under their cover Loulou was sick.

Yasha seemed puzzled about Dushan. "What drove them to *that*?"

She hiccuped but the nausea diminished and she felt readier to talk. "He was repulsively anti-Semitic."

"What's that?"

"He hated Jews."

Yasha whistled and inspected his nails. "In our village that's a state of mind. You don't get gold bars for being one but you don't get crucified either. What did he do for a living?"

"He engaged governesses and nurses. He was good with horses – they used to lay their muzzles along his sleeve and munch the padding of his coat."

He's a pimp, he was a pimp in Vienna, and an abortionist . . . Kostya, how can you say that?

"Nice work," said Yasha. "Where was he from?"

"What business is it of yours? He can hold no interest for you." She was impatient to be rid of Dushan, and for part of herself to go with him.

"I've got my reasons." Yasha frowned. "Number one being that we're in the same hole, you and me, and I want to know who I'm sharing it with, what you're like, who you are. Tell you a lot about people, their friends."

The boy had a point. "Very well," said Loulou. "He came from somewhere in Bohemia – Pisek, I think. My father met up with him at Soden when I was a baby. There was a lady he looked after – a patient. She was convalescing and Papa knew her. He became acquainted with Dushan in that way."

Byeloselskaya, a St Petersburg grande dame *recuperating after her third abortion.*

"I loved him when I was little. He used to let me play with his watch, such a lovely watch. The face had enamelled nosegays round the moon and the figures were carmine pinks."

Yasha's face lit up. "Where'd he keep it?"

"I don't know. In a long pocket, I seem to remember, inside . . ."

He scrambled up. "Answer to a prayer." He dived into the rhododendrons. "Don't budge. I'll be back."

Voices came from the far bank of the lake, skittering across the water, distorted by mist. She peeped through the leaves. A group of peasant women was skirting through the reeds, their red headscarves giving them the look of a troupe of strolling players in an open-air show.

Alone for the first time since dawn, Loulou became afraid. She did not doubt that the boy would come back but without him she felt lost. As countess, her life had been lived so apart from the people now roaming the park, who had looted her rooms and murdered her staff, that in the house she had still managed to keep aloof from them. Inside there her person was sacrosanct and they had kept their distance, but in the open air she felt hunted. These people were on their own ground, the overgrown gardens were reverting to nature and soon landscape and figures would be one.

Dushan had been run down in the open. A month ago, when the railway was still working, he had left for the city, promising to bring word. A message came by his valet: "Situation deteriorating hourly." Then nothing. He must have been coming back to warn her to leave – or to stay. No one would ever know. Too late, in any case. The killing had started with the valet. They drowned him and then they murdered the young schoolmaster, his wife and children. The bodies had been brought to the foot of the grand staircase at night and left for her to find next morning.

Not a word was said.

Yasha approached soundlessly and tugged at her sleeve. His finger-nails were black and sticky. "Right," he said. "On your knees. This is where you learn some fieldcraft."

Loulou followed him on all fours under the rhododendrons. At the edge of the plantation, he stopped. Directly ahead was the tennis court, its net almost disappeared under sorrel and bindweed; beyond, two hundred yards distant, was the squat frontage of the boathouse.

The boy turned. "It'll be safer by water. See that door? When I give the signal, double up and run."

2

Since Yasha had last visited the boathouse the door had been criss-crossed with palings nailed to its frame. He smashed a window at the rear and scrambled in ahead before helping Loulou through.

The interior was wrecked. Down the slipway to the lake lay the boating fleet of the Alekseyevs: Kostya's racing skiff, the double-oared scull, the lakeman's dory and the ladies' varnished clinker boat with its flag. All had been holed by the ferrule of a punt-pole.

"Bastards," panted Yasha.

Brushing herself down, Loulou looked round. "My old punt," she said calmly. "They missed that. It might do."

Yasha nodded and dropped to his knees a few feet from the window. The flooring was made up of small gridirons fitted together like tiles and the excess water from upturned boats flowed down to the lake through the perforated slots. After lifting aside a grid the size of a doormat, he squeezed the upper part of his body into the sluice.

"They thought of everything, they were clever blocking off the water route, but we've still got the punt and our legs and they didn't find this."

He emerged dragging an oilskin bag twice as big as himself.

"What have you got there?" asked Loulou.

"What keeps body and soul together," he said proudly. "Our hard tack. Want a look?"

He gripped the toe of the sack, and with a jerk whipped away the waterproofs. The grating vibrated to the sound of glass and tinplate.

Loulou surveyed the heap. Yasha's providence was God-sent, no doubt, but what kind of iron rations were these?

Cherries in maraschino, mussels in red sauce, pears in kümmel, water-chestnuts in brine, salted almonds, saveloys like babies' fingers, pink mousses, nectarines in brandy, dried apricot rings, white chocolate, goose liver, langoustine and crabmeat, *petit fours*, wafers, preserved ginger, sweet Easter cake . . .

Mama's. Of course, Mama's. Loulou remembered the marzipan in that fine glazed paper which stretched like goldbeaters' skin, slab upon slab in the ebony wardrobe under the feather boas.

Mama's second cardinal sin.

She had laid in supplies of relishes against the surfeit of a nursery diet foisted on her by Papa. And now Yasha had tumbled out her clandestine store, packet by packet, from holes in the wall, under floorboards, and had collected them up in tarpaulins to put by for a rainy day, never realising how old they were. Mama herself had died before her secret banquets were exhausted.

Yasha noted her frown. "No dice?"

"I have no idea," she said slowly, "*what* you are talking about."

"No . . . I mean, isn't it any good, this stuff?"

Loulou toppled a little pillar of tins with the point of her toe.

"Yakob Pavlovich."

"*Grafinya*, milady?"

"You have been stealing."

Yasha glowered at her from under his fringe. "*Stealing!* I'm not the cat that thieved the dripping, lady. And what have that crew been doing back at the dear old homestead – helping to polish the mistress's spoons?"

Loulou put out her hand. "I'm sorry . . ."

Only much later did she learn that in blaming his moods and attitudes on her own crassness she was often wrong. He was beset by images from the past and they served only to enmesh him in memories of times when he had been a spectator of events too vast for him to accommodate.

The men in the park had seemed as unafraid as the boys from Yasha's street, years ago, who cornered a rat in the outhouse. When the first stone struck it reared up and gave a fledgling squeak, covering one eye with a pink, thumbless hand. Yasha was full of pity, not because the rat was to die under Grisha's boot but because, for a brief time, the rat too knew this. Yasha had never forgotten. So that in Russia, when some Grisha became a village hero for throttling a rabid dog, or a Vanya was given sweets for hanging a litter of kittens, Yasha kept quiet. That was simple prudence. They grew up, those lads. After a drink, a treat, a threat or an order, they'd turn on you.

He slid a hand down the leg of his right boot and brought out Dushan's watch. "We better get some shuteye. Can't make a move before sundown." He flipped open the casings and the watch spun between them like a winged seed. Inside two miniature hammers beat out the hour. The chime sounded sweet and piercing.

Loulou sat back on her heels and spoke unsteadily: "I'm sorry I accused you of stealing."

He shrugged. "I didn't reckon it counted as stealing. It was part of the plan, you see. I thought we'd need sustaining if you wanted to make a real run for it. Could have been a trek to Semipalatinsk for all I knew. How could I have figured it was a one-loaf-and-a-sausage trip to drop in on the neighbours forty miles downstream?"

If you didn't think about it much, didn't take your nose from the book, nothing sounded cosier: a dawn spin in a flat boat, a couple of hundred miles over land with a pack on your back and snugly fitted up; tins, matches and smokes; a torch and collapsible stove; and a cool head, well-stocked with decoys and wheezes to put the hounds off the scent. Live rough off the land, on your wits, independent and resourceful, your life in your hands. They all did it, the 'tecs, incognito among the crags, tracking their man, drenched with rain one minute, burned black from the sun the next. Tough as hell, gnawing roots, spearing fish, dowsing water in sand; and never giving up until the bracelets snapped on and the adversary came clean.

In the hut by the river where his parents bickered and regretted their fate, Yasha had craved hardships. The big free-and-easy stand-up, bare-knuckled scraps where you took on your life, knocked out its teeth, then stamped on its hands. Let them all come: the jolly close shaves, brushes with death, near things. That was the stuff.

All right for them, though, the lean guys with gimlet eyes and lantern jaws, they had the chance to make it on their own. He'd never be able to get up a good run for a flying leap at an evil Chinaman, let alone unmask an international drugs ring – not with her, not with a woman. Especially not this woman, he wouldn't.

Her lackey-fying instincts were still up to strength, thank you very much, milady:

"Yasha, do try to be more careful with that pole. I'm positively soaking." She lay on the cushions at the bottom of the punt watching bugs jumping up and down on the water. "Such a lovely name for them, *Daphnia* – don't you think?"

Yasha grunted. "For what?"

"Water-fleas. They're everywhere."

"We had them at home. The dry kind. They bit."

Loulou sighed and trailed a hand over the side of the punt. "Yasha, you're still dribbling water over me."

"It's the pole, it's too long," he said irritably. "It's daft making them so long. By the time I get to the top, the rest of it's all under water."

"You'll get the hang of it," said Loulou languidly.

He was making hard going upstream against the current of the rivulet which bent tortuously through the expanse of marshes to the east of the park before finally straightening into the cut to supply the Alekseyevs' ornamental lake. With its stone bottom the cut had been easy. Once into the twisting marsh stream the punt slipped this way and that among the weeds.

They passed out of the shelter of feathery rushes into a stretch of open water, ribbed with stiff little waves which slapped the blunt prow making Yasha wobble. The pole ceased to touch bottom and, without its power, their craft was in danger of being nosed back into a clump of grim-looking reeds.

Yasha reflected. Loulou saved him. "Is this any help?" she said holding up a paddle.

He shipped the pole quickly, snatched up the paddle and breathed again. "You bet."

Once in clear water Loulou relaxed. The night was warm. They struck shallows again and Yasha discarded the paddle. At each clack of the pole she felt reassured, and the ripples flip-flopped beneath the boy's burblings, his language now quaint and comforting, keeping them in touch when she could not see but only imagine him behind her, scuffling with the pole on the flatboard stern, fearful of toppling off his short legs into the dark.

When she woke, the moon still hung above the willows on the bankside but dawn was near, the sky to the east a washed-out grey.

Even under the greatcoat which Yasha had draped round her in the night it was cold. Hitching it tighter, she looked over the side. A bough overhung the punt. They had stopped. In the thin light she made out a line stretching from the prow to the undergrowth. He must have moored them. Poor boy, all that work.

The voice came to her as a whisper: "Listen, lady. Listen."

Her limbs went rigid. That terrible man with the saw, he must be here, in the boat. She was captured. Done for.

"You ditch those rags *now*."

The punt eddied, silhouetting a hunched figure at the bows, hair sticking out in barbs against the yellow-plum moon.

It was Yasha being silly.

Loulou flung aside the greatcoat and scrambled to her feet. "You foolish boy, scaring me like that, I nearly died of fright."

"We'll both die if you don't do exactly what I say. This is no kiddies' outing. We're on the run."

At the best of times Loulou had difficulty with this cloak-and-dagger aspect of Yasha's outlook. Now, refreshed by sleep and at a safer distance from the house, she was ready to argue. "What on earth has that got to do with my clothes?"

His voice became unpleasantly grating. "Soon we're going to hit the big river, and that's where we scuttle *this*." He banged the paddle, making Loulou start. "And I'm not slogging across country with a fancy-piece dolled up for a supper party. So I'm doing you an alias and a disguise. Get me?"

She giggled. "Come along, Yashichka, you don't seriously believe . . . ?"

"And you can drop all that. Let's get something straight. I'm in charge now and you'll jump to my say-so because without me you're dead meat. I won't tell you again – get it off. All of it."

Loulou felt up her back. Her fingers touched the topmost pearl button. "I can't." He said nothing and she floundered on. "Not if you watch me, I can't."

She felt like a whore rustling behind a screen, the man's silence palpable until his exclamation when she stepped out, unclothed.

Smiling, Yasha turned towards the prow but this was not enough.

"Do something. For the love of God make a noise."

Yasha laughed. "How about a tune, something stirring?"

She wrenched at the button, breaking its retaining loop. "Anything, anything, this is so humiliating. *Schnell, Knabe.*"

Softly, Yasha began to hum a waltz. The sound of her nails grazing the tussore of her bodice hissed in his ears.

She felt the dawn wind on her spine as the puffed shoulders of mimosa silk bagged on her upper arms. They don't even need to look. Some men never look, but just lie there, antennae eavesdropping on the fall of brocade. He seems like a boy, but how could you tell? Unequal development . . . that's possible. Bizarre.

Withdrawing one hand from the sleeve to the fingertips, she held back the stiff cuff and pulled first one arm through, then the other. Damn the boy, why couldn't he have told her about this before, back at the house? The warm bodice dropped forward, spilling over the front of her skirts like a skin emptied of its animal. Red-blonde hairs on the nape of her neck tingled at the roots as curls of mist smoked up from the watercourse.

I shall freeze.

"Sun up," called Yasha cheerfully. "They'll be unleashing the bloodhounds any minute. That's what they do, you know, with runaways. Once they get the scent . . ."

His head moved. He was turning round. She screamed: "Don't you dare!"

Yasha chuckled, slid on his belly, arms thrown out over the

gunwale, and splashed his hands in the stream. "Don't take on, lady. Water throws them off the trail."

The motion perturbed the set of the boat and Loulou staggered, then recovered herself by jamming the heels of her high-laced Spanish shoes between the slats over the planking at the bottom. Yasha had begun to make rasping sounds with his lips in perfect three-four time. About to unloose the drawstring ribbon at the centre of her chest she lost courage. "Yakob, I can't go uncovered. Not underneath. Let me keep . . ."

"All of it, woman, I'm telling you. Get rid of it all."

Woman. Insufferable. But what was the use? He seemed to know what was best. She drew out the bow and flung wide her arms on a line with the points of her shoulders. The cord untightened and, with a jerk, she freed herself.

Exhilarated for a moment she stood forward in the attitude of a Winged Victory breasting the air, until the gnats, catching the odour of orange-blossom. Pin-pricked her soft skin.

"Where is it then? I need something this instant to cover my . . ."

"Where's what?" Yasha called back. His head was over the bows, his nose level with the jigging water-boatmen.

"Yashichka – the *disguise*."

"Are you ready?"

She crossed her arms over her breasts, looked down at the unravelled camisole top and shook herself, trying to detach the boning which had caught up in the neckline of her frock.

Surely not. Not Yasha. He wouldn't, he couldn't. But they were alone and no one would ever know.

Weed floated past into the dank burrows at the bank. Afterwards, he could throw her in and hold her head under until the algae stained her teeth green. Had he ever? Ever with a grown woman? They were probably going to die soon. Wouldn't she want to, if she were a man, the first and last time? The reflection of her figure stared back from the water. Drowning was too horrible. At that moment she decided to offer herself to him.

"These." Yasha hauled himself back, still without facing her. She had not had time to say anything. In Kostya's picnic hamper he rummaged for a collarless shirt and a pair of canvas trews of the kind worn by the yardmen in the stable block.

"Not altogether?" she whispered, knees trembling from relief.

His eyes came round. "Naked," he said. "Must be naked as the day you were born." Without another word he twisted back, flicked his body half out of the boat and, submerging his head, began to blow bubbles.

The submissiveness of a moment ago carried her on and she bent to Yasha's authority. He was the only one with a plan. Whimpering in her hurry, she tore at the back fastenings below her waist, bruising the quicks of her nails on the tightly-stitched eyelets. When the man's clothes came flying through the air, Loulou clutched them over her and Yasha turned his head from the morning light.

"That's equality," he said. "Leaving everything, taking nothing. Nothing left to strip us of now, except our lives."

The clothes were rough and male but inside them Loulou felt safer. "The alias, Yasha? You forgot to tell me who I am."

"That's gonna be a laugh." He drew Semyon's shears from his boot. "You're going down in the world. In two shakes we'll be related, so you better live up to me. Ever had a brother, lady?"

The vessel dipped as Loulou shifted on her elbow to watch the great flat horizon emerge over the flowering reeds to separate itself from the bluish slopes a long way off.

Yasha took out the long silver pins from the braid and shook hard. The heavy plait unloosened, bushing at her waist like a hand of cards. Her grandmother had counted each stroke: ". . . seventy-nine . . . eighty . . . nearly there . . ." The ivory brush smelled of cardamom and pears. "Eighty-one . . . eighty-two . . . ginger-cake, chestnuts, salmon in the raw, good strong Russian-baked red brick – which colour is my Nathalie this Christ's new day?"

Loulou always replied: "Red as the bloodstone in your hair," and, at the end, she received a kiss and a green fondant dusted in sugar.

Yasha whistled. "This is some mop." He sliced vigorously and she bent her head, helping him, thinning the hair into a fan for the shears, then shaking free where the blades sprang apart.

Under the cobalt sky, the clumps darkened and fell away over the splashboards of the boat, floating nests of deep auburn onto the current.

The bed of the rail tracks had been gouged from the soft rock of the bluff. Above the line, boulder and scrub clung to the face which rose sheer to the tree-lined summit.

From below Yasha and Loulou took almost an hour of scrambling and slipping on the loose shale of the gradient to reach the foot of the stone revetments which buttressed the cutting against the drop to the river. Out of the sun's glare they rested, too worn out to speak. A quarter of a mile beneath, their waterlogged boat, trapped by a freak eddy between sandbanks, was refusing to sink and the stern sat up bobbing among the green and orange cushions which had settled on the river bottom.

In this light all was visible.

Yasha knew that since the track hugged the river, sooner or later it would arc south-west along the boundaries of the Laskorins' estate. The wood-burning locomotives were slow movers even on straight runs but here on the bends and twists of the valley they would be especially sedate. A hitch on a freighter could drop them within range of their objective before nightfall.

There was shade at the base of the wall and they had food and drink. "Here," said the boy, digging in the bag and bringing out a bottle of lemon cordial. "Grab this while I get something to wash down with it."

They ate shortcake biscuits and the drink was warm and sticky.

Yasha licked his fingers before bringing out Dushan's watch. "No hurry," he said, after the chimes had struck twice. "All the time in the world."

Loulou stretched back unseating a shower of pebbles. "Time for what?"

"To wait," he said nodding up at the wall. "And eat. And not to walk."

He must think she was tired. Well, so she was, but not as tired as he. He should have seen her leap from the saddle as fresh as a child after a forty-mile ride. "Yasha . . . You're not expecting a *train*?"

He began a tuneless whistle. "Might be," he breathed between flat chirps. "Could be."

She laughed. "My dear boy, there are no trains for a thousand miles."

He stopped whistling. "How come you know that? It's not all gone to pot yet. Anyway, I expect you don't know everything about trains. You been on them much, for instance?"

"If Papa hadn't died I might have been on more but then I probably wouldn't have married."

"That makes a whole lot of sense, that does," began Yasha sarcastically, but she went on talking in a high, oddly formal voice as if he had no part in the conversation. They all talked like that about themselves. Like you weren't there. Nor were you, not when things worth happening happened. You were round the back, in the yard, on the other side of the door.

"Oh, that last train journey before the war! Hundreds of miles in a train like an apartment on wheels! We had a salon all to ourselves, my friend and I . . ."

Insulated. Up in the air.

On the journey from Poland Yasha had escaped from the sweltering third-class and hopped down into the pits in the engine sheds. "It was winter when we came over by train at Brest-Litovsk . . ." Mechanics were swapping bogies to match up with the Russian gauge. Among the axles and wheels a man in a cap held him up to see the diners whose meal went on as the restaurant car was run up like on stilts and lads as little as Yasha himself rammed into place the great axle-boxes and flanged wheels. It stank down there worse than Yasha's family's compartment.

A pretty lady, thinking he was a grease-monkey, pushed two fried dabs to him through the top of the window and her whole party waved and grinned. The man in the cap looked at her so hard that she blushed and, without removing the cigarette in his mouth, he shot spit along the coachline where it said *Wagons lits*.

He reverted to Loulou's memories. "Go on, don't tell me, you had velvet button-seats and a wash-place, all with china doings."

Loulou searched his face. The expression was bland. "That goes without saying."

"That's the way to travel," said Yasha, rolling up biscuit wrappings between his palms. People like her always had somewhere to go, and went, without saying.

"Quite," said Loulou, getting into her stride once more. "The views! Morning and evening we watched mountain after mountain, glittering with snow. When we got out it was windless but so cold, like bathing in spring water. Only to breathe that air was enough to make you light-headed."

"Where'd you go then, for these mountains?"

Her manner became exalted. "Does it matter? We were together."

She didn't even need to know where the stations were. No mad scrambles at halts for a pie.

"Caucasus?"

Loulou spruced her hair with crumby fingers. "Oh, eastwards, that way. The train was so slow. Sometimes we stopped at every tiny station and even places without stations at all."

The fireman was probably drunk.

"The coaches were decorated with pictures and children used to crowd round to look."

They were after fags and half-empty bottles of wine. Sent to the signals by their picturesque dads and beaten if they came back empty-handed.

"Young ones pointed to the pictures and said *beautiful*."

Crafty, slant-eyed, bent from the day they were born. They knew what to say.

"I can see it all," he said.

"The further we went the more the wildness came to us, bounding like a gazelle from the deep, eternal fastnesses of old Russia. The skies, the plains, the space, the sheer amplitude of that primitive world, made me faint. You know, things even smelled barbarous – and old, so old, even the people."

"Yup," said Yasha. "That figures."

"You know about such things? One would be quite overcome unless . . ."

"You had a home to go to?" he suggested.

"Not that," said Loulou breathlessly. "Unless you had someone to share it with. To have someone whose spirit was so free, independent and fine that he could sweep away convention and just *live*."

Ah – a man. A lucky man who could call his soul his own. "Did he?" said Yasha.

Loulou took a moment before coming to. "Did he what?"

"Defy convention."

Running her hands through her unfamiliar hair again she brushed against the tiny studs in her earlobes. "Damn! My sleepers. Why didn't you notice?" She unhooked the studs before resuming. "Well, yes, I would say, to a certain extent. He wished I hadn't married . . ."

A real free-thinker.

"He used to say he wished I was a grocer's daughter . . ."

Yasha stuffed the ball of biscuit paper into his mouth and began to shake.

"We had that one week together." Her eyes brightened again. "Just one week with the one person to whom one can say everything. I hid nothing from him. You wouldn't understand."

I bet he did, though, thought Yasha, fighting for breath. One will have understood, one would.

She shook her head. "You'd be shocked."

"Ha!" gulped Yasha, tears in his eyes.

"If only he could have worked, Martin might have been a great artist." Her mouth trembled and she looked away. "But my presence was so necessary to him that without me he had no heart even to make a sketch. That week he wanted to paint snow."

Yasha coughed and accidentally swallowed the ball of paper. He got up and thumped his chest. He had an image of a long thin man in a frock-coat with an easel under his arm and tubes of Chinese white brimming from his pockets, clapping a hand on the shoulder of the man at the firebox and telling him he wanted the brakes on so he could knock out a canvas or two at thirty below.

"No shortage of that," he said. "So your man did his stuff?"

"He couldn't," whispered Loulou.

"A sudden thaw?"

"*My husband, my husband.* Martin couldn't. He kept thinking of my husband."

"Why? Was he on the train too?"

"*Ach, Dummkopf!*" cried Loulou. "Martin said his spirit hovered between us and robbed him of inspiration."

"Left him plenty of snow, though, I expect," said Yasha giving in to a spluttering laugh which fluttered the wings of the waterfowl on the river below.

Loulou was patronising. "Yakob Pavlovich, have you no soul, no eye for beauty?"

Yasha eluded the question with a sneer. "Ma must have. She cried when she saw where we had to live. Ma said Pa had deceived us, promising us another life and then burying us. When I lay down under the bench I watched their snow-boots clomp on the earth floor and heard the axe whistle as Pa split logs for the stove and my mother wailing. I thought that any minute they'd get swallowed up for keeps in the dark. That was Russia to me, lady – a hungry black belly waiting to gobble you down."

"You are being silly," said Loulou.

There was a pause. In spite of himself Yasha wanted to hear more about her Martin. There was nothing else to do, anyway. He thought he could size up the competition and see how they ticked, these guys whom these ladies went in for up to their necks.

"Go on," he said. "Tell me about him. I'm usually a good listener."

Back came the drawing-room voice. She straightened her arms in front of her as if pushing at an invisible wall. "Well, after that journey he never stopped writing. It was so embarrassing. 'Let them think what they like,' he said. He was always so arrogant. 'Your mama, your Kostya. None of *those people* ought to be considered. Why should we submit? In years to come no one will even remember their names, while our love will make one glorious high summer of the whole of our lives.' A few weeks more and he would have come for me."

She looked out tenderly, beyond Yasha to the brute expanses of marsh and inlet which they had traversed. Nothing moved.

"Back there I was waiting for him, you see."

Martin the masher, shooting a line, collecting nice and handsomely on his star-crossed lover stake. The artistic temperament was obviously a cinch for folding up anything in skirts. Where's the use in educating ladies when they can't discriminate?

Anyway, time had passed him by, her paintbrush loafer. He'd

dallied too long. If he turned up now Parfuta would soon knock the dreamdust out of his eyes.

"That's bad," he said. "I keep trying to tell you – no one's coming for you or me, except with a chopper in his hand. You can kiss goodbye to the snowman. He can't book tickets no more, not for your line."

He expected her to flare up, but she only nodded. "I know, I know. No going back. But still, he may live, he may come to me, wherever I am."

He looked her over. She trusted men. Now it was his turn. She trusted him. A sudden sense of responsibility caught him off-guard. Was he up to it? Anyone'd tumble she was female. What a pair they made: the dwarf and his beautiful sibling hiking to fairyland. God, they were done for.

She sat in front of him, knees drawn up to her chin, eyes glowing from recollections of her dissolute drawing-master. A victim if ever he saw one.

A breeze sprang up lifting the shale-dust.

She was blind to him, murmuring: "The train . . . the painter. A painter on a train."

Yasha slung the cordial bottle into his bag, thoroughly glum. Give it a rest. The bastard had come between them. Soon she'd start comparing. He wanted to be on the move, out of reach of all the talking, looking back, remembering.

"*Raus Bruder!* On your feet, we're striking camp."

"A train?"

"Didn't you hear it?" he lied. "That whistle down the line?"

Loulou got to her feet obediently.

In true detective fashion he kicked at the unparted gravel on which they had lain, in order to cover their trail. Without a word they scaled the low embankment. The rails sang in the heat and in amongst the double tracks dockweed flapped.

Yasha hitched the bag tighter over his shoulder and turned a slow circle on the crunchy infill between two sleepers. "Aw, God blast his eyes!" he shouted. "I don't believe it!"

Loulou followed his gaze. The lines ran smooth and undistorted. "What's all the fuss about?"

He screamed: "*Fuss! Fuss!* You should have poked your nose under that bloody dauber's train once in a while, and then you'd know what to call a fuss."

He hopped down the track, twisting up her arm and forced her to her knees beside the rails. "See that?" He pushed her head down.

The heat from the iron vibrated on her mouth bringing with it a tang like that of dried blood. What it was she saw she could not interpret. "There's . . . nothing."

Yasha pushed her sprawling across the metals. "That's the up line, lady – the one we want. And that," he bawled in desperation, stubbing his boots against it, "that stuff on it, good and thick, that's *rust*, r-u-s-t. Get it?"

"What do you mean?"

"It's not what I mean, it's what that bloody means – this side hasn't seen a train in weeks."

He slouched to the rails crumpling his fist in his eyes. He wanted to weep from disgust at himself for making out he knew it all, for being shown up as the fool he was.

"Pull yourself together, boy, stand on your feet."

The words of his father came down the railroad. Uttered in her ladylike drawl, they were even harder to bear. Loulou seemed to have taken heart from his bullying collapse and was already a hundred yards or so ahead, nimbly skipping from sleeper to sleeper.

She turned gracefully. "Come along, dear, we can make way till sunset and then hide up for the night. We should be in time for a morning dip at the Laskorins."

Yasha drew in his mouth, made the sign against the evil eye and pulled a horrible face at Loulou's departing back. She did not turn again. Eventually, he shouldered the bag and lumbered after her.

Two heads were better than one. If he arrived on his own, the Laskorins would whip him off like a dog. They needed one another, like he'd always thought: her with her chums, him with the know-how. They could drop down to the valley and reconnoitre the house from the river.

He began to run along the rail like a tightrope walker. Stake it out first, that was it. They might be a bit tardy with the red carpet round the front.

Times were hard even for bosom pals, nowadays.

3

The riverside approach to the Laskorins' house was blocked by a maze planted between two dense patches of undergrowth which had been left untended for eighty years and now zig-zagged down to a landing-stage on a steep incline formed from thousands of tons of earth which had been shipped up river on barges.

The intention had been to cut off any view of the house from the banks; ensure that persons landing could easily be seen; and to discourage them from going further should they try to do so without invitation. There was no fear of danger or reason for privacy: the estate demesne extended three hundred and sixty degrees to the horizon. But landward, on the carriage-road side, all standing trees had been uprooted and two villages demolished to provide a stretch of waste scrub reminiscent of the free-fire zone between the inner and outer works of a fortress.

To the new visitor it was explained with apologies and much laughter that Laskorin *grandpère*, old Mitya, had been so dunned by creditors in his youth that he swore that when he made the family rich again he would rebuild the country house, not on architectural but on gun-laying principles. On both counts he was as good as his word. Having resigned his artillery commission to marry a railway heiress, he laid out the grounds strictly in accord with the tactical requirements for enfilade fire, maximum range and the view over sights.

As she negotiated the puddles barefoot, Loulou recalled his face surmounting the tight uniform stock in the salon portrait, like a purple-cheeked tortoise exasperated with its shell. Across a narrow strip of garden planned *au naturel* in the English fashion, the ramparts of the maze reared before her, stacked against the upward drift of the slope like steeplechase hurdles.

Yasha splashed up, his boots tied on a string round his neck. Loulou looked him up and down.

"Do you always wear your boots that way?"

He showed her the soles. "Only in the wet. They leak. See?"

Enjoying the feel of his feet on soft ground, he stared about him cheerfully. From a little grotto a grey face peered down at them through criss-crossing branches of golden rod. The limestone smile was sardonic. As if recognising something along the wall of the maze, Loulou nodded to herself.

"What's this then – his place?" asked Yasha.

"Oh, I don't know. Some Roman, a long way from home."

"That's good," said Yasha. "Then he ain't gonna give us no trouble."

Loulou was struggling to remember. Of the two entrances to the maze, one was bogus: taking that way you ended up at a fountain somewhere near the centre. The other used to be masked by a pair of indecent Renaissance figures which stood on columns where the biscuit-coloured gravel of the path began. Supposedly cupping their infant *pudenda* from bashfulness, they always provoked giggles from less well-bred callers.

At the edges of the walk Loulou found the impress of the columns in the earth. The yew hedges towered above them, trimmed very neat along the curve of the path. She called Yasha.

"Wait a bit," he said. "This stuff hurts." And he sat down to put on his boots. "Here, have a look at this. There's more of them stone people."

Under the hedge clippings two statues lay on their sides: poor cupids, if you could call them that when one was so obviously female. Off their columns they seemed very small when Yasha set them upright against the hedge.

"That's disgusting," he said, standing back. "What kind of person would do that?"

She was about to rebuke him for his prurience when she saw her mistake. To judge by the freshness of break and mark the figurines had been mutilated quite recently; the little boy's sex neatly chipped off, the little girl's incised.

"Savages," she replied at length, looking towards the house.

"You know some nice folk, I must say," said Yasha.

"I hope I still do. I hope for both our sakes I still do."

The path curled and doubled back following its circuitous, time-wasting line, but Loulou had recovered her childhood imprint of the route and pressed forward.

"Pyotr used to work here every morning. Perhaps we'll see his ladder." She stopped occasionally, hummed to herself and then darted off. "I think we go this way," she would call, disappearing round a corner. "And then this."

The last time Loulou had walked through this maze she had been with Laskorin's eldest, unmarried daughter, an old maid of around thirty (which seemed to her then to be ancient), a tall creature who wore a pince-nez on a ribbon and talked excitably of female emancipation. She was an atheist, too, and anti-monarchist, but only shocking to Loulou because she chain-smoked and dropped the cigarette ends. Afterwards one of the gardener's boys had to go down on his hands and knees to pick them up and then rake the gravel.

"I'm sick of this," muttered Yasha. "My legs are too short. We had a lousy night and now we're having a lousy day, and you keep running so I can't keep up." He rubbed his forehead and gazed at the sky. "It's too hot and it'll get worse. I'm fed up. Can't we have a breather?"

"Here we are," said Loulou. "I knew I hadn't forgotten. We're right in the middle."

There was a rustic bench and a pole holding up an oval board with the Imperial coat of arms at the top. Yasha lay along the bench and crossed his legs while Loulou read out the metal lettering on the board:

Le 4 juillet 1887 LL Majestés Impériales L'Empereur et L'Impératrice ont ordonné le placement de cette plaque d'argent au milieu du jardin de Son Excellence M Le Prince Laskorine en commémoration de la belle journée . . .

"Yiddish I could read," said Yasha sleepily. "But the French is a mystery. What's it say?"

"Nothing much," said Loulou. "Someone came here on a day-trip and didn't want to let us forget it."

"That painter guy you told me about?"

Yasha knew this was sly; Loulou had not mentioned the man since yesterday but he was intrigued. Was he becoming jealous?

He handed Loulou a jar of preserved raspberries from his bag. Tipping the fruit back she took a long drink. The juice dribbled down her chin into the linen shirt.

"Not as important as him," she said, wiping her mouth with the back of her hand. "But Martin did meet the Laskorins once."

No plaque for Martin, or the Fifth Army. Would there be, after the war? Something austere, she thought, would be decorous. A cairn in the highest Carpathians.

"Some guy," said Yasha, hoping to draw her. "Where is he now?"

"I don't know. In the snow." Did it ever melt there? She hated being so ignorant of where he had been. "In the mountains, where they're fighting."

"A soldier, I get it. Beg pardon, an *officer*," said Yasha, distancing

29

himself from this other man she was so taken up with. "They wouldn't take me."

"Why not?" It was an absurd question but Loulou was not listening to him.

"Obvious why not." Yasha chuckled and wiggled his feet. "I couldn't see over the side of a trench."

"Not trenches in that part, surely? I thought it was a war of – what do they call it? A war of . . . ?"

"Movement?"

"Exactly. Of movement." She imagined gun limbers being raced among boulders in a great sweeping charge.

Yasha became excited by this talk of war. "That's just where you're wrong, sister, there's sieges round there and bombardments, more big guns than on the West Front. Pa's brother told me – he was wounded at Lowicz and he saw Mackensen closer than you are now."

In her mind Loulou saw Martin, not under fire, but on that day here, so long ago, smiling imperturbably when Kostya made a drunken scene in the presence of the Grand Duchess.

"Things happened, Pa said, horrible things, you wouldn't believe . . ."

A blustery wind began to play at the tops of the hedges, conveying sounds from the house.

"Listen," whispered Loulou. "Can't you hear it?"

The noise had been faint. There was a beat and a sort of peahen screeching gusting down.

"It's music," said Yasha. "They're having a dance."

As they concentrated the noises took on shape: the peal of a harmonium, the jingle of tambourines.

"At this time of day? Don't be stupid."

Yasha pulled a face. "Well, they're drunk, then."

"You don't know them, the Laskorins. If they were they'd keep quiet about it."

Very starchy, dear, aren't they, your friends? I left off hock and seltzer in kindergarten. Don't they ever relax?

Martin, Kostya. *Wo sind sie jetzt im Böhmen?*

They came out of the maze by an iron-work gate which stood at the foot of a grassy rise leading to a flight of stone steps shaded by cedars. Glass splinters littered the steps. The trees blocked the view to left and right but ahead Loulou could see that the glass side doors to the west wing were wide open. Above them was the governess's sitting-room, its windows closed up with green canvas blinds. Not a single pane was intact.

Yasha hung back. The music had stopped the moment they passed through the gate. Who was watching?

A grotesque individual lurched out of the gloom of the hallway and came down the stone steps. Yasha stiffened, ready to run, but as the figure advanced, hands held high like a tightrope walker's, he relaxed. It was a little girl in preposterously high-heeled shoes, several sizes too large; a red blouse hung loose to her knees over a stiff taffeta petticoat. At the foot of the steps she made an awkward curtsey and stood silently in front of Loulou. She might have been a pretty child but there was no way of telling now her face was whitened with powder from forehead to throat, her cheeks and lips bright red and her eyelashes blackened. No visible part of her was unadorned, from the pearl choker at her neck to the flowers wreathed in her brown hair.

Yasha, feeling safe, laughed out loud.

The child slopped up in her ridiculous shoes and smirked at him, the orange rings of her eyes unnaturally bright.

"What's so funny, mister? Never seen a lady before?"

Before Yasha could reply, from inside the house the music struck up again very loudly and the girl performed a curiously antiquated dance around him, bowing every so often as if he were her partner. The hurdy-gurdy noise ceased as suddenly as it had begun and the child started to scratch herself under her blouse.

"Wouldn't have any smokes on you by any chance, would you?" she said.

"You little slut," shouted Loulou, recovering from her astonishment at the apparition quicker than Yasha. "Those clothes don't belong to you."

The girl gave her an appraising glance. "You're a fine one to talk – fit me better than yours do, and that's a fact."

It was true. Loulou was forgetting herself. She tried to deepen her voice. "Where's your mistress?"

"You might well ask," said the girl tucking up her skirts before doing a cartwheel on the grass slope. One ill-fitting shoe flew into the air and Loulou snatched it up, a court shoe, silvery white but now stained with green on the heel.

"This belonged to her, didn't it?"

The girl sat on the grass, her legs widespread. "That's as maybe, I really couldn't say. Besides, there's no masters and mistresses now 'cos we're all nature's ladies and gentlemen."

Yasha was making two fat cigarettes from the strong black tobacco in his bag. The child scrutinised the movements of his clever little fingers as if trying to catch out a conjuror in his trick.

"Me, too?" he said, handing her one of the cigarettes.

"What?"

"A gentleman."

"Depends," she said, sniffing the tobacco. "Depends on whether you're one of us."

"And who are you?" said Loulou blandly, itching to pull the clothes off this insolent little trollop's back.

"The chosen people, that's who."

Yasha grinned. "I'm all right, then."

The girl stared suspiciously into his face. "What's your name?"

"Yakob Pavlovich Rubin."

"Phoo," she said. "Not *that* chosen people."

"Ah – been a fresh selection, has there, since my day?"

"I'll tell you what," said the girl, accepting his light. "*Confidentially*, there has."

"I might have known."

"No, no, *anyone* can be chosen now." She blew out a long stream of smoke. "I do like a whiff when I'm in company."

Yasha pointed at Loulou who watched open-mouthed as the little girl inhaled deeply. "Even him?"

"Who is he?"

"My brother."

"Brothers is in," said the child airily. "That's family."

Yasha squatted down on the grass and pulled hard on his cigarette.

"We all share," said the girl. "My sister Debbie, she got the silver earrings and the red velvet dress and the bracelet with the gold links and the half-moon glass bits hanging down."

Yasha scowled up at the trees. "So your sister's in there, is she?" he said. "Who else?"

The child considered. "Well, we're all there. Ma, Pa, the Ivanovs, Yefim, Mr Schmidt and Fedya. Then Father Mikhail, he used to be, except he's gone away – and Valerian, he's our real father now."

In the pause that followed the music revived. Over an old polka tune they heard a man's laugh.

"That's him," said the girl. "That's our Valerian." She pinched out the cigarette with her dirty fingernails and looked to Loulou. "Pleased to meet you, his brother. I'm Becky. I'm ten. What's your name?"

Yasha had forgotten to give her a name. Loulou swallowed. "I'm . . . I'm nineteen," she said, lopping seven years off her real age.

Becky scrambled up and went to Loulou. "You've got nice smooth hands. Have you done a girl yet?"

Yasha caught Loulou's eye and winked. "Hey," he said. "You're making him blush – he doesn't even shave."

32

"Oughter grow a beard then," giggled Becky. "Like them at home. Ever such big beards they've got."

Loulou took Becky's hand and pulled her into the shade of a magnificent camellia japonica.

"Now, Becky dear, tell me what happened."

The child crumbled her dead cigarette and squinted round at Yasha. "Is he really your brother? Doesn't look a bit like . . ."

"Step-brother," said Yasha. "Same mother."

Becky seemed reassured. "What happened when?"

"When Father Mikhail went away. Where did he go?"

Becky piled the tobacco into a heap on the palm of her hand. "To heaven, didn't he?"

"Do you know where heaven is, Becky?"

"Don't be daft, course I do. Valerian told us."

"Where did he say it was?" said Loulou quietly.

Becky flapped her free hand at the maze and blew ash up into the air. "Down there, somewhere, not far. Give us another, then."

Yasha gave her his half-smoked cigarette. A small round face appeared at one of the upper windows. "Was he the only one?"

Becky shook her head. Her white make-up was beginning to melt and run into the hairline. Droplets glinted on the tiny fair hairs over her upper lip and her little teeth were streaked scarlet where the rouge had rubbed off.

"All except the grandpa. When he fell down Valerian put him in the stables. Oh, and the man with white shoes. He stayed in the room with the big piano."

Loulou turned towards the house and began to climb the steps. Yasha shouted after her but his cry died away when Becky skipped up to take the countess's hand.

"Come on," she said. "I'll do the honours."

4

The baignoire fluster of Mimi Laskorina's small sitting-room made the cool interior seem overheated. The hangings and papers were in matching tones of that carnal puce which Mimi favoured for everything from underclothes to lampshades. Clustered on one peach wall hung a set of oil sketches in japanned frames done by an amateur in the 1830s. Confronting them, Loulou imagined the artist, an exiled officer, a duellist perhaps, clutching his palette in the dusty nullahs of Caucasia with not a live thing to be seen for miles and miles. The pictures seemed to have soaked up every drop of moisture in the hot room and burned it off in their varnish.

Mimi had no family, not one, at least, that could be decently spoken of, and she bought such things at sales, "picked them up", carefully scattering them around her like someone else's discarded, expensive clothes. After breakfast, she lounged here plumping up cushions and sipping orange liqueur, attempting from the mementoes of strangers to imbibe a style of life which she fancied they represented.

The clutter had not been touched. It looked as though Mimi had not yet got up but would soon come down in her wrap to pore over some bankrupt merchant's stock of majolica, or the Venetian glass which straitened circumstances had obliged a general's widow regretfully to dispose of, murmuring incessantly: "A quality article"; "A fine piece of its kind"; "A rare little item"; to the farm-bailiff who bought for her and despised her for this procuring of other people's dead lives.

Becky gazed at the soft furnishings from a respectful distance.

"They give this to me," she said proudly. "No one's to lay a finger on anything in it, not till I've worked out what it's all for." She lit her cigarette, coughed and pointed to a collection of gilt patch boxes on the gerode table. "Yefim wanted them, but Valerian told him he could only have them when he . . ." She hesitated. "'Understood their purpose' – that's what he said."

"Do you think she understood – the woman who put all this here?"

"Oh yes," said Becky. "Be bound to. She was a lady, wasn't she?"

"I really couldn't say," replied Loulou truthfully.

With a timid, proprietorial air like that of a bride showing off the matrimonial home, Becky walked through room after room. To the child, every object was intriguing and she made no distinctions of value or taste. Whether it was a bentwood chair, a silk blind or a Della Robbia roundel of infants embracing, she drew it to the attention of the visitor as if believing that only totality of the contents could yield up the genius peculiar to the house and its owner.

"They must have needed it, otherwise, what's it all doing here?"

To this reductionism Loulou silently assented. Dwellers in mud-huts could parley only mud-hut philosophy: nothing transcends use. As they stood in the long gallery which led to the great drawing-room, Loulou could understand the girl's puzzlement at the lack of obvious meaning in these strange surroundings. If Mimi had found no place here, except in that stuffy parlour, and had had to invent a bogus history for herself, it was because she felt about most of the house as Becky felt about it all: nothing had any reference to her. Becky would never work out, as Mimi had, that there was no equanimity to be gained from the property of others unless you eradicated its pedigree.

Becky left Loulou in the centre of the gallery listening to the music coming from below. At the tall white doors of the drawing-room she turned and called out in her high voice: "This is my very favourite. Close your eyes and don't open till I tell you."

Loulou obeyed without a word.

As the doors opened the music stopped. Through her eyelids Loulou sensed the light and remembered how the sunshine blurred the outlines of the windows on summer afternoons. The drawing-room had always been the most intimate of the family's rooms. Husband, wife and children dined apart but they all gathered here once a day, after dinner. Across the wide barrel vault of the ceiling an imported French painter had devised an incongruous scene: gentrified shepherds in satin knee-breeches were pasturing lambs on a pocket-handkerchief of green, watched over by half-naked nymphs. The Frenchman had left in a huff when Laskorin's grandfather lost patience with the artificiality of the painting, and the background was completed by a serf artist. At a loss to understand the foreigner's visual logic, the serf had introduced a vast herd of ewes, two horned rams, hurdles and a well.

For over half a century the Laskorins' sullen fatstock had gazed down on the Broadwood and the rose marble dais where the orchestra sat on gala evenings sweating into the gold lacings of their professional serge. An idle tympanist once looked up, saw an army of sheep the colour of mud and gave a loud snigger. But in general the aesthetic clamour on the ceiling was seen as piquant, *charmant* and *tout à fait Russe*.

Here Martin had spread out his drawings on the floor; here Loulou had first played piano in Beethoven's *Archduke*; and here she had surprised the middle Laskorin daughter in the arms of a minor official from the next county, half-naked at three in the morning.

"Well I never," squealed Becky. "He's not moved."

Loulou opened her eyes on the white room.

Becky was standing back from a high winged chair. When Loulou came up the child put a finger to her lips:

"Sssshhhh! Doesn't he look nice?"

A man with over-brilliantined hair lolled in a corner of the chair. On his face a wry smile, his mouth gently parted.

"Lovely teeth," whispered Becky.

It was true. They were much admired – his strong point, in fact.

"Here he comes, old Walnut-crackers," Polly Laskorina would say when he leapt the net and skipped up to them waving his racquet. Still impeccably got up in white flannels and blazer slumbered vapid Gerald, the coach, who thought playing tennis with them put you on the same level as the people who paid your wages.

If he opened his eyes now he would know her: they had flirted together often enough. He was the least phlegmatic Englishman Loulou had ever met and would inevitably awaken with some broken-Russian compliment on his lips. Out of gallantry he would give her away. Until she learned the fate of the family she could let no one, not even the child, know who she was.

Loulou perched on the arm of the chair. "Becky, dear, would you like to play us a tune?"

The girl was reluctant to part from her dark young man who slept so handsomely. "It'd wake him," she said. "Besides, I can only play the tambourine and I lost that when we come from the village."

"I'll teach you," said Loulou.

Becky followed her gaze. "On that?" she exclaimed, nodding towards the grand piano. "Oooh, I dursn't. I might break it."

"Don't worry," said Loulou. "That instrument was built for the hands of strong men. Have a try. Get used to it first and then we'll have a lesson."

Becky skipped over to the piano. "I like lessons." Wiping her fingers on her skirt she began to prod the black keys.

Quickly Loulou leant forward, speaking in rapid, soft-toned English. "We're in great danger, don't speak, listen carefully, do just as I say."

Gerald appeared to listen intently, not moving or opening his eyes.

She poured out everything into his tranquil ear: the seizure of her estates; her journey; about Yasha; all the time watching Becky, and moving closer and closer.

Gerald gave a sudden belch, banged his head against her cheek and slid down in the chair. Loulou started from the abrupt movement, nearly overbalancing, and grabbed at his lapels. The blazer fell open; blurting through the gap came a loose slush of uncoiling intestinal tract.

At Loulou's scream Becky's hand flew in the air and caught the piano lid. It came down with a crash on her fingers.

A short figure appeared at the double doors. "What's all the blasted row? Kept telling you, didn't I? What did you expect?" Yasha was shouting. "It's a bloody slaughterhouse all over the place. They've been at it for days, drinking, murdering . . ."

Becky sprawled on the floor, howling and sucking her fingers.

"Here, crybaby," called Yasha, diving under the dead man's chair. "Have his racquet."

The child tried to console herself. "Will he get better?"

"He's better already," said Yasha. "At least he won't have to smile no more for his wages."

"Valerian done this," wept Becky. "It always ends up the same way with Valerian."

Another child came running into the drawing-room. "Hey, you never waited for me, you promised . . ."

This girl was bigger than Becky, smaller than Yasha, but painted up to look like an infantile tart. Her blue-black eyes stared expressionlessly from a little rice-powdered face. Her long plum-velvet frock was too hot for summer and sweat shone at her rouged lips. She wiped it away with a bulgy, ring-covered hand.

Becky ceased to snivel and gave the newcomer a malevolent look. "Aw, shove off, Debbie. What do you think you look like? He wouldn't be seen dead with a little rag-bag like you."

Bile-green droplets from Gerald's ruptured stomach began to merge and spread over the seat of the chair. Loulou wanted to be sick. "Oh God," she murmured, hand over mouth. "Oh God, that poor man. My head's going to . . ."

Yasha grabbed Debbie. "See him?" he said very quietly, pointing to the body of the tennis coach. "He never saw nothing. Just like going off to sleep it was. Right off like a sleeping baby, no trouble, to heaven and never a squeak. And if you don't shut your bleeding little trap, darling, you'll be up there with him."

Debbie stared. "You wouldn't . . . ?"

"Oh, wouldn't I?" said Yasha. "A desperate lad like me . . . I'm

on the run, I am. You didn't know that, did you? The police of four
continents is looking for me."

"I want Matryona," howled Debbie.

The children raced out.

"We'd better scram too, lady," said Yasha.

"Oh God, oh God," shrieked Loulou. "For how much longer do
I have to suffer that *ludicrous*, that *juvenile*, that *lunatic* gutter chat?"

Yasha was unoffended. "Sorry. It's the thought that counts, isn't
it? I mean, you're doing yourself no favours hanging round this dump.
I seen them, you seen them – they're crazy people."

Loulou almost threw herself at him. "You can't stop it, can you?
It's a disease, a horrible linguistic disease. Go away, let me think."

Yasha was shaken but held his ground. They had to have a plan.
They couldn't just sit around indefinitely, playing footsie with a
corpse. He hopped onto the piano stool, whirled round a couple of
times before opening the lid and walking his stubby fingers along the
keyboard.

The air filled with discords. Yasha sang quietly to himself: "I don't
care . . . I don't care . . . We can't stay . . ."

Loulou sank into the plush of a deep settee, opposite Gerald. They
could have been an awkward pair of guests who had nothing in
common and had fallen silent after their introduction. She drew up
her knees and began to shake violently.

From one of the distant rooms came a feminine screech: "You stop
that blasted racket! I'll give you what for, just let me catch you!"

Yasha shut the piano lid with a bang and kicked the stool. "Say
something?" he asked Gerald's immaculate trousers.

Loulou bared her teeth. "*Aaah*, you stunted little blow-fly, get out
of my sight or I'll kill you – I swear it – I'll smash your stumpy
legs . . ."

Yasha swaggered out of the drawing-room whistling. On his way
through the next room she heard him muttering: "If that's the way
you want it, lady, fine by me. See if I care."

An intense desire for sleep was overcoming her. She wanted to
creep into a hole and shiver herself into warmth, buried under the
weight of silence. To hide from this horrible house, its sluttish
dwarf-children, horrible sheep on the ceiling, watching, lurking, their
green teeth waiting to unskin the gross thighs of their mistresses. Vile,
vile.

The house fell silent and she seemed to sleep.

When the man came in she thought she was still asleep. He was
very dark. Deep dark from the woods, black from the sun. A thing
that you cross yourself after seeing when you pass him on a sleigh in

the city. His hands take the bridle of the trace horse and still its champing just by grip. In the breath of the animal he watches you get down. Dumb. Motionless. A thing that ate you up in dreams.

He wouldn't go away. She trembled and knew by the movement of the cushions that she was out of sleep; in touch, coming to. Upside down in his belt was a bottle, over his shoulder the twin-barrels of a gun. Loulou shrank further down in the sofa and kept still.

The man gave her a quick glance and, in turning, caught sight of Gerald's white tennis shoes. The blood had reached all but the last lace hole.

5

"Sweet Mother of Christ! Is there to be no end to it?"
The man fell to his knees and, eyes shut, crossed himself. A smell of bracken and rainwater carried in with him and Loulou saw that his hair and long jerkin were stained with mud.

Another of them – marauding, sentimental, drunk. Face him before he snuffles you out, this pig among acorns.

A brass bell sat on the flap of a secretaire. When she rang it the tiny peal was so familiar that she half-expected Laskorina's maid to appear on the threshold.

The man whirled round, still on his knees. "It moves, then," he said, showing his teeth. "Paler than death, but it moves." He stumped towards her, eyes lustrous from drink. "I thought they'd got you with the other barrel. Are you one of them? Did you do it, then?" He pointed to the body.

She did not speak. The man seemed unsurprised, got to his feet in one smooth movement, unslung his gun and stood above her, cradling it in his arms and stroking the cross-hatching on the stock with his thumb. It looked too good a gun to belong to him.

"Valerian . . ." he began, looking over her head. Loulou's breasts prickled under the shirt. "Valerian thinks his time has come, Valerian stalks the ricks and metes out justice, pruning hook in one hand, severed heads in the other, St John the Divine in his pocket, just for information . . ."

He allowed the gun to slide so that the metal plate on the butt touched her hair. "Why did you leave him uncovered?" he shouted, suddenly angry. "Isn't he dead?"

Weaken and they'll have you by the throat, these people. Strike first, be firm, command, Kostya had drilled her.

In the broad spaces of the room her voice sounded unnaturally loud. "How should I know that? Touch him."

She expected a blow but Kostya was right: the tone of an order is what makes it obeyed. The man leapt over the sofa and she could hear him beside her pulling at something.

"Nearly," he grunted. "More than winged."

A blast rattled the window-panes. Two doves rose from the plum-tree by the orangery. Ears ringing from the detonation she turned to see him breaking the gun. A brass cartridge case shot out, clipping the gilt mouldings on the recessed wall panelling.

"Out of his misery," he said brusquely.

Striding over to the long casements through which, on clear winter days, could be seen the domes and crosses of five churches, he ripped down one of the heavy velvet curtains and carried it over to the high-backed chair, its headrest smoking from the spread of shot. The bluish-green stuff swished on the floor as he flung out the curtain, twirling it like a matador's cape, so that it settled flatly over the space in the centre of the seat where the dead man hunched against the stiff cushions, hiding the jagged hole in his chest. The curtain stretched from top to toe, enrobing the tennis coach in its lining of sun-bleached calico.

"What kind of man are you, lad?" he murmured. "This is no place for cow-eyed boys. Valerian has a mission for boys with white hands. The cutting has only begun. Don't wait to have that cream of yours pinked."

Spitting on his hands he began to manhandle the chair behind the Broadwood.

"There's a great time coming. First to go down was the war, then our little Tsar – the Kingdom of Heaven be his – and now judgement is upon us with the Lord in all His wrath unseating the stars from their places, driving up the price of wheat, and I don't know what else. A great weariness to hear our Valerian, but there's a queer education to him."

All this exalted gospelling was accompanied by a wild grin. She could not decide if this were his normal speech, or if he were imitating someone madder, but she watched him with growing fascination, forgetting to be afraid.

He gave a kick to the rear casters of the chair which described a slow arc on the glossy boards before coming to rest under a group portrait of the Laskorin males dressed in the costume of Tartar Khans.

"Are you educated?"

Loulou huddled down in the sofa and peered over her knees. "Fairly," she said, taking her time, offering the kind of answer which might please him. "But abstract things never seemed to stick in my mind."

"No!" he shouted. "What I mean is – can you speak with tongues?" As he waited for her reply the man took up the bottle at his belt and uncorked it.

"Tongues?" She focused on the pin-point irises of his staring eyes.

He took a mighty pull at the bottle and screwed up his face as if the taste were disagreeable. "Tongues! Has thou been touched by the Pentecostal fires?"

"I doubt it," she said uncondescendingly.

"He doubts it," he simpered, raising the bottle to the portrait. "He can't say, your excellency, his tongue cleaves to the roof of his mouth. See here, bag of bones, can you talk German?"

Loulou's face lightened. "Oh yes," she said. "Reasonably."

"And French?"

"And French. At Smolny I won the medal . . ."

"And English, too?"

"Best of all," said Loulou. Perhaps the deserters were not all Russian. They might need an interpreter down in the village.

He bent over her slowly passing the bottle under her nose. "Then drink, my little baa-lamb, the ash is on your muzzle. Drink before they lead you to the shambles."

She felt faint at this unexpectedly threatening response and the reek of liquor was making her head swim. "Have I said something wrong?"

"Not to me," he whispered close into her hair. "But Valerian, now, Valerian is the one prophet, Valerian alone has been given the gift, Valerian speaks the tongues – the kitchen-menu French, the 'This Way Up' and 'Fragile' on the German boxes the masters had from Petrograd. Why do you think our dear departed tennis coach lies here, staining his flannels?"

"I don't . . ."

"Don't know!" screamed the man. "Know, know now, because I tell you – for his 'mackintoshes' and his 'dogcarts' and his 'milady' – for all the whirring foreign noise his mouth could make, presuming to outspeak Valerian."

Loulou giggled. "That's nonsense. You simply want to frighten me. Can't you talk like a normal person?"

The bottle went again to his lips and he gulped deeply. "As well to be frightened. Here, at night, the women wait for the moon to fall out of the sky."

He passed the bottle to her and she drank, pleased for the first time, since assuming her new identity, to be taken as so unquestionably male that she could become the drinking partner of this man. How easily men recruited one another as comrades.

It was cognac, brackish from age. Someone had resealed the old cork with sealing-wax and the spirit tasted greasy and burnt. The spoor of the Laskorins' major-domo: helping himself, then adulterating. She remembered Kostya's whitewashed cellar, and the big cellar-book, and the acid taste of the staves she had licked as a child playing among the broken casks. Her father drank little but loved the ageing of wine: "For Loulou's son and the Reds, for their coming of age together."

As she took her lips from the bottle a picture came to her of the butler's split thumbnails, but she went on drinking. The cognac bit deep into her empty gut.

"Here, that'll do," said the man, surprised at her appetite. "I'm not here to make a man of you." He pinched her ear, looked hard at her and she stared back boldly. "I know you from somewhere," he said. "It'll come back . . . Eyes like that . . . Ungodly eyes . . ."

The French window stood open. A fine dust bowling gently over the lawn had clouded the acacias. Loulou and her companion continued to regard each other until the man threw himself down on the sofa beside her. "An illustrated paper," he muttered, finally averting his gaze. "The guards at Krasnoye. Some balcony or other. Same old faces. Women's faces. All of them waiting. Ladies-in-waiting, waiting . . ."

His voice fell away and he seemed to doze. Loulou relaxed his fist from the neck of the bottle, and making a stoup of her hand poured out a little of the liquid into her palm. His eyes were closed. She bent down and supped up the spirit. Now it had less fire. She dabbled her throat and temples with the moisture. Head arched back, she allowed it to dry off in the air, filming her skin with sticky warmth.

As if conscious of her movement the man gave a short violent snore, then jumped up. "Skirts! Skirts! Only the men were in breeches. Your legs are disguised." He laughed. "What are you? A spy with lace drawers down her gaiters?"

Her head began to spin again as she struggled to work out the time it would take to get from the sofa to the door. She had lingered too long. He was fit and would catch her. Where was Yasha?

"No." She leaned back against the cushions, suddenly resigned from fatigue, brandy and the overpowering presence of this strange man. "Not me."

"No drawers? That's no way for a girl to go about even if she is a spy." He laughed again. Perhaps he wasn't dangerous, after all, just curious. "After you," he said, waving a hand towards the bottle. "Ladies first, I know, even though there may be nothing between them and their buckskins."

Why had Kostya been so abstemious? It was delightful to be sensuously fuddled. Think how that side of their lives could have been made bearable. Pleasurable, even, had he brought to bed one or two of those musty bottles over which he gloated in privacy. Then there would have been no need to tear her.

"All the same to me," said the man morosely. "You all look the same – in clothes, out of clothes. Whoever made you, made you with one piece. Peeled you from the solid bolt."

He took out a clasp knife and began to scrape at a dark stain on the front of his jerkin.

Outside, the afternoon silence closed in over the house, stilling the sedge along the ponds, the rustle in the shrubberies and the tap-tap of the family thrush cracking snailcases on the cobbles of the great court. At the mis-chime of the stable-clock the lizards twitched in Polly Laskorina's vivarium. Loulou sensed the mob in the park, bedded down, pillowed by their axe-hafts under the sticky-budded larches.

The scraping went on and on. She took more of the cognac and marvelled at the man's persistence. It must be blood and he wanted to be clean. At last the blade clicked back and he carefully smoothed down the leather.

"Take *me*," he said, picking up his previous train of thought. "Strip me naked and who have you got? – Jack."

He looked to her for confirmation.

"Is that your name?" she said. "Don't you think we ought to be introduced?" She knew the remark was silly, coquettish even, but with the cognac in her she felt suddenly reckless: she passionately wanted to make him like her and protect her from whatever might happen.

"Belyakov," he said, stretching his legs. "Vladimir Ivanovich. Huntsman."

"And I'm . . ."

"You!" he shouted, for no apparent reason. "I don't need to know your name. I've seen you before. I was seeing you before you were born."

When he groped for the bottle she steadied him against her side and passed it to him, hand over hand, like a baton. His eyes were as watery and blank as a dead man's.

"Our Father . . . Who art caught in . . . the act of giving them our daily bread . . . Valerian knows it, Valerian did his own words after he hanged the priest with his own belt and put on his cassock. 'Lead us into temptation, deliver us to evil' . . ."

Suddenly frightened, Loulou began to slide along the sofa but Belyakov grabbed her by the arm. "Lady-eyes, daisy-eyes," he slurred. "I won't hurt an eyelash of you, young master."

She hollowed her back and sank inwards away from his other hand. He seemed puzzled. "Don't you trust me, boy? Why, you and me could be friends. A man needs a friend, a boy needs a friend."

The hand pressed at her right breast through the shirt. He paused, mumbled to himself, spanned the entire breast with his fingers and squeezed. Loulou jumped from the pain and gave a squeal.

"How dare you, you great ugly pig! Take your foul hands off me or . . ."

Before she could formulate the threat he had twisted up her arm behind her back and was thrusting her across the room.

"Stupid bitch," he grunted, pulling the shirt up from her midriff to confront her with her own image in the gilt Rococo mirror which hung between the two long windows. "Are those all you've got to hide?"

The exposure was humbling. Not because she cared that he looked but because this man stared flatly, unvoluptuously, and shamed her, as Kostya had done, the first time, by his disappointment at her girlish figure.

The bony upper part of Loulou's chest flushed from physical self-hatred.

"Just look at yourself," said the face over her shoulder.

Her face was streaked with dirt. Her hair was filthy and seeded with tacky fluff from bulrush plumes and the tortoiseshell flecks of dead birch-leaf. She felt like a naughty child caught rolling in the mud. Only her lips were improved, set clear in her face, cosmetically rouged from the raspberry juice.

After gazing coldly into the reflection of her grey eyes Belyakov gave up, lurched away and sat down heavily on the sofa. Loulou raised the hem of the shirt again and stood before the glass, enjoying the touch and sight of her own hand on her breasts.

"You won't get far, not here, not with those," rambled the deep voice.

"What do you mean?" she said dreamily. "I'm not big, I can run, they don't get in the way . . ." His dismissal of her would have been painful enough had she been sober, but the liquor provoked her to exhibit a spasm of annoyance, masking even her panic at the intimacy which, Loulou knew, she herself had provoked.

He laughed. "That's for a certainty – more ribs than a pontoon bridge, but that's not where you stop, dearie, is it?" He nodded at her waist. "There's a bit more to the rest of you, and a whole lot more obvious when they liberate you from your breeches."

Loulou swayed back slightly. "What are you talking about? Those people – out there – are they so different from you?" She let the shirt fall and followed him as he went to the east-facing window. Beyond the flagstones of a terrace, one floor below, a grassed scarp fell away to the plantation where every autumn after the forester had thinned out the saplings the Laskorin daughters had made a tree house in the coppice from stripling trunks.

With a marked change of manner Belyakov took her arm gently this time and pointed over the tree-tops to where the village lay in the hollow.

"Down there is a man leading men, pointing them like a setter pointing for guns. He'll scent you on the air, and freeze for them, dead in line for this, here." And he pressed his hand between her legs. She did not move away but stood rigid.

"Why?" she said at last. "Why me?"

"Oh, it's nothing *personal*. He doesn't know you, not as an individual. It's all of you, all together. 'Justice indivisible and indiscriminate' he says. You might as well ask why *him*?" Belyakov jerked his head towards the body under the curtain. "Five years out of England and scarcely a Russian word in his head."

The draped chair loomed big in the afternoon shadow. Loulou shuddered. "What harm have we done you – that pathetic Englishman and me? A real man would be in the woods, stopping up the earths of those night prowlers." She felt Kostya round her, smiling, snarling, touching, as many-armed as a Hindu god, that terrible first time. The memory instantly quenched her desire to be taken up and protected by this Belyakov man, at the very moment that he began to show her more particular attention. She tore herself away, shivering in spite of the heat, and folded her arms, gripping the loose flesh at her shoulders with spread fingers. "Diabolical," she murmured. "Hanging priests is one thing, but excusing animal appetites . . . that's night talk, the slavering of unclean things . . ."

Belyakov whistled and frowned at her. "Tell that to the priest. Dead is dead. See what indignity he wouldn't rather have suffered."

He picked at the window shutters with the spike of his knife. Fragments of paint floated down to the sill, their coat-upon-coat laminations unpeeling like the pages of a miniature book.

"Women," he said moodily. "Women can wash off the stains. Ours have learned to, at any rate; and your sort is our sort under all that delicate talk."

She opened her mouth to shout but he turned and prodded her away with the knife. "Your sort . . . Who do you think you are now? Aren't you ashamed to have come to this? Where's the honour in you? Fight if you don't deserve what is coming to you, don't try to enlist me for your protection. Oh, I know that's what you thought. Fight or run. Don't wait like a doe for the ferret – not like *him*, their brilliantined racquet-master with manicured nails." A flush spread across his cheekbones above the dark beard. "I've killed no one from

malice, not yet. And as to the desires of the unclean of the earth, they
are better visited on the bodies of others than on your own."

Kostya, what did you teach me? *There are martyrs of the devil who
put to shame the saints of God.*

"Be merciful, be practical if you can stomach it. Go on," he said,
pointing to the shrouded chair round which greeny blow-flies had
begun to circulate. "Lay him out, wash him – if you can find any
water in the tanks that Valerian spilled for his baptisms. What do
you want me to do – carry the buckets for you?"

She strode at him and raised her fist. "I know fear. I have waited
for the hammering at the porch, and the lighted torches, and the
uncouth railing of men like you, canvassing my fate, all in the name
of some newly-dispensed legality."

Belyakov was not listening. Half-way through her speech he had
thrown open the casement and peered out across the terrace into the
trees.

"See there," he muttered as she came up to see what he was so
intent upon. "Jesus Christ himself – come to make a neighbourly
call."

Through the spinneys of young timber wound a straggle of bearded
men, the younger pressing forward, sweeping the uncut tussocks of
grass with staves, the steel tips flashing. They strode ahead like a line
of skirmishing pickets, prodding clumps and slashing as they passed
through coppices. What they were searching for Loulou could not
guess, but in case it had not sprung out at the touch of the staves
or had lain still, they were backed up by another line, this time of
older men limping and stumbling in the high, springy grass, scything,
each his patch, in wide intersecting circles. Behind them lay untidy
swathes of bark-strippings and yellow grass. The wind had stilled.
Nothing carried up to the great house except for the far-off tinkle
of steel as the blades clashed, or an occasional shriek from a woman
who had broken away from the party skirting the line of cutters
to pounce on some small animal or nest overtaken by the march of
men.

Some way ahead, booted, and stepping high in the wide savannah
of the pampas growth came a tall youth in a black robe hitched to
the level of his boot-tops. Every now and again he stopped, snatched
at the spearpointed grass, and chewing at a blade like someone out
for a stroll, turned to the followers and shouted something which,
far from Belyakov and Loulou, died on the still air. A rolling chorus
came back from the men who were evidently obeying some signal
and they rested at their upright scythe handles dark against the white
grass roots. The youth looked about, lolling his head to the sky as if

to warm his face against the sun. At a wave from him the men and women resumed their progress up the slope.

"What are they doing?" said Loulou, the third time the lines had stopped and moved on.

"Hunting," said Belyakov, keeping back from the window as the cries of the women grew shriller and nearer.

"What for?"

"People," he said. "See their dogs?"

Over the expanse Loulou could see no sign of an animal.

"There, there." He nodded to the band of flower-kerchiefed women. "Bitches have the best noses."

Loulou leaned forward across the wide sill. It was like the theatre, only better, for the scale of the set was limitless to the horizon, the colours unhazed in the sparkling light. For a moment she felt like the wolf which viewed his own hunting in the snow: a lovely picture until it came home to you that the convergence of their tracks was the point of your eye.

At the edge of the terrace the youth disappeared from sight into the Laskorins' ha-ha. Suddenly his white fingers appeared on the rustic cornice, then his head, framed between two stone posts of the balustrade. Loulou looked down on him from the window, secure behind the glass made opaque by the slant of the light. A low straw hat wreathed with ivy and bindweed flowers hugged his face.

Two of the younger men detached themselves from the group and ran down into the ha-ha. Evidently they made a platform with their staves for the youth rose up just below Loulou, his hands free, and bounded over the coping of the balustrade onto the flags of the terrace. The stock of his single-barrelled shotgun clattered onto the stones as he flexed his knees low to break his fall.

First over after the youth was a short, bald man with a beard half-way down his chest. One of his shoulders was higher than the other giving him the appearance of being always about to unsling his Schneider rifle. He turned his back on the youth and shouted down to the crowd in the ha-ha.

A chair leg knotted to a rope sailed overhead. The bald man made it fast between the pillars of the balustrade. One by one they followed up, arm over arm, each carrying a weapon strapped to his back. Their possession was evidently a gauge of loyalty because the youth's followers, as soon as they found their feet on the terrace, made an awkward presentation of arms before seating themselves at his feet in long, ragged file. Half a dozen swarthy fellows with blue scarves knotted round their forearms stood by one side. Belyakov noted that these were equipped with Martini Henrys, Chauchats and the standard Imperial infantry arm, long-barrelled rifles from the Putilov works.

When the women climbed up the gabble became deafening. They passed along the lines of sitters handing out round loaves of rye bread and little boat-shaped pies from deep bags at their waists. The men ate noisily, but with eyes averted from the youth who was staring up, arms behind his back, at the massy pilasters of the great house, like a sightseer in a strange town. There was some kind of mute communication between himself and the swarthy men with rifles because all at once, perhaps after catching sight of some movement of his hands which were hidden from Loulou and Belyakov, they took six bottles from a hat box one of them had carried up, and rolled them down the terrace along the lines of men.

The noise increased. While the men drank, the women stood grouped behind them like a church choir setting up a rhythmic chant which lifted up through the buzz of male voices. Debbie and Becky were visible in the group, clapping their hands and smiling.

Safe from view, Loulou had leisure to inspect the youth. Under the jutting blond eyebrows his blue eyes seemed very pale; above the fair skin of the face already darkened from sunburn were clusters of near-white curls emerging from beneath the plaited straws of the hat-rim.

Suddenly he moved, clicked his heels together and raised his arms. The shotgun bumped against his spine. Instantly, everyone went quiet.

II

VALERIAN

End of May–beginning of June 1917

6

"Dearly beloved brethren, who are we that are gathered together, breaking our bread in the shadow of the tents of the unrighteous?"

At the window Belyakov spat and muttered something to Loulou which she could not catch.

"Hearken to me, toilers in the vineyards of the earthly lords, and let each man answer to himself – who is he?"

The women, apparently unperturbed by this exclusion, began to screech, exchanging among themselves dry-throated but musical cries which made Loulou want to move her feet in a jerky kind of dance.

"Who art thou . . . ?" "I am thee . . ." "And thou art I . . ."

Their bare feet stomped as each woman sang her response. The men shifted in the sweltering heat and the bald man mopped his head, but none answered the speaker. Loulou realised that their silence was part of a ritual, and they were waiting for the moment of their ceremonial entrance.

"He is a grain of the unnumbered sands upon which immemorially have trod the feet of the unjust!"

He sounded thrillingly, magnificently mad and Loulou wanted to giggle and, simultaneously, cry out in the same archaic words: "Aye! Aye!" like one of the rabble at an illicit prayer meeting.

The youth lifted his bronzed face to the sun and screamed melodiously: "I am sent to become one of you, to lead you up to the high places!"

No one showed the least surprise. The uplifted voice filled the listeners' expectations. From their throats came cries of exhortation: "Zion in Glory!" "Hosanna!" "Jerusalem is ours!" The bald man began to weep, fingering the silken knots of his priest's rosary.

This was only the beginning. More was expected from Valerian and they settled themselves before him, the partly-eaten food discarded; but, amongst the men, the leather bottles still plied their way along the line. They were waiting for that moment when they would cease to be individual men and women and come together as a congregation, making their devotions manifest in one body.

Valerian removed his hat and passed a hand through his fair curls.

"I came among you to partake of your tribulation. Who are we, my people?"

"Scum," said Belyakov distinctly this time, clearly enough for Loulou to hear.

Valerian paused and, for a moment, she froze, fancying that the youth, too, had heard, but his pause was only to give space for more cries from the listeners.

"White wolves that roam abroad fearless at noon," shouted the tallest of the swarthy men slapping the bandolier across his chest and stepping forward out of rank. Valerian smiled, his grave eyes sweeping the line from end to end. At the silent movement the tall man fell back, reproved. Valerian waited. No person dared further to divine his mind.

"What is our quality?" he whispered in a rising tone. "What nature has been bred into our bones? What men have we been made? *Made, made, made!*"

Seated directly before Valerian was a very old man with a trim white beard. As the speech had gone on he had been struggling to make his mark with a cry or comment, but every time he opened his mouth he was overtaken by the readier wits of the younger men, and had fallen simply to looking round, his lips working soundlessly.

"Spit it out, Gerasim," said Belyakov to himself.

In the silence the old man's voice shook: "Meek, oh Lord. Poor in heart."

The crowd stirred in irritation and Gerasim stared at Valerian's boots.

"Hearken to Gerasim," said the youth, "who has grown old in the service of earthly powers."

"Blacked their boots, emptied their pots, lifted them dead-drunk off the naked bodies of splay-hipped peasant girls in every town from here to Simbirsk," murmured Belyakov.

"We were the captive prize tied at the stirrup of every prince. But now, my people, we are come into our own. The Kingdom of Saints is upon us and our rule shall be of iron."

Loulou could have clapped. A roar went up from the crowd, and the women cast dried flowers overhead.

The young man adopted a graceful stance, one leg straight, the other crooked at the knee and Loulou was reminded of an amateur player taking bows in the very salon where she and her companion now crouched, after hamming singlehanded through *Othello* in Mimi Laskorina's sables. Timidity seemed to have overcome Valerian after those ringing phrases and, like the actor come down to earth, he coughed politely behind his hand in the face of his audience's clamour.

Between the balustrade and the women, Debbie and Becky were playing knucklebones. When the noise subsided the women began to fidget and Debbie saw that one of them would knock into her or Becky and upset the bones. She got to her feet, grotesque in the oversized lady's tea-gown, raised her arm, fingers together, and pointed skywards.

"Child?" said the youth with genuine tenderness.

Debbie's face was clown-like from purloined rouge. "Valerian, tell us about the Beast."

At this, Gerasim's right-hand neighbour rattled an abacus and raised his runny eyes to the sun. "The Beast, Valerian, the Beast! Let me number him, let the beads ride up to the vile sum of his abominations!"

Valerian's voice became rasping: "In a dream I have been visited. I have beheld him, truly, running on the clouds of night, leaping from mountain to mountain. He is vast, my brethren, swelled with enormities, but he jinks like a hare in his grace. I have seen him, a rider upon a great horse, blood-red hair streaming to the wind, the smile of heaven on his brow."

"What is it?" whispered Loulou. "This Beast?"

Belyakov groaned quietly. "Christ only knows, but you can count on his telling of it to make them forget their bellies and sharpen their hooks."

"The Beast cometh," shouted Valerian. "The Beast cometh to raise servant against master."

"Glory be to the Beast," moaned a young woman in a floral scarf. "Our babes shall be suckled."

"Believe it," answered Valerian. "For the truth of my heart is sprung into my mouth."

He stepped to one side and viewed the great house front like a builder contemplating his work, outlining its extent with a flourish of his hands. "Necessity dissolves all laws. Hunger will break through stone walls without respect of persons. All this before you is henceforth your common demesne."

Valerian spread out his arms as if to embrace the vast Laskorin estate, which rolled behind his listeners over the tree-tops on the ridge, across the river and into the swampy meadowland miles beyond the formal gardens and parkland within sight of the terrace. "Where they ploughed not, there we shall dig! Corn shall be rooted in the place of the rose. Oh, men of the north, who are reckoned the least of nations, out of ye shall a branch spring and a star arise!"

This last cry boomed out of the depths of Valerian's breast and spilt over the heads of the peasants like a bow-wave. Its modulation was no longer that of a youth, but of a youth become man, a man inspired, glorying in his access of strength. This was the moment which all had been waiting for. On the word "arise" men, women and children rose to their feet, and at a signal from the silver-haired man, called out as one: "God save thee, our Valerian, dear Father and Provider!"

But Valerian overrode the encomiums. "The vagabond Christ is at your head! The fat swine of the earth shall be bled from the throat! Our vine shall green from the root-sack of their bones!"

A squat broad-shouldered peasant, dressed in a long armless garment with silver tassels which flapped around his soldier's boots, suddenly unhitched his rifle and, with a practised twist, locked a barbless French bayonet along the underside of the barrel. For a brief moment he was at the centre of a turbulent circle of younger men who, seizing on his example, drew from under their shirts and from the tops of their boots kitchen knives and saw-edged flexible blades thieved from the cabinet-maker's workshop. As the blades whirred in the sun Loulou shook and saw in her mind scalded hogs on the trestle, their flaccid quarters inert to the knife. The peasant with the bayonet vaulted onto the balustrade and disappeared. Others followed, the less athletic cursing and tripping on the mossy stone.

"Where have they gone?" she whispered to Belyakov when the terrace was half-depleted and the women had begun a weird keening song.

"To the vaults. That short one, Anton, is running his own game. Last night they murdered the menservants and they're rolling every tun in the cellars up to the gatehouse."

"Why? I thought he said . . . Valerian . . . I thought he said they were sharing . . . ?"

"Not Anton," said Belyakov feeling for the cartridge pouch at his waist. "Not that bastard Slovene. He was our quartermaster sergeant in Galicia. He sold the field bakery to the Austrians for rum."

Below them, a seraphic smile on his face, Valerian was walking among the women. Loulou was intrigued. The chorus skirled higher as he dallied, fondling the curls behind his ears, affecting unsureness about whom to pick and the singers shrank back into a closer circle where barely enough ground was left for their feet to cover. When they threatened to squeeze to a standstill the circle opened out and the chosen one was extruded, rotating in step to the beat. The women seemed to know instinctively who was required but no preference for beauty, grace or youth was discernible to Loulou. The reward for young and old alike was an anointing brush from Valerian's fingers, a touch which the woman would cover, cupping the place with her hand before curtseying back into the circle.

Twice Valerian walked the ring watched by several of his older male followers and with the bald-headed man one step behind. The women were unremitting, their cadence soaring from tremolo to the high pitch of village part-song with its peculiar edge of enticement. In some country hamlet Valerian would have improvised an answering call but here he was meant to make his mark upon them in a different way.

For the third time he resumed progress when a blow racked his body back upon itself and, given the time it took him to fall, Loulou thought he must have been shot. Her first impression was that a bullet had caught him in the ribcage and traversed, shattering his spine. But the impetus had come from behind, as if an animal had burst from a gap in the flagstones burying its teeth in the small of his back.

There was a cracklish bang like that of a discharge and a flash the colour of blood, but the noise was Belyakov's stabbing his fist through the window glass, the scarlet, the bald man's Solferino blouse flung over Valerian's chest. "Hermann Schmidt!" he bawled, hacking at the jagged edges of the hole with his elbow. "Do something useful, you gutless Prussian bug; if any harm befalls him I'll take it out on your pudding face! Get something between his teeth before he goes tongueless as well as mindless!"

The register of the women's voices degenerated to a whining growl. They stopped dancing but instead of offering help to the German who was frantically casting about for a gag, they snatched at their skirts and pressed closer to one another. A shrivelled old wife at the centre of the crush lifted her cataract-shrouded eyes and screamed. When the rest took up her lead, it was too much for Hermann who turned away from the body and began to scream back.

Belyakov poked his shotgun through the hole and fired both barrels at once. His yell unfroze the ensuing silence. "Rip up your blouse, dodderer, before your little Jesus-bell bites back on his clapper!"

Hermann nodded and fell to stuffing red rag into Valerian's mouth.

"And you can get those dry-uddered witches out of my sight. What's the matter with them? Lost their legs with their voices?"

Loulou surprised herself by enjoying the exchange. Belyakov was the only one unafraid at the scene being played out before them. Clearly he had some affinity with this young man whose forehead stood out pallid against the grey paving of the terrace-walk. Unpolluted by that reverence which had made the women ludicrous with their bobbing and ducking, Belyakov knew Valerian as a man and knew of his falling sickness. Under the buskin and gobbledygook he must be more than a green-man totemised by rustics. With the pentecostal fire of his mouth he had broken in that pack of wolverines cavorting on the terrace. One day, just as easily, he would turn them aside like a coulter slicing fallow.

Hermann looked up at the window. "You'll pay for that, Vladimir Ivanovich. It's the master's people you've been disparaging with your harum-scarum. He sets his face against remarks in the personal vein. And mind the people's goods — the Lord has not yet granted us the boon of a glazier."

Before he could finish Belyakov smashed more glass and leaned out, waving his gun. "You prating Christ-pimp, Schmidt, talk to me like the Junker horse-arse you were born, not a Judas with his hand on his heart. Tend that man while I come down and shoo off those hags when I tell you."

This seemed to exhaust the fight in Hermann who cleared his throat and barked at the women: "Well! What are you gawping at? Out of it, out!"

The women departed, struggling over the balustrade in their heavy skirts. Only the two little girls stared dispassionately as Valerian twisted and gurgled under the inept touch of Hermann's fingers, the ictus in his neck palpitating like a gland. The wild screwing of his limbs had ceased. "You ain't doing it right," said the elder girl, joggling the knucklebones in her net purse. "Is he, Beck?"

"Naw."

Becky drummed her sister's tambourine and they both began to skip around Schmidt, rattling the golden sequins under his nose. The German swung round and made a grab for Debbie's ankle but she was too nimble. The other men laughed. "Oooh," said Debbie. "You're forgetting yourself, you are, in the presence of the master."

Valerian suddenly arched his back. Through the rags his teeth ground alarmingly. The girls abandoned their teasing and stood side-by-side with Schmidt who was kneeling at the body. "Would it be right to be buckling his legs with this belt?" he asked, knowing that the children felt no fear at Valerian's fits and had shown others exactly what to do when he was taken in this way.

Debbie considered. "No," she said. "It's a little 'un. See his eyes — when it's only a little 'un, it goes to his eyes and his lids they fuzz like bee-wings."

When Belyakov came onto the terrace he grabbed Valerian's hat and waved it at Loulou who had poked her head through the smashed panes. "Here, you, daft lad! Get the cushions off those sofas and make a bed on the floor. I'm bringing him in out of the sun." As he and two of the other men staggered up the terrace with the body, Belyakov turned to Schmidt who was keeping step with them. "My nephew," explained the huntsman.

Loulou piled lemon-coloured cushions into a heap by the secretaire. Afterwards, in the presence of the men, the prostrate Valerian and the dead tennis coach who still lay swathed in the wing chair, she found that her hands were trembling and she tried to shield the outline of her breasts by folding her arms and hunching her shoulders. Against the glistening satinette Valerian's curls spread unkempt, several tones darker than they had appeared in broad day.

She turned away and crossed the room to the opposite rank of windows overlooking Mimi Laskorina's private garden. On the tiny four-square lawn women were hacking out turf round a grey stone fountain shaped like a goldfish. Beyond them two old men scythed down the bushes in the rose-walk, crimson-flecked white petals drifting under their blades. In some hidden place the terrace chant resumed and Loulou screwed up her eyes at the nasal screech of children's voices.

"Water, boyo. Fetch us water." Belyakov was shouting at her.

She hunted round for the obvious – glasses, decanter, bowl – but none contained water.

"Find the pump," said the huntsman more quietly, jabbing downwards with his thumb.

"Where on earth . . . ?" she began, but Schmidt scowled and the two other men, twin brothers called Ivanov, one with a limp, looked curiously from her to Belyakov. Afraid suddenly of giving herself away, she ran to the far end of the drawing-room from where, she remembered, the double doors opened eventually onto a stairway. Behind her, his voice carrying hollowly under the high ceiling, the huntsman was giving her a family tree for the benefit of his strange companions: "My sister's boy, not the brightest but a good lad at heart . . ."

7

Beyond the formality of the great room where Valerian lay, extended the family's more private apartments. Yet another drawing-room, but much smaller, with ochre-washed walls and a plump green settee upholstered in rep. This was the hermaphroditic mix of Millie Laskorina's suite leading off from the greyish study where her foreign illustrated papers still strewed the circular table.

In these parts the old house was still replete with the ease of well-being. "I pride myself," Millie used to say in her mannish slur, "on my in-dep-endence." Up here Millie had maintained her self-sufficiency and no one had yet disturbed the little blue alcove where she had eaten alone at a folded card-table surrounded by her glass-cased Italian majolica.

Loulou fingered the banding of an oblong table and stared at the bell-pull which was looped, out of her reach, at Millie's height. "I always ring at ten. I always have coffee brought up then. I never trouble Gerasim." Always. Never. Until now Loulou had not given much thought to Millie's emancipated positivism. But how, she wondered, was the food brought? Given old Laskorin's sense of decorum not, surely, via the grand staircase?

She found the door in the next room let into a gesso *trompe-l'oeil* of a Roman banquet which towered above the iron hoops of Millie's bedstead. Wooden stairs led steeply down. Leaving the door open for light, Loulou descended awkwardly, misjudging the drop from step to step. Just when she achieved a rhythm, the stairway veered left and she came upon another section, even steeper, but well-lit from a doorless archway situated at the bottom of the flight. The last two steps were unexpectedly tall and, in her eagerness to be out in the daylight, Loulou stumbled and almost fell onto a flagstone floor pitted with gravel specks that shone like sand.

"Nursey, nursey, what a wedding day shall be mine . . . Noises, noises in the head . . ."

A tiny old woman in a headscarf had emerged from behind a dresser. At the sight of Loulou she fell silent and wiped her eyes on the fringes of her scarf. The wavering song of the peasants digging up the croquet ground floated into the kitchen.

Loulou flinched back against a table, scoring her hands on the hard edge. "Forgive me," she said. "I seem to have lost my way."

The woman stared at her and dived a hand into the bodice of her black dress. "You're late. Now, where's the list?" Without taking her eyes from the countess she produced a narrow roll of butter paper and began to unfurl it, patting it down against her breast. "All here," she sighed. "All on Frossya's list. 'Frossya, I can count on you,' she said. 'Everyone is to come to make my day glorious. Let streamers fly from the cedars.' The Laskorins know everyone. Telegrams here, telegrams there . . ."

By now the end of the roll of paper was touching the floor and Loulou saw that it was quite blank. The old woman felt the paper with twitching, yellow fingers as if it were embossed with letters. "You, now, who are you, eh? Late, careless, late."

"You wouldn't know . . ." began Loulou.

"Ha!" said Frossya. "Every last one, late-coming reprobate is known to me." She moved closer to Loulou, spat and poked a finger through a rent in the man's shirt. "You're the governess from his estate in Tver, the one she found him with, the one she flogged and sent away."

Although the old woman had no strength and could not have hurt her, Loulou shrank back further, feeling that the finger would pierce through her skin. The table overbalanced with a crash. "I don't understand . . . I don't belong here . . ."

But before she could finish Frossya was dexterously rolling up her paper which curled back to her bosom like a chameleon's tongue. Her eyes dulled and she began to mumble: "Governesses . . . What need had she to turn her mouth to foreign talk?" She turned up her eyes and grinned, showing her gums. "He'd die, he said, that one, if his girlies didn't speak better than any master's French whore. What a host we were to have! All gabbling out foreign telegrams, and lawns as smooth as a ballroom floor. Ah, the glass, the figured satins! All promised, all drawn up in the lilac shade."

After staring blankly at Loulou's chin for several moments, she shuffled to a doorway set in the far wall and beckoned her down three brick steps into a tiny room off the scullery where it was even darker. Without changing expression Frossya looked up to a photograph in a long nickel frame hanging below the red ikon lamp in the corner and began to weep again. When no tears came she picked at the corners of her eyes. Finding no fluid trickle she dabbed a fingertip to her mouth and smacked her lips.

In the photograph a group of children wearing curly ramswool hats and padded coats was lined up against a sleigh in order of height, their feet invisible in the snow: Millie, Lola, Petya and Polly Laskorin, not a smile on their puffy faces. The driver had his back to the camera but his companion was taking a surreptitious glance. Much younger, but still toothless. She was Frossya.

"Nursed them all," quavered the old woman. "All those girls and the boy until he drowned."

Loulou made out a box-bed under the sacking-covered window, a rough plank bench supported by trestles and heaped with old clothes. There was a small stove. Without waiting to be asked, Loulou sat on the bed. The horsehair mattress rustled as she leant forward. "Frossya, darling," she said lowering her voice. "Where have they gone, and who let those *persons* in?"

Where the inner rim met the glass Frossya ran a finger round the photograph frame. The change in Loulou's tone did not seem to affect her. "Incapable from the blood, *sudarinya*," said Frossya to the sleigh-driver's back. "Cloven natures, dearie."

To Loulou, the quivering in her legs now subsided, this seemed less than an answer. "Who? Who, darling . . . ?"

"All!" cried Frossya banging the photograph till the glass rattled. "*All*, all drunken from supping on themselves like chalices gilt, inside and out." She turned to Loulou, sudden cunning in her dry eyes. "I should know better than to say so, dearie, but with them all asunder now no one will be wanting me to embroider their trousseaus, will they, dearie? No more starched skirts to goffer and dentelles to blind myself over, no harebell lace to trim . . ."

When the old woman began to cackle to herself Loulou gave up her questioning.

In the silence she sensed the weight of the house above her, suite upon suite of rooms piled overhead which in the afternoon warmth were gently breathing off the accumulated wet of spring. The timber frame was drying beneath its load of stone and plaster with tiny creaks and murmurs. From the posts and rafters of Frossya's cell came the rustling of mites eating their way out. When she banged on the wall above the bed the rustle stopped only to resume seconds later.

The sound appeared to have a tonic effect on the old woman who straightened her back, waddled across to the plank bench and sat down heavily, stroking the clothing which, Loulou now saw, was too fine to be her own.

"I always loved the touch of them," she said, as if confiding a secret. "The touch of their bodies and their clothes, the fittingness of them, one for the other. It was right they should be so. My people were always hateful to my sight with their sordid ways, Lord forgive me. But death comes to all, unaverse to the clean and unclean."

"Who has died?" asked Loulou.

"Did I say dead? But there are no certainties now, unless stiff on the bier before you. Three weeks since the *barinya* was to send my chicks to Petersburg. She stamped and swore when I said no good would come of it. I can't read print, I said, but I can smell that pest-house from here, and if there's troubles this far-off – for this was when the villages were going up in flames – then they'll be worse up there amongst the godless ladies and gentlemen. 'Pack the trunks, Frossya,' she said, 'or I'll turn you over to the wild men for a witch.' 'Ha!' I said. 'Watch they don't spill your blood in a corner and smother you in your muslins. If it's old women they want, they've had seventy years to put the torch to me.' *Barishnya* Polya was supposed to be marrying, so she cried and wouldn't go. In the end, none of them went. The village elders had already thought up this religious stunt. So then they came and told the mistress. Quite nice they were. 'Darling *barinya*, we can't do your gardens any more. We can't gather your crops. Valerian said they all belong to us.'"

The kitchen was warm, the old woman harmless, so Loulou lay back and let her go on, hoping to extract some sense from the tale. In the end, when the sun had come round and the lime-washed walls of the little room were dazzly from light, Loulou gave up. Frossya was lost to the present: her time had stopped with the advent of the strange youth, this Valerian boy-man, who represented a threshold across which her memory could not pass. Every reminiscence concluded with the words: "Valerian said they all belong to us." Then she would regress, *da capo*, every story culminating at this unbridgeable gap.

At first exasperated, Loulou eventually became party to the old woman's indifference to time, forgetting Belyakov, the water and the entire hubbub which raged in the rooms above. Mimi Laskorina had taken heavy toll of Frossya, who unburdened herself of this bane of her life disparagingly: "A speculator's daughter, blowing money around to get herself a family."

The patriarchal snobbery was bizarre in one who had suffered from it – after all, Laskorin had married Mimi precisely because her money would secure the upkeep of that very style Frossya so adored – but Kostya had taken a similar line: "Jumped up, those cousins of yours, no roots."

Frossya knew. "Thought I couldn't tell but it showed." Mimi's

huffs, Mimi's meanness, they all sprang from that. "Didn't belong."
Mimi's death?

Mimi's death the old woman could not absorb, but she tested it
out to herself as an idea. She might have gone away, she was never
satisfied, always coming and going, buying and selling. And what if
she were? Dead? Then the Kingdom of Heaven be hers, if she had
the education to understand what that meant. "Worked us on saints'
days. What could you make of that?"

Valerian, too. Frossya had known him from before, had known
his mother and father (if it were his father). Despite them, he had
been to priests' school. Beside the look of him, his high way of talking,
both of which he had had since childhood, Frossya would go no
further, except in condemnation. He was neither fool nor holy.
Nothing but the cruellest fraud would take in such simple people.
"Feathering his own nest against the days of reckoning. Then he'll
run away as he did before."

If it were all as ugly and wicked as Frossya believed, why did she
stay? The answer was Loulou's question: where could she go?

*   *   *

"Down in the forest
Where the grass grows . . ."

Debbie came skipping down the stairs. On the bottom step she
dropped the dressing-gown cord and hallooed to her sister whose
scuffles could be heard at the turn of the first half-flight above.

"'Ere," she called. "Told you I knew where he'd be. Made himself
at home already."

When Becky dropped down the children stood together, figures
outlined in black cut-out confronting the light. With a titter Deb
pointed at Frossya. "She's off her head. Can't even remember her
name. Go on, you ask, 'is brother."

"What's your name, cabbage patch?" jeered the younger girl.

Frossya gestured helplessly and began to weep again. At this the
children lost interest and crowded up to where Loulou sat.

"You're in trouble," said Debbie. "People are out looking for you.
You better do what you're told."

"Think you're *lo-orst*," chanted Becky, climbing onto Loulou's
knee. "Don't take no notice, though. They're all the same, upstairs,
always shouting." She wriggled happily on Loulou's lap as if settling
to listen to a story. The naturalness of the child's desire to be close
gratified Loulou who reciprocated by encircling the little girl's waist.

"And who are you to give me orders?"

64

"Leave off, why don't you?" said Debbie, smacking her sister's fingers as Becky explored Loulou's cropped hair. The younger girl only simpered and pressed closer. With affected nonchalance Debbie wandered over to where her skipping rope lay in a patch of sun and began to braid the cord into her own curls.

"What's the matter?" asked Loulou gently.

"She's only jealous," confided Becky.

Loulou's voice was soothing: "What's happened?"

"If you must know," said Debbie, "while you've been dilly-dallying with that old house-slops over there" – she gave a toothy leer in Frossya's direction – "that Vlady Belyakov and the rest of them's had problems."

"'S right," put in Becky. "Mr Schmidt, he went off to the cellars and Vlady puts our Valerian to bed."

"That sounds very sensible," said Loulou.

"Yeah," said the older girl. "Except he's not come round."

8

Valerian looked dead.

In the chapel light filtering through the stained-glass windows of the Laskorins' melancholy bedroom, his blond curls had turned the colour of soap. The blue eyes stared upwards, unblinking. He reminded Loulou of a hanged man, cut down for dissection.

"Why is his hair so long?" she whispered.

Belyakov gave a moan. "I don't know, do I? Can't you do anything without asking stupid questions?" He touched the smooth forehead. "Cold. Anyway, whoever heard of a bald prophet?" He cracked his knuckles and looked behind him. "That's a point," he muttered. "Where's that Schmidt devil gone?"

Outside the room there was no sign of Schmidt but the Ivanov twin with the limp was snoring on the ottoman, a rifle propped against his bad leg.

"Why don't you just stay away?" said Loulou. "I can manage."

He took no notice but watched respectfully as she bent down and put her ear to Valerian's chest. The grey hessian shirt was open across his hairless flesh and one neat pap lay by her mouth.

"He's breathing," she said and closed over the shirt. "Hand me that."

Belyakov took the priest's robe from a black chair at the foot of the bed and she covered Valerian up to the neck.

"Who was his father?"

"Father, mother – how the hell should I know?" he said going over to the window. "Does it matter? Or do you reckon they still want to claim him after all this?"

Leaded into the sheet glass were elongated panels depicting whey-faced ecclesiastics in queer hats, and fat girls carrying lilies; the colours were acid and mournful.

Beyond the windows was a view of the park. Stakes had been driven into the croquet lawn and the Laskorins' boxwood mallets lay here and there amongst heaps of palings. A division of property had evidently been taking place before the sun got too high and the peasants retreated to the cool of the artificial wilderness. The rose garden, the walled garden, the paddocks away from the house, all bore the marks of sharing and individual allotment. In one or two sheltered corners where the soil was particularly good or the new owner was energetic, work had already begun. Trenches had been put down, roots of rose briars disinterred and even strawy manure brought up from the stables ready to sink at the base of the diggings.

The soil was poor, they knew that; it was their livelihood to know it. The time was wrong, they knew that, too. Why, then, had they listened and wasted their labour when the vast arable of the estate was out there spanning the valley from hill-top to hill-top, intact and undisturbed?

Belyakov despised them, these so-called practical men, who prided themselves on their cunning. Their whole lives had been consumed in quarrels with neighbours over boundary posts, in shaving a few yards off one another's plots, stealing timber and cheating the farm bailiff — only to be gulled at last by this crazed artilleryman on the bed whose only experience of command was to run about an emplacement at Lemberg pelting himself with latrine shit because a shellfuse detonated in the breech of a one hundred and fifteen and strewed his gun-crew's offals on the sandbagging.

Covering himself with filth might be Valerian's way of expiation, but what had they done, these vacant, credulous, ignorant day-labourers, hired hands, gleaners, share-croppers, mothers and fathers of ten or fifteen weakly children, half of them still-born or dead before they were one, to be walk-on parts in his private catastrophe? He couldn't hoe a turnip patch, yet they turned up their eyes to him for bread. He had them by the ears, by their insane desire for justice; and they gave him what was pleasing for him to contemplate in the destruction of this house: a symbolic redressing of wrongs.

In the shade the men and women slept on. A silvery cone of midges hung over the ornamental fish pool. At the edge of the wilderness a couple began to make love. The woman's petticoat was all bundled up on her shoulders and the man knelt in front of her. As his hands clasped her bare waist she ruffled his hair with her feet, turned away and smiled into the grass.

Loulou sat on the end of the bed and touched Valerian's face. He felt chill in the afternoon heat and his long fingers trembled.

"Well?" said Belyakov, hearing her move.

"Utter prostration. With rest it will pass." A term she had so often heard in the convalescent wards of her Moscow hospital. It meant that the doctor did not know what had happened but did not consider cause to be important when, from experience, he knew that such patients recovered.

After a long silence Belyakov turned away from the window. "What will pass?"

"This nervous attack, his collapse . . ."

He hunched up his shoulders and threw out his arms.

"Don't you dare, lassie, don't you fucking presume –" He pushed up against her like some ruffian inciting a brawl, jostling, barging until she was flat up against the wall. "Don't you try to tell me that what that little bugger's got can be put down to *nerves*."

At such proximity she inhaled the smell of cordite and lilac coming off in his sweat.

He articulated terrifyingly slowly and with extreme precision: "He's not an old lady who can't stomach her gruel, he's a bloody man, that lad, in spite of those buttermilk tits you'd love to scrape your nails along. He's something you'll never understand because he's been in places you've never seen, done things you've never imagined could be done, been called upon to do them, had that demanded of him, been told it was the most ordinary thing to be required of any gangling little homespun who swung on the wicket-gate kicking his heels in the sacred dust of Holy Russia."

Abruptly his voice fell, and he tapped her cheekbone with the knuckles of his fist. "And who for, miss, who for?"

"I don't know . . . What do you want me to say? It was his duty . . . I don't know . . ."

"Did you say that to *them*, the ones that came in the night, prodded your thighs and ran their hands to the tops of your silk stockings – that you didn't know why, you couldn't imagine what they meant by it, what they wanted to . . . to *express* – as your sort would put it?"

"I never told you that. I never said . . ."

Before Loulou could finish Belyakov had pushed her to one side and she almost fell across Valerian's face.

"You didn't need to," he said conversationally, as if nothing had happened. "I've been a wallflower at those parties myself – too shy, you see, too well brought-up to want to make ladies dance that kind of jig. We could get away with it" – he nodded towards the figure under the robe – "him and me, babyface and uncle, but we had to watch, they made you do that."

"Dirty, filthy brutes," sobbed Loulou. "What for?"

"To make themselves felt, that's what for. To make you notice they'd been. Look round this place – what do they do, that bunch out there, that scum I call them, what do they do as soon as their toes stub on marble? First they piss on it, then they carve their initials: they want you never to forget them again. Never. And they want to turn this place into a great monumental masonry yard. *By their works ye shall know them.* If they do nothing else they'll take it apart, brick by brick, and you, you, when they've done with you they'll stone you to death in the rubble."

"God," wailed Loulou. "You're as mad as he is."

"Oh no," said Belyakov. "He's totally unreasonable. I'm just talking common sense."

"You can *joke* about it?"

"It's no joke, I'm telling you," said Belyakov, tucking the hem of the robe round Valerian's feet. "I'm prophesying, and if you want to save your skin you hearken, not unto *him*, but unto me. I've had more practice at getting out of tight corners."

Loulou hoped she could believe him.

For a time they sat quiet and unmoving. Valerian's respirations were growing stronger and his chest rose and fell steadily beneath the covering. Both were relieved. Quite why, in such circumstances, neither had any idea. Belyakov, perhaps, because Valerian and he had gone to the Front on the same troop train; had returned and got back the same way together. In those intervening years Belyakov had bullied, cajoled him, protected and eventually loved him when he finally broke.

For Loulou there could be nothing so binding. Yet after what the huntsman had told her, there was added to a natural pleasure she took in the simple physical being of the youth a sort of compassion; not understanding – he was too far gone to be followed – or even sympathy (he might have her killed) but the sense of pathos a child might evoke by falling sick and protesting because to him disease was inexplicable.

From somewhere far beyond the park a locomotive was blowing off a head of steam. For the second time since her arrival Loulou remembered the railway and Belyakov noticed her change of expression.

"Yes, they still run, occasionally," he said. "If you have friends."

"Where has it come . . . ?"

Her voice trailed away but he understood. "From nowhere *you*'d know. Waiting for someone? Husband? Father? Lover? Someone to get you out of this?"

She did not look at him when she answered. "Everyone's waiting for someone now in this country. Someone or something. And when it comes everyone will be there to meet it like the peasant women by the tracks who peer down the line through their fingers, hoping it will only pass through."

Belyakov gave a short laugh and rocked to and fro in his chair.

Outside it had begun to rain. At the first drops the sleepers awoke and abandoned their workings, leaving their tools in the wet.

Loulou sat on in the deepening shade, unspeaking, pleased that the failing light obscured Belyakov's face.

"Am I dead?" came a voice from the bed.

Loulou jolted herself upright. The room was in darkness. She must have been asleep since sunset. A match flared and Belyakov held a candle to Valerian's face.

"How would I know?" he said. "Aren't you the expert on dooms-day?"

The youth smiled feebly and put up his lips to the huntsman's brow. "Vladimir . . . Vlady . . . It's you. Always at my side."

"Maybe we've both copped it, then," said Belyakov watching the candle flame dance in the vitreous humour of Valerian's eyes.

"Not a chance," laughed the youth. "When the time comes you and I will be getting off at different stops. This has happened before. Remember Przemyśl when you had to dig me out? I knew you'd come."

Loulou was astonished: he sounded quite normal, greeting Belyakov as if both men had just met at a regimental reunion.

"More light," said the huntsman, turning to her. "Over there – in the chest, you'll find a store of candles."

While Loulou groped for the lid in the dark, Valerian raised himself on the bolster. He took a deep, shuddering breath.

"I saw fire and heard a great voice," he said quietly.

Loulou found candles and lit up a six-branched candelabrum which stood before the dressing-table glass. She watched Valerian in profile. "Like Moses?" she asked.

He took no notice. "A voice proclaiming the day of Armageddon through the cities and governments, khanates and suzerainties of all the Russias. End to end, the land will be rent . . ."

"That's a mouthful to hear spoken," said Belyakov gloomily as if irked at Valerian's reversion to the apocalyptic. Nevertheless, he crossed himself before going on: "But your voice says nothing that we didn't know for ourselves. You may be called to preside over the massacre of the innocents but I want to avoid being bloody rent. Can't it tell you anything useful, this voice – like how we sort out your old messmate Schmidt or that weaselly Anton? That'd be something, a few practical hints."

Valerian propped himself up on one elbow: "I cannot ask, my dear friend, but only wait to receive."

"In other words you haven't a thought in your head," said Loulou contemptuously. "You're just like the old frauds in beards and dirty sandals who used to bless our scullery-maids at the side door for a hunk of cheese. Prophet indeed! Tell me what the dawn will bring."

Wary of blows, she kept an eye on Belyakov but he heard her out, all the time anxiously watching Valerian.

The youth yawned and stretched. "Have faith, child. Believe on me. Is it not good for those poor wretches below to make merry in the liberty of creation?"

"No, it isn't," said Loulou.

"The Lord will provide . . ."

"No! No he won't, that's just the point! The only Lord the hem of whose garment those miserable sinners ever touched has ceased to provide because they've cut off his hands!"

"And who are you to dispute the rightness of that, boy? Why should they care for the fate of others when those others cared nothing for them?"

During this exchange Belyakov had listened intently – much to Loulou's gratification, since she had a desire to impress him, if not by her courage, then by her determination not to be cowed – but when Valerian shut his eyes and clasped his hands to his head, the huntsman rose and stalked off. The room was very large, more like a small assembly-room than a family bedroom, and Belyakov was swallowed up in the darkness.

Loulou persisted. "I doubt that I admire them any more than you do. The owners of this house may be greedy and idle and tasteless and self-important, but they're not cruel, not on purpose – they don't enjoy seeing people suffer. They're too feckless and silly to find the will for that."

She sat up in her chair very straight. Valerian opened his eyes wide. "You say that because you are one of them."

Loulou's heart fluttered. Did he know her? From her visits to the Laskorins perhaps? It was inconceivable that they had ever met socially – a pity really – he would have been a treasure in the stifling boudoir of the Laskorin females. Seen her on some outing? In some newspaper? She felt sure that even her best friend would fail to recognise her now as a woman, let alone as Natalya Igoryevna, Countess Alekseyeva. With her cropped hair and gardener's cast-offs she must seem like some juvenile outlaw.

"How can you assert that so glibly? Is this the great principle you hand down from on high – those who are not with us are against us? I have no home, no family. All I had is lost. Yet I pity your followers as I pity myself and those who had more to lose."

Slowly the youth turned to her, spanning the gap between them with his outstretched arms. "Come to me," he said.

Loulou wanted to giggle, but gave an involuntary shiver. Having no idea what to reply, or even if a reply were called for, she drew herself up even straighter and stared back, her eyes very bright.

Valerian put one hand to her head and with the other raised her chin so that her face was presented to him at an angle. In the candlelight she caught sight of herself in the glass: disembodied fingers starting out of the void to caress her skull, pondering the lie of the bone, weighing . . .

She tried not to flinch. At length he allowed his hands to drop.

"Woman," he began.

"Woman?" exclaimed Loulou. "You really are out of your mind."

He smiled. "Woman, be not too forward but hold fast to your liberty."

Loulou was about to deny herself again when there came a crash at the far end of the room. Belyakov had flung open the double doors, and in a broad shaft of light from an oil lamp held aloft by someone in the passage-way, the elder Ivanov was catapulted through the doorway over the body of Georgii, his twin with the limp.

"What's this then, Makar?" said Belyakov, hauling him up by the ear. "Taken it literally then, have we, all that stuff about creeping to Jesus?"

"Waiting our moment, that's all," said Makar freeing his ear with a jerk and pulling at the top of his breeches.

"To enquire of the master's health," added Georgii from the floor where he was sprawled, good leg pointing to twelve o'clock, bad one at a quarter to. "And to make our . . ."

Makar bent down and Georgii whispered something to him. "Our *repord*," he said, and saluted humbly in the direction of the bed.

"Can't even say it, Makar, you toothless old bugger, never mind do it."

"Ah," cackled Georgii, having untwisted his leg and attempting to rise with the aid of his rifle. "That's just where you're wrong, Vladimir Ivanovich. We may be a bit unhandy, like, with the words, but when it comes to carrying them out, we're still spry enough . . ." He broke off in a spluttering cough, hacked out a laugh through his tears and waggled the barrel of his rifle at Makar. "Tell 'em, Mak, tell 'em what we just found."

"A dainty dish," said Makar, showing his gums.

"Hagar," said Georgii. "A solace in the wilderness."

A pettish shriek came from the passage as a short figure was thrust into the room. It was a woman dressed in a grimy white satin frock. Georgii, half-way to his feet but still clinging to his rifle, put out a hand as she passed in order to smooth out a ruck in the skirt, but the woman sprang away and he slithered to the floor, whimpering as his knee banged on the boards.

The frock was cushiony from underskirts, at once concealing the true form of the woman's body and exaggerating it by padded shoulders, tight sleeves, nipped waist and bustle. Apparently more affronted than afraid, the figure pirouetted in the lamp beam with a clumsy attempt at elegance.

By this characteristic exhibitionism, Loulou recognised her: the thick black hair hung in rats' tails over her eyes, her chignon was tilting over one ear, but this was Polly, silly, snobbish, dense Polly whose bedroom was full of half-done jigsaws, stuffed animals and balaclavas which never got posted to the Front; the Laskorins' nineteen-year-old daughter.

Damn her, thought Loulou, damn her. Any minute she's going to say: "Gosh!" with that lisp and I shall want to kill her. And what, for God's sake, is she doing in that ridiculous get-up?

The light grew brighter: Schmidt stood in the doorway holding an oil lamp lashed to a broom-handle. The tulip shade cast green stripes on the dome of his bald head.

When she caught sight of him Polly screamed loudly. "Don't you dare lay a finger on me, you disgusting *cweature*!"

"That's the spirit," said Schmidt. "That's how I like them, screeching from down in their white bellies." He never drank, but when moved, had the habit of wiping his mouth on the back of his hand, very quickly and very often. When he did so now, the Ivanovs took it as a sign, and began themselves to be appetised.

"Let me sort her out," said Makar unbuckling his belt. "Such noise in the face of the master. Take up them skirts, brother. I'll give her something to scream for."

Schmidt said nothing but lowered the lamp until the hot funnel was smoking under Makar's chin and oil dripped onto Georgii's outspread boots.

"Now, lads," he said sweetly, "we wouldn't want to damage our goods, would we? Not before we'd taken our time over easing them out of their cladding."

The dialect was so thick that Polly understood almost nothing, sensing only from their jabber that they had some plan in mind which concerned her.

Catching Belyakov's eye, she frowned questioningly. "*Qu'est-ce qu'ils disent, ces monstres-là?*"

The huntsman shrugged, unwilling to admit that he did not understand.

"Here, I thought she talked funny," exclaimed Makar. "She's a Frenchy piece."

He took off his leather cap and bowed with a flourish. "Bonzhoo."

"*Mon Dieu*," shouted Polly moving towards the bed where Valerian sat up smiling. "*C'est un cauchemar. Aidez-moi, messieurs, protégez-moi, je vous implore, je suis la plus jeune fille de la famille Laskorine. Dites-moi ce qu'ils veulent, ces salauds?*"

"*Ce bonhomme-là,*" said Loulou, indicating Schmidt, "*est amoureux de toi.*" At this Polly became less flustered and peeped sideways at the German. "*Mais . . . c'est un peu difficile à exprimer . . . ses amis sont charmés par tes belles fesses et voudraient . . .*"

"Loulou! I thought there was something queer," Polly burst out. "You vile tease! What are you doing in my house with these old horrors – and in *twousers*!"

She flung herself into Loulou's arms burbling excitedly in her schoolgirl French.

Schmidt bent forward and slapped his knees, chuckling obscenely as the women embraced, not understanding a word.

"How about that?" he wheezed to the Ivanov twins. "Young love, lost and found. Better than a picture. See how she throws herself at him. Takes your old breath away, that. And her a virgin, I expect. I do love a virgin, a pretty educated young one like her, with that dark curling hair." He stretched out a hand to Makar. "See how thick it sprouts. More of that than the eye can see, a rich coverlet . . ."

But Makar had lost interest. "She's took, Hermann, spoken for. See, the lad . . ."

Schmidt's eyes were dreamy: "Then he'll ream her slit for us; we'll strip her bare for him and stand her to him like a stallion, and she'll squeal and plead . . ."

The lamp globe shattered with a percussive bang which zinged from wall to wall. Loulou's inner ear fizzed. The flame was doused in the sputter of unvolatile oil welling from the brass reservoir through a neatly-punctured hole.

"Spare us, Hermann," said Valerian, thumbing the ribbed hammer of a cocked revolver and sighting the German on the blob-bead. "And you too shall be spared."

9

Polly had been hiding in the cellars for two days.

One morning peasant women had appeared in the dairy demanding food. When the dairy girls refused out of fear of the domestic steward, the women lay in wait behind the churns and big Matryona fell upon him when he came to do the rounds, wrestling him to the ground. As he lay tight in her brawny arms, they beat him to death with wooden butter paddles and threw his body into the store below ground, where it bled into the great cheeses stacked in the dark.

In the kitchen it was easier: the cook, an old man, fled at the sight of the women's bloodied clothing; there were no other male servants inside the house except for the Laskorins' Finnish butler whose Russian was sparse. At first he affected not to understand but they caught him blowing down the newly-installed pneumatic speaking-tube which communicated with the floors above, and they cut his throat from behind.

When Mimi came down to investigate why lunch was so late she found him propped under the meat-safe, the stopper of the tube still clutched in his fist. They had taken his shoes and his bare feet were yellow. The dry cupboards had been ransacked and all the uncooked meat removed; but a *macédoine* of fruits, *paupiettes* of veal and a *savarin* – all dressed for the table – had been strewn over the floor.

To begin with, Mimi had not screamed, her legs had simply given way. But when the warm syrup from the *macédoine* seeped through to her skin she thought it was blood and her shrieks fetched her husband. Without a moment's reflection as to the reliability of the remaining servants, he entrusted Mimi to her maid and the house-keeper, harnessed the two-wheeler and set off for the neighbouring gendarmerie.

Polly had been with Frossya in a bedroom, high in the house, where the old nurse had been making a fitting of the girl's wedding dress. The last she saw of her father was in the fly, bumping across dried cow-pats.

The housekeeper, a surly woman whom Polly detested, gathered all the women together and made for the wine vaults to which only she and Laskorin had keys (the butler, being a new man, was not yet trusted by his master). Not wanting to spoil her white frock, Polly ran back to change. Upstairs, struggling with buttons, she saw a bunch of men in army caps without insignia loitering at the end of the drive. The frock half-undone, she raced back to the vaults where the housekeeper, having locked the doors, refused to let her in.

This saved Polly's life.

By the time she had left off hammering at the door, the passages above were echoing to the shrieks of marauding women. A little longer and men would be joining in the hunt. Not knowing what to do, except run, she darted from one cellar to another, directionlessly, trying to kick off her court shoes and do up her frock at one and the same time. She took a turn which led away from the wine vaults to a stretch of store-rooms where long packing cases and steel tins lined the walls on every side. Here she waited, regaining her breath and listening.

Faint squeals penetrated the buttressed walls. Polly had pressed onwards until, quite unexpectedly, she had come on Frossya in her kitchen quarters at the back of the house, in the act of covering the butler's corpse with sacks. At the sight, Polly let out an accusatory screech of rage and fear but the old woman was too exhausted even to protest. All she could do was to gasp exhortations: "Run, run, let him guide you, take you away . . ."

Who?

"Him. The decent one. Belyakov."

Papa's keeper, ranger, huntsman, whatever he was, had gone to the Front two years before. What was he doing back here? But Frossya had come to the end of speech and began to mumble unintelligible names. If the old woman were right Polly might have a friend. She had gone out of her way to be pleasant on the rare occasions they had met on the estate, and the huntsman's deference had never been sullen. How he could now be in league with the criminals and deserters infesting his park and covers was beyond her. In spite of Frossya's testimonial Polly had no intention of throwing herself on his mercy. To be alone was better, alone and out of sight. She knew where to go until things quietened down.

She had made herself as comfortable as possible in the refuge she had found as a child, a cavernous enclave beneath the western foundation of the house where the air was fresh from the river. There she had breathed free, hidden from her mother, father and sisters, and had wept for the death of her brother. Although the timber baulks ran with water, and in autumn the river seeped all over the floor – the reason why this cellar had long been abandoned – it was her own familiar territory. A passage led out to a gap in the river bank, just below the maze, where she could scramble up and watch the main entrance to the house.

Down here, in the dark, she had holed herself up, intending to sit out the siege. But next day the German had found her in another part of the cellars, filching sacks, almost frozen to death, her resolution all but destroyed from hunger and the terror of another night alone in the cold. From his grim manner, Polly took him to be a representative of authority, which indeed he turned out to be, dragging her up through her own house to be put on display.

The one word in three she could distinguish of what he said was so queerly high-flown that she gave up any attempt to understand what was happening.

When Belyakov presented himself, showing no sign of recognition, Polly had crossed from his blank stare to the leering suggestiveness of the other men, and gave herself up for lost.

That had been in the beginning, before Loulou, about whom, above all, Polly had been inexpressibly shocked. Not so much at the breeches or cropped hair, or even at her turning up in the midst of such scallywags – Loulou was known to be eccentric to the point of flagrancy – but at her *gaminesque* intimacy with the young man who reclined on the Laskorin marriage bed with his boots on.

For the first time in her life Polly had doubted her hold on reality. Perhaps she had never lived here at all, perhaps only these people belonged, and had come back from a long stay elsewhere, to take up their rights; even to the bed on which she, and her sisters, and Petya had been conceived.

Loulou was deeply impressed. A simple act of violence had restored Valerian's authority, the shot quelling everyone present, including her. Even Polly almost behaved, allowing herself to be escorted from the room between Belyakov and Schmidt. The Ivanovs cleared up the mess and resumed guard duty. Nothing seemed to have happened. Valerian rucked back the coverlet with a thrust of his boot, crossed his legs and smiled at Loulou as if he had known her all his life.

She took the smile as an invitation and responded automatically by moving closer. After two or three steps, she faltered, overcome by light-headedness – the brandy, the acid scent of nitrate smoke still hanging on the air? – and put out a hand to steady herself by the rail at the foot of the bed.

Valerian toyed with the revolver, rolling the chambers between his palms.

A gun made things easy. It looked easy, what he had done. Anyone could do it. One shot, and back to the old times. The gun was heavy. One shot and the creature would be headless and jerking. She knew what to do, Kostya had shown her: slip the catch, thumb back the hammer and *squ-e-e-eze* away every indignity, past, present and future.

"Light more candles," said Valerian, watching her as he spoke.

The candelabrum was quite within his reach but she crossed to his side, found the wax taper and matches, and did as he asked. The new wicks sputtered and fire-cracked, before flaring up. While he watched her back, Loulou heard the soft click-click of the bearings in the spinning cylinder.

The boy was mad, a law unto himself. He could do anything. Afterwards, they would come in, remove her corpse, scrub the carpet and right the furniture. All in a day's work.

In the glass Valerian's face was invisible, obscured by the shadow of her body, the room's solid furnishings dissolving at the penumbra into a blur of japanning and gilt. The thing without a head stretched on the white sheet still tumbling the magazine round and round past the cocked pin. She tautened against the stab at the small of her back where the bullet would go in, and the fieriness of it, and the bursting of her spine. Her eyes closed.

Do it, do it *now*.

Behind her the bed creaked, there was a laugh and Valerian spanned the nape of her neck between his thumb and the trigger guard. The simultaneous touch of warmth and cold made her tremble.

"You disgusting, disgusting," she panted, groping for words that would pierce him. "*Animal*."

His weapon still primed, the boy leaned back, tapping the burred handgrip with the tips of his fingers in the fashion of a concert-master acknowledging applause.

"What have I ever done to you?" Loulou faced him screaming. "The vindictiveness. The positive *vindictiveness*."

Only now could she begin to understand his nature. With the knowledge of her own terror came the knowledge of her own reaction: having endured it, after it, she too could kill. Not as she dreamt, not as some fulfilment of vengeance inwardly nursed, but a pleasure after which part of her hankered. The desire was almost physical, a release. She would enjoy it. The house was infected with this same pleasure, and she had taken on the contagion. Her body felt intoxicated with a feeling which could only express itself pointblank, right between the eyes, clean through the heart.

The boy looked down on her, lingeringly, reading her face, porting the gun at an angle away from himself as if fending off an anticipated detonation. A slight shiver along his outstretched arm trembled the brass lanyard ring protruding from the butt. With a sudden pinch and pull at Loulou's scrubby hair he yanked her beside him, then down onto the edge of the bed. Before she realised what was happening he had taken up position before the candlelit mirror and was standing exactly as she had stood moments before, confronting the flame and the glass. Barrel reversed, he rested the revolver on his left shoulder and waited.

In the soft play of shadow and fire at the contour of his neck, the haft of the gun bulged and shrank, alternating qualities: foal's hoof, claw-hammer, wood and iron, grain to edge. Loulou's mind searched for origins. The dressing station. It was there. Paralysed limbs, un-severed, bolted in calipers. Dead and alive, like the weapon.

The tweak of his fingers still stung on her scalp. One smooth movement and the gun would be hers.

"Weakling," he said suddenly. "Inadequate. Chatterer. Scum of the earth." Words passed from his mouth like spittle dribbling onto embers. Kostya on the point of spasm. *Up, lift, up, do it now.*

She sprang at his neck. The voice slid into darkness: "Get it right, bitch, for once in your life . . ."

Between her fingers the gun revealed its true nature; not as a thing for itself but as an instrument for perfect culmination. Loulou fired, two-handed, level to the inward curve of Valerian's back. Waiting for his fall, she fired again, intent. Only when the third shell ratcheted into line, did she begin to register. Was shooting like being shot, with no time to overhear the noise? After the third, she knew, but still fired. Again, and again, and again.

Valerian found the gun where she had flung it, under the Boule cabinet by the window-seat. He lay on the bed, knees drawn up to his chin, patiently cleaning off the fluff adhering to the metal parts. Loulou eventually stopped weeping.

"Bravo," he said, tapping out the hinged magazine so that the six chambers stood free from the barrel. "You should congratulate yourself. If motive and will count for anything, murder was done back then."

A smirk, a triumphant set to the mouth, a joke even — any of those she could have endured, but Valerian's plain matter-of-factness enhanced her sense of shame.

"Always check," the boy went on. "One day your life may depend on it."

Not on that, not on a machine, not again. Next time an infallible poison to work discretely, leaving her intact – that would be her choice. He thought she was stupid. A schoolgirl.

"Or death," she said.

"As you prefer," said Valerian, accepting this possibility also, without changing his tone or moving into that weird liturgical speech which flowed from him in moments of high emotion. Loulou was learning: the transition was dangerous. Now he seemed spent, unrestive, almost lackadaisical. Once she could predict the change would she be safer? At present he was simply a youth, anxious to instruct her in technicalities. The stub of the magazine centre pin was between his fingers. "Look," he said, encouraging Loulou to peer closer. "A little pull and there you are." Six empty cartridge cases flew backwards onto the bedsheet. He could have been a child on a river bank extracting a hook from the lip of a fish. He showed her where the hammer had pierced the percussion caps. "All done," he said with a grin. "Hermann's lamp cost you your chance."

"You knew."

"I always know about things of that kind."

"Damn you." She sat down on the bed.

"Ah well, as for that . . ." Without finishing the remark, he dug into his blouse belt and brought out a live round. The leaden nose seemed dumpy, homely even, squatted on its elegant brass stock. She said so.

"Snug and cosy," murmured the boy breeching the bullet into the top chamber before clipping the cylinder to, thus aligning the round with the barrel.

Loulou edged away.

"The Lord has protected you."

Not again. This must be his quiet madness, a dull, rolling fugue which harked back to theme, time after time. Oh God, let him not begin again.

"Little savage," he said, almost caressingly. "Spitfire, creature of spirit."

All the time he was holding out the gun as if it were some sacred cup. "Take it, seize your opportunity. Take me up. Now your time has come again."

This time she aimed. Not at him, but stylishly at the chandelier. The recoil buckled her right arm and the revolver flew from her grasp. Valerian picked it up, relaxed the hammer and stuffed the gun under his belt. "Cold blood, my dear young person," he said, picking chips of leaded lustre from his curls. "Cold blood is what makes the man."

Outside Polly Laskorina heard the shot and threw herself on the

Ivanov twins. "Just you wait," she was screaming. "My Papa will come home soon, he'll know what to do. And then you'll be sowwy . . ."

10

Yasha shouldered aside the ivy overgrowing the high wall of the kitchen garden. The brick was crumbling under the suckers of thick tap root, and loosened mortar sifted down through the leaves. In this place you couldn't put your hand to anything and take it away clean. He rubbed off the red dust on the knee of his trousers, listening to the rustle as the foliage sprang back and re-composed itself, scarcely lifting to the thin breeze.

Creepy. Toads must piss there underneath, in the dark.

An hour ago Frossya had fed him on bread and God knows what meat but he was still hungry. In his pockets were two spiced rolls. One for sunrise, one for noon. Half the day provided for – more security than usual in this crazy hole. He hid the food behind a heap of pea-sticks.

Behind him lay the great house swathed in mist. The ground floor was a milky blank but one level up shadows moved behind a blind and he heard laughter. Women. In there the beds were soft. Why couldn't they sleep, the women, warm from the men who had tired upon them? He longed to make that impress on a woman, but you needed weight to be a man. What breath could he knock out of anyone?

The lawn was slushy with vapour. By the time Yasha found dry footing he was at the gravelled approach which he and the countess had crossed the day before, looking for the maze.

A white owl bulked soundlessly out of the mist, skimming the grass for voles. God help the short-legged, marooned in this bog.

He went on between the trees in his soft, rolling gait, a townboy nervous of blundering into the sailplane wings of the owl, hating the bird's superb indifference but fluttering his hands above his head where the talons might drop to his skull. It was an involuntary gesture, left over from childhood when he had played under the table and the gate-legs loosened, threatening to scissor him, head and foot.

"A strange boy," his mother would say. "So quiet."

His father was less fond. "He'll get too big for that table one day. Then where will he hide?"

With the onset of puberty Yasha's legs ceased to grow. His mother bought a herb brew from the oldest woman in the village, but his father favoured the scientific and when his son turned fourteen he sent for a machine advertised in a weekly horse-racing paper. Strapped to the machine, Yasha was stretched twice a day for a week. It was useless. After that they sold the machine to the keeper of the Jewish cemetery, a cheerful man with a hook instead of a hand, who used it to wind wool for his wife's knitting business.

In the end they all gave up on Yasha's body and concentrated on Yasha's mind: Granny taught him Yiddish and German, and he read books from abroad. In these the heroes were always musical and very tall, so he identified with the murderers and outlaws whom he imagined to be like himself. When, invariably, they were murdered before the last page, he learned to hold himself aloof from literature.

Every night, on putting down his book, Yasha had murmured the prayer: "OhGodmakemegrowsoonplease." By the time he was fifteen he had almost turned against God. Other boys grew but even this banal grace was to be denied him. But perhaps now God had given him a role; it was a compliment to be placed at the focus of evil. You brought out the worst in people.

Where the gravel walk ended, Yasha left the avenue of trees and pushed through the undergrowth bordering on the railway embankment. Above the rise the sky was already yellowing the hills. At the foot of the bank he searched out a spot where the brackens grew thickest, and diving under the fronds, he flattened out a burrow. Inside he lined it with last summer's dead growth. Dry, rainproof, perfect. Even the browns and greens merged with the colours of his clothes.

Here he could settle and wait.

The detectives would come along the railway. Eventually they would. They always did. You could rely on them for that. They went by the book.

In the wrecked salon a half-shuttered lantern smoked at the centre of the library table where Schmidt and a local boy called Yefim sat up, playing cards and arguing.

"Don't you ever want a woman, then?" said Schmidt, flicking the court cards in his hand.

"I told you, I'm married," said Yefim. He wasn't but how was Schmidt to know? It was safer to appear competent in this sort of talk. Gerasim had warned him about this Volga German's dirty mouth, but there'd been no one else to stand guard with him tonight. The rest were sated and hopelessly drunk.

"What does she do for you then, this wife of yours?"

Yefim began to describe his mother. "Well, for a start, you wouldn't believe how clean she keeps the place, not like those sluts who hang about the . . ."

"What are you, lad, soft in the head? Try again. Your woman: what does she let you do to her?"

In all his young life Yefim had only spoken more than three words with two girls in his village. One had lifted her skirts for him at the creek after church, when he was fishing. He was so frightened that he dropped the line and lost his father's tackle. The other was his sister and she had married when he was ten.

"Oh, that," he said, trying to think of something the one with the skirts might have wanted him to do, but finding himself unable to put words to it. "Oh, the usual. The usual."

"That's just it," grumbled Schmidt. "That's all you get with wives, the usual, and usually not enough of that."

Yefim waited, hoping that Schmidt would go on to explain, but the German pulled on his pipe and took another card from the deck.

It was cold in the salon. Schmidt had put on a red smoking-jacket with gold bugles down the front. The sleeves were too long and he kept pulling back the cuffs in irritation. Yefim observed him over the cards: shiny and bald, deep trenches round his mouth. He'd seen things.

For half an hour the game went on in silence broken only by the declaration of cards and the ticking of the German's steel alarm watch at his elbow. Yefim was a novice and relied on his companion to mark down his points correctly.

"King and queen of hearts? *Marriage* – twenty," Schmidt would say to the cards Yefim placed face upwards on the table. Then he made up the tally on the flyleaf of the church calendar which lay between the two decks. He was one card short of double Bezique and had become so intent that his pipe went out.

Yefim grew confused and bored. To break the monotony he rolled up a long spill of paper, lit it at the lantern top and passed it to Schmidt who leant back and sucked the flame into his pipe bowl.

"Know where I'd like it? Haven't had that for years," he said through his teeth.

"Like what?"

"With her, that daft lass in glasses. What I'd like with her."

"No, I can't say I do," said Yefim. The German might fall quiet again, and then there'd be only the silence and this awful game.

Schmidt drummed his teeth with the pipe stem. "I'd make her. She'd do it," he said.

"Ah," said Yefim laying down a king and queen of trumps. "I daresay she would. No gainsaying you, I expect. Is that *Marriage* again?"

"*Royal Marriage*," said Schmidt. "Forty. You'll get the hang of it. Perhaps you'd like a turn?"

"Never was much good with figures. You'd best carry on with the scoring."

"Not that, you imbecile. *Her*. At her."

"What at who?"

"God in heaven, lad, the same one. The little dark piece with the almond-sugar mouth – the one I'm playing for."

So that was why Makar had joshed him about some girl when he came back from patrol and then winked at Schmidt. Yefim had been too busy checking his kit to take much notice. It explained the choice of card game, though: Schmidt couldn't lose with all that adding-up to be done.

"How's it going to be, then, . . . H . . . Hermann – the usual?"

Schmidt began to shout: "The *usual*, the *usual*! Don't you know what's going on here, boy? It's anarchy, it's nihilism, that's what it is! Everything's permitted – outrage, sacrilege! We have the right to commit any horror." He pushed away the score chart. "You're one twenty down. Had enough?"

Although vague about the prize he was being asked to concede, Yefim refused. At the turn of the sixth card he was beaten.

After sweeping the steel watch and chain into the top-pocket of his jacket, Schmidt strode off to the high double doors of the salon.

"Hey," called Yefim. "We're stood together till dawn – remember? You can't just walk away from your post. Turn and turn about, you know that, all night."

Schmidt smiled. "All right, fair's fair – turn and turn about. We'll toss for it."

"For what?" said Yefim. He looked round, nervous at the idea of being left alone in the echoing gloom.

"What for, mother's milk, what for?" grinned the German with a jerk of his fat thighs. "For whose bearded oyster is first going to slip down the lady's white throat."

It was dawn. Loulou lay on her back, picking at the hem of the sheet. The smell in the room was suffocating.

As soon as Valerian left, she had looked for the door-key, then remembered seeing Schmidt at the far end of the passage, working his way down, fiddling with his haversack outside each room. The door was locked and he had taken the keys.

Without another thought she had stripped off her clothes and looked round for water. The basin and ewer in the dressing-room were empty. By force of habit she reached for the bell-pull and was about to yank it when she realised that she was no longer the summer house-guest of childhood friends but a prisoner amongst criminals.

In the whole house there was not one drop of water to be found. What use had *they* for water? Not to wash, not to drink. The dogs rolled in their own dirt and soused themselves in wine. Loulou burst into tears, and her weeping was the more bitter on account of the trivialities of her privation: now she would not be able to get clean.

In Mimi Laskorina's dressing-case lay a snug row of bottles with cut, sloping shoulders. Loulou whisked off the silver-gilt tops and sent them rolling along the table onto the floor. She sniffed at the contents of each jar: some colognes, some scents, the perfumes all different. Poor fat Mimi! How vulgar she was.

By the jug was a huge bottle shaped like a pear, three-quarters full. She slid out the ground-glass stopper and sniffed. So *that's* what he smelt of, old Daddy Laskorin, when he kissed her in the morning in the breakfast-room. Orangey and tart. Trust him to know the best. She poured it in with the rest, until the chrysanthemum-flowered basin brimmed over, then plunged in, face down, dousing her evil-smelling hair. She took Mimi's hair-glove to friction the rest of her body, rubbing at her fair skin until it was sore. They said Napoleon made his toilet like this. But it was disgusting: her scalp prickled with fire, her hair was no cleaner and the grime on her limbs seemed immovable. There was nowhere to empty the basin. The candle burned low and she climbed into the bed, damp, dirty and afraid.

She woke some six hours later in a sweat from the warmth of her own body. Blue roundels of painted glass set high in the far wall glowed faintly. She remembered how once she had stayed here, in this same room, as a child with long hair. In the mornings she used to creep into her mother's bed.

"Lou,Lou,Lou,Lou, lie still, watch."

The light had thickened in the glass like a blue sweet, then struck out amid the warbling and squawking of fractious birds, making shadows on her mother's closed eyes.

"Mama, it's time."

But Mama only smiled in her sleep, and flung an arm over Loulou who was a good child and lay still under the weight and tried not to mind being bored.

Mama only kept her promises to men. She and Kostya had been so close that if Loulou had not been in love with him herself, she might, before her marriage, have suspected them of being lovers. Her father had. Kostya told her after the wedding that he had enlisted Mama on his side – her father disliked Kostya for his patent attractiveness to women – by leading her to believe that an affair was a possibility, but only after he had married Loulou. The arrangement appealed to them both: to Kostya's indecent pleasure at having mother and daughter simultaneously; and to Mama's moral sense. To her, marriage was an institution within which any kind of sexual behaviour was permissible. So she had promised Loulou to Kostya, and Kostya obtained her.

Loulou was not shocked at Mama but saw her as merely being true to her upbringing: that in a woman there was no requirement of honour and that ladies, in any case, could never be accused of telling lies. Whether or not Kostya kept to his side of the bargain Loulou had never known. And with such a woman as Mama you could not tell. Her selfishness was ungovernable. She saw the war only as an opportunity to be idle. Had she lived she would have seen the abdication of the Tsar as a slur on her caste and bemoaned the present disturbances purely because they interrupted the supply of game from the estate in Tambov. But she died. Died as befitted a woman of her station: serene in the knowledge that the world had existed only to pass her by, her last words not Russian but French.

How strange it was, not to have seen at the time that Kostya was such a crook.

Loulou's head itched from the cologne mixture. She sat up and rubbed it against a bed-post, trying to remember how he had felt beside her.

That last time a white veil covered me to the neck. My face in the mirror over the bed: dark, brooding and seeming to lengthen by the second. The gramophone playing a regimental waltz. I ached.

"There is nothing I can do," he said afterwards. "I shall never change."

"Now that I am not in the least afraid of you," she had replied, watching the snow bank up outside the window, "I can be alone."

How coolly arrogant she had intended to sound. It was only later, when she learned about him and Mama, that she realised the pleasure it must have given him to repeat that remark to others.

What would Mama have done? With Belyakov and this Valerian? No doubt about what Mama would have done: "Such boors, my dear." The voice slightly drawling, over-rolling the "r", throaty and muffled, as if chocolate were melting under the tongue. "So *louche*," she would have said, and undressed them with her round, candid eyes.

And to think that for years she had treated Mama as that one person to whom simply everything could be told, when all the time she might have been having him do to her the things he had done to Loulou.

Thank God she was dead.

Loulou wriggled deeper into the lumpy feathers of the Laskorins' conjugal mattress, husbanding her fatigue. The men had gone. They would be sprawled out somewhere, not waiting for cock-crow. Everyone was tired. Polly would be tired, they would see to that. Polly was a snob, they would soon bring her down to earth.

Close your eyes . . . don't look up . . . rest will come. With the movement, image after image: Mama on the bolster over the arm of the sofa, her unpinned hair streaming, skirt thrown up, face invisible . . . A thumb nearly buried in the fissure . . . Valerian's eyes upon her . . . having seen death . . . alien, a naïf . . . bumping along the seabed, flayed, toes turned up for the eels . . . the anchor chain running between them clanking, clanking . . .

"What the hell do you think you're doing?"

Belyakov was standing over her jangling a great bunch of keys. "Make yourself decent, for God's sake. We're moving out."

In the dimness Loulou could just make out the outline of a woman. It was Polly, still in her white dress with the long train.

"I'm taking her with us," said the huntsman. "Come here, girl, you're hobbled like a bullock."

Polly stood motionless in the crumpled satin as he wrenched off the train at the seams, muttering: "That Schmidt's a mad bastard, wanted a lady in a wedding dress, wanted to paw the stuff of quality. Won her at cards, if you please." He threw the material over Loulou. "That's it now, get your clothes on under that if you think I might see more than's good for me. You're coming with us if you've got any sense. They might make do with you once they run out of women with flesh on their rumps."

Loulou grabbed her boy's clothes and began to dress frantically, careless of modesty. As she wriggled into the breeches, the satin slithered away and Belyakov chuckled.

"A rare brushless fox, you are, missie, hardly enough to colour your trophy. Couldn't hide behind that bush, could you?"

"Get away," hissed Loulou, now more than ever hating the revealingness of her fair complexion. "You're all the same, animals . . ."

He only laughed louder and turned to Polly. "There's two minds about that – ask the *barishnya* here, who safeguarded her intact?"

Polly put on her spectacles and glared short-sightedly at her ruined frock. She did not seem particularly frightened but then the stupid never are, thought Loulou. She's probably costing the yardage. With Polly things took a long time to sink in.

"Are you all right?" said Loulou.

Polly frowned. "Me? Yes, I think so. I don't seem to be able to find my cingle though."

"Is that all you've lost?"

"I think it is," said Polly, slowly feeling all over her bodice. "But Mummy lent it me, you see, and . . ."

Belyakov ignored them both. "With any luck we can make the station before they dry out." Dragging a blanket off the bed he expertly twisted it into a hollow roll. Down the middle he stuffed several loaves and two brace of plucked grouse.

While he was stringing up the parcel, Loulou heard herself say: "And Valerian?"

His eyes glinted. "Now why should we concern our heads with him?"

"He's dangerous, running about out there, he'll lead them to us again."

Belyakov punched the blanket roll and tossed it in the air to test its firmness. "*Him?* Dangerous? After one of those attacks he'll be as meek as Jesus. He's out there all right, but he'll be pecking chaff with the quails, communing. Don't you see how it works yet? In the pack the tail wags the dog. Valerian, he's an emblem . . . A figure-head . . ."

Out of Polly's mouth came that prim, querulous treble, reserved for speaking to men, which always gave Loulou neuralgia. "She *likes* him. Mummy always said Loulou was obsessed. With some girls it's cakes, or necklaces or small animals, but with that family, Mummy said, it's always," she lisped babyishly, "theckth."

"Her use of that word," said Loulou morosely, remembering Mimi's pendulous flanks, "was certainly the nearest Mummy ever got to experiencing anything *loose*. But Daddy, now, Daddy was more practical, darling, wasn't he – in that howwid, howwid thphere?"

Polly stamped her foot. "Why do you have to spoil everything, Natalya Igoryevna?" Her use of Loulou's full name and patronymic showed how deeply she was provoked. "Every one of my birthday parties was ruined by you with the spiteful things you said about my young men. You're just jealous, yes, jealous, because you're so skinny."

Belyakov gawped. Polly waved him towards the door: "You go first with that thing. I'm coming. Don't wait for her, I want to go now."

To Loulou's surprise the huntsman did as he was told. Alone in the room she was struck by panic: Polly seemed so sure of herself. Something was going on between them. Some men liked spoiled bitches. What if they really left her behind? She grabbed Mimi's comb from the dressing-table and hurried out.

The silence of the house was broken by the swish of Polly's dragging skirts, and Loulou caught up with the couple at the top of the grand staircase. They all stood for a moment under the pierced cupola through which the weak morning light lifted the murk of the stairwell. A perfectly hideous place to live, thought Loulou, staring down the marble steps, past the nape of Polly's neck. A bank, a railway station, a place built for customers, an investment.

Thank God I have the imagination to be a snob.

They passed out, unmolested, into the sharp June morning, trembling a little from relief and the breeze. To the east, distant by about a mile, was a long windbreak of firs planted by Laskorin's father to stall blizzards which every winter massed on the ridge. Beyond, lay the rail-head. Belyakov strode out leaving the women to stumble on as best they could.

Barefoot in the furrows, Polly swore picturesquely. Belyakov stopped and waited. "Not your sort of exercise, missie."

"How much further?" asked Loulou.

"Not far," he said, taking Polly's arm and guiding her to softer ground. "Not for a brisk lad like you."

"Oh, shut up."

Polly smirked.

Without another word they eventually reached the tree line and flopped down in the shade, shivery and hot. Polly whined about the pine-needles digging into her legs while Loulou rested and looked back at the house.

Burn it down; please God, they'll burn it and the earthworms will level it once more to the lie of the land.

In the far corner of the wheatfield they had just crossed was a grey blur. Something was moving across the curve of the ploughland. Presently Loulou recognised Emir, the old grey lead horse of the Laskorins' carriage pair. Rejuvenated by freedom or the open space, he came lolloping over the rows, sporting with his hooves, raggedy-docked tail erect. A rope hung loose about his neck.

"Holy Mother of God!" breathed Belyakov. "I thought we'd seen the last of him."

A dark figure on Emir urged him into a stately gallop. They careered along the line of the slope, equidistant from the house and the little group of figures under the trees. Loulou admired the control with which the rider guided the animal by the strength of his calves.

He might have been any fine young man out for a morning's ride, except for his robe and the gun across his back.

11

Since dawn Yasha had listened for trains. Twice he heard a brief whistle; then, later, the chatter of pistons. Somewhere there must be a stationary locomotive under steam. He hopped out of his burrow, scrambled up the incline and put his mouth first to the rails of the down line, then to the up. Not a tremor.

A quarter of a mile along the embankment, just before the track began to tilt on its long curve away from the outskirts of the estate, he spotted a water tender set back from the line; one edge of its rusting tank overhung the side of the embankment supported on timber piles. The chute had not been drawn back, and drooped on the sleepers, wobbling in the breeze. When he reached it, Yasha was breathless and he rested, one knee on the rail, looking out over the wooded river flats to the house which stood small and yellow in the rising sun.

Two miles away to the east a string of carts circled by half a dozen outriders was fording a tributary of the main river. One cart was evidently stuck fast in midstream for the driver had got down from his perch and was waving to the men on horses to halt the line. Other drivers leapt down into the water and began to help by thrusting their arms through the wheelspokes in an attempt to get the wagon rolling. Two horsemen remained at the far bank, stationed on a knoll from where they scanned the woods behind the convoy.

Yasha's point of vision was not high enough to comprehend what they sought for among the trees but he knew they were afraid: they sat the horses stiff-legged, ready to spur away.

He sprang up at the chute. Futile. He ought to have known – it was set at the height of a normal man. Under the tank, almost covered by nettles, was a long box for storing the platelayer's tools. Yasha split off the lock with his heel and found a length of iron with a spanner-head used for tightening bolts on the sleepers. It was as long as he was tall; with it he pulled down the chute by the lip, clambered up to the top of the tank and looked out, past the river.

Hidden from the watchers on the knoll was another rider. Seek as they might, Yasha knew now that they would never close with him:

instead of plunging in along the path they were expecting, he had veered away at the last moment and flanked the wood, slowing to a canter, aware that the convoy had a rear-guard which would be straining for every sound. A mile downstream from the carts which, by this time, were again making some headway, rider and horse swam the river undetected and disappeared into the undergrowth north of the point where the first cart was now just reaching land.

Yasha shivered and blew on his fingers. He recognised the lone rider from his streaming hair: that crazy man who talked behemoth-talk about beasts and justice and Christ-knew-what-all. His *grafinya*, Natalya Igoryevna, looked all in, tagging behind that black-faced huntsman and the other woman in the frock who was holding his hand and looking up. Don't listen to women.

Yasha himself should never have been taken in by Natalya Igoryevna's big grey eyes. His father had warned him: "She's the educated type. Just take the wages. Leave the rest to me. I'll deal with her. I understand that sort."

That was the trouble with Pa: he'd always understood the wrong people.

The men who had come one day to the wood house by the river where Yasha and his family lived, they didn't, they knew Pa's game. "Well, Dad," they said. "You've been a good and faithful servant. How do you want it, your reward – up the arse or through the head?"

It was bayonets then; you couldn't get ammunition for love nor money.

Yasha had cried: "We're not gentlefolk. You've got it all wrong . . ."

They thought he was a kid and left him where he was, over the stove. His mother took longest, but he couldn't get down. He thought they'd come back.

The stove went out and there was no food. He had gone to the great house for help but ended up giving it.

"Us? Help *them*? Help that lot? God in heaven, what good would that do us?" His father's last words. No one was impressed. Not even Yasha.

At the great house his existence took on meaning – at last he had a start in life; a mission to accomplish; adventure beckoned – just like the book said. Then, yesterday, he had fled, out of pique, after Natalya Igoryevna had humiliated him in front of those kids. The question for him now was whether his loyalty and his guilt – he shouldn't have talked so big in the first place – were enough to outweigh his instinct for survival.

It was Pa all over again: "Look after number one or you'll cop it."

They should have put that over his grave as a warning against damnfool principles. Live like a dog, die like a dog. No son of Yasha Rubin's was going to say that about him.

Under the Norway pines Polly stretched flat on her belly. If the ground weren't so beastly damp she might almost be enjoying herself: the air was fresh, she wasn't hungry, a man had taken her under his wing and, best of all, Loulou looked dreadful; quite an old woman as she argued with Belyakov.

"I've not seen him since yesterday. For all I know he could be lying there dead."

"And for all I care," muttered the huntsman. "Keep quiet, blast it. I need time to think."

Polly pretended to concentrate on the landscape. Pretty as a picture in the sunshine, the embanked railtrack gleamed northwards to the blue-green woods. Loulou meant that dwarf – what on earth did she see in him?

The voice was bossy. Loulou on her high horse again:

"Vladimir Ivanovich, aren't we really rather making fools of ourselves out here? I can't imagine that the boy means us any harm. Surely he has gone off on some business of his own, nothing to do with us? Why don't we simply get up and make our way . . . ?"

Out of sight to the north-east, a colony of rooks burst from the tallest of the trees. In the briefly perceptible moment before the noise of their cawing reached the line of pines, Belyakov detected its cause: a hiss, then a report shrinking to a brittle pop on the broad air.

Before any sound reached him, Yasha knew what was happening. Twenty feet or so from where the dismounted men were heaving at the near fore-axle of the beached wagon, a gentle concave pit opened on the unruffled surface of the water. The men had only time to stop dead, unprotected, before a cone of water shot high overhead, feathered with shrapnel and pebbles from the bed of the stream. The lead horse caught the side blast full along its neck and dropped without a scream. Its pair, a roan with a chest like a beer-vat, kicked out in terror, hooves churning the unstable footing of the stream. With one desperate plunge it stood upright for a second, lost hold and crashed against the centre shaft, canting over the entire wagon.

Only Polly remained unalarmed as the pin-prick spurts of sound built into a pattern: one – two – three – four – break – one – two – three – four.

In silence Belyakov worked out the tactical system: continual movement laying fire every four rounds from a different angle, closing nearer to the target with each salvo. A favourite technique which gave him Valerian's cipher *en clair*, and his favourite weapon, a trench mortar, light enough to run with. He must have been expecting trouble.

"What does it mean?" asked Loulou in a sudden access of fear which made her move nearer to Belyakov. He regarded her speculatively, loosened the cap of his bottle, thought better of it and screwed it back. Loulou's throat was raw from thirst but she did not ask to drink.

"What does it mean? Well, missie, I don't know exactly, not at present. We're safe here, for a bit, don't you fret. Out there, they're settling scores between themselves – none of our business, like you said."

With relief at his words came the return of Loulou's parching thirst. Suddenly uninhibited she snatched the bottle away from him and took a huge gulp. It was spirit, stinging like gall, which went no further than her mouth.

Belyakov had hunted over every inch of this country and could have navigated them safely through it night or day, but at the moment his knowledge was useless because their vantage point at the tree-line was too low to give a view of the action. He had been tempted to shin up the highest tree for a quick survey but remembering the dense cover of the eastern woods, decided not to expose himself to snipers.

Besides, the skirmish seemed to be progressing to their advantage. It sounded like an enemy being driven off and pursued into open country. Although more intense and concentrated, the crackling rifle fire was receding by slow degrees and eventually the mortar action ceased. Best to sit it out until nightfall before making a move.

He tried to explain to the women. It was some time before Polly grasped that although the railway looked so invitingly near, a three-mile zig-zag across semi-impassable wilderness was needed to bring them within striking distance of the line.

After that, she was quiet for a bit, then began to complain in a teasing, whining monotone: "This is awful. We should never have listened to you. We're quite cut off. Why did you leave it until daylight to run away? We should have left the house ages ago. Now it is too late and those beasts will find us . . ."

While Loulou tried to rest and forget her thirst, Belyakov took Polly on until his head was near to bursting from her muddling talk. "Anyway," she said, without reference to anything which had gone before, "I thought you told me last night that you and Valerian were comrades and that Schmidt person was a comrade of Valerian's, too, so what I want to know is why you don't appear to have the slightest influence over either of them? I mean, you just seem to let them walk all over you."

The huntsman gave up. "You don't understand, Apollonya Dmitryevna. Valerian is different from other men." Polly looked up sharply but said nothing. "He's not the sort you take issue with."

"Unpredictable?"

"Yes." He was glad to agree. "Not reliable in any way that you know what he's thinking or how he'll take something."

"What would he do if he knew that you were running away with us?"

"That's just it," said the huntsman. "I don't know so I didn't discuss it. You don't, not with a man of his type."

Yasha felt his way through the high spear-grass to the edge of the fir plantation, and watched armed runners from the house sweep into the eastern woods less than a quarter of a mile from the fugitives. From here it was an easy run to the top of the tree-line where the Bible-spouting huntsman would be standing guard over his women. Too easy. It was his country and the fellow was probably handy with that long rifle, could probably pull down a moving target smaller than Rubin, Y., no matter what bobbing dodges he made from tree to tree.

Better take it easy, think it out.

He crept a little way into the shadow of the trees and lay on his stomach among the shedded cones. No, that way the hunter would let fly, think he was being flanked by some other party from the house. Yasha empathised: touchy as hell he'd be, pinned down by the mortar fire, thinking it was for him; hungry too, and thirsty – if what Yasha had heard about his habits was true.

With a pang he registered his own hunger, cursing his ill-judged providence in hiding the last of his food in the kitchen garden. He wouldn't have minded sharing, not with Natalya Igoryevna, so why hadn't she trusted him?

The opening bars of the waltz he had sung two mornings since came back to him with the picture of her undressing in the punt, so reliant and obedient then, almost his own. He began to whistle, softly at first, then louder and louder, stopping every so often to interpret the silence. At the third *rallentando* he sensed the bouncy thud of someone approaching at full pelt, and before he could roll away his head was smothered in petticoats as a soft body plumped down on his back.

"Told you so," came a high triumphant squeal. "It's him, the sneaky little beast. I'll teach you to spy on me," went on the voice as Yasha's shoulders gave under the battering of heavy thighs. "On me, of all people, me, me, me!"

She would have gone on pounding his nose in the dirt if someone else hadn't yanked her off.

"Yashichka! Darling . . . Thank heavens!"

"Oh, dear heart, our little treasure!" mimicked Polly, casting about for her spectacles in the torn folds of her wedding dress. "What would we do without you?" She called back into the trees: "Over here, before Natalya Igoryevna bathes the creature's nasty little feet with her tears."

Loulou stroked away the impress of furze from Yasha's cheek and kissed his brow. "Poor child," she said. "He's as lost as we are and came to find us."

He softened to her embrace. Shadow ringed her eyes: she was filthy and looked about twelve years old. "Hullo, lady," he said.

Belyakov dispelled all by his glare. "Keep your hands to yourselves, *mesdames*," he said, kicking Yasha to his feet. "This one's for me."

By noon the sun was striking high through the pines. As their area of shade reduced the women felt vulnerable and crawled away from Belyakov and Yasha into the dark recesses between the trunks. Polly was watching the men who sat in the open, out of earshot. "Just look at them both. You'd think they were goat boys on a hill-top admiring the view. I do dislike that kind of showing off."

Polly's hoyden giggle floated to the ears of Belyakov who turned and gave a grimace.

"Right, ladies," he called. "Quiet now, we're on the move."

When the women came over he looked Polly up and down. "The boy knows a track that should take us up to the line. It's a crawl, though – can you hoik up those skirts? Be better if you left them behind."

Polly refused point-blank to do either.

"As you please," he said, lifting the rifle crosswise to his breast and stringing the loops of the bag round the bolt-stop. "But remember, Apollonya Dmitryevna, this isn't nursery games. Your first squeal could be your last – and ours."

With Yasha racing ahead, pausing every so often to turn and wave the women round the dips and hollows in the lumpy pasture, the way down was easy. Once they reached cover at the edge of the wood

Belyakov took command, plunging straight into the heavy undergrowth between the trees without a thought for those who followed,
struggling to keep up.

Avoiding trackways and clearings, the huntsman led them into an
almost impassable tangle of quickset brush which scratched and tore
at the women even after the weight of his body had broken out a
passage for them. After an hour of this work they fell to crawling
single-file, elbow over elbow, in the sour mash of rotting leaves. When
Belyakov showed no sign of slowing down Polly began to whimper.
Yasha, struggling to keep pace with the huntsman, tried to ignore
her but she grabbed him by the knees.

"Is it much further?"

She looked such a fright, tears dribbling clean through the muck
on her face, that he paused, glad of a moment's rest. "Ask him," he
said, feeling the cramp in his right leg ease under the warmth of
Polly's clasp.

Belyakov stopped and rolled on his side.

"Where are we?" said Polly.

The huntsman wiped the sweat from his face with the sleeve of his
jerkin. "What's up with her?" He addressed Yasha as if the question
were a message to be passed along the line.

"She's had enough," said the boy. "She's not used to it; if you
want to know, she thinks it stinks round here."

The huntsman kicked back at Yasha's head. "Shut your mouth,
boy. And she'd better shut hers. We've got company. Listen."

Helpless in the murk, the two women followed Yasha's example,
their bodies crushing new-fallen blossom into the ripe slush of black
earth. In the silence they sensed nothing except the dark air filled
with a scent like that of molasses transpiring from the rotten foliage.
At the back and feeling very exposed, Loulou fought off a craving to
leap up and scatter to the wind like a flushed hare. By now she no
longer cared what became of her, if only the waiting would cease and
the hunters come into view.

Suddenly, in the far distance, the small-arms fire resumed. A short
volley crackled back from somewhere in the wood and the noise
of that was nearer. Soon one staccato exchange followed almost
continuously upon the other. At the first clash Loulou's animal
wildness froze, and she clung stiff to the earth. Belyakov had heard
the first report while Polly was whining: a high sighting shot way out
of range. From the advance of answering fire he worked out the
sequence: a rider was closing up to men on foot, driving them back,
and their axis of retreat was straight this way.

The next fusillade was on the right and near enough for him to smell powder. Thirty feet? Twenty? He fondled the haft of the long knife in his boot, and raised his head very slowly.

Nothing moved across the green-black tangle of branch and leaf, hanging impenetrable above the backs of his companions. Animal, man, trap, mine, concentrate upon the hidden life and it would quiver in the ear or eye, sooner or later.

A whisper of sound, the faintest tick at ten o'clock, and then he knew: the drift of a leaf-sight wafer as the target bulked up.

"Undershoot," said a voice. "Go for the horse."

Seconds passed. The tick-tack of minute adjustments, gearing up a hammered long-rifle. Belyakov had the feel of it along the flesh of his thumb.

"That'll do," said the voice.

Overhead leaves scuffled in a clump of alders as the marksman relaxed, taking his time. Boxed in, head to toe by the huntsman and Polly, Yasha could not move. He wanted to twist onto his back like Belyakov in order to see what was coming but he could only listen, and while he listened it was worse because the voice was indistinct, making no sense, and he had the desperate feeling that the one who was speaking was listening to him, too, waiting for an inadvertent rustle which would reveal Yasha Rubin, tracker and hero, flat on his belly, rigid with anticipation of the muzzle-touch at the base of his skull.

A man screamed: "Bastard, God damn him!" and immediately after the springy detonation of a heavy-calibre bullet recoiled from beneath the alder saplings. Belyakov jerked himself into a sitting position. Already the rifleman was scrambling back the bolt. "Again, again. Right centre," came the familiar voice. "See. On the polder. You've killed a loose horse. The bugger's on foot."

The gasp was audible to Yasha, and the marksman abandoned his aim, firing indiscriminately into the dense cover.

Either having exhausted his ammunition or lost his nerve, the man with the heavy rifle ceased fire after a final wild sally. "I can't, Anton Ivanovich, I can't any more." It was Ignat, the sergeant musketry instructor, Belyakov's former patrol leader in the Carpathians. An ace.

"Scum," said Anton twice.

There was a squawk like a hen caught by the neck; a meaty squashy thump, then silence. Yasha felt Polly's head juddering uncontrollably against his shins.

From the direction of the narrow water-course at the bank of which Ignat had first concentrated his aim, rose a high, triumphant call. "Anton! Ant-on! My shot! My shot!"

The invisible killer of Ignat scampered in the ground elder, irresolute. The call came again, nearer, and Anton crashed blindly away from it, slipping and sliding on the dark leaf mould.

Barely two hundred yards from where Loulou lay paralysed by the thought of her imminent death, Anton turned, dropped onto one knee and fired off half the magazine of his carbine. For a third time came the call, stalking him forward, further and further into the depths of the wood.

At a sudden popping noise like a cork being drawn Belyakov flung himself across the prostrate bodies of Polly and Yasha. Something tumbled end over end above the highest tree before bursting the ground in a crack and whoosh of orange flame. In Yasha's mouth the earth tasted salt. The following pair of explosions touched off in the air with the pealing blast of a great bell dropped on flagstone. After, there was quiet in the sough of the alder branches and the distant antagonist seemed to turn away, the sound of his laughter gradually losing itself in the swish of bracken.

Just when Yasha felt safer there was a creak in the emptiness, then an accelerating rumble. He looked up. Someone had set in motion the two wagons which Anton and Ignat had been guarding and they were slowly trundling towards him over the flattened undergrowth.

The impetus of the wagon's roll had gouged out a long wedge of scrub through which Loulou could now see a clearing by the water's edge. No one appeared. The owner of that ringing voice which she had instantly recognised as that of Valerian, showed no sign of riding up to inspect his handiwork.

On the fringe of the clearing wisps of smoke rose from the smouldering grass; the centre was pockmarked by three small craters close enough together for the diameters of two to intersect.

"Fine placing," said Belyakov, but nothing more was said and none of them moved. Already the birds were hopping down to peck at the disturbed earth in the holes.

The leading wagon, its central shaft in splinters, had heeled clean over crushing part of the load, and a braided uniform jacket from one of the crates hung from the rim of the topmost wheel. There was no body, no blood, no aftermath. All had happened so quickly, hidden from view, that Loulou felt absurdly disappointed: as if she had missed the crucial part of an act and would have liked the man who had done this to take it again from the beginning.

Evidently satisfied that the danger had passed and would not return Belyakov got to his feet, strolled to the tilted cart and spun the front wheel, humming to himself. For a while he poked about in the crates in an idle, half-hearted fashion, before making a closer inspection of the second wagon which had come to rest upright almost unscathed, twenty feet or so behind the first.

Although the load had been tightly secured top and bottom by broad thongs of plough harness strapped right round the body of the cart, the covering was not only the oilskin which Belyakov expected, but additionally several layers of white linen bedsheets. Between the cross-bands the unstarched material caved in beneath his fingers. He stood back, tapping his long knife against the heel of his boot. Loulou watched, guessing his thoughts. Irregular, disorganised shapes, nothing hard, angular, efficient-looking. In the brindled shadows of the clearing the jagged nose of the wagon seemed to take on an animal snoutish aspect which Belyakov was warily circumventing.

Weapons, ammunition, fragile loot – all those would have been in containers. Then why had so much care been taken?

Belyakov ripped back the layer of oilskin and pupa-white sheeting. He saw the hair first, matted, strawy. Female.

Yasha had already guessed and willed himself to move closer without alarming the women. Just a stroll to stretch the legs.

By the cart the smell was unmistakable. "How long?"

The bodies were face down. Belyakov touched flesh under the hair of the nearest. The nape was slightly bloated. "Twelve, fifteen hours. In this heat . . ."

Yasha smiled towards Polly and Loulou. "Many?" he asked, still smiling.

The huntsman counted. At least ten, there could be a dozen. They were crammed together, hair intermingling, but one wore a badly-matched chignon which he recognised as Mimi Laskorina's. Apollonya Dmitryevna's two sisters lay with their mother between them. He felt Polly's gaze at his back as he pretended to rearrange the coverings of the load. "Hard to tell," he said.

Yasha clambered up to where he could see over the duckboards. "Christ Jesus." Belyakov kept on pointlessly smoothing the sheet. "Oh God."

At the shock in the boy's voice Loulou instinctively gripped Polly's arm but the girl tore herself free. "I must see, you shan't stop me, Natalya Igoryevna, I must see."

Yasha tried to fend her off by an impassioned burst of swearing but Polly gathered up her tattered bridal frock and leapt onto the boss of the wagon wheel. The boy hissed at Belyakov: "You stupid bastard. What do you think you're up to? Gag the little cow before the whole world hears and she beaches us high and dry."

Behind him Loulou wrenched at the girl's skirts until the seams burst. "Polly, darling, no, no, darling, you mustn't. . . ."

An hour later, while Belyakov and Yasha were still heaping broken branches over the corpses in the wagon, the women sat well apart at the edge of one of the mortar bomb craters.

"Silly nonsense," said Polly. "They're dead. Who cares if the dogs get them now?"

Her reaction on seeing the bodies had been no less astonishing. After identifying the heads as if they were so many wigmaker's blocks she had bathed her arms in the nearby spring and returned, quite undistraught, licking droplets from her fingers. The men put her calm down to grief. Loulou knew better and had been accusing.

Polly was viciously cold. "You only think it ought to matter because it would matter to you, and we're the same kind of people with the same inbred feelings. Well, you can grovel alone in the ashes for them, and for me, too, if you like. Bawling at me to be anguished won't do one bit of good. I *can't* care much, that's the thing."

In the face of the girl's apathy Loulou suddenly realised that she was no longer capable of calling up words appropriate to this or any other occasion. Conscious only of her own helplessness she stood up and strode out like a man for the stream. Behind her Polly gave in to immediate sensation. "Ooh, I so want to slee-eep . . . I must be feverish . . . feel my temples . . . I can't stand . . ."

From the far edge of the clearing Loulou took a last sight of the leaf-topped cart and the men bending over the girl urging her up. Mother and sisters finally set aside, Polly had entered on her martyrdom:

"My whole body aches . . . I can't breathe . . ."

Unnoticed by them all, Loulou slipped away between the trees.

12

In the deep of the wood it was cool. Picking her way barefoot through the wettish leaf-mould towards the water, Loulou dodged between the trees. Everywhere the noise felt near, drawn up from the running stream into the air which moistened the earth under her heels and chilled her legs; but when at last she saw the bank she was already tired and began to regret having given herself so long a journey back to Polly, Belyakov and Yasha.

The ground became more open and she felt the sun on her back. The tributary had shrunk to its summer's width; in autumn, the gentle slope now dense with meadow-grass and tiny yellow flowers over which she padded, was black with water flooding down from the hills.

She tried to avoid the flowers but soon it was all she could do to keep upright, for the grass gave way to mud and she almost fell headlong into the wide treacly opening broken into the bank by cattle where the river meandered into shallows and they could herd together to drink.

The way down was fretted by hooves. She waded in up to her waist and rubbed her hands together under the surface of the water. They turned very white. She knelt in the silt and pulled the shirt over her head, holding one sleeve in her teeth as the material billowed out in the current of air along the water. The breeches flapped leadenly around her legs, wavering in the cross-current made by the breeze. About to undo them and dive about, white and free, like a pup with a slipper in his mouth, she remembered Belyakov at dawn in Mimi's room and the way he had looked at her as she dressed: contemptuously, without interest, as if her unclothed body were an affront. She hauled back the shirt and stumbled to a steeper part of the bank not trampled by cattle. There she spread the shirt beneath her and lay on her side staring up into the sky.

Only when the breeze rose did Loulou realise that she was not alone. She felt suddenly cold, sat up in a panic and thrust her arms into the sleeves of the drying shirt. A continuous human noise separated itself from the rush of the water, rising then falling, with a

low harmonious lilt. Behind her the tree-lined path she had followed
down to the stream wound as empty as she had found it.

On her feet now, she scanned the more open ground of the opposite
bank.

A saddleless white horse stood in a patch of sun, a man on his
back. The man's face was tilted to the sky. Even from a distance she
knew it was Valerian and that the sound came from him.

"Save me," the boy was saying. "Save me."

Emir jostled the gnats with a flicker of his ears.

The overhead sun dipped hollows under Valerian's cheekbones,
the line of the mouth was jutting; square to the light, his shoulders
bulked angular and heavy.

Loulou had started to wade across to him but out of fear and
exhaustion collapsed to her knees.

"Help me," she whispered from the water's edge.

Only the horse caught the sound, swivelling an ear to where she
lay amidst the gold and yellow loosestrife on the bank, but her gasp
lost itself in the chatter of water over submerged pebbles in the
stream's bed and Valerian continued his prayer.

Yesterday, when she had the chance, she should have killed him.
Even the horse, shuddering his rump under a cloud of flies, was less
indifferent to the world. In the dazzle of sun between the trees
Valerian could have been Martin.

Gathering the last of her strength, she called out: "*Help* . . .
me."

Valerian felt for Emir's mane and did a bareback roll to the ground.
Once on his feet he circled, protecting himself with the body of the
horse. When she crossed his line of sight, the boy relaxed, allowing
his chin to rest on the bump of Emir's flank. He smiled. This was the
last thing she had expected and Loulou felt cheated and, suddenly,
quite unafraid.

"Hark at you . . . Prayer-mongering in the wilderness. I ought to
have known better."

Horse and man came nearer.

The sea-blue of his eyes was so healthy, so insolently clear, that
scrambling up, she yanked clumps of willow-grass from the bankside
and threw them towards him.

"Oh, you're so sure of yourself, aren't you? The pair of you, God
and his one elect. Cocksure soldier-boy! Always so absolutely in the
right."

The vulgarity which came so easily to this girl with the round-eyed
look of a kitten left Valerian untouched.

In the seminary Father Joachim had goaded him: "Young man, I do not believe in your vocation. In your heart you know nothing of God." This would happen in the sacristy or in the garden and always the old man scrabbled at his beard before jabbing an elbow under the boy's breastbone. "Why are you here? Come, boy, surely, you can tell me. I insist."

The question was never answered except by the words with which the master had initiated his novice. And which made the novice insuperable. The truth was unspeakable, a crime. God was a deaf-mute whose utterances Valerian alone could interpret.

Her voice held above the ramble of the water: "Betraying all we hold dear . . ."

The theme was familiar. Again and again Father Joachim had come back to this, until at last he could scarcely bear to eat at the same table with his novice.

Then Valerian had wanted to die.

Yesterday this girl had gazed at him along a pistol, knowing him without understanding. The same strength as Joachim's; the same indolent conviction welling up from health and instinct to shake him with its purity. Her "Lying scum!" equivalent to Joachim's: "What you worship in your heart is not God."

Loulou twisted in the grass. "Deadeyes, deadeyes!" *Now he will kill me*. Russet strands of her hair caught bright in the sun. On the way across the horse lazed behind him at the end of the rope, baring his teeth to take gulps at the stream.

When Valerian's shadow fell across her Loulou kept very still. Her bare legs were stained from moss. "I do beg your pardon," he said, bunching Emir's rope rein round a fist sticky with burrs and grease. "For alarming you, I mean. How can I make amends?"

Emir sneezed.

Until she had eaten, nothing was said. The food was a miracle, bread, warm from his body where it had lain in the folds of his belted blouse. Only bread, but it was enough, for a while, to cure her tiredness and fear. He waited, kneeling in the flattened willow-grasses, teasing Emir's out-blown nostrils with a larch shoot. Her body felt thick from the sudden heat of food. She did not wish to speak and curled away to rub at the greasy patches on her knees. The moss green stained as vivid as murex.

"They were justly punished," he said, thumbing the bark from his switch. "The blood of women was on their hands."

How absurd he was to apologise. Did he not think he had the right? Wasn't there scriptural authority for just killing?

"Even normal people can desire the death of someone, I believe."

"I do not glory in their deaths," he said.

"Then you should," she said, smudging the flecks of humus which underlay the moss clinging to her knees. Her heart slowed at the remembered image of the butchered Laskorin women heaped on the cart, cheeks uncomplexioned by the draining out of blood. One glimpse of the clasped hands beneath the oilskin covering had been enough to make her rejoice that the boy had lobbed his grenades. To kill without remorse was his privilege.

The sunlight dazzled on his half-smile, furring the golden cilia at the margin of his profile. In this light and this space he was the twin of Martin, lurid as a yellow cat basking in the green shade. Both had that effrontery which stirred her more than beauty. *Look at me, simply look.*

With the boy, of course, there was less polish but that only allowed him to come deeper within her. Had Martin been before her yesterday the hair of the trigger would have trembled off spontaneously to shatter the turn of that perfect neck. The boy faltered under her gaze, the rod half-stripped and runny with stick-lac.

Bastard! Why had Martin failed? But she had never believed in his plan of escape: fetch her away from the Alekseyev estate, carry her off to Constantinople, Rumania, to a flagship from England in the Odessa roads.

"Take *me*," she said with an unexpected breathlessness. "Yesterday I would have taken pleasure in your death."

His white fingers stood out clean against the pear-flesh gleet of the under-bark. The remark sounded more daring than she had intended but the boy found nothing to catch at.

"When my mother died I was glad."

God help us in our isolation, thought Loulou. He knows nothing. If I could have been *had* on my mother's grave, the defiance would have been ecstatic. "Why?"

"Because I loved her. Can you understand that?"

His eyelids were hairveined with turquoise. Loulou would listen because she did not need to understand, because he wanted her only to listen. Emir crunched shale underfoot and snuffled himself in the toil of the current.

"She was a child once more and I was happy and resentful too because I wanted to be like her, a child again."

"Your father?"

"My father I never knew. I dream of him."

Loulou pillowed a cheek slant on her raised knees and wailed inwardly. This boy must be sick. Obviously he was sick. Behind her closing eyes Valerian's past resolved itself into pictures: the hugger-mugger torpor of a provincial monastery where house-martins screeched beneath the cupolas, liming the iconostasis with river-mud and feathers; an Ophelian mother whose mad gold hair leapt into fire when the boy beheld her face in the glow of a Mass candle. And the father from nightmare, mounting her in dreams. The images rioted, divesting Loulou of the last vestiges of wakefulness and she fell asleep to the *fioritura* cheep of lazuli-finches massing in a blue cloud above the Capella of the Winter Palace.

Before she awoke she felt herself blush from the intentness of the boy's eyes upon her, and she knew that he was still smiling.

"You sleep like a soldier," he said. "A comrade-in-arms, dead to the world."

The interlude seemed to have refreshed him; he stood the horse out of the stream and began to tighten the rope harness at the headstall. "Here," he said, threading out the end of Emir's leading rein. "Catch onto this. I've something to collect."

Loulou watched him leap midstream into the shallows and take the go-down on the far bank in a single stride before disappearing into a clump of spruce. She speculated. The horse was elderly, tractable. She could make a run for it, saddle or no saddle. For all his verve, the boy would never reach her before she had worked Emir to a canter. There was no safety with Valerian. Even if he had not done her kinswomen to death, his companions had, and what was his genuine relation to them? That dark Belyakov was one; he had helped her and Polly and Yasha, and had expressed similar respect for women, but she remembered his hands. One twist and she could be wrung like a crow, and hooked up like her cousins *pour encourager les autres*.

With one hand she clutched Emir's rope at the knotted bit end and held the loop of slack with the other. The horse was over sixteen hands. Loulou searched with her feet for a rise in the ground which would give her spring to mount. Valerian had been kind, yes, Belyakov had been kind. Kind for no reason. She realised again the terror of her situation: they had made her the object of an inexplicable mercy which could also be denied at will.

The horse circled, there were no footholds. The stream flashed mica from the drumming pebbles. With a harsh cry Loulou swung her right leg at Emir's flank, managed to straddle him with the crook of her knee, but fell back from the insufficient spring of her left foot which slid away, carrying her with it into the mud under the horse's belly. Unalarmed, Emir rolled his neck, gave a neigh and fussed at her hair.

High above, bark shattered among the top branches, exposing pockmarks of yellow tree-flesh where bullets sank home. The boy had made his collection. With his blue-black carbine unslung he stood over against her, a man again.

With the advent of her independence and of his weapon, Valerian's entire manner changed. This time he tied her hands. With the short butt end of his gun he broke off half a dozen thickish branches from the nearest tree clump, trimmed them with a hand-axe taken from the smallest of the bags he had dragged across the rivulet, and fashioned a kind of Indian travois by lashing two shafts across Emir's hindquarters. After criss-crossing the projecting part with smaller branches, he proceeded to line the sloping platform with brushwood. All this was done in silence, efficiently, morosely. When he tipped out the sacks she saw green stick-grenades, hemi-spherical magazines of brass cartridges, flighted mortar bombs and boxes of small-arms ammunition, boxes with webbing handles each stencilled with a foreign lettering.

"Where is he?" said Valerian in a grating voice, snugging down the containers in the brushwood bed. "Where is he?" came the voice again. Valerian was bent over the travois, his back to her. When she failed to reply a third time, he turned round and threw a calico bag full of long-rifle magazine clips which split between her legs in a welter of copper casings.

"Why has he denied me? The whole region is under my command. My people are searching him out."

Belyakov, of course: the untrue disciple.

"He was trying to save us."

The boy was contemptuous. "From what?"

"Can't you see that not all your people are enthusiastic for sacrifice? He was sickened and despaired of you and promised himself to us, to Polly, Yasha and me."

Valerian laughed. "There is no hiding place," he said, and resumed his stacking of the travois.

By the time the last box was lashed to, shadow narrowed the gaps between the trees. In half an hour it would be dark. Valerian tested the secureness of the load by leading Emir into the water. Patient up to now, the horse grew restive and swished his tail at the contraption strapped to his flanks. Valerian twisted the bridle-rope around his fist and pulled the old horse down the bank, all the time soothing him in a monotone:

"Schurr, schurr, schloop, boy, shshsh."

Wake skittered beneath the fronded overhang where Valerian stood up to his knees in the stream.

"Gently. We're together now. Aren't we together, aren't I here with you, part of you?"

At this repetitious, strangely intimate speech, hairs prickled at the nape of Loulou's neck. The boy was addressing both her and the horse.

"Gently. Schurr, schurr . . . Vlady Belyakov will be found . . . And we shall be together again under one roof . . . And the dark-haired girl with the governess's spectacles . . . And the little man . . ."

He let fall the rope which snaggled away on the current before lining out straight from Emir's bit.

"Why did Vlady turn against me?"

Against the fading sky he was tawny black, sleek as a muskrat.

"I don't know . . . Don't hurt me . . ."

His face was unseeable. "Swear never to leave me."

She promised. Nothing else would do.

"Then," he said, "I will help you."

Once physically in his power Loulou felt safe. He had only to stoop, circle her waist with one arm and jolt her to her feet before she was overtaken with that paradox of feeling which had dogged her mature life: what a man did, coming close enough to touch, was what she wanted to be done.

She made no struggle when he tipped her backwards, almost horizontal, in order to seat her astride Emir's forequarters. She shut her eyes and marked the variations of his breath as he sprang up behind, gripped her to him one-handed, and flicked the rope rein. Soon they were on the rough country of the far bank where the load snagged on tree stumps and the fallow unlevels of grassland where the slewing canter of the horse unsettled her.

"I don't know you or your family," said Valerian after dismounting to untangle the edges of the travois from a hazel thicket. "Or have I forgotten? I often forget."

She stretched out her wrists. "Untie me first."

The smile was unchanging. "Now, why would I do that? You're a bolter, *baba*, a bolter."

This word infuriated Loulou. *Baba. Woman.* Peasant woman, crab-handed, stooping on the threshold to unlatch her *barin*'s shoes.

"I have some dignity left. Address me properly when you speak. My father was . . ."

He listened to the roll of her father's entitlements.

"There is more," he said when she thought she had finished. "Allow me." And he began to gabble in scarcely-recognisable French:

"*Membre du Conseil de l'Empire, Sénateur, Ministre des Apanages, Ambassadeur Extraordinaire, Archi-grand Maréchal des Couronnements des Empereurs, Chef du Kremlin et des Edifices et Arsenaux Impériaux, Conseiller Intime Actuel . . .*"

Loulou remembered Belyakov yesterday morning at the house: "kitchen French", pentecostal servants' patter.

". . . Which made you *Durchlaucht, Serenissima* – Madame la Comtesse Natalya Igoryevna Alekseyeva . . ."

"Makes me," she said.

Valerian remounted and whispered into her ear: "Only I am left, milady, to make and unmake."

Over a rise the house came up like an orange eye peering over a wall.

They skirted the main approach at the north front making for the cobbled yard on the river side where the Laskorins had kept their brood mares in a row of eighteenth-century loose-boxes. Before they reached the low white gates by the smithy Valerian gave her instructions: "If your promise to me was good, Natalya Igoryevna, you will be safe and so will your friends. There are some decent women amongst the community. They will care for you if I ask. No one will harm any of you. As long as I remain alive."

Too tired to twist away Loulou allowed her head to droop back and touch his shoulder. "Why?" she murmured. "Why should you want our dependence? What good can it bring you?"

Valerian hushed her with the sing-song jingle that had calmed Emir. "One day I shall owe you my life," he said with a broad, unexpected grin.

Before she could express astonishment he had put his hand over her lips. Emir forced apart the gap where the unbarred gates met and clopped into the yard. At the feel and clatter of the cobbles under his hooves, he whinnied and stopped dead.

Except for a single hurricane lamp hanging from a pole between the central columns of the portico, the house was unlit. Valerian shrugged round on the motionless horse.

"Yefim!"

Yefim was Emir's favourite stable-lad, and at the sound of his name the horse ambled forward in the direction of the head-boy's tackroom. They had almost reached the first of the loose-boxes when the nearside strut of the travois caught in a drainage runnel, skewing the load, and two ammunition boxes smashed onto the cobbles. A latch clicked and in the light pouring from the upper part of the open half-door Loulou recognised the shiny bald head of Schmidt. At the sight of horse and riders he raised his arm as if in a signal and from behind boyish cheers rang out. Then, spilling into the yard, came a straggle of loutish youths – half-men, half-children. They tumbled around Emir's legs, whistling, patting and shouting. The horse seemed to take it as his due, allowing the tallest to close a broken-nailed hand over his bridle.

After his horse, the boy had eyes only for Valerian. "We got 'em, Master," he panted. "Just like you said, in the woods. That Vlady, him too. We found 'em . . ."

Schmidt stood apart, almost lounging, and made no attempt to help the riders dismount. "Master," he said, without looking at Valerian but screwing up his eyes.

Yefim began to stutter. "We weren't sure, you see . . ."

Schmidt and Valerian had words only for one another: "Intact," said Valerian. He dismounted, one arm round Loulou's waist. "Make a check and then put it in store."

Schmidt's voice sounded through the yard, giving orders. Under his breath, he praised God. Not for the prisoners, nor for Valerian but for the cache.

Yefim watched Valerian set Loulou down on a heap of horse-blankets and cut the cords around her wrists.

"Is this one to join the other blasphemers, Master?"

Methodically, and without reply, Valerian disarmed, unclipping the carbine from its sling and withdrawing the magazine; next came the grenades, looped to the inside of his belt. He handed them to the boy. When he had finished Yefim tried again:

"It's not another lady, Master, that you've brought us?" He seemed afraid even to look at Loulou. "Because I ought to inform you, Valerian," he went on in imitation of Schmidt's pompous manner, "we got one already." He indicated a barred door at the end of the walk abutting the horse stalls. "And she made no end of trouble till he slapped her. Hermann. Mr Schmidt, that is."

The flame of Loulou's pine-splinter torch splashed red in the darkness. Polly was sprawling on the earth floor of the store-room sobbing bitterly, her black hair filthy from oil and sand underfoot. When Belyakov tried to rouse her she kicked out and scrabbled on the soft earth. Only Yasha had the heart to take note of the light.

"Lady," he croaked from his hideaway among the tar-barrels and brooms. "Thank God. Safe."

"Caught," said Loulou flatly. Behind her Valerian chuckled.

One word was all Polly needed to identify the countess. "You wretch, Natalya Igoryevna, you disgusting fraud," she wailed without getting up or even rolling over to confirm who it was. "Do something, can't you? They've said they're going to do the most horrible things! I can't stand it . . ."

Belyakov put his arm round Polly and this time was not repulsed. He eyed Loulou dully with no attempt to understand why she was there.

"Well, you can thank me, miss, for saving your life."

Again Valerian chuckled.

Yasha sank to a crouch. "Oh, that's fine, that is. As far as it goes, lady. But what me and him want to know," he shouted, waving at Belyakov, "is what about us?"

Polly shook herself free of the huntsman and sat up, all tears gone. "That's quite another matter," she said with a dab at her inflamed eyes. "I don't like to be superior, but after all, you are *men* . . ."

Valerian spread out his arms, his smile embracing them all. "They are no less loved for having been afraid and trying to flee our kingdom."

"Tosh," muttered Polly.

"Remember we are brothers and sisters in God. And who more so than my old comrade-in-arms, Vladimir Ivanovich?"

The only answering sound was the crackle of pine. Transfigured by embarrassment, Loulou hung her head and watched the hot resin plop into the damp earth. He might go on for hours. One simply could not tell.

"I love him as I love you," called Valerian. Yasha cringed at the inclusion.

Loulou felt warm breath on the back of her neck. She turned as far as she could without unbalancing the torch. It was Schmidt, grinning, his priest's robe thrown back to display a bandolier fully restocked from the cartridge boxes.

"Speaks the good word wondrously," he whispered, huddling against the line of her back and reaching down to feel for her hand.

Alert to the protocol of these impromptu sermons the youths left off their work and shivered in the biting river wind which swept over the yard.

Loulou manipulated the torch so that when it fell, the sudden flare-up engulfed the back of Schmidt's hand before dousing itself in the hem of his robe.

III

APOLLONYA

June–September 1917

13

Below the sun the clouds were sparse and narrow with bright edges and black, liquid centres. Figures dotted the path. Six girls were pulling a brown cart with big wheels. Hooked over the shafts on the harness points were sickles and blue calico aprons. At the turning by the fish pools, the girl in the green and gold headscarf began to sing, dragging out the tune alone until a little blonde joined in. At the foot of the incline leading to the upper meadows they stopped, shaded their eyes and searched the horizon. The girl in the green and gold headscarf was the only one to look back towards the house.

Seventy feet up on the roof Loulou lay flat on her stomach and peered down through the gapped parapet. She knew why they were up so early, and why they looked about them. Even at this distance she felt she knew the very song they sang. Since the rain, sounds and colours appeared so vivid that every detail was brilliant.

The girls hauled on, their ankles thick against the white path. Loulou had passed a short night in the open, alternatively star-watching from the roof and reading by candlelight. She stared at the book. *Un Journal Intime*. A disconsolate lady bemoans her fate in language once felt to be appropriate while girls sing in the dust and pull haycarts. God would reward them, Valerian had said. But they did not look to God for reward but to Valerian. It was him they reached for on the horizon, lingered after, longed for, like timid beasts. The taut Valerian, the bronze youth in the white shirt, gun-belted like one of Yasha's *pistoleros* from the Sierra de la Estrella in Indian Territory. Not the Spirit but the Body and the Blood.

Loulou rolled on her back and confronted the sky. Light-headed from waking dreams she craved a place in which to hide away from this dawn-bright alertness of things in the world. Daytimes were a nightmare of heat and idleness. From the moment she had been brought back from the woods after the failed escape a month previously, she had merely existed uneasily within the community; had been tolerated but spied upon, watched over but resented. Everything done to her was done upon authority: Scripture justified all.

Her fate and that of Polly, Belyakov and Yasha had been subsumed under Divine Will. Sinners repent! Prodigal sons and daughters be embellished with Valerian's love! There was much talk of that, but she knew most of the boy's followers simply ached to put a bullet into each of them. At times Valerian seemed to be drawing attention to the captives by his remorseless charity. He was no comfort.

Except for Yasha, Loulou began to avoid her companions. They were free to roam the house and gardens, but Polly had insisted that they kept together. Loulou wanted privacy and, after a brief squabble, she got her own way. Already she had found the place. Each day, at any time she chose, she could withdraw to the Laskorin roof where she hid in the shadow of the dome over the grand staircase and listened to the noises below.

Worn down by the June heat, poor diet (food was scarce and, to the community, she was a useless mouth), the daily problems of keeping clean, decently clothed and, above all, secure in her hiding place, Loulou had quickly passed beyond those false notions of dignity which had so amused Valerian. The previous night she said to Yasha: "That tall man who always wears the yellow scarf. I pass him on the steps to the kitchen garden. Yesterday his hand shook on the verandah railing when he stopped to let me go by. Do you think he would help me?"

As a last resort she had considered offering herself to one of Valerian's men in return for protection.

At first Yasha was shocked, then pensive; and finally, practical: "Have a heart, lady. Not that one, not Osip. He's Valerian's tactician, a wizard with maps. They went through four campaigns together. Anyway, he's out of reach. Got made a lieutenant. One of the band of brothers."

Valerian had formed an Inner Council of six. All power was now in their hands.

Loulou threw out her arms and groaned aloud. "Wretched troupe of clowns, giving themselves rank, military rank too. What had their God to do with titles? It's quite ludicrous."

Yasha tidied the heap of books which her sudden violence had toppled onto the blanket he had spread out for her. The evening had been sultry. They were both irritable and sweaty. "Don't you let appearances fool you," he said, wiping his forehead with a corner of the blanket. "That crowd's no circus turn, lady . . . When the likes of that Osip says 'Bang Bang', you stay dead." She had this snobby way of looking at things and wouldn't be told. "Sure, dress up funny, don't they? But ludicrous? Not ludicrous, milady. Any other kind of 'ous', yes, like *murderous, disastrous, torturous* . . ."

"There's no such word," said Loulou.

Yasha buffeted dust from the leaves of *Collection des Modes de 1897*. "You know what it means, though. Like you know what 'lieutenant', 'master' and all that stuff means. Call them what you like – the pure in heart, children of the light, God's anointed. They've got it in for *you*."

This would have made more impression if he hadn't mentioned Valerian. When he said "master" she'd got that funny look and began staring at nowhere, wittering in her fancy way: "What a bore, I do believe it's going to rain, Yashichka. Oh, how I long to be cosy somewhere, looking out at the storm."

Well, he'd done what he could. He'd even pitched her a tent out of tarred paper and drapes from the nursery. "Midsummer Eve last night. Never rains Midsummer Day, everybody knows that."

"Delightful," she said sliding into a huddle beside him. "I adore all that country lore. So picturesque. Tell me the names of the wild flowers and hedge plants."

There was nothing rural about Yasha, the backyard town boy, so he made it up: a florilegium of spurious Jesus-all-Fire, St Mary's Thumb osiers and sputterkin apples. She loved them all the better for not knowing a single one.

Yasha was enjoying himself. "Round about here, in the old days, on Midsummer Day, they lit their St John's fire and watched for Jacob's ladder . . ."

Well, they were doing something pretty queer, the night before, down by the river, leaping over hot logs barefoot and calling out to be cleansed. He couldn't tell her – she thought he never went far from her at night – and God knows how it would have fitted in with her ideas. A bit of nature magic. That's what it looked like when that stable-lad, Yefim, took off his footrags and jumped and shouted; with Schmidt, Valerian and Matryona kneeling like the Holy Family in the open on a huge shiny table from the library. But when Osip tripped through the grass in nothing but bandana and pipe-twill riding breeches to walk a twenty-foot smouldering pitchpine trunk without a twitch, Yasha knew it for something else. A test, an initiation.

"Words are dead," shouted the new lieutenant, bowing to the table. "They no longer trouble me."

Valerian had boots, though. You could hear them squeak on the coppery grain of the table. Daisy face. He was always covered.

"Well," she said. "Did it come?"

Side by side they were, as warm as two mice in a jug. He was dozy. *The ladder. Jacob's.*

"I wouldn't know," he said. "Not being a native. Besides. I told you, that was the old times."

If it wasn't, something like it must have been. Did he come down the ladder or go up, this *Yakob, Yasha, Yashenka?* Down, down. Where else for *Yashichka, yid, zhid, kvas zhidok*: Jew small-beer. Down to the bottom where old-timer Schmidt fingers his lariat, boot on the rung.

When Yasha woke, the sun had risen fat and still. There was a smell of wood smoke. Her upturned face was bluish in the light. He gave her sugar and white bread stolen from downstairs. Mornings were best. In the morning she didn't ask questions. Yasha took himself off to his corner, out of sight, and tried to guess what was coming. Valerian had divided his rule: north, south, east and west. Each lieutenant had absolute say in his sector; each was level with the others and each was equally under Valerian in perfect obedience. That was the theory.

Milady at her breakfast had dismissed them – and the system.

"Religion under arms, my dear! But of course! How else could Valerian ensure the observance of his commandments? But no one could take it seriously for a moment. You know them – they'll put on a little swagger at first, but the practicalities of keeping the peace in a community let alone defending it from attack will soon come home to them. For a week they'll be bullies, in a month they'll be whimpering drunks and going to pieces like everyone else."

Yasha knew too much to be sure. They might strike a woman like her as hucksters, tap-room keepers, light-fingered valets, draymen, money-lenders and tramps that had once existed on the other side of her drive-gate, but to him they were army. That's what the army was – less all that Martin-Kostya froth-on-the-top she went on about. This was the trench-digging, mine-laying lot; NCO professionals, survivors. Come the showdown they'd stand shoulder to shoulder with the infantry of Valerian's pitchfork regiments and fight to the death for what they had. It wasn't much and was getting less: the country teemed with riff-raff but Valerian refused to turn a soul away from his radiance.

Four from six left two. Makar the old one. And Schmidt, the veteran, made up for honour's sake. Now Schmidt was different, as vicious as a straw-yard bull eyeing for his chance. Morale was his business, not fighting, and it kept him close to his master. Valerian, they said, only slept because Schmidt never did. He was everywhere.

Yasha threw his bread over the parapet uneaten.

* * *

Loulou nibbled the dry skin on the ball of her thumb and watched the girl haymakers disappear into the mealy dawn haze.

I have been nosing the dust for days. I eat and drink the burning sun while they sing and walk in the shade of trees. They worship Valerian because he is the light. Once I too shone. Now I am shut in the dark scrabbling at the doors of my own house.

In her hand was the Laskorin children's scrapbook. Different-sized letters had been cut from periodicals and stuck down with lumpy flour-paste on the sugar-paper leaves.

Lola – Petya says hide the bread in the toad's cabinet.

Petya had been the only son, long-dead. The house was to have been his, and all the banks of gilded books. Then he drowned, and now she was killed, the sister, and the code was lost forever, indecipherable as their scattered bones. What did it matter? Girl and boy would only have perpetuated their parents and continued a moronic line. Look at Polly, the sole survivor. What was the point of her, except other Pollies? *Ad infinitum.*

We are better finished, all of us, stopped in our tracks, our biographies unreconstructible.

The messages spread thicker, almost blocking out the blue of the pages: *We are getting a new friend called Pavlushka . . . He's pretty big for a friend really.*

The illogicality was mordant, too universally childish for her not to picture the child who had written it – the boy again, admiring a bigger boy as only a boy would. Interspersed were spindly drawings of trees, and flowers with wiry petals. Hiding bread and wanting big friends described Loulou's own situation almost entirely. Once men and women had crossed themselves at the sight of her and bowed, but *en masse* they had outlasted her and the race-course crowd she was being driven to meet in the white open tourer. When she was gone from this place the village children would come up here and make kite-tails from the commonplace book *des enfants Laskorine.*

She had no gift for people. "You cultivate the wrong types," Kostya used to say as if the world were a garden border. But with the people here any thought of entrée was absurd. Yasha's folk-lore had eventually left her depressed because of its exoticism. To think you could become proficient at understanding such people's lives was to expect the impossible: if you learn Chinese you don't become a coolie. There must be a knack of simply fitting in, going unnoticed, which was outside her intellectual scope. Without a thought in her head Polly could do it, but Loulou, however hard she tried, could not overcome her sense of the scale of the reversal which placed her outside the experience both of Polly and those who held her captive.

Once they had kept their distance, muddling in the dust, night-watching the boundaries of her life, the grateful recipients of what she chose to discard. Now they were in the dressing-room rummaging her clothes. Close-to they had a dignity – she could appreciate that – and there was pathos in the wondering looks which they gave her even when they were being shooed away on Valerian's orders. But the sheer catastrophe which their nearness signified made Loulou's head ache. She had been too well educated in the niceness of degrees of proximity not to be fearful of their total collapse.

At home Kostya had employed a schoolmaster for the village children. The last Friday of every month his wife would come to Loulou's boudoir to stammer out requests and complaints. A gentle bird of a woman who worried about the falling school roll. Last Easter she had been murdered publicly at the door of the church. Her husband fled with a priest but the mob caught both and hacked them to death.

Every day Loulou anticipated a similar fate but could not prepare herself. *Hide the bread* drummed in her ears. But there was no toad's cabinet.

I know my friends. To expect the worst is to know everyone. They will save themselves and then conspire to offer me up to Valerian as a final sacrifice. Yasha is gone, thieving for scraps. If he knew where the toad's cabinet was he could find bread.

His voice came to her now, beating down the voice of the child, a threatening infuriated drawl: "You and your fancy friends, you and your Laskorins: they've done us no favours . . ."

Yesterday he almost slapped her face because he thought she had betrayed him by speaking to a man and touching his arm while she spoke.

"I only wanted some news."

The man had been by the wall of the garden rigging trellis for the south-facing espalier of pears. He went so peaceably and orderly about the work that she had wondered who he had been before coming to this place. A straight-backed practical fellow, somebody's headman. When she approached he turned away politely, but she grasped his arm and begged him to tell her what was going on in the neighbourhood. Was the war over? Pouring from her came a tumult of names – friends, anyone he might have seen, met or heard of. Three women in the distance who were collecting dead branches pointed, shrieking with laughter.

The man was dumb.

"You and your bright ideas," Yasha had bawled afterwards. "What is it about you and men?"

Privately he had drawn his own conclusions: there must be something repulsive about her. Must be. Nearly a whole afternoon alone with Valerian in the woods and nothing coming of it. That's not leading a man. *Next time, pick a talker to prance round the garden with.*

So she closed herself up and waited.

Don't be too long, squiggled the messages in and out of the skeletons of pasted-down flowers in the blue book. *I'm just going out and when I come back you'll be here, I know you will . . . I can't wait until Daddy comes home . . .*

14

As the sun climbed in a clear sky the leads quickly soaked up the heat. At the same time every morning Loulou sought shade in her favourite place. The trapdoor to the ladder down which Yasha had gone, via the garret, on his foray for supplies, was set in a box-like projection as tall as a man. Hoisting her books and cigarettes onto the top, she settled in its shadow and drowsed.

Barely had she had time to make herself comfortable when, above her, came a slithering and bumping noise and the books tumbled onto her chest. Yasha must be back early. She sat bolt upright prepared to shout at him for his inconsiderateness. The trapdoor rose up, black against the sun; surmounting it a head, the features indistinguishable, but of a shape she recognised. Not Yasha but Belyakov in his floppy summer cap, liquor on his breath detectable at a good six feet.

He swore quietly, dropped back the flap and jumped down at her feet. His eyes were orangey and the cap, a shapeless thing of felted cloth, was pulled well down. It was early but he was drunk, and when drunk evilly disposed. She took note of his characteristic flush and wished she had drink to offer. Only more of the same would undo his truculent melancholia.

He glared as Loulou wriggled out of range of his breath. "Typical," he grunted, surveying the litter of books, bottles, cigarettes, cushions and tins lying scattered over the leads. "Slut's mess. You need a housekeeper, missis." Picking up a book at random he broke it open at the plates. "All dirt, inside and out. Typical. So this is how a lady whiles away her leisure. Scavenging in filth while we beseech the salvation of her soul."

"My soul is my own to salvage," said Loulou. "So you can leave me off your chanting list. Not that you would understand. You never listen to anything except priest babble. Besides, you're drunk."

"Oh, shocking, shocking!" he called out to the sky. "A depraved four-footed beast am I!" He stood over her and banged the book shut against his knee. "There's sin and sin, and iniquities outreaching wine."

She turned away. "Am I never to have any peace? What do you want?"

"Peace, is it? Down there," he shouted, grinding underfoot so hard with the heel of his boot that the dulled lead gave way to silver. "Down there are those who would give you quiet with a hayfork through the eyes. Listen to me, woman, and thank Christ for my charity. I come with a warning."

Loulou was by the parapet. The peasant girls had long ago disappeared but now, by the lake, a gang of little boys skimmed stones at the ducks. "Warn me then," she said, turning. "And then leave. I have my occupations."

With surprising deftness Belyakov hopped from joist to joist and brought his mouth up to her ear. "In the kitchen, a dark woman . . . begging. Blackish, the colour of molasses, but dry." Loulou felt him tremble momentarily. "Husk-dry."

She leaned away and ran her hands along the warm lichen on the stone, murmuring: "Poetic, poetic. And did she cast fates, and tell you what lay between the cusps of the moon and touch your pointer against mange?"

Her detachment sent him wild. "Witch! They will hang you!"

"Witch – me?" she said quietly. "Oh God, no, not me. My powers are not so great – otherwise you would all long ago have been turned to blossom and puffed away on the wind."

Belyakov almost believed her. It might have been sisterhood talk. He took care to distance himself by invoking her names: "Grafinya Natalya Igoryevna Alekseyeva – she knows you."

While she watched he took a long drink from the flask he always carried at his belt. Afterwards he seemed less troubled. "There is no work for your ladyship, is there? While women toil the lady lolls, fancying herself the heroine of a wicked book."

Loulou's tone became pedestrian, apologetic. "I do try but I am out of joint with those boors. Sometimes everything here seems ugly and cruel beyond words. I feel I am simply waiting to die . . . Tell me about your black woman. What did she say?"

"Wasn't to me. I just happened to be on my way through. No, she told the women and I watched their faces when they told me. They knew all along you weren't a lad. Or claimed they did. They'd been watching you. Matryona, the big one, lifted her hands and praised God that the truth had been revealed."

"Will you help me?" She lived apart like an animal, untended, but her skin was fine and clear, her body scent sweet. "Help me." The ring in her voice was true.

"What help is there?"

Loulou stretched out her head to him. "The help you give trapped things. *C'est ton métier*. Kill me. Break my neck."

The demand was so unexpected that Belyakov clasped his own neck and squawked: "And who'd be left to wring mine?"

With a shivering laugh Loulou seemed to come to. "Matryona, of course. I've seen her, she'd do anything for you." That fat widow, she would, too. Always pushing her daughter at Valerian and causing discord.

He bared his teeth. "Meat for the pack, one day, missie, that woman, but while she can walk, keep her in view."

"But what should I do? I've run as far as I can. It's impossible."

For an hour they smoked her cigarettes; Belyakov astride the parapet, she in the shade. "As for running, it's too late. Remember old Prince Dorokhov's place at Yarosovka where they had the show every summer?"

Loulou remembered the great draught horses nineteen hands high imported from Belgium for the deep ploughing that Prince Dorokhov prided himself on. Every year he showed off his brood mares and their crop of foals. Papa was his friend from student days and used to heave her up to pop sugar into the horses' mouths. She remembered and smiled at the memory. "The one they called 'the model agricul-turalist' because he built a lying-in hospital for his labourers' wives?"

"That was him," said Belyakov. "The best sort. A funny old devil – and hard – but one of the finest. When he took it into his head to run foxes in the two-thousand-acre forest at Yarosovka we bought the hounds, him and me, in Petrograd. And a red coat. A lovely man."

"Well?"

Belyakov pulled on the bridle of his imaginary horse and slapped his rump. "Gone," he said.

"Where?"

"To the end of the world with his high-handed stallions, to the stinking crupper of this stinking world."

In the cold shade Loulou sweated.

"Squashed like a fruit, that old man, pulped with his old lady."

Yarosovka overlooked the sand-shoaled river, about thirty miles upstream. A spare house, cool even on windless nights of June, as indestructible as the waters running before it. "Who?" whispered Loulou.

He knew exactly what she feared. "Not *him*, not Valerian," he said, resuming his former pose and lashing out with his boots at the leads. "That's not his fashion; leastways, not when he's in control.

No, when he talks of salvation and promotes himself to saviour, he means it, in his heart, he means it."

"Who, then?"

"Hard to tell, cooped up here. Don't think I'm privy to the news his patrols bring in. No one knows much except the few closest to him, and they don't tell. But they're gut-tight scared, I can tell you that."

"You must know something; you've just told me."

She waited while he drank from his flask and made another cigarette without offering her either. "The black woman – she knew what I have told."

"What else?" cried Loulou. "The house, is the house still there?" If the house stood, she felt obscurely, not all would be lost. People come and go but the house stands.

"They anchored barges midstream, took winches and hawsers to your precious house and it came down in splinters and stone, along with him, and her and their children and their children's children, spread in the mire of the horses. Bonemeal, blood and hoof, they made of them, dung for trench and furrow."

"Oh Christ, spare me!" screamed Loulou. "Make an end of me! Take me so that I do not have to bear it!"

Belyakov watched the hot colours of park and woods flush intermittently black under the skim of the clouds. A task lay before him, one for which he would require her advice, if not help. She would quieten spontaneously in her own time. They always did. Meanwhile, be glad for your own peace which came out of practical knowledge that what you described could never be what you had seen; and what you had seen was more terrible that what could be imagined; but having seen it you could smoke, rest, stretch and gaze on the world and still meet it in the eye.

Eventually Loulou ceased wailing, sobbed once more, stopped and rubbed her eyes. She was unsatisfied. She asked for more; for detail; for everything; for nothing to be kept back. The whole story. He sighed and obliged, but knew how to stop her. When he came to the children, the Dorokhov children, that stopped her. To bear the recital of their fate you needed to be not a man or a woman, but a veteran who had proofed himself against consolations. She shrieked and closed up his mouth with her hand. "Tell me something else, drive it away, tell me how you know. The woman, the dark woman, what about her?"

Nothing about the woman mattered, except as a point about which her mind could turn.

"You know the sort." He affected a weariness he did not feel. The important change had been worked: she was electrified into fear for her life. "They trade on portents – shooting stars, bearded comets, women bringing forth litters of rabbits . . ."

"Pelagya!" cried Loulou. "I knew it. That she-devil vagrant from one of our villages. Always pretending second-sight. She used to say she was pure *tsigana*, but no gipsy lives without family. The little boys holed her up in a cave until the priest drove them off and kept her locked up in a compound below the apse for her own safety. The louts at the posting station wanted to flay her for a sorceress." A burst of sunlight caught her and the huntsman studied her haggard eyes. "Surely," she said, "no one believes what she said about me?"

"She said nothing of you."

Loulou was perplexed, then afraid. "But you said . . . ?"

"She said she knew you."

"Of course she knows me. To know me is to know . . ."

"That you are here? That is all she needs to know."

Even though Pelagya knew the only thing about her that it was vital to conceal – her whereabouts – Loulou was grateful for the intervention, relieved that Pelagya had kept secret what she knew about the Alekseyevs, husband and wife. "This is dreadful," she said. "I hide away, scarcely daring to breathe, only to be found by some hideous mischance. Can this draggleskirt madwoman put me in danger?"

"Look at you," said Belyakov with a grimace. "Hair shorn like a lamb's, rump overfilling the seat of a man's breeches – they know their own sex. A word at the wrong time and they wouldn't need an excuse, not those women; they'd slit your flat belly down to the cleft."

"Then why not now?" moaned Loulou. "Believe me, I'm ready, I'm pleading to go."

He led her to the edge of the roof and made her look over. "Out there," he said, "where he is, so are they. They go to the fields at sunrise in case he rides by. They stay there all day, broiled by the sun, for the chance that he may come. They want him to see them. He is their divinity. While you . . ." He spanned her temples with his hand. "You trouble him and because you trouble him they hate you. 'Where is our little brother with the agate hair?'" The mockery was fierce in the huntsman's voice as he repeated Valerian's words. "Do you think those drabs don't hear him? They cut up his meat, and bob and serve at the knee, but they listen and they know that what you have, they have, and at a flicker of the lip theirs can be his."

Loulou pulled at the long fringe which had grown down to her eyebrows since Yasha hacked off her hair a month before, and peered at Belyakov. "Why doesn't he take one, then, or two, or the whole gaggle – there are no rules for him surely? He could have a harem if he wanted."

The answering look made her feel like the last of some rare species which even a poacher might hesitate to shoot. "He wants you. Only you will do. And being wanted may keep you alive. I can't help you any more and I won't go against him. I shall be taking the oath of allegiance." This was a vow which the rest of the community had already made to hold their crops and animals in common under the protection of God and Valerian. "I need security," he continued. "Soon I shall be a married man." This was said slowly, as if staking a claim to a position in the world of respectability.

Loulou was nonplussed. "You mean you're throwing in your lot with these savages? For the sake of a woman? I can't believe it. And don't count on me," she went on, wanting to revenge herself for his betrayal by calling up the future. "When the . . . When the . . ." *Detectives come* was how Yasha always saw the day of reckoning, but it sounded silly and she let the threat trail away. "Who is she, this woman, this fortunate bride-to-be?"

"She's not a woman," he said with dignity. "She's a lady."

"A *what*? A lady – here?"

"There are such, in spite of circumstances." He breathed in heavily. "Apollonya Dmitryevna and I are to be wed."

"Oh my God, this is agricultural farce. What is she to be – a shepherdess?"

Belyakov stiffened. "Never you mind, missie. I shall protect her and keep her."

"My dear man, that will take some doing."

"Does as she's told. Not like you," he said.

"And the women, what do they think? Doesn't she stick in their throats like me? We're blood cousins, don't forget."

"The women know what's good for them. Valerian approves and I have told them that Apollonya Dmitryevna was a paid companion from a poor family, a sort of junior governess."

"But she can hardly read."

"Neither can they," said Belyakov. "So I don't see much trouble in that direction."

"You're a heartless schemer," exclaimed Loulou. "I am to prostitute myself to your priest so that you can safely play mothers and fathers with a featherbrain."

He blushed. "I know you think I'm not good enough."

"That's not all I think. By the way," she said, looking past him to the tree-topped horizon. "Have you asked her or is it Valerian to whom you propose?"

The blush went deeper. "When a man has no friends he has the right to approach the father."

"*Svat, svakha, svashenka, svakhin, svatovshchik, svatovshchitsa!*" exclaimed Loulou, the words for the intermediary in peasant marriages tripping off her tongue. "Valerian! The Heavenly Matchmaker. I ought to have known."

A whistle came from the trapdoor. "Trouble, lady?" asked Yasha sticking out his lower lip at the sight of Belyakov looming over Natalya Igoryevna.

Loulou shrugged and gave him a brooding look with her great grey eyes. "I am not sure, Yashenka," she said through her teeth. "Vladimir Ivanovich wants to take us all under his wing. Your disguises don't work. Everyone knows who I am."

Yasha threw a wicker basket onto the leads and climbed down after it. "Yeah," he said, addressing Loulou but fixing his eyes on the huntsman. "I've heard he gets around. People's his business, so the word goes."

Belyakov vaulted up to the trapdoor. When only his head and shoulders were visible, he beckoned to Yasha. "Listen to me, boy."

"I listen good, massa," said Yasha. "From where I is."

Loulou laughed.

"Take charge of her, make sure she changes her ways, and for God's sake find her some skirts."

The boy tugged at the hair on his temples. "Sure thing, boss."

The huntsman frowned at the queer dialect. "You from Little Russia, son?"

"Nope," said Yasha. "Cat Fish Fork, Texas."

"What's eating him?" he asked after Belyakov had disappeared.

Loulou was unpacking the basket. "He's in love."

"Anyone we know?"

"The Laskorin girl," said Loulou absently. There seemed to be nothing in the basket except a tablecloth.

"She's daft."

"Of course she is. But he's not marrying her for intellectual stimulation."

He grinned. "Loco, the people in this place."

Loulou brought out seemingly endless folds of white linen. "Yasha, this really is ridiculous. What on earth do we want a tablecloth for?"

"Good, isn't it?" he said.

She shook the cloth out to its fullest extent. Patches of iron mould were clustered at the centre.

"Some stuff, eh?" Yasha was eager to show off his prowess at foraging. "Guy with the gammy leg tried to grab it off me, so I swiped him one. Dog eat dog down there when it comes to napery. There's a feast day coming round and spick and span ain't in it when altars is in question."

Loulou sank down, the cloth sagging over her hips, and gave a piercing whine. "Never mind the table linen, I haven't eaten. Where's the meat?"

He dived both hands into the deep basket. "Getting to be knottier, sweet-talking Frossya." At Loulou's feet he laid a whole rabbit, fur intact, and still warm.

She recoiled. "What's that?"

Yasha twitched his nose and made long ears with his index fingers. "They're all like that at first. A bit primitive until they get into pies."

She went behind a chimney stack and lay down while he skinned the rabbit, jointed it and made a stew of meat and apples over the gun-metal basin in which he kept a charcoal fire smouldering day and night. Before they ate he folded the cloth into four and spooned the food into wooden bowls with flowery rims. "Good for morale," he said as she wolfed it down. "A bit of civilisation. Some folks have no manners."

Loulou licked the spoon and her fingers. "Do you think we will be expected to eat with them, now that Belyakov says we are to be no longer shunned?"

"You'll have to wait, then," said Yasha, piqued that she had not praised his stew. "The women don't eat till the men have ate first, fit to burst, and all the praying gets done after. Horrible dinners, too, all seeds and beans."

In spite of the warmth from the food they both shivered. The sun was declining into a haze and the air sharpened. For a while they strolled back and forth along the flat edge of the leads by the parapet. Yasha glanced down the swollen curves of the columns. "The sons of bitches are coming back home."

Along paths made biscuity from the light teemed doll-like figures hurrying from the four corners of the park. A bell sounded.

"Watch those females," said Loulou. "Guess what they'll be doing in a moment."

Male or female, Yasha couldn't make them out. What did it matter? In this place the sexes were equally insane. "You don't want to bother, lady, it'll only wear out your nerves."

"Look! They're prostrating themselves. It's disgusting."

A white blodge showed up at the far end of the main driveway. As Valerian bobbed up and down in time to old Emir's rocking-horse canter, figures scattered to the verges and lay prone. "There!" shouted Loulou triumphantly. "What did I tell you?"

Yasha sighed. A pity the girls didn't lie on their backs so that you might have got a flash of something worthwhile.

"He can be charming but he's such a *fool*," she murmured. "Diabolic, too. Those sneaks in their gaudy scarves hate me, apparently."

"Who says?"

"Why Vladimir Ivanovich. He has told me so."

"Oh, *him*," said Yasha, glugging from an imaginary bottle. "He sees Redskins under the bed."

"No," said Loulou. "I believe him in this. He knows the real world."

Emir had disappeared under the portico slashing his cropped tail at the hornets. The women below arose, brushing pollen from their aprons.

"I got a show for you tonight," said Yasha suddenly.

"Not the stage-coach one again, I'm so sick of that story. Couldn't you think up something – I don't know – less *ferocious*. All that shooting and whooping . . ."

"You're just ungrateful," he said. "Anyway, it's not out of my head this time. It's the real world like you say your John Barleycorn knows."

"Is there a witch in it?"

Yasha pondered. "Could be," he said guardedly.

"Because if it's anything to do with that ugly Pelagya then I simply won't listen. And I don't want to hear how I shall be done to death eventually. And no love interest, *please*."

"No Jesus, no hags, no lynchings, no hick preachers, no weddings," said Yasha. "Promise."

Loulou ran her hands over her face and through her hair. The touch of her red curls felt raggedy at her ears. "Polly eats with those smug brutes, you know. She'd spoil my appetite with that ghastly smile. Revolting girl."

"I wouldn't mind. Not for a square meal." Yasha was displeased that she would not be persuaded away from her morbid train of thought. He had a big secret. Not that it couldn't wait. He would show her in time. He had blazed the trail. When the sun went down they could follow the tracks.

Loulou rounded on him. "Creatures! Appetites! And you're just as bad! Always pushing conversations to the point of indecency. Let me sleep and be silent."

Yasha covered her with the damask tablecloth and lulled her to sleep. "Prickly Pear City," he crooned. "Old Dirt Village, Boggy Depot, Fire Steel Creek, Main Red River, *Keche-ah-nue-ho-no* . . ."

15

O ut on the lawn the children had made an altar from the sundial and were sacrificing dolls. The present victim was French in Second-Empire costume and the tang of frizzled hair wafted through the half-open window of the yellow drawing-room.

Polly Laskorina stepped back from her easel wiping a paintbrush on her smock. The fumes brought on her hay-fever and she sneezed in staccato bursts. Iridescent droplets winked on the surface of her panel.

"Oh, for heaven's sake!" she exclaimed, suddenly feeling hot and tickly.

Kicking off her clogs she pattered up and down the makeshift studio, cooling the soles of her pretty little feet. At one end hung Valerian's unfinished picture of Our Lady of Sorrows. The Virgin was as pink and swollen as the dropsical udder of an unmilked cow. Polly stopped wriggling her toes on the resinous planks of the floor and railed at it in silence and contempt.

There was no modelling to the figure which seemed simultaneously fat and flat. The work was so two-dimensional that it would have been at home in the ante-chamber of a pharaoh or in a Japanese wood-and-paper house. No talent. That was obvious to the merest amateur. The man was a fraud. The Virgin embraced herself with leg-of-mutton arms, arrested in the act of twiddling her robe with sausagey fingers. Puffy, boneless, rosy and flat as a board; packed with meat but wooden, like jig-saw charcuterie.

The odour of burnt doll's stuffing thinned on the breeze, losing its pungency. Polly rubbed her nose as the prickling in her nostrils subsided, and peered more kindly into the slitty plumbago eyes of Valerian's Our Lady.

"Holy Mother of God," she murmured. "What is to become of me?"

From childhood she had retained the superstition that images, if long enough contemplated, would move. For a long minute she stared, excited by the experiment; but as ever there was no return and the face of Christ's Mother, fixed by Valerian in a catatonic whimper, continued to engross itself in that deadpan exclusivity of suffering which Polly had come to accept as the mark of saintliness.

Perhaps she wasn't holy enough. Millie had tried to raise the devil by staring at a whitewashed wall; Lola thought they could hypnotise tumblers into movement. Their minds were unclean, said Frossya — under their blankets they must have been touching themselves. In any case, how could Polly succeed with this Virgin? Altogether too hideous. What else would you expect when that warped Druid had done the painting?

"'Blessed are the pure in heart for they shall see God,'" quoted Polly to herself. There you are then: no varichrome Jesus would be stepping off the picture plane for Valerian or for her.

Still, thank heaven it had begun to rain and the children had gone. Squeezing out rose carmine and cerulean blue onto her palette, Polly set to work again with her brush laying on the colour in wodges, in time to her own Beatitude:

"Blessed are Mama, and Papa, and Millie, and Lola, for they are . . ."

What? Dead? No. That would not do.

"Blessed are Mama, and Papa, and Millie, and Lola, for they have been . . ."

Mine? No. Rich? No.

Oh God, where do such thoughts come from and why do I feel nothing?

Blessed *were* Millie, and Lola, and Mama, and Papa; and the Bichon Frisé dogs; and the mulberry Abyssinian cat; and the golden Palominos in the stable champing at the bridle; and Mama's Arab with the forelock of an angelic child. All the animals and those who fed and tended them. And us. And everyone who came to us with their six pairs of brogues bought in Scotland, silk hunting hats, parasols, Alexandrian cameos, ivorine flasks and sal volatile, pill cases, turnip watches of gold that played waltzes; all their frocks and stuffs and suits and silks layered and tissued, bursting from traps and hampers; blessed was each one of them, and the things which they brought to diversify that unnecessitous charade played out under the leaves on sunny afternoons which they called their lives.

Jolly lucky, in fact, not to notice at the time that they were of the blest. Not that she had done so herself, reflected Polly, spearing with the point end of her brush a cranefly which had mired its legs in her paints. Only now that the advantages of her former life had become appreciable was she cold to their sense. Then she had nothing in her head and no one had time for her. It was a nice feeling, that was all, to be more comfortable, to be rich. At the time she had given no thought to such things; now she dismissed the opportunity she had overlooked in not knowing their value then, as a nostalgia for ignorance, and took pleasure in this new awareness of herself.

Mama and Papa were so queer. She used to wonder how they came to conceive her. They were always praying. Polly could not remember a time when either had kissed her without the attendant religious performance of crossing her on the forehead with a cold thumb. Just before bedtime usually. Without the cross, Lola had said, kisses made you pregnant. And for years she had believed this because Papa kissed Mama so and Mama had no more children after Polly herself.

Not once did they come to her bedroom. Frossya used to leave a lamp burning, just in case. But they never came. No need, of course, said Papa: one is never alone with God.

Things had not changed much. There was a banner stretched like a playbill between the trees in the park: TODAY, THE FEAST OF THE TRANSFIGURATION OF THE LORD GOD OUR SAVIOUR JESUS CHRIST. *Their* days were not Papa's and Mama's days. Today is a feast. Today we can eat meat and drink wine. Today they pray, and Valerian with them. "'And as he prayed the fashion of his countenance was altered, and his raiment was white and glistering.'"

Out there, among the formal parterres of the French garden, the wild men stood waiting for the voice of the Lord:
"'This is my beloved Son: hear him.'"

Their very own prayer-book, picture-book Jesus with his robes and wavy locks.

"'There came a cloud and overshadowed them: and they feared as they entered into the cloud.'"

Polly giggled and bit her lip. I'll say they did. I bet. Pitilessly she recalled her mother's sallow neck and hard eyes. Put down like a sick kitten by the man in white who transfigured countenances for all eternity.

Nevertheless, prayers mattered – if only to those who pray. God's wrath might have been loosed on the parents but their least-loved child had been spared, and she had seen Him blow up their murderers. He had a sense of humour as well as unpredictable ways.

Art could be an offering and she liked to see her paintings as a sacrifice. *Moses in the Bulrushes.* Look how *he* started and how he ended up. One never could tell. She had done the basket and the bulrushes and now she was on the eyes of Pharaoh's daughter. Very slinky, heathen princesses. To be dandled by one must be rather exciting, if you were male, of course. For a girl it would be like a tickling from a False Pretender or a Tartar Khan.

Sun flooded the room again. The brush hairs spread evenly into her paint. It was nice to be working well; to feel slightly fatigued but to want to go on. If it were not for Loulou hanging about always moaning about headaches and how tired she was and drawing attention to herself, the last few weeks might have been delightful. Of course, there was the noise to contend with, but one soon got used to gun-shots and wood-chopping and ranting. The whole house was stuffed with awful people, of course, but then it always was. No doubt the authorities would arrive one day and expel them and set everything to rights. After all, now everyone was dead it was her house, so there was undisputed possession to look forward to.

There was something soothing about painting. It was quite fun, too. No one had let her do it properly before. People had always been telling her what she ought to do, pushing her from pillar to post. Now only Vladimir Ivanovich tried to be bossy, but she could deal with him. Besides, he did what Valerian said and she and Valerian had their art in common, so she had a protector. And, since Valerian had *his*, who was Boss of them all, Polly could afford some free-play for her artistic temperament. Nice. Better not to desert those who spoke to God when you could interpret for them, like Moses – or was it Joseph?

When Valerian told Mr Schmidt (the one who looks at a girl in that creepy, goggly way) that all the pictures in the house were awfully decadent and immoral, Mr Schmidt was sure Polly herself could paint nicer ones and he was right. Nobody had ever taken her seriously before and Mr Schmidt almost wept when he saw how keen she could be when the chance came her way of painting pictures for the new community. Her pictures could help purify young minds. How pictures from the Bible would put a stop to those beastly little girls parading round in Millie's tea-gowns and plastering rouge on their cheeks, Polly had no idea; but who could complain when Mr Schmidt had promised to supply all the materials?

Belyakov had become very respectful since she began painting. He primed the wood panels and stretched canvases for her. Polly felt valued and important. She had set to work immediately on backgrounds, blocking in a field of golden wheat for Ruth and Boaz, and banks of green rushes for the Moses child.

Then Valerian had to come and spoil everything. Absolutely in character. God always ruined things when He thought you were enjoying yourself too much. Valerian had insisted on painting an angel for himself. A big one, very fat with squalid little wings. Then he did an even fatter Virgin in all the wrong colours. When she had tried to explain to him that nobody painted like that nowadays, except awfully ill-educated people, he got quite shirty and shouted that when he had been at the seminary everyone just adored that kind of thing. In any case, that was how the Virgin really looked. And the saints, too. Once upon a time they were actual portraits. At that she became diplomatic. Very religious people were weird and if Valerian wasn't quite God he had got pretty close (in his opinion) and with that sort, Papa always said, it didn't do to throw caution to the winds.

The worst thing about Valerian, though, was his niceness to Loulou. She was a pagan idolatress, Mama said so – a nature-fiend. Adulteress, too; and the husband was worse, only one never learned what he got up to (in private, that is). They had brought the county-folk into disrepute with their goings-on and Polly had been forbidden to speak to either of them. Typical of Valerian to be interested in her, the unrepentant Magdalen. Loulou was allowed to do no work at all, and just lay about all day like an odalisque, never going to prayers. And she'd stolen heaps of clothes, and went round looking an absolute fright in blacket velvet trousers, ruffled shirt and pink stockings. Quite tasteless and unladylike.

When Polly protested, Loulou only laughed and called her stupid. Perhaps she was, and perhaps it was better if that's where cleverness got you – to go thieving and prancing about like a kept woman. Anyway, talent was above intellect any day.

Enough of unpleasant things. She tossed her head and tested a drying area of paint with her palette knife. The eyes of Pharaoh's daughter sparkled like quartzes. Fine. Fine. Time to add a few touches to the other work on the go – her Virgin and Child.

Belyakov should be here any minute to varnish two of her paintings. His admiration could be counted on. When he saw her he always took off his hat and bowed. Sometimes he spoke in a funny way: not quite out of the Bible but like he was making up bits of it on the spot. Once she had written some sentences down but they didn't seem to make much sense. That was not surprising in this topsy-turvy atmosphere of holy gardening and day-long chants. Instead of writing up the things that had happened perhaps she ought to put down her thoughts. *Pensées d'une belle esclave.* Something of that nature. A lot of thoughts had come to her lately.

16

Belyakov came into the room without knocking, wearing his cap. Polly did not greet him but stared. After a while he remembered and snatched it off.

"That's nice," he said, waving the cap at her picture.

"I know," she said and began to dab in the gold stars on the Virgin's mantle with her finest sable. He didn't know the first thing about pictures but it was gratifying to be praised even by the undiscriminating. "My family wanted me to go in for an artistic career." This was flying Papa's lukewarm responses rather high but, drat it, Belyakov couldn't cross-examine her relations now that they had passed on. Besides, talent ought to declare itself and be respected. "All of my friends said I had the gift but, you know how it is – I simply hadn't the time to spend hours and hours in front of an easel perfecting my technique."

"No," agreed Belyakov humbly. At least, it sounded humble. With those moustaches all over his mouth you never could quite catch the tone.

Eventually he turned away and caught sight of Loulou's chaise-longue. "Does the ladyship take a hand too?"

Polly concentrated on her palette. "At this creative moment," she said, "nothing is further from my mind than thoughts of Natalya Igoryevna." For some reason he was always bothering her about Loulou. It was discourteous and extremely boring.

Belyakov turned his back to her and smiled. "You've been busy, then." His voice was formal and awkward; the conversational equivalent of cap-twisting.

Yet Polly felt able to answer. Young men said that sort of thing to you in the drawing-room. It was neutral and answerable. "Yes," she said. "I am really quite exhausted." Shifting back on her heels so that Belyakov could get a clear view of the picture, she began to clean her hands in the bowl of turpentine which Frossya had provided. "Once one gets started, one has really no idea where line and image will lead one."

"Like Valerian?" said Belyakov.

She frowned and made a charming bow of her mouth. "Oh, I don't think so. He's so *constrained*, wouldn't you say? Illustrative."

"Sloshes it on, too." The huntsman was unclear as to her drift.

Polly cleaned her brushes in silence.

At a loss to revive the exchange Belyakov lifted up Polly's Moses panel and carried it over to the window. The sunlight brought up interesting yellow patches in the wet oils. Back at the easel he scrutinised Valerian's fat angel which was hovering benignantly above a flame-red shack. "Nice," he said again, less certainly.

Polly screwed up her eyes and looked sideways at the angel's legs. "He's no good at figures. Look at that." She prodded the thick ankles. "Adipose. Compared with my work, there's no sinew, no fire. What is it children call the ox?"

"The bull's uncle?" Belyakov felt relieved to be attuned for the first time.

"Quite so. Compared with my work, that is a fat ox."

"You don't take to his stuff, then?" This was a surprise. Criticism of Valerian was rare on any count, but no less welcome for that.

Polly had meant to be combative, not critical. With these people it was risky to be open. In any case, he had no right to lead her into confrontation. So bad-mannered. She allowed her disapproval to show and Belyakov's conversational gambit evaporated.

"I expect you know all about art," he said weakly. "With a house once packed with artistic gems."

She nodded enthusiastically. "A young woman of intelligence with a modicum of dash just couldn't help having her taste *formed* by her surroundings. A kind of osmosis, if you know what I mean."

"Yes?" said the huntsman.

"And then we were forever hearing so many different opinions and ideas. Papa had masses to stay – artists you know – that sort of person. And they talked and talked."

Attributing Belyakov's silence to awe, Polly burbled on complacently. "Not that we had a *salon* exactly. Not like Natalya Igoryevna had in Petrograd. Her soirées were simply agonising from all the brainy people she introduced one to. Household names, that sort of thing. They wrote for the papers and thought up novels and plays. Their names slip my mind but dreadfully famous, very literary, always gossiping and snarling and quarrelling. I couldn't stand them myself. Treacherous creatures! One kind word and they gaped for the next, and if you couldn't think up more compliments they turned nasty and said things behind your back. Appallingly tempestuous but excessively *terre à terre*. Ugh! I like artists because they don't have their feet on the ground." She shook her head ruefully.

The huntsman grunted into his beard and began to sort through a stack of unvarnished paintings propped up against a wall. "Temperament – that's the devil."

"Well, they were all spoony about Natalya Igoryevna, I know that." Polly thrust out her bottom lip. "Do you mind if I ask you something?"

He straightened up only to bow. "Please be so good, Apollonya Dmitryevna."

These formalities made Polly blush and look away. By the time she decided to put her question, he had moved a little nearer. Her mouth twitched slightly. "I used to be awfully jealous of her, you know," she said. "Do you think she's fiendishly attractive?"

He frowned. "Not compared to some."

"What was that again?" Damn the man's mumbling.

Belyakov cleared his throat and enunciated ringingly: "Not – compared – to – some."

Polly went pink. "Gosh," she said and clasped her hands.

He came even nearer. They stood close together, the bowl of turpentine between them.

"Rather skinny, isn't she?"

Belyakov nodded.

"Of course, if one's built that way," went on Polly a little unnerved by their proximity, "there's not much one can do. A richer diet, perhaps, but she exists on nuts and vegetables, or so they tell me. It does detract, I feel, from a woman's *presence*, somehow, if she's so physically . . ." Polly searched for the word, and not finding it, gazed more intently at him as if it were to be found in his face or on his person. For a moment she almost sensed his muscular fingers at her temple, cradling her head. When the word came, she shied at its impact, flinging out her arms involuntarily.

The bowl went spinning onto the folds of her smock. "*Insubstantial*," she got out before her face crumpled into the first of a series of sneezes which both she and he were helpless to control.

Afterwards, the moment gone, he polished the lenses of her spectacles, handed them back and watched as she resumed painting and the familiar high-toned voice.

Polly spoke of her upbringing: "Of course, you wouldn't know what it is to be sheltered, would you?"

He made some kind of noise and set about stirring the varnish.

"Inconceivably restrictive," she sighed, lifting a mournful face to the cornice. "In town practically the whole winter, paying calls with my aunts. I so wanted to travel, to broaden myself . . . Hand me that daubstick, would you? These starpoints are smudging."

Belyakov did as he was told but a trifle ungraciously it seemed to Polly. She remembered his weakness. "There's a bottle of wine in the cupboard. Do help yourself. Valerian said we can have wine. And oil. Isn't that funny?"

No answer. Oh, he was moody.

What had come over her a few moments ago? Such thoughts for such a man. A bear, a grouchy bear. Neither said a word until Polly marked the end of her afternoon's work by dropping her brush and leaning back to stretch.

"Want me to start?" he said, almost inaudibly, dribbling varnish off a wooden spoon onto a strip of panelling.

Although she disliked the idea of turning her back on him when he seemed so *farouche*, her nose began to tickle again and she went over to the window for air.

"Is she sophisticated?"

"Who?"

"Natalya Igoryevna. You know who I mean."

"I don't know what sophisticated means, though," said Belyakov.

Polly was stung. She had hoped for an answer similar to the one he had given before. Her voice went up a semi-tone: "I'm good family. As good as hers, if not better. Mama said I could have been, I could have been *anything* had I put my mind to it. Aren't I sophisticated?"

"I told you, Apollonya Dmitryevna, I don't know what . . ."

"Tcha, tcha!" exclaimed Polly, twirling round as if to catch her reflection in the window glass. "Knowing about the world and its ways. Rather superior and above things. Cutting with men – that sort of style."

She could hear him. He had got up and was probably dripping varnish onto his boots. A smile came over her face. "Yes," she went on. "Men hang on their necks. You know. Temptresses like her. Men ought to have someone to protect them from sin."

"They do, *sudarinya*," said Belyakov. "Valerian says: 'God's precepts safeguard men.'"

"Goose!" squealed Polly. "I don't mean protected all over against every – what does he call it? – 'manifestation of themselves'."

The thought of protecting the big rough man behind her made Polly feel a little faint. Her hands plucked at the thick weave of the peasant skirt beneath her smock and she tried to think of something further to tease him with, but he broke in on her.

"I've got land. I've got a house," he said thickly.

Oh dear, oh Polly, you have gone too far. He'd always been quite fun when he was Papa's ranger, showing her wolf-cubs and baby birds and things, but she'd been a baby herself then – well, almost.

"I can take care of a woman."

This was intended to lead somewhere. "Unpredictable when in liquor" his references said but they took him on because he was a shot. What would Loulou do? Head him off – but too late, he had started again.

"She doesn't have dark curls."

Polly took her chance. "Who doesn't?" she said, trying to sound icy.

"Natalya Igoryevna."

"Of course she hasn't, she's red-haired. What's that got to do with anything?"

"She's not to be compared," came the slow voice prickling the hollow of her back, "to some." Now she knew. Now it was all going to come out.

"I know how to look after a woman."

"That's what Aleksandr Borisovich used to say." She turned to him and repeated the name, as if bidding it goodbye. "He was very well-bred."

"I don't believe I had the honour . . ." began the huntsman.

"No, to be sure, and now it doesn't matter one jot." Empty man, empty name. "I was supposed to have been marrying him."

Aleksandr Borisovich had been at the war so long that she had forgotten what he looked like. Papa and Mama had been so pleased when he proposed for Polly. It took him simply ages to make up his mind.

For a moment Belyakov looked hangdog.

"He bred cocker spaniels," said Polly. "And kept them in his bedroom. That's all he ever talked about, his dogs and their complaints."

"Valerian was nearly a priest, you know," he said brightly. "Before . . . before his . . . Well, before. He can marry people anyway, that's what he reckons because he's in charge."

"Like a ship's captain?"

"That's it," said Belyakov. "Because of his position. He's going to marry Masha and Yefim."

"I thought your women were emancipated, like my sisters."

Belyakov switched the stick from one hand to the other and back again. "I don't know about that, but they'd rather die than be unwed."

Polly laughed. "How primitive."

"It's only right," he said huskily. "Nature."

"And what do you know about nature?"

Belyakov threw down the stick. "As much as you do, Apollonya Dmitryevna. I know I'm not good enough, but I'd do the right thing by you."

"No, you're not, are you?" said Polly. "But you would, wouldn't you?" His face was hot and red and did not smile back. She looked at him sideways. She wanted him to go on talking.

"Breeding," said Polly.

He looked down. "I know . . ."

"Breeding," said Polly, "is what dogs have."

Before the huntsman had time to pursue this remark, the double doors opened with a crash. Valerian strode in and went straight for Polly. "Where is she then, your friend?"

Still charmed by the genuineness of Belyakov's incipient proposal, Polly dawdled with her curls. "You don't look at all well, my dear," she said. "Too much excitement is not good for one. Try to relax."

A hard line creased above Valerian's nose and his cheeks went skull-white. "That woman, that woman, the one with the bay-red hair, where have you hidden her?"

"I don't know any such *woman*," said Polly languidly.

Valerian began to shout: "Boy, woman, girl, that one, you know her. Where is she?"

"Oh, *him*," said Polly and pointed upwards. "He's always up there, reading and lazing about."

Valerian stared helplessly at Belyakov. "What does she mean?"

"On the roof, Valerian. She's camped out on the leads."

"And the dwarf?"

"With the dwarf."

Valerian stamped up and down the room, swinging his arms. "Good, good," he repeated. "Concealed, concealed. This must be handled carefully. Tactfully." Halting by Polly's *Moses*, he tossed back his hair and struck a pose before them, hand on hip. "You must know that the news of this stranger in our midst has reached the congregation and many are troubled."

"What stranger?" said Polly. "She's not a stranger, she's related to me and I'm not called a stranger. Why, I thought . . ."

"In the spirit and in the flesh, thou art as one of us, Apollonya Dmitryevna," said Valerian.

Polly looked hard at Belyakov who avoided her eye.

"A dark woman has come many miles to accost our brothers and sisters with rumours and strange troubles."

"Well?" said Polly. "What has some old gossip got to do with Loulou?"

"Be sure that her sins have found her out. The woman knows of her doings."

"Phoo," said Polly. "Slit the woman's nose and send her packing. My relations are very respectable."

Valerian took this in. When he spoke again his voice was changed. "You see, I must find her before she tries to flee again. To reassure her that . . . no harm will befall her."

"Humph," said Polly with a smirk. "I knew there was more to this than meets the eye. She's been at her tricks again."

Belyakov glared at her. "The master knows his mind."

"And so does she," said Polly, taking up her palette. "You will excuse me but I have work to do." With this she swept up to her easel and planting her legs astride, began to measure off a space for the baby Jesus's head with the stem of her brush.

"With the woman you can do as you like, Valerian," said Belyakov. "But I don't want nursemaiding. If I choose to take my chance then I shall leave, harm or no harm."

Valerian was darkly ingratiating. "My dear friend, you shall not leave my side. I love you too well. You shall always be with me and all that I have is thine."

Polly was shifting the pegs of her easel. When this biblical note was sounded she snatched them free and her picture fell to the ground. "I shall not be of the company," she shouted and ran out, slamming the door behind her.

The two men talked into the twilight.

"There's no agreement yet but it will come," said Belyakov. "She must be angled like a fish. It's expected by them. Marry us and I shall settle and your peace shall be kept."

Valerian held out his arms. "Beloved companion, I am truly blessed. We shall be together as we have always been. That child will be an ornament to the tabernacle. Tell her friend that she too is our sister in Christ. I give my word. Ask her to mingle among us. She will be safe."

Belyakov was less impressed than Valerian intended him to be. There was no arguing with the young man when these states of elation arose in him and the huntsman knew that rational opposition would only rouse his fury. But Polly was unlikely to submit to any proposal which involved Valerian being some kind of surrogate father to her. She had not told Belyakov she would be his wife, but he was content with the start he had made. Her first engagement would have been fraught with the same pretended reluctance. Women were all the same, no doubt.

Valerian knew that escape was impossible and refused to consider that Belyakov was as much a prisoner as Natalya Igoryevna. The estate was picketed and ringed like a fortress. But if he was to be a prisoner Belyakov wanted the comfort a woman could provide; and if Valerian did not say this, he knew it. With him it was always a question of language: love was a force, a force compelled, force was then love. A simpler man would have said: "Take her." Valerian preferred: "Love her." But it came to the same thing in the end.

Valerian wanted Natalya Igoryevna. Even Polly saw that. If he had her, would he leave them alone?

17

As he searched for her she triumphed in the knowledge that she could kill him. She was blameless but this time she had a knife. She watched as he came nearer, feeling the blade in her hands: long, smooth and deadly. An object to be caressed and loved, even more than a man.

He loomed above her and she thrust upwards with all her strength. His face changed into a woman's with a pock-marked jaw-line and gold earrings. She screamed and the woman doubled up, clutching at the knife blade as it went cleanly past the breastbone into the heart which Loulou had thought was Kostya's.

She opened her eyes. A dark head stood between her and the sun. She went on trying to strike, shouting: "Not dead yet!"

"Take it easy," said Yasha, wrestling her arms down to her sides. "A dream, that's all."

He bathed her face, then rolled a cigarette, lit it and put it between her lips. She drew in the smoke with a comfortable sigh. "How long was I asleep?"

Yasha glanced at the sun. "That purple shadow under the oak, see? Must be getting on for a quarter past five. I'd guess a couple of hours." The Dakota Kid could tell the time from shadows. "If you'd read as much as me you could tell too. From grass-colour, that sort of stuff." And Dushan's watch before the hands had begun to go backwards and then stopped altogether. Only Valerian and his disciples were permitted clocks but Yasha suspected that half of them couldn't tell the time.

The flavour of the dream still with her, Loulou only nodded. On her side, elbow on a cushion, a blanket under her legs, she watched Yasha rinsing some clothes. A devotee of all those hard men, and yet he kept so clean.

"You must have read such heaps about murder, Yashichka. Tell me about murder, give me your opinion."

A piece of cord ran above his head from chimney stack to parapet. A shirt dangled there, dripping. "Whose murder?"

Loulou considered. "The Laskorins. Do you think Valerian murdered them?"

Yasha slowly wrung water out of the breeches which Frossya had made him out of a pair of child's jodhpurs. "Word in the settlement is that Valerian hanged the priest, so he's a killer all right, but that was out in the open like, opposite the dry-goods store. Your friends got plugged in the dark. Cellars, from what I heard."

He stared at the breeches' buttons meditatively and then turned to her, leering. Loulou shuddered. "But that old Papa Laskorin," he went on with detachment, "he caught a packet in his dog-cart. Personal, that was. Ran into a squad of little treasures he thought he'd seen the last of when he fiddled the levy and got them called up, two years underage, just in time for the big push in '16."

"How can you say that? He was an honourable man. I liked him."

"Oh, that's logical, that is," said Yasha giving the wet clothes a fresh pummelling. "He must have been a decent guy because you liked him. Must have been how his bodyservants and his grooms and his butler and his coachman reasoned, too: 'Nice man, the master, always sees you right. Thank you, sir, excellence, please be so kind as to kick the arses of them down the village before you kick ours.'"

"You're not making sense."

"Oh no," shouted Yasha. "Defective in the head, am I, as well as the legs? Well, I know, see. I *know*."

"Who told you such a tale?"

"People, that's who. Their people. Their mothers and old dads, that he took them off when they was no more than kids, and pushed a good old Russian rifle in their mitts that came taller than their heads. Got told, they did, to get stuck into some Prussian pickelhaubers who had mountain howitzers, torpedoes and Christ knows what other shots in their lockers."

Loulou looked round and stubbed out her cigarette on the wall. "I've told you before, Yasha, you have no concept of duty."

He dropped the wet breeches and stumped up to her, hands on hips. "I'm looking at it, lady. And duty's done what duty's always done in this wild beast cage you call a country: it reclines on its back while someone else does the washing."

Loulou slid off the blankets and brushed at the cigarette ash on her blouse. "I was forgetting," she said. "Give me that. You should have said. I'll always do my fair share."

He pushed her back. "Bit late, isn't it, for that? Sit down."

Loulou did as she was told. In these moods he could be nasty.

On the brickwork, cross-legged, Yasha raised his index finger: "First mistake. They didn't all cop it out there. And before they was going to be *made* to cop it in '17, the Army falls apart, and they get it into their shaven skulls that duty's like stale bread to a horse: the more you feed it him, the more he eats and the more he swells, till either he stops or bursts and they drag off his carcase on a winch. So they say: 'Have a bite yourself, sir, your honour, makes you feel good, makes you think of self-sacrifice and the Motherland, and other people.'"

"I don't follow," said Loulou twisting her curls.

"*Second*," went on Yasha, ignoring her. "The officers get excited and won't stomach this ranker piffle about them owing a duty to convict-head scum . . ."

"What duty?"

"Ah. That's what *they* said."

"Well, then!"

"Can't see it, can you? Never clouded your brain with other people's point of view. Their duty was their *job*, see? And they couldn't do it. Next time, they said, next time we'll do it. Just hang on, and one more crack and we'll do it."

"Do what?"

Yasha almost screamed. "Win! They kept blasted losing!"

"Ah," murmured Loulou. "I knew there were setbacks."

"You know what that means – setbacks?"

Loulou nodded. "Of course. The troops withdraw and yield ground to the enemy."

"That sounds nice and straightforward. What happens to them as can't?"

"What do you mean, can't? They're under orders, aren't they?"

"Can't because they're wounded." Loulou had never considered the details of such an eventuality. Yasha's voice fell to a whisper. "That huntsman, sweet on your kissing-cousin, that Belyakov, he told me what happens after a setback. They dig a pit, the ones taken prisoner, a pit as wide as this house, and they fill it with the likes of those Ivans, Yefims and Pavlas that Papa Laskorin got drafted before their time to do their sacred duty so as he wouldn't be without a man to shave him or rub down his hunter."

"Not all of them, surely," said Loulou. "Not all of them died. Some were saved."

"Saved themselves. Chucked duty, stuck up a train, came back. And when they reach home, what a stroke of luck to happen on him, making a run for it, just like their officers said it was treason to do."

"I knew someone had been filling you up with nonsense. What other lies did he tell? What did they do to *him*, old Laskorin?"

"Their duty, like they was taught."

Loulou covered her face. "And the women?" She saw fat silly Mimi in a huddle with Lola and Millie, crying and waiting her turn.

But Yasha had finished his lesson and was once more up to his elbows in cold, grey water. After hanging up the clothes, he emptied the basin by throwing the contents clean across the parapet, and dried off his arms on a rag. "They never touched the women, that Valerian's bunch," he said at last. "Against their religion or something. A woman has to be – there's a term for it – what they call a 'consecrated object' before she can be interfered with, if you know what I mean."

Loulou believed him but doubted the efficacy of the rule. They were men, they were brutes.

"That tennis-playing foreigner thought they was after the parlour maid when they broke in here, so he rushed to protect her, all chivalrous, but she wouldn't believe that they'd come to save her from him, and they wouldn't believe that he wanted to save her from them. Not till she stopped screaming and by then he was dead."

Dear Gerald, he never was a good umpire.

"But the women were murdered in cold blood . . ."

"Who says?"

"Polly says . . ."

"That one never makes much sense." Squatting on the leads Yasha again raised a finger like a schoolmaster admonishing the class dunce. "Not by Valerian, they wasn't. He'd already stormed the house, taken their land and had the whole district running his errands. Where's his percentage in doing in the ladies?"

Loulou screwed up her eyes. "The simpleton's best pleasure," she said. "Revenge."

"There you have it," cried Yasha. "Only the wrong way round. That's why he exterminated Anton and his cronies. It was vengeance on them for doing it."

Momentarily she was relieved that Yasha could defend Valerian, if setting one kind of murder against another could be called defence. But she was so much in a murderer's power that it was literally vital to distinguish his motives for killing. "What's that Wild West expression you use – to cover his trail?"

Yasha sneered. "Tracks. What tracks? This is war. There's no tribunals or public prosecutors in these bushwhacking parts any more. He wouldn't have shot those women. Where's the glory in that? No danger, no revenge, no satisfaction, not for his exalted kind." His voice darkened with suspicion. "What gives you the right to sit in judgement, anyway? You were with him, weren't you, the night they got hit?" Beneath his penetrating stare Loulou dropped her eyes and blushed. "You said he was flopped out, swoony as a maiden on her back. Remember?"

The "remember" was unnecessary. He knew where she had been when Anton took those prisoners on their last *shlep* to nowhere. Now she was cut up because she had spent the night patting Valerian's pillows and taradiddling instead of getting wise to what antics the menagerie stooped to when their keeper was temporarily indisposed.

Disgust made Yasha feel energetic. Hopping to his feet he passed before her, took up his knife and began to mill the hollow edge on the soft stone of the parapet. As he silently bellied a groove, Loulou was circling round the question she longed to ask. It was contemptible, craven, this self-concern, but how could she prevent it? He despised her already, so let him despise her even more.

"Does that mean I'm safe, Yasha? That Valerian won't murder me?"

He did not reply and she watched the powdery calx film the knuckles of his grinding hand. "Yashichka," she whispered. "Dear. Say that Valerian will not kill me."

The boy tempered the heated blade with spittle, set the edge with a last long stroke and ran it along his lower lip. "That's crystal-gazing, *barinya*, religion. Look to the front and you get it in the back James-brotherwise. But who knows what miracles may happen?" In exasperation he rammed his knife into the crumbly cornice. "There's no justice except what you fix up for yourself. Grow up. If you stick around this hell on earth any longer I reckon you'll croak. Why don't we just beat it?"

She came up behind him and put her hands over his eyes. The setting sun glared above the sweep of the horizon. "How do you picture it, *golubchik*? Where do we fit in?"

Obediently he translated the world she could see into the only images which made it bearable for them both. Under covered wagons rutting virgin pastures pioneers straggled, ever watchful for Indian smoke and a sight of the brown fort beneath whose shadow they could recuperate.

Tears blobbed the sharp corners of her eyes. "The well is poisoned, *milii*, the garrison has fled. There are no more forts for us, dearest, not here, not now. The eagle's feathers have been plucked. We have no strength."

Yasha felt the tip of his knife. She was in a worse way than he had realised. Inactive, kept short of food, shunned, Natalya Igoryevna had weakened and would succumb. Gently he pushed away her hands. "Clever bastards, really, the way they make it dawn on you that your time's up before you're even dead."

"But you feel it too. You must."

He might have done before she started on all this, but her spineless-ness got on his nerves. "That's hostage-talk, lady. You're not staked out on an anthill. Hang on a little longer and the cavalry'll be here." Not that he believed it. Not for a minute. But she seemed to fall in with the prospect and gave a throbby sigh. Time to waken hopes. "What about that big blond guy you were expecting? He might still make it."

God above, why couldn't he shut up? He had about as much faith in this Martin character as he had in cleft rocks spouting water but she looked like she was dying for a heartwarmer.

To his surprise Loulou made no response.

"Need liquoring up, lady, to get tough? That it?"

At the thought Loulou's face cleared and she sighed. "Ah. What a gift that would be. Simply divine. Could you manage . . . ?"

"Oh yeah," he said sourly. "Now you're talking. Yasha's supposed to know how to part God's children from their Paradise-juice. Well, he doesn't. They lock it up like muskets on a man-of-war. Can't be done."

Down below a gong boomed in the silence and the air began to fill with voices. Yasha thought of tortillas and sidewinder steaks while Loulou headed back to his earlier conversational ploy: "I'm no longer a young woman, Yasha . . ."

Nope. Her idea of romance'd put years on anyone.

"I cannot believe in dreams any more . . ."

Ha. ha.

"Martin will never arrive . . ."

Him? He'd never got going, had he? Stuck at the points in his cradle.

"Oh, shut up," he said aloud, dreading another onslaught. "He might still get his boots on. What's his proper name, tell me, in case I shunt into him?" He pretended to be organised, busily smoothing out a paper and licking his pencil.

"Martin Aleksandrovich Kabalyevskii. But you'll never meet."

Yasha wrote down the name in full, nevertheless.

"He always used to get carried away and make promises he couldn't keep."

Lost his timetable, probably. Not used to making his way without a bunch of retainers unrolling the carpet in front of him.

Yasha watched the sky, calculating the moment of twilight when it would be safe to make a move. The name Kabalyevskii bothered him. Someone had said it before her. And in his presence.

* * *

150

The dark closed over the roof and they sat almost cosily, back to back, now and then letting fall a remark but largely content to be silent, eavesdropping on the house beneath.

The sounding of the gong had been the call to evening prayers, and for an hour there was quiet. Loulou shuddered when the devotions ended, as they always did, in the banging of doors and shouting. The brutality of the din reminded her of Belyakov's visit that morning. Would he come again, having made his preposterous offer, to solicit her blessing? Deep in the house a waltz crackled on Lola Laskorina's phonograph. Loulou smoked her next-to-last cigarette and rippled the burnished edges of a French romance. The downstairs tune and the book had the same jaded, calamitous feel: "Oh Yasha, will we ever survive?"

Yasha leapt to his feet, furious. She was getting maudlin again. Something had to be done. He shook her. "You never listen, do you?"

"The music," she whispered, blinking away tears. "I only hear music."

"Excellent," he said, taking her hand. "Nothing. Night comes and you've heard nothing. All day. Nothing." Self-acclaim swelled in his voice.

"Except the music," Loulou was about to repeat when Yasha narrowed his eyes. A breath of air lifted his fringe. He was on his stage, striking the attitude of best detective, the park behind forming up under the moon in a dark-olive backdrop blodged with trees the shape of sleeping lions. Dots of yellow light wavered beside the distant railway.

"The train," she breathed. "Of course, the train."

Yasha bit his knuckles in sheer excitement. "Could hear it from up here, couldn't we? Last time, last night, I heard it then. Close, close." Loulou held her neck erect and listened. The waltz cascaded into the warm air. "Forget it," said Yasha in triumph. "It's done the last haul. That locomotive won't never clank again, lady."

"Why not?" She did what he desired, showing her fear at his superior knowledge. "Why, why, why . . . ?"

Yasha danced madly round her like an unstrung puppet. "It's over," he shrieked. "I've got a secret, lady, a big, big secret. A dis-covery that's going to get us out of this mess!"

"Tell me, you little wretch!" she screamed back, giving in to his antics. "God, you're so unbelievably tedious, boy."

He liked her that way, irritable and feverish. "Guess what Valerian was up to today?"

"*Ach!*" she flounced back at him with the folds of her blouse. "Is that your great secret? Bays alone to his God, my dear, like any white wolf . . ."

Yasha looked all round before bending low to her. "And between times, *my dear*," he repeated. "Between times he's with his mates, smashing up the rail tracks."

18

If someone had asked Loulou she could not have explained why Yasha's news so affected her. She had long been powerless, existing only at the caprice of those who held her captive; no fresh privation could be imposed since she had nothing left to lose except her life; and her isolation was no more or less absolute now that the railway was wrecked. But affect her it did and she slumped down, covering her face.

Yasha was all gentleness, smoothing back the wrist ruffles on the matador shirt which had once belonged to Millie Laskorina. "Don't take on so," he said. "Your Martin doesn't have to come on a train. There's ways round. They can easy lay the track again."

That morning he'd scouted the highway, even the dirt lanes. Barricaded, every one, really professional, in three-line depth and covered from hedgerow and ditch with mortars and a couple of Hotchkiss machine-guns. A toad couldn't have wriggled through. As for the railway, sappers from a crack mountain battalion had run two locos with flatbeds in tow, one on the down line and one on the up, and ripped out the sleepers with steel cutters five miles in either direction.

Sunset *wagons lits*.

"I shall die here," wept Loulou. "I know I shall die. We are cut off for ever and ever. Why today?"

Today, yesterday, the day before. To Yasha the date was superfluous: they were in *schtuck*, permanent. There was work ahead. He couldn't do with her flopping like a spaniel.

She had to be roused.

"That's the stuff. You'll feel better after a good cry." This was a statement much used on Yasha's mother by Pa. More often than not it had shut her up. On Loulou the effect was quite opposite. She seemed to take it as licence for turning thoroughly unstrung. She lay down, got up, clutched parts of herself and lay down again, howling and sobbing. Between outbursts, she gave in to despair:

"I just don't care any more. Go away . . . simply abandon me. I want to cry and cry and cry. I want to dream of one last day, being happy, sitting in a sunny place, picking violets."

Yasha clasped his head.

Standing on tiptoe he looked down from the parapet to the terrace far below. "Put a sock in it, lady," he said at last. "We've got a job on and the coast's clear. Let's go to work." Pride and excitement were in his voice.

Mitya Laskorin's serf builders had driven deep into the swampy riverine earth characteristic of the region, testing for bedrock on which to found the house, but when at depths above ten feet or so they invariably struck water, the old man was obliged to compromise. Hardwood piles of twice that length were sunk below the waterline, and the house stood on a free-floating structure of stanchions which had been slowly degenerating for over a hundred years. Now, in places where the wood was pulpy, sections had been cut away and restored, but the new timber was soft and in the equinoctial rains the house palpably slithered on its footings, cracking the plaster on walls and ceilings. When damp rotted the floors at ground level, Polly's father had had the soil beneath excavated to within a yard of the water table. The space which Loulou now occupied was a tiny part of the gap which extended beneath the whole building, up to the edge of the brick-lined wine cellars.

Out of the honeyish glow of Yasha's lantern she peered into the darkness. All around them, stacked on iron battens resembling sections of rail track, loomed huge coffer-like boxes shiny with wet. Recoiling from the touch of their bitter-cold metal, she thought of Spanish kings tiered in lead, casketed heap upon heap in the Escorial.

"What are they?"

Yasha held up the lantern, pooling them together in the light which hardened the jut of the containers into sinister-angled shadows. "Can't shift for them down here." He kicked one of the smaller boxes which littered the floor. "Enough for an army."

She asked him again.

"Here," he said, handing her the lantern. "You'll soon get the picture."

He dropped to one knee, fumbled with his boot for a moment, then stabbed the point of his knife at several of the crates on the floor until, apparently satisfied, he dragged one towards him and began to prise off the lid with his blade. "Some wood, some tin, some webbing. See?"

She did not but bent to give him more light. Inside was a silky white integument. It was like breaking into an egg. "I don't understand."

Yasha was tearing away the greasy top wrappings.

"Just as I thought. Hotchkiss stuff. Ammunition, see?" He burst out the neatly-packaged magazine strips each embedded with thirty rounds for the French machine-guns positioned on the village road.

Loulou took the lamp and began to wander among the mounds of boxes. "And this? And this?"

Yasha excelled himself in explanation, having spent long hours alone down here in the dark, deciphering the numbers and legends stencilled on the packing cases. "What you might call over-provided with shot and shell," he said, mooching around the ammunition boxes. "When there's a definite shortage of weapons to shoot it off with."

"But they have guns up there. I see them all the time."

"Wrong mix. Those for instance." He took the lamp from her to pick out the dun emblems on a pile of greyish tins. "Light machine-gun. Bergmann, forty round boxes, enough for a month of Sundays, but where's the gun? Same with these," he went on, stalking through the narrow passages between containers. "Madsen clips, belts for Maxims, Spitz rifle bullets, but not a weapon that'll take them."

Loulou struggled to understand. "Do you mean . . . all this . . . It's not very good?"

"Not very good, no, in fact, it's no darned good at all – for them."

"I see," said Loulou, carefully siting the lamp on a projecting batten. "Then why is it here?"

Yasha sat down on a long metal cylinder marked *Doppelzunder 16* and made room for her.

"They robbed a train down south, about two months ago. Supposed to be a secret but there was so much night-time coming and going to unload it that by the time they'd finished every kitchen girl knew the details. Laugh was, the engine was ours but the wagons was German and Austrian loaded with captured stuff all hitched up to be shunted back in the retreat. The railmen – and you know what political types they are – these railmen passed the word to your wide-eyed chum up there, that the People were about to be deprived of their means of self-defence, and Valerian, who'd got himself a reputation already for general brigandage and mutiny, your man, he killed the crew, and steamed north with the goods. Must have thought he had a brain on him, pulling that. I know the others still do because the young gentleman omitted to inform them that they'd dragged twenty trucks of garbage into their own back yard. He really earns his keep, that one."

Loulou looked around at the black boxes. "Don't they work then, those . . . things?"

Yasha's laugh was as unexpected as a footfall on soft earth. "Now

and again, lady, when the bits fit, but most of it's as useful as his
front end to a horse when his backside's missing."

"Enough for an army, you said."

"That's right – High Explosive, enough amatol, enough nitro-
cellulose, ringpulver, ékrasit, dinitrobenzine to blow your Valerian
straight up. But it's like this, you see." He clattered the lamp down
on the cylinder. "In the wrong tin cans. There's hardly any shells."

"Shells?"

"*For it to go in.*"

"Oh. Are they necessary?"

Yasha almost stood up. "What d'you think he's going to do when
the time comes to defend this place – carry it up in armfuls and throw
it from the roof? Of course he needs shells. *One* needs shells; shells
he needs more, *barinya*, than he needs you."

Back on the roof her initial excitement at the possibility of release
gave way to horror.

Yasha's logic was simple. He was no expert but explosives were
ticklish enough stored under ideal conditions. After two months of
being dripped on, with the frosts to come, then a thaw, followed by
another stifling summer it'd be more than touch and go with that
stuff underground. Why wait until it had sweated itself unstable,
ready to go off on its own? Better, surely, to take advantage now, set
a fuse (God knew there were enough of those – percussion, time,
delayed action, the lot) and beat it to the river.

"Yashichka, Yashichka, that's criminal. You've forgotten the children, the babies. You can't hate *them*. Even Apollonya Dmitryevna
is little more than a child. You might not care for her, but that's
hardly an excuse. Why, dozens would die . . ."

"It'd be quick. Pouf. Whizz. Wouldn't feel a thing." His relish was
artificial and she knew it.

"*Golubchik* darling, you are terribly brave but far too drastic to
make an efficient murderer."

"How do you know?" he said. "Anyway, what suggestions do you
ever pop up with? Unless you reckon the hags won't do for you if
you talk to them nice."

"I've done little to antagonise them."

"Oh no, 'course not, just by *breathing*, you haven't. Besides, it's
not them or us. Me they tolerate. It's them or you. They say Valerian
treats you too special."

"Well, then, I shall resist," said Loulou grandly. "I know how to
use a gun. Surely you can find me something in this arsenal down
there."

"You're crazy. Those women'd rip you apart before throwing you to the men. I'm better off out of it."

He continued to argue: the lady's squeamishness could be catered for; no need for a massacre; he could pick a time when the women were out in the fields; Apollonya Dmitryevna could be let in on the secret.

But in his heart Yasha was forced to recognise that Natalya Igoryevna's hesitation was as contrived as his own apparent lack of scruple. For some reason, unadmitted to herself, she wanted to stay; and knew that, in the end, if she did, he would not desert her. Her complacency might infuriate him but he could only submit. The prospect of the long winter nights so filled him with dread that he had devised his plan as much to escape from his dreams as the house. Already his sleep was broken by nightmares of being strapped helpless to a landmine on a thirty-second fuse which he had to extract with his teeth, and he woke in a fever with the taste of indigo bitters seeping under his tongue from the charge of 2-4-6-trinitrophenol.

19

"Parents and masters of families are in God's stead to their children and servants . . ."

Cheek, thought Polly. Papa all over again, yelling at us.

In another part of the garden Yasha was climbing onto a chair to see over the heads of the congregation. "Would you just hark at that crook," he said loudly to an old woman. "He's got more on his back than a Texas whore."

The old woman twitched her shawl and shuffled aside.

Valerian had matched his costume to the autumn tints. On top of a stepladder at the spot where the net-judge once dozed, he stood resplendent in a chasuble of white, red and gold.

"Every chief householder hath the charge of the souls of the family . . ."

It was Polly's wedding day, *alfresco* amidst the yellowing grasses of the tennis court. To Polly, without spectacles, Valerian was only a hot blur in the distance, going on and on. Wretch! It was supposed to be her day.

"To fathers within their private families Nature hath given a supreme power . . ."

I know what my father would have given him, if he'd caught him making holes in the tennis lawn. Fathers were beasts.

Loulou found Yasha. "Where's the man who puts the black bag over his head?"

"Any minute now, lady, he'll come out with his magnesium tray and say: 'Keep it like that and *smile!*'"

"Just like an Arizona hanging?"

"Or a lynching in ole Tennessee."

Becky appeared at Loulou's knee, her hair plaited and intertwined with poisonous-looking berries. "Hey," she said. "His brother, save a dance for me."

Yasha kicked the parchment of her tambourine. "You're too short for him. It's indecent."

"Course I'm not – it's all the rage now, younger women. Anyway, *you* can talk, Arse-stumps."

Yasha cuffed her nonchalantly.

"We got mutton," she called out, skipping away. "And tarts for afters."

The autumn sun burned. Polly longed to be out of her frock. That cross-eyed Frossya was supposed to have repaired it. Peasant invisible mending indeed! The stitches grated like cat-gut. It was all so awfully crude. The Becky girl had even offered her rouge.

"Every father of a family under the love hath the liberty in his family to use services and ceremonies according as he perceiveth out of the holy spirit of love . . ."

None of *her* family. The officiant had shot them. No one left even to give her away.

"When we're wed will you do me every day?" shouted Becky from the shade of the tarpaulins which had been stretched overhead from the wire fence around the court. Gerasim, cropping hay over white tennis lines, prodded her with the heel of his scythe. "A dwarf wife has litters, hairy, like cats," he said serenely.

"Let an hundred vagabonds and renegades play the filthy persons . . ."

Polly blundered forward on the arm of her groom who had to guide her under the tarpaulins and down a wide swathe cut through the green. As the couple drew level with the lines of onlookers on either side, men bowed from the waist and women bobbed in part genuflection, part curtsey. Coming into Polly's focus below Valerian was a carpenter's trestle covered in damask. Behind that a silver band, the sheen of the instruments dulled in the opaque light. No sound came forth as Polly and her groom, followed by Yefim and Masha who were also to be married, stumbled along the uneven turf.

On reaching the makeshift altar Polly looked up and saw that the funnels of the horns and tubas and euphoniums had been stuffed with raspberries, damsons, apples, pears and every imaginable regional fruit of the season to form gigantic cornucopias between which peeped the eyes of children swathed in mantillas cut from the lace hangings of Mimi Laskorina's matrimonial bed.

The congregation hushed then broke into a wild anthem which Polly had never heard in any Christian church. The wordless noise throbbed in her ears and made her sweat into her gown.

As she fretted in the heat, Belyakov squeezed her hand. At the start she had felt, if not *chic* then reasonably *svelte*, even though Frossya's rough washing had slit the satin at the tucks, and the old-gold facings had turned beige from sun-bleaching. Now, with damp-stains under her arms and the stench of patchouli from Masha, she could have screamed out loud and been sick.

Valerian silenced the congregation with a wave of his hand and brought his homily to a finale: "This brings no discredit to the father, but if the daughter that is brought up with him in the family shall do any such things herself she hath not the blot alone, *but bringeth also an evil report upon the family.*"

Yasha looked at Polly with interest. "What's she done, then? Not eaten up her cabbage or got herself pregnant?"

"Answered back," said Loulou. "Stamped her foot at Daddy and said 'Won't'."

"Didn't he want her to marry Vladimir Ivanovich?"

"Not good enough for her, he said."

"Fine start to a marriage, that is," said Yasha.

"Fairly standard, I should say," said Loulou.

For the bride Yasha experienced a new-found respect. She might be daft but there was mettle to the soul in that featherdown body. Valerian wasn't the man to be talked down easy. Crook was too feeble: he was a mobster in the gang of fallen angels. If Lucifer had mates this one'd be hanging on his stirrup right into hell. He was the thing in the broom-cupboard that your Ma told you came out in the night to skin naughty boys and girls alive. Not a lad to give lip to.

Valerian climbed awkwardly down the steps. Loulou composed herself and tried not to laugh. The climax was approaching.

In the grey frock-coat too tight for his full backside the huntsman looked a ninny bending tenderly to Polly, the tips of his pomaded moustaches brushing her ear in a cat's-whisker kiss. Whichever way you looked at it, such ceremonies were absurd. Bridegrooms were gross, no matter how slickly fitted into their clothes; brides wriggled their understraps and were ogled by the bystanders; and priests obsequiously pimped for all mummies and daddies, extant or elsewhere.

This was no worse. The moral was the same, nothing differed except a mere quibble over style.

Masha had on a lady's evening gown in lavender pastel with frilled bows at the shoulder knots. A debutante's first-night glad rags, the hem dipping over her bare toes like a knicker-satin shroud. Yefim's spine was brittle as lump sugar under the frippery stripes and gold wire of the number one walking-out uniform jacket thieved from a staff-sergeant's corpse. Men in a hatter's paradise of Homburgs, opera hats, brown Derbies, the slouch caps of Sicilian vagrants, women in cartwheel panama straws askew under swags of gardenia.

Tricked out like a voodoo crowd eager to be bloodied in the gore of the cock.

At the high point when Valerian held out the chalice, Polly sneezed, her eyes brimming with pollen from the floral crowns held above her and Belyakov's heads. Masha wept real tears noisily. Perceiving each bride to be equally moved, the women pelted them with tiny paper chains and more flowers while the men chuckled and leered.

Becky crept from behind and stroked the thick plaid of Loulou's trousers. "Nice bit of stuff, that," she said. "Tailored, I expect. You can always tell a man by his things."

The first bride and groom came towards them, her hand laid on his, and the crowd whistled and clapped. Grass clippings spattered Belyakov's patent-leather pumps.

"Dead men mayn't tell any tales but their clothes does – look at him – a regular pawnshop he is, done up in 'is borroweds."

"Clothes don't make the man," said Loulou.

Becky nestled up and plucked a loose thread from her blouse. "Naw. She might not be fussy but what I'd be bothered about, if I was *her*," she said, nodding at Polly whose brown eyes were luminously circular from short sight, "is where the man inside them had been. Got a reputation, he has."

"What for?"

Becky winked horribly and squeezed Loulou's knee. "Oh, this and that, big boy, this and that."

The ground floor of the Laskorin house took the form of a horseshoe, the gap bridged by the grand stairway set directly under the pierced rotunda. From each side of the stair the family could pass from room to room. On formal occasions these were thrown open. Now, for Polly's wedding, Valerian had decreed there was to be no departure from tradition, and when Loulou came in from the great brown garden there stood revealed through open double doors the grandiose sweep of the reception rooms where old Laskorin had once staged levées for the princely and rich. Never in her time thrown open *en suite*, each of these tall cool rooms had been a separate venue for pettier, more domestic functions. Loulou knew every inch of the enclosed spaces, but the light which now poured from one into another so reduced their size and content that she was obliged to hold to a chair here, a desk there, for the reassurance of the familiar. Little had changed except for the dancing beam of the sun plying the afternoon glare from floor to wall, wall to ceiling, and bursting out around her as she lingered on the threshold of Papa Laskorin's daytime study.

Here, on the green leather sofa from which his little daughters had prised the buttoning, he had reclined in judgement on disputes over boundaries, the allocation of timber for firewood, the marling of land, weddings, inheritances and the paternity of bastards; dividing dowry-money, finding matchmakers, ordering searches for stolen goods, organising festivals; all from the same unsprung seat across which, as a child of three, biting his lip in wonder and terror, he had watched his mother and two serfs spreadeagle an adulterous bride of sixteen and so dog-whip her naked back that she bared her teeth and screamed to heaven; and where he genially lay on Christmas Eve to supervise, while Lola and Millie handed out painted dolls to peasant girls and wooden swords to the boys, before distributing red and green sweetmeats to the assembled company. Here, in this clean place replete with huge furniture, where the unremarkable Laskorins had observed their public obligations with stoical relentlessness, Valerian now stood, flushed and shy, to greet the guests streaming into the light.

If Loulou had not felt so weak and ill she could have thrown something at him.

A moratorium, he had said. A truce. He had come up alone to her attic refuge, sponge and comb in hand, and commanded her to make ready and come to the feast. It was his will, and theirs, the huntsman's and his bride's and all the simple people below. They wished for her presence in reconciliation. She was to be an outcast no longer.

Now the swine was daring to ignore her.

A giant in an astrakhan soutane was evidently in charge of protocol, leading brides and bridegrooms to kiss hands with Valerian, then calling up guests of honour, two at a time, with a nod of his shaven skull. Loulou doodled on the blotter of a bow-fronted writing desk, awkward and close to tears. After the brides had distributed their favours and moved into the slant afternoon shadow beneath the farthest window, she stared directly into the light around the figure of Valerian. His face was a mask. Had he noticed her plight? Would he make a sign? His eyes were the eyes of a portrait. Wherever she looked the eyes looked back into hers saying: Behold, see my power. Wait.

It was the first time she had seen the lieutenants whom Yasha had described. Against the light they bobbed in ragged silhouette, grouping around Valerian, awaiting the order to be seated. Loulou watched. The shaven giant beckoned to her with an operatic heave of his cloak. She stared back and kept still. The man did not call out. So Valerian had kept the secret — they still had no name for her. When Becky curled her sticky fingers into the palm of Loulou's hand and tugged on her sleeve she allowed the girl to lead her through the silent crowd.

As she came up the steps Valerian called for water and did not look at her.

In the total quiet on the dais her mouth was dry from shame and relief. A chair was placed for her. She was conscious of her slightest movement under the watching eyes. The lieutenants remained on their feet until she was seated. As they followed suit she wanted to cry out herself, not for water but for wine.

Perhaps there were miracles. Perhaps she was saved.

From the tail of the procession, in amongst the small stuff of the holy-rollers, Yasha watched them both.

Look at me, he says: Schnorrer, shyster, horse-wrangler, dude. Any lame-brain could have marked his card for a chiselling two-bit no-good. But holy, holy, holy, that was what got them: the expectation of miracles. Look at her, gorging on his Bible-eyes, believing she'd done something it took a crook like that to forgive her for. But forgiveness was for Christians who worshipped conjurors and confidence-men.

Yasha squirmed through the crush of peasant topboots and unhobbled skirts. Talk, jokes, salty couplets, folk-wisdom about first matings all mellowed into a thick growl above his head. From waist down the guests sweated out their characteristic smell of clotted felt and neatsfoot oil. In the fug with the children he marauded from trestle to trestle where painted beakers stood high among the dishes of meat.

With a wink a big-bellied farrier handed him a thimble-glass brimming with colourless spirit which Yasha drank off in one gulp. The fumes cleansed his palate and made him feel warm. Propped against the cross-piece of one trestle he separated bunches of fruit and let cherries fall into his mouth. Overwhelmed by the noise he stayed there with the children he did not know but who shared their spoils with one another and with him. The grown-ups rattled on and fell about, finding themselves wittier and more fetching, moment by moment.

In the cold eye of the boy they were a rum bunch: Belyakov grinning and parting Polly's teeth to receive a hunk of widgeon; Loulou chewing on dark meat while men hung over the back of her chair, and Becky tipped bonbons into a tray at her feet; Valerian holding an empty glass to his temple while Schmidt searched for well-water among the jugs on the table a few feet from Yasha himself.

Broad-boned Matryona in French jet braid and starched lace mouthed big enough in the hubbub for the boy to lip-read: "Easy on yourself, *batyushka,*" she was saying. "Hermann, my darling priestly man. At Christmas they'll pluck her and us women'll lard her white breasts for the spit."

Polly? Yasha shivered enviously at the image, nursing his chin between his knees. Before long that fat would be for the loutish huntsman's dipping.

"Now tell me this," the black and white woman went on. "Why should people even stoop to rub shoulders with that foreign cat, outlaw that she is?"

Schmidt listened without answer, waiting for the crowd to thin out and give him space to cross back to his master. Seeing her advantage the woman leaned over him, brushing the dome of his head with the stiff fleur-de-lys along her breastline. "We'll straggle her finery, white crow, you'll see . . ."

Milady Loulou, then. White crow for a white wolf. The wrinkly hags had matched them up already.

"A gaping skull at our feast . . ."

Hermann spotted a chink in the wall of revellers and was about to slip away when he faltered, slopping water over the broad woman's chest. Framed between two of the lieutenants, Osip and Titus, Loulou stood face to face with Valerian, beaming upwards into his eyes as sweet as a china milkmaid. Valerian drew her to him, lifting her clean off her feet. Yasha watched as Hermann, without so much as a twitch, mastered himself, righted his jug and slid up to his master's elbow.

Watch the distaff side, Hermann, they had advantages of nature for making themselves amenable. Like the fat lady knew.

At a signal unsighted by Yasha, quiet fell on the company. By the great doors an amateur bugler sounded a voluntary. After that the noise of yelling and cheering brought Yasha out from under his table. He clambered onto a trestle top where he sat up tall with the children and watched for the show to begin. That there was to be a show for which the ceremonies before had been merely a prelude he now realised from the grouping of figures on the dais. Presentation time had arrived, the moment of gifts.

A line of women bustled in through the side doors carrying deep reed baskets which they emptied into wooden cutlery trays. Yasha sniffed. Like the standard country wedding offerings, except poorer and queerer. Like gipsies had dug them up, or tramps: wrinkled crab-apples in a fancy shoe-box, two voles laid out on a cheese platter, six tumblers of dried pulses, a pattie-pan of meal, dried rose-petals sprinkled over honeycomb. Fruits of the earth in tribute. Seeds, re-growth, that sort of idea going with that sort of stuff. They looked about as sprouty as a gin-trap, but after a hard summer under Valerian the givers themselves appeared as shrunken as their gifts. Not that these barrel-scrapings evidently mattered because every so often when the heap became too straggly a haggard woman in round spectacles slid the excess into a grain bin by her feet and kept an eye on the real goods stacked to the nearside.

Yasha's neck tingled at the sight of this luxury. Bolts of velvet in red and silver-grey enclosed a long rectangular space into which more rich gifts were being tossed: a set of silver knife-rests shaped like spurs; ivory button-hooks; monogrammed razors; ebony knitting-needles. Pickings from dining-room, nursery and dressing-table. Handy sort of loot which could be stuffed into game-pockets or twisted up in a shawl.

As the mound grew, more and more guests came to watch, to gasp and, occasionally, to jeer. Whenever an article of ladies' wear appeared — a pair of lisle stockings, a hat with dried wallflowers on green silk — the little band burst into a loud and jaunty tune, and the women squealed in delight at the coarseness of the men's jokes. But not all the things were given as thoughtlessly as they had been snatched. The weapons were gifts of choice, selected at leisure. The crowd hushed, the band played down. Here was beguiling work that obliged a man to appraise.

Yasha watched a dagger laid upon the heap, the tang of its blade embossed in leaf-gold with a scene of lion cubs pawing a deer. Then a high saddle studded with gunmetal bosses on the pommel. A naval telescope, night glasses with heavy cowls projecting from the lenses. Then another saddle and another, cow-punching military issue blackened from the thighs of riders, and cut about with slashes. Short whips, bridles and a string of brass bells from a trace horse head-band. Battlefield litter, dead men's mementoes, stripped off them like footrags.

But the best was coming last. The lieutenants and their followers were snaking up in platoon strength, booted and bandoliered, each with his item: a pair of long-barrelled Daghestan rifles with curly butts, a rimfire pocket pistol, gun after gun; and the men who gave them pored over them as they stood waiting in turn with the men who had already given or had nothing to give, snicking breech-bolts and yahooing like pirates round a rum barrel.

At the drop-leaf end of the gift table Belyakov and Polly began the first argument of their married life. She wanted to inspect some of the objects more closely. He had mislaid her spectacles. Her lisp was pettish: "But I thimply must have them."

While the bridegroom looked for pockets in the unfamiliar suit, Polly nosed at the heap. "I'm sure I noticed that brooch of Mummy's.

Shaped like a langoustine with emerald snappers." When she turned to him Belyakov was slapping the insides of his thighs. "How can they be there, stupid?" she shouted above the noise of the band. The huntsman twitched. "Remember?" Polly went on more considerately. "She always wore it on her saints' days. Papa —" But she had forgotten where she was and what had happened that day, out on the lawn. Her new husband had come too late to be introduced to Mummy socially. She giggled at the idea of such a meeting and gave the huntsman a peck on his moustache. "Of course you don't, my love. How could you? But Mama would have adored you. So, so *farouche*, my dear, with the neck of a bull."

Belyakov took this correctly; the sneer in her voice was for Mama, not him, and his self-esteem revived.

"Thieved," he said, poking amongst the pill-boxes and silver-chain reticules. "Along with this lot. Still, it's six of one and half a dozen of the other. You're getting given what isn't yours either. We'll find a home for it."

At the mention of home Polly brightened. "Something borrowed," she hummed. "Something old, something new . . ."

Over by the huge *vieux-Saxe* stove in the corner women had begun to pack away the wedding presents. On the dais Becky held a coronet of juniper berries and strawberry leaves over Loulou's head. The countess looked dazed. Belyakov shook his head. How many of them had been taken in by those tartan trews and the short hair? Or was it only him, because only he knew what went into that boy's dress and had witnessed the pallor of her whole body? He felt his hands protruding unnaturally from the stiff sleeves of his jacket. Loulou had something Polly would never be able to give. He took a long drink from a wooden beaker. "Look," he said, very loudly. "Our little *grafinya* wants us to see her coronation."

Big Matryona overheard and broke off her conversation with Schmidt. "Now that's a queer way of talking for a man on his wedding-day. Or is he Bolshevical about women as well as property?" The tone was bantering but she looked at him hard.

"Hah," snorted Polly. "He's mine, he knows that."

Belyakov looked sheepish.

"Always was one for the ladies, though," said Matryona. "Full of talk about them. But it was just talk, missie. All talk, eh, Vladimir Ivanovich?"

She froze her broad lips in a taunt. Polly shook off the implication with a lie: "That's all *you* know, my good woman. In actual fact he's had oodles of girls, haven't you, my dear? Quite awful." She stuck fast to her husband's arm.

"Well, I never," boomed Matryona. "To think we never noticed the dark horse in our midst."

Belyakov knew his wife wished to parade her man's reputation, but in private she would test the sincerity of his claim. With the procession to the bridal bed setting off any moment he felt only dread at her coming demands.

Schmidt glided up to Polly. "Look upon your bridegroom as a true child to Father Valerian," he said, rippling her curls. "One who loves all living creatures regardless as to sex. Ah, the innocence of him, in the midst of worldly troubles. Be thankful, my dear, for the saintliness of his disposition."

Botheration, thought Polly. Just my luck. I knew it. "Tcha!" she blurted out as Matryona tut-tutted over the nonplussed Belyakov. "It's simply too wicked what we women have to put up with."

At that she swept Schmidt aside, leaving Belyakov to follow, his ears burning from Matryona's titters.

Polly found Masha, and both women stood hand in hand glaring at the revellers as if challenging their husbands to emerge from the crowd and claim them. Masha's Yefim could scarcely lift a leg and when his friends half-walked, half-dragged him to the appointed spot at the head of the retinue, his eyes blinked alarmingly. The bride hid her face in her hands.

"Come along," hissed Polly when the huntsman drifted up fiddling with the points of his starched collar. "Make a decent fist of it now you're a respectable married man." He coughed politely, covering his mouth with his hand and planted himself firmly at her hip. "Time we were on our way," she said, giving him a speculative glance. "If the worst comes to the worst at least I married someone who could stand on his own feet."

Abashed as he was at his unaccustomed prominence Belyakov beat down the resentment he felt at Matryona's insinuations and decided to be ungrudging. In her own way his wife had sought to compliment him. For her it must be a come-down, this farcical Nature-union, but she was making the best of it and so should he. Breathing in heavily, he placed her hand over his and smiled. In front of them, the smallest girls and boys strewed garlands at their feet.

Rose-briars caught at the hem of Polly's frock, swirling her train into a mass of petals and green shoots but she stepped radiantly onwards, casting short-sighted smiling glances at the fuzz of people surrounding her. Almost blind without her spectacles, she halted on the threshold of the ante-room which led out to the main entrance, thence to the steps and the estate through which she would process past the throng of villagers, and so down to the bridal chamber in

Belyakov's house. She turned around at the spot where the vast double doors would soon fold back to hide her, Belyakov, Masha and Yefim from the sight of the congregation. She thought how beautiful she must be in this frock, how fine her figure, how appreciative they must all be at the sight of her. Now the men would be undressing her. Her limbs warmed under their eyes. Now she wanted to be undressed. It was time for disorder, for hands to be upon her, underneath, within, everywhere. Her gaze directed itself aimlessly, floating over a pool of faces which she could not distinguish but which flowed over her body. When she slipped between the closing doors the smile was still on her face.

Beneath his table, sunk deep in the terrible heat of the feast, Yasha was snoring.

20

The racket was ghastly. Loulou left the feast early, threading her way through the mob of revellers, past the little pipe and percussion band, now quite out of beat and melody yet the players still grinding away at syrinxes and kettle drums, their coronets of thyme and mimosa slipped back to rest on their ears like headstalls; past the twin prie-dieux and the rustic altar, the tipsy and the paralytic: head up, arms stiff at her sides, in the way that Grandmama had taught her a lady vacates a room.

Yasha had been filling himself up with yellow wine. Soon he would be drunk and rolling those lovely eyes. Some slattern might accommodate him.

To have the remnant of this night alone would be luxury.

At the foot of the monumental staircase a cool haze from the marble enveloped her. She paused in the quiet and looked up to the translucent rotunda. The double doors were closed now, the feast was shut away from her and the sun had gone down but there was still enough light.

The palm of her hand was dry to the touch of the balustrade as she felt her way up. No work, yet the skin crackled. She was becoming neglectful of herself. Perhaps those tart little girls could spare a tub of cold cream and a mirror from the dressing-case they had rifled. Trulls, princesses, jades, ladies, they all suffered similar inclinations. Had to keep themselves – What was Yasha's phrase? – "Dolled up."

Loulou smiled at the fig-leaved Apollo at the turning of the stair. Polly was grotesquely painted and powdered. She'll need it tonight for face-saving when wolf-man slips out of his encumbrances to reveal all in that malarial shack by the river, full of giblets and feathers and rainbowing game-meats.

This was Valerian's day too. How would he while away the night? Abstemiously? In prayer? Then rise at cockcrow to inspect the sheets?

One flight from the top a footfall made her halt. Schmidt was padding up behind. Round his bald head was a trim garland, in his hand a shepherd's crook wound with helical ivy.

"Well, my titled missis, this is a fine turn-to-and-run. Too good for the paltry lads and lasses, are we, sneaking off on a night as rare as this?"

A dozen steps separated them. Against the elegant lines of the balusters he looked fleshy and out of place. She remembered her father's shout to a baker who had once called with his account: "You can go to hell!"

He stared back and raised his foot to the next tread. "So I could, milady, so I could before I was saved. But now there's saints from heaven come down to earth and under their rule it is your kind that treads the path to hell."

A tortoiseshell crucifix swayed under his chin. Was the creature trying to hypnotise her with his superstitions? She backed up to the central landing. Schmidt took the steps carefully, one at a time. "Come down," he called softly. "You're an educated woman, you know where your duty lies, no one knows better. Those of your sort there may be who are parasites, leeches, idlers, but you know when to pay your dues, you do." He seemed genuinely anxious to get a point across.

"Pay?" said Loulou. "What with?"

He stopped one stair below her. There was no smell of drink on his breath. "You must have something," he said, fingering the crucifix. "Ladies is never without."

"Money! You think I have money?" They all thought that. Kostya had. Old name, old fortune. "I thought you had abolished money."

He regarded her with unaccustomed gentleness, his eyes filling with tears. "There's other commerce besides coin."

"Pig!" screamed Loulou and snatched the crucifix from his neck. "Easing your lusts on defenceless women. Touch me and I shall blind you!"

The cross had been a costume brooch and along its back was a thick pin which she flicked out. But Schmidt was an old hand-to-hand fighter. One bob of his head and she was stabbing air; the handle of his crozier shot out and hooked her behind the knee. A jerk and she was sprawling.

He was quick but not quick enough. On her way down Loulou lashed out with the pin and cut him from eye to jaw.

"Bitch!" grunted the German and deliberately fell across her with the whole weight of his body. Lying awkwardly over the angle of the stair, Loulou caught the shock at the base of her spine and went dead to the knees. For a moment they lay intertwined, both thinking that her back was broken. "Bitch!" he repeated, the warm blood from his gash dripping onto her eyelids. "Your legs aren't done. I'll have you high-stepping for me yet."

He was right. She could feel herself kick, the thick carpet had saved her – that and his trench-practised skill. He knew all the tricks.

Forcing back her head with the butt of his palm he slapped her twice with his free hand, then wrenched open the ruffled collar of her shirt. As he explored her, pinching and scraping the nipples, her head was being pressed so far back that she was brought to the edge of unconsciousness. Without allowing her to faint he kept her at the point of strangulation while his mouth closed over hers, his breath oddly sweet.

Afterwards he whispered: "I could kill you now and swear it was an accident. One less idle mouth to feed. Or shall I brand you, burn you, mark you for the corrupt slave that you are, who defiles all she touches?"

Taking care not to break the skin he pricked the tip of her nose with a gouging spike as shiny and smooth as a sailmaker's needle. "Scar for scar, milady. Where shall it be? Eyelids? Mouth? At the parting of the hair?"

"Why not?" she said exhaling so deeply that his chest rose above hers. "Why not now, why don't you? A cross on my breast. A bloody cross to guard you from my kind. No one will come. You can do as you want with me." She locked her arms behind his back and began gently to score his shoulder-blades with her fingernails. "Think of it," she murmured. "How I shall howl for mercy when you feel me, and whip me, and feel me ..." She knew the words by heart and recited them with a burr of inviting sensuality which Schmidt had never heard and which shocked him profoundly.

"Yes," he said, disengaging himself. "You'd like that, you would – to sully a man – that's what your sort's for, isn't it? That's all you think about."

"Don't you want to?" asked Loulou catching his arm. "Oooh, how I would beg."

"It's not natural. This is sin." His voice rose. "Woman should keep to her place."

Immediately Loulou let the fire in her voice die and lifted his hand to her cheek. "There," she said. "No harm in this."

Unhurriedly, Schmidt ran his fingers into her hair like a boy fluffing up the breast-feathers of a pigeon. The bobbed ends at her neck bristled pleasantly. He acted the playful lover, almost gentle, placing her in profile with a thumb beneath her chin so that the flood of crimson light from the cupola fell into slantish shadow along the planes of her cheek and nose. Loulou relapsed into voluptuousness: the sensation of being handled and held fast thickened her flesh. Under the skin the blood surged like heavy oil.

"Look on this," he murmured.

A square of grey pasteboard. He bowed it between his fingers with a card-sharper's flick and an image formed against the falling light. A portrait, a court portrait, embossed *Hofphotograph des Kaisers*; brownish but highlighted pink at the temples and swell of the cheeks, a gold tint on the yellow pear-drop diamonds at breast and ears. Heavy eyes gazed candidly from a face turned to one side.

In life Schmidt had modelled her to the precise angle. "Woman, look upon thyself," he said. "The bride decked in her bride-price."

No wonder he had thought her rich. But the diamonds were ill-cut, antique and never her own. "Tcha, tcha," said Mama. "Loulou is so innocent! Heirlooms! She cannot keep such jewels!" And they were whisked back the day after the wedding. And Kostya saw that the bride-price was taken out on the body of the bride.

Loulou's great slatestone eyes gazed back from the print, pupils blotty from headiness. How could she not have seen? A serene little puss he must have thought her, enough to tempt Cain with that inviolate stare.

There had once been a Levant morocco frame, blind-tooled with roses, which he always carried to make other women quail before that imperceptive smile.

Schmidt had released his hold, but continued to fondle her brushy hair. "At first I didn't see you in her," he said, tapping the photograph. "Not without her crowning glory. That's a woman that scents her fingertips, I thought. A fragrant woman. Now, what's she doing with this little fellow who put her in his pocket-book along with pictures of Berber whores pissing into chamberpots or raising their rumps to be stuck by black fellows like so much swine-pork? Was she his mother?" He stroked the side of his nose with the photograph. "You see my point? His mother I could understand. Somehow she wouldn't get tainted by the . . ."

"Proximity?" suggested Loulou.

"That's right," said Schmidt. "You don't . . . not with your mother. But a wife now. You see my point?"

He would never see hers: not with his mother but hers. She never saw it until afterwards.

"Lucky he was, though," went on Schmidt. "Had the devil's reward in this world, strumpets and fine women and high-style. Till he fell among us on the road from Stochod."

"Tell me how it was with him."

Schmidt drew himself in, cross-legged on the broad stair and reflected. "Now, how do I bring him to mind? A dark slip of a man he seemed, fluttery with his hands, black and white, flip-flopping like a cavalry chevron on a lance-pole. But when you stepped up to him he was solid like a tree. Couldn't fathom it, a man that size having those hands, until I thought, Jewish, *Schwarzenjude*, a Rabbinical hair-splitter with hands white from washing off the blood of children and Christ.''

"Was he your officer?''

Schmidt laughed. "Nobody was nobody's officer then, milady, unless he was mad.''

"He *was* mad,'' whispered Loulou.

The German laughed much louder showing the hollows in his back teeth. "There speaks experience.''

Loulou could almost have liked Schmidt for perceiving Kostya as a fool.

"Mad, she says, and mad he was when last he trod this earth.'' He coughed and politely covered his mouth. "Seeing him was like being back at musketry school. Him spanking fresh in his bottle-green twills with a red stripe up the leg like a painted coachline and his fringy epaulettes, and the lacquered peak of his cap twinkling in the dawn sun. A regular strutter he was, and no mistake. Taskmaster and bandbox, all rolled into one, your glass-eyed Jewboy.''

"He was not a Jew.'' Her lips were stiff and sore.

"No more he was, no more he was. Didn't like Jews, did they, in the Izmailovskii?'' Apparently it was not a question, but a joke, for Schmidt, not waiting for a reply, laughed again, this time more quietly. "Proved he wasn't beyond peradventure we did, in the end. Anyhow, there he stood at the ditch side, got up like his beloved sovereign's dandy dog, and behind him a squad of the ugliest tosspot marauders I'd ever clapped eyes on. 'Guards,' he said. *Guards* – you wouldn't have trusted them with the cook-house swill-bucket. In Galicia there was thousands like them, burrowing into the skirts of the Army, 'Kids' we called them, scavengers, jail-dross who'd bayonet Joseph himself and do the Virgin Mary just for fun. 'Who is your commanding officer?' says your prune-eyed Israelite, frolicking his moustachios an inch from my nose. There was us three – the master, and that bridegroom from today, but he speaks to me because I'm the boldest and oldest and so stands more to attention like one of his own Guards NCOs. I looked sideways at Vlady and he looks down the barrel of his Schneider like there's a bug in the rifling. 'Killed, your honour.' That was a fact. How, we weren't going to spill. 'Where's your unit?' He's a stickler, this one. We could see ourselves being strapped to the triangle for a flogging. 'Couldn't rightly say, your honour.' That was a fact, too. Three-quarters had chucked their weapons into bogs and gave themselves up to the Germans when

Prince Leopold of Bavaria caught us on the hop over the Stochod in April. He knew that. He knew we were on our way home. '*Guards,*' he screams, prancing at us with his little kittenish hands. 'Place these men under close arrest!' I thought God's judgement was upon us and Belial was about to crunch our bones to flour. But the big bastard Lett that had charge of the troop, he fingers his ear and, God be praised for His mercies, he winks behind Izmailovskii's ramrod back, straight into the eyes of Valerian, our master. No one moves. With his whiphands your officer pantomimes blows, executions, the crushing of unrest. Brute Lett grins then sniggers and your officer's eyes go far back in his head like dots. Valerian steps forward. 'If your honour will permit me,' he says, polished as a master of ceremonies. 'By virtue of the authority vested in me by superior powers, I hereby relieve you of your command. Be so good as to surrender your side-arm.' This is better than a play. We stand to attention all honourable while the Lett's Chinese navy rock on their heels fit to burst."

He paused and wiped his mouth. Loulou heard her own voice, sounding unfamiliar, ask: "And what did he do?"

"What Guards officers do," said Schmidt. "Did what they chose him for. He salutes, doffs his cap, sets it firm again on his head, unbuckles his pistol and passes it to Valerian laid across his hands. Then three times, very loud against the morning birds: 'God save the Tsar!' he shouts. 'God save the Tsar!'"

Mad. Beautifully mad.

"And?"

"And the master shot him."

"With his own pistol?"

"With his own Mannlicher. Clean. Stood rigid for a fraction, then dropped without a word. One bullet at the meet of the eyebrows blew him clean as a sparrow's egg all over the fatigues of the Lett."

Christ, thought Loulou, slowly crossing herself. How well I knew him.

She wanted to crawl away but Schmidt had not finished. His recollection was now in spate. "What to do with him then? I would have left him where he fell. Valerian wanted him buried and Vladimir Ivanovich still had his back-pack with entrenching tools intact. But the Lett's Guards, they mobbed us, snapping like weasels. He was booty, he was pickings. Theirs. We couldn't argue. They were three to our one. So I superintended while they yanked him out of his boots, had off his spurs, his trews, down to the soft linings under the frogged jacket. Everything they tampered with – inspected his parts totally, you might say. Clear to the day, then, that this was no son of David. And that worried the big Lett. Looked worse, murdering a Gentile officer, so they shook out all his pockets, took the little spirits-flask, the gold repeater watch and cigar case, made a heap of his papers to set fire to with a lucifer from his silver box. I stamped it out before they was round the bend of the cut. It's why they're charred, see?"

She looked again at the photograph, a widow whose suttee pyre had been doused below her. So that was how the frame had finally served. Her youth saved from the fire.

"Hermann is always a shade on the providential side," he said. "A last scrabble under the frogging may make all the difference, just to see if there's anything worth keeping. Not a man for papers, Major Graf Konstantin Maksimovich Alekseyev. All passe-partouts for official business. One letter, unfinished."

"Darling Andryushka," read Loulou. "Aunt Natasha and I were delighted to receive your chatty letter. When you come to us again it will be winter . . ."

"I kept the picture out of respect. A wife or sister? Or a mother? Innocent, naturally, pure in heart . . ."

"And the others?"

"Those," said Schmidt unfurtively, "are texts for sermonising the heathen, to be brought out like rotten apples, fortifying the wholesome against sin."

Kostya, Kostya, you will have said too much in that wayside sunrise, smiling that derisive smile. "What has got into you people?" What he always said to the bearded labourers from the demesne fields who came up to the house on deputations, bowing from such a distance that she could never distinguish their faces, and he strode out to them, to be kissed on the shoulder and to give orders in an incomprehensible patois.

He said he knew them better than their mothers. So they led him out, her dark man with the drawn look, to a place of execution and mocked him for his presumption.

Schmidt was embarrassed by her silence. "Happened a lot," he said. "Out there. Him or us. Man has his choices to make and no deferral. Dead, your man, among many such lordships."

He cradled the photograph and brought it to his lips. "The women weep and are comforted by them who knew not solace. No hard feelings, little missis? I have lain with your face beside me and now I know you."

When Loulou did not respond he bent over to look into her face and she spat into his eyes.

"Bitch!" he screamed and struck her on the temple with his fist.

* * *

"A little accident, Master. The ladyship fell and fainted on the stairs. I was rendering assistance . . ."

Valerian fixed him briefly with a suffering Jesus-eye, then looked upwards. "Hermann, knowest thou me for thee I knoweth. Touch her once more and I shall drop you naked from the point of that dome, on a wire, for all the world to witness the last spurt of your damnable seed."

21

"Orphans are children," said Belyakov. "You're not a child.
Leastways, I've never seen a little girl with those." And he gave
Polly's left breast a timid prod, wanting to tease but uneasy about
translating words into action.

Unconscious of the touch she lifted her face to him and stared.
"Rot. Orphans are orphans. It's a state of being, not a stage you go
through. Mama and Papa are dead, so I'm an orphan. So there."

"My sweet," said the huntsman, permitting himself the first endear-
ment since the wedding. "Let me be a father to you."

"Pooh to fathers! I wanted a man. Why do you think I married
you according to those obnoxious rites? A man, a man!"

Belyakov examined the backs of his hands and coughed. "Well,
there you are," he said. "You've got one, a nice one, a good one, one
who could eat you he loves you so much."

"I don't want a nice man. I've had enough of *nice* men, thank you
very much. You've never been a girl, you don't know how sickeningly
clumsy nice men can be."

Belyakov got up and lounged by the unshuttered window trying to
look at ease. She turned, took in the pose at a glance and then
concentrated on her own reflection in the glass. The clear sky was
black and thick. Outside the autumn night-warmth chilled, sparkling
the edge of the panes with frost. Tilting her head first one way, then
another, she shook out loose pins from her slate-coloured hair,
catching them expertly before they fell to the earth floor. The eyes
that looked back from the dark were hazed and caressing. For all her
regard for his presence he might have been a lady's maid.

Two strides away from the surrender of a newly-churched bride of
nineteen, together with her, alone, their union already well-rehearsed
in his and her dreams, and he was as limp as a trapped hare. Much
more of this and he'd be as redundant as Daddy.

"They dropped things and simpered and never knew what to do
with their hands. When are you going to get out of those frightful
clothes?"

This last was said with such a brisk, unnerving grin that he completely lost his tongue and could only fret at the long-stemmed rose in his button-hole.

But any hurry she might have implied was swiftly lost sight of as she continued to brood on her image in the dark glass. "Just think," she said, as if to herself. "Just think how low I have sunk. An orphan at the mercy of man." She stretched out an arm and laid it bare along the stuff of his sleeve. "Hefty," she said. "You could pick me up with one hand."

Polly's onsets of seductiveness disconcerted him. Did she know what she was doing, or did she speak the first thought that came to mind? He shifted back and regarded her warily. The thundercloud hair curved down the slope of her shoulders tangling front and back with the bride-lace and ribboning which tipped the loosened rim of her boned corset. Belyakov rubbed his hands on his knees. What was he waiting for? Before he could work up any idea into action, she turned full face upon him, gave a tug on the drawstrings and breathed out, luxuriously. One wide nipple lifted outwards and upwards against the cambric lining and fluffed to a dark point. Absently Polly looked down and freed the other breast which quivered lightly before coming to rest.

"Well?" she said. He tried to follow the jerk of her head, but the movement shuddered her breasts and held his gaze transfixed below her chin. "Well?"

At the loud and businesslike voice he glanced down at himself. The cloth over his knees felt thick and hot. *Those?* Not yet, surely; it was all too quick. In a panic he scrabbled at the loops of his dress braces.

"Oh my God," sighed Polly. "Have some pity on a girl. I mean, little by little, everything, but bit by bit. Starting at the top would be showing proper consideration for a newly-wed, don't you think?"

Why should she tell him that she had played this game before? Gone so far, yes; stripping herself at a distance. Yes, always prudently out of reach, and never quite of everything. But she had enjoyed inciting the man, with only the length of an ottoman between them.

Belyakov shrugged off the jacket and began to heave at the tapes of his waistcoat, keeping his eyes on her face. Debbie had edged the high bone of the bride's cheeks with a white-wax rouge which glistened in the lamp-light. They had tried it on her lips but Polly was sick at the taste and the girls who attended her had taken turns to bring up the blood colour by pinching and scrubbing at her mouth with their hard-bitten nails so that it now stood out scarlet and contused.

When his coat fell to the floor, she matched him unselfconsciously, and sat like a schoolgirl on the dormitory bed, caressing her underarms and stretching back to stiffen her breasts in a pose of innocence which, she had learned from giggly play-room jokes, ought to send men mad.

Belyakov felt his arms grow heavier. He had always thought embarrassment at such a time was exclusively feminine, and he made the mistake of telling her so.

"Mmmmm," said Polly. "That shows how much you know about women. What on earth have I got to be embarrassed about?" As if to persuade him of this truth she cupped her left breast in the palm of one hand, springing out the tip from the brownstain flush of the nipple with the little finger of the other.

He had expected her to be mute, paralysed, and had already prepared a speech in which he would offer to sleep in the loft. Instead, she was pursuing him into immobility and silence.

The long low room where for a couple of years before the war Belyakov had skinned hares and oiled his guns, slept and eaten alone, had been done out for their first night. The oldest women of the community had relaid the earth floor and kindled a fire of apple-tree branches. For that he was grateful. Knowing that he slept on a heap of skins they had dragged in a bed from the house and set it up by the hearth. Although it took up a quarter of the floor and was hideous from mahogany and inlay, he took the bed as a kindness. But when it came to decoration, the women's fancy had overreached. Bulbs of garlic hung beneath the sill of the high window; vervane and daisies twined round the bed-legs; everywhere he looked, greenery and grasses overspread the timber walls. The drying herbs tickled his sinuses and he pinched the bridge of his nose until his eyes watered.

Half-naked, Polly scrutinised him in the lamplight. "I saw a cask of white burgundy being brought up here from the cellar this morning. I know what's the matter with you – you've been drinking all day. To think what might have been," she continued, getting up to turn down the lamp. Against the deepening glow her bust was ripe and sharp. "A woman's touch is all that's needed."

In the half-dark Belyakov responded to the gentleness of tone, eased his torso out of the crackly shirt and shook himself like a retriever.

A basket of figs stood on the lone table where he laid his shirt. For no reason he took out a fruit and offered it to her. Polly split the rind with her big teeth and white juice spattered onto the ribbing of her discarded corset. All day she had complained of hunger but had hardly eaten. Now at last, skin to skin with this man, she did not wish to faint from weakness.

He stood in her light, watching. The second fig went down almost whole. Afterwards she smacked her lips and dabbled her fingers dry on the verdigris *eau-de-soie* of her top petticoat.

"Aren't you wildly in love with me, then?"

"How d'you mean?" he said, miserably handicapped by her directness and the problem of removing all his clothes in front of a woman.

"Oh, my giddy aunt!" she exclaimed, slithering off the petticoat with one twist of her waist. Underneath was a shorter one in transparent bobbin lace. The line of her thighs showed up pinkish. "I mean, if you do, aren't you supposed to want to do things to me?"

He couldn't work this out immediately. Love her, she must mean. He did. But at the present moment he couldn't *do* a thing. In spite of the fire he felt very cold. "Yes," he said after a long interval.

Skipping past him Polly grabbed the basket of figs and vaulted backwards into the billowy goosefeather mattress of the bed and began to juggle the remaining fruits across her chest. "Golly, I mean, don't you know *anything*?"

Belyakov eased the back of his neck where the muscle was knotting. It wasn't him that didn't know, it was her. He was in no condition with her going at him like a snow-cat.

"Where's the wine, then?" she said immediately after, unconcerned that he had not responded to her insult. Glad of a job, he tapped the baby firkin of burgundy which Gerasim had trestle-rigged behind the bedhead. He drank from the jug-eared loving cup, one of Valerian's presents, refilling it when he had done, stretching across the bed to hold it to her lips.

Polly sank back and allowed the wine to tipple into her mouth. "This is simply ridiculouth," she said after a long swallow. "I mean, things can't remain as they are. We're man and wife." The wine glossed the down on her short upper lip and trickled to the well of her right eye. With his back to the fire the huntsman felt warmer as Polly dishevelled herself in the depths of the goose mattress, kicking against the folds to reveal long pearl-stockinged legs. Her breasts lay apart, spanning wider than her back. In between, the rib-ends flared like wing stubs.

She asked twice again to drink and left none; but apart from an increasing lisp there was no perceptible change to her speech. The wine had reached her, nevertheless. "I am entitled, you know," she said, "to my birthright."

Belyakov's gaze fell on a pike nailed out for smoking on a brick baulk of the hearth. The smell of its drying flesh mingled unpleasantly with the aroma of sweet applewood from the fire. On a raft of timber which ran the whole length of the room hung the desiccating corpses of leverets, wild song-birds and bundles of tiny fresh-water fish. Guilt made the huntsman tender and respectful. "No place for a lady, Apollonya Dmitryevna, I realise that, but trust me – I'll make a proper home for you."

Polly sat upright, puffing the feathers away from her mouth. "Home?" she almost shrieked. "Don't you understand? Home is what I'm trying to get away from. I didn't marry you to play houses. My birthright as a woman, Vladimir Ivanovich, a *woman*!"

He held her off with Valerian's catch-all slogan. "But nobody's entitled to anything any more. We're all equal."

"Oh yes! And brothers and sisters too. What hoodwinking cant! You don't believe it, do you?"

He contemplated the sharkish eye of the pike. "Well," he murmured. "Share and share alike, where's the harm in that?"

"They do that here, all right – at least, the men do." She caught hold of him by the hairs round his navel and peered up at his chin. "Or don't you know – really?"

"Know what?"

"That fraternity doesn't mean brothers and sisters not playing at mummies and daddies?" When she told him what she had overheard the men discussing and the entertainments they had planned for after the wedding feast, he had to sit down.

Polly's spectacles had lodged in the left leg of his trousers and fell out undamaged when he took off his patent-leather pumps. Since she had gained equanimity after telling her story, he felt freer in a loose-limbed kind of way, and they sat, hand in hand, on the edge of the bed, enjoying the closeness of a shared secret. At the foot of the bed stood Valerian's fat Virgin picture, its shellacky blues unnatural against the organic tones of decay which frothed around them.

"Repellent," said the bride. "And quite out of place. Was it someone's idea of a joke, sticking it there?"

"Her ladyship said Valerian thought it might make you . . ." *Fruitful* was the word he could not bring himself to say.

"Make me what?" said Polly sharply. But she had already guessed how Valerian's mind would work on this day of all days. "Nonsense," she went on. "It's that spiteful Loulou making trouble again." Her glasses flashed in the log smoke and she leaned forward against her husband waggling the ring on her wedding finger. "She has a very immature attitude. Just because she's no longer a . . ." The implication was left outstanding while the new bride pounced on Loulou's defiance of correctness. "Just the two of them quite unchurched and left together in Daddy's old apartments. I heard those depraved children giggling about it. Her and him. Alone. Without a scrap of respectability. It's disgraceful."

Belyakov fondled her ear through the flood of hair and she drew closer.

"Well, isn't it?" she said in a more submissive tone, but persisting when he took her by the shoulders and kissed her forehead. "Don't you think?" Polly yielded to his silence, allowing her body to be slowly borne down into the mattress-heap. "Well, it's jolly bad form," she called out from under his chest. He shook her upright by the waist, plonked her down so heavily that she sank to the midriff in the feather-bag. Then he sat out of reach, glaring at the contour of her stately neck.

"Is this how we're going to spend our wedding night? Talking about somebody else's?"

Polly pushed out her lips. "They're not married." She gave a curt tap at the place over her breastbone where a crucifix would normally have hung. "That's all I'm trying to say."

"Not like us, eh?"

Polly shook her curls in triumph. "There, I knew you understood. They're not entitled."

Did she really believe that the mumbo-jumbo in the tennis court gave him the right to her? His glare became fiercer. "A man takes his pleasure where he finds it."

At the harrowed ring in his voice her eyes sparkled. "Oooh," she murmured stroking herself from temple to hip-bone. "That's what a girl wants to hear. When do we start looking?"

The nightgown was Mummy's. Shot-silk with a Paris label. Between Polly's legs and at the bodice, citrous-yellow folds battened on her warmth like the flesh of a clingstone peach, reeking of oil of camphor. A present from Papa. Made out of guilt after some flagrant indiscretion, and never worn by Mummy, it had lain in her press to be ravished by Debbie and handed back with a leer – "Bit of trousseau" – at the wedding breakfast.

At Belyakov's insistence, Polly had completed her undressing with the wick of the lamp turned down to its lowest, and she kept her back to him when slipping the nightgown over her head. Her impatience subsided under the run of the silk on her skin and she sat expectant but by now slightly afraid, on a low wooden table set at the foot of the bed, a battery of votive candles for Valerian's Our Lady unlit at her thigh. In the hearthside murk Belyakov still struggled with his remaining dress clothes, becoming more agitated. He knew where the nightdress had come from, to whom it had once belonged, and by its camphorated reek he was reminded of death. Polly sensed nothing except pleasure at the tickly, familiar smell of her mother's bedroom, and the rough hiss of the fabric across her body.

"Of course, you'll have to tell me what to do." She tugged at the silver-lace tassels suspended from the underside of the open-work bodice. "Everything. I'll need to know everything."

"You're a cool one," he gasped, clawing down the shiny material of the left leg of his trousers with his toes. "Aren't there any nerves in that body of yours?"

"I wouldn't miss the littlest moment for the whole world. I mean, one doesn't get married every day, does one?"

He put it down to education. In his restricted experience, tears, fainting fits or plain horror were more in the natural way of things than enthusiasm. Yet Polly was not as poised as she wished to appear. Under the linked chrysanthemum medallions which made up the straps of her nightgown her shoulders heaved rapidly and she did not turn round. And, as if deliberately trying to delay him, she broached an irrelevant topic:

"Loulou told me . . ."

Naked by now, he groaned at the name and covered the lower part of his body. "What are you bringing her into it for? Haven't we had enough of that wretched woman?"

"I only meant . . ." Polly felt an onset of dryness in her mouth. "Let's see, well, *naturally*, there are some things I *don't* know. Loulou wouldn't tell me about what people do *exactly*."

For the first time that day Belyakov was gratified. Now he had an edge, and he prayed that she would allow him to keep it. "Is that so?" he said without taking a step to where she sat but instead contemplating the quickening rise and fall of her spine.

"Oh, yes." Her voice shifted down a chord, like an adolescent boy's. "But she said a lot about what isn't done."

Except for a noise equivalent to a nod, he kept quiet and let his hands fall away. Suddenly he was conscious of the hairs on his body bushing together like a pelt through which a sharp male sweat dribbled onto the smooth planes of his upper arms. A powerful urge swept over him to thrust his hands under the rear panels of the nightgown and break the straps where single fine stitches connected the tips of the petals.

"Nice people, well, nice, well-bred people . . . women, refined ones . . . *ladies* . . . Ladies aren't supposed . . . aren't supposed to *look*."

Before he knew what was happening, she had whirled round on the table top knocking over the candles and was peering at him through her spectacles at an angle which cut him off at waist-level.

"Oh," she said with the start of a giggle. "I suppose I see what Loulou meant. I'm awfully well-bred but I don't think I'm very nice, am I? Not really refined. Do you think I'm still a lady? Didn't Valerian say there were no ladies or gentlemen any more?" After each burst of candour she approached a little nearer, the silver tassels weighting the silk against the lines of her figure. An arm's length away Polly reached out and he allowed himself to be taken and led forward very gently to the lamp which she snuffed from behind with her free hand.

"Let's pretend," she whispered in the orange firelight. "Let's pretend we're equals."

It was no good. Experience had made him shy. Ignorance had made her forward. The combination was inept.

In the deep bed she pulled at him. "Kiss me." The kiss was as infantile as the demand. He managed to snuffle at her cheek with his moustache like a horse nudging for sugar. It tickled. He tried for her lips but she twisted away and pawed at his lower body. It was no good. Even she ought to have divined that by now.

"Stop it."

She wouldn't, so he took a deep breath and pinioned her wrists at the small of her back and forced his lips on her mouth. The response was instantaneous and he shot back to relieve the hold of her teeth on the flesh of his underlip.

"Beastly, utterly beastly," she squealed, sticking out her tongue. "That's not at all nice."

With any other woman this might have been the finish but Polly's fit of pique reduced him to blundering forward, undeterred. When she flinched and raised her eyes to the ceiling, baring her mouth with tight, efficient teeth, he swore.

"This business is incredibly tedious," she said after he had lain face down beside her. "And my legs hurt when you drop on me like that. What about sideways?" Without waiting for a reply she arranged herself. When he showed no sign of life she licked the back of his neck. "Come along, now, don't be a baby."

The backward jerk of his head banged her teeth on his skull bone. "Holy Mother of God, why can't you stop ordering me about, woman?"

Suddenly desolate she began to howl. "Nobody in the world cares about me. Mummy, Daddy, Lola and Millie are gone. I want to go home. I want my nice things back. I'm so horribly miserable I could die."

Belyakov cursed the brute in him. "Now, now," he lullabied. "Who's a silly, then?" As he tried to soothe her with murmur and touch he felt pride in his absence of desire. Although her breasts swelled at each sob and her belly was warm, he was quelled by her tears and was regenerated, along with the after-effects of the wine, by calm, undemanding brotherly affection. "Uncle Vlady loves you, my sweet, let Uncle Vlady love you . . ."

"Does he?"

"Of course he does, my dear. He can't tell you how much."

She sprang up like a clockwork doll. "Oh yes, he can," she said grimly. "For a start he can help me get out of this frightful old shroud thing."

The passage of years would never efface Belyakov's dismay at the subsequent events of that night. He was a solitary man, unused to women, even, at times, shunning them out of inexperience on the rare occasions when they had presented themselves as opportunities. His occupation had enabled him to dismiss his need for them. Few women would have wanted to share the regime of such a life as his: for days he could be gone, winter and summer, on hunts which had been old Laskorin's chief pleasure. Out there, in forest or marsh, he had learned from childhood that your only hope of survival was self-reliance. He might track bear for thirty-six hours, quite alone, then hole up for the night in a snow-filled gully, waiting for the gentlemen to come at dawn and take their shots. It was a hard business to be in, but he was proud of the vigour he felt in being able to perform it single-handed.

The Army had restricted his independence, yet, at the same time, he had discovered a solace in the company of men, men like himself, at his level, which was distracting and comfortable. It was then that he began to see those years lived apart as misspent, even perverse, and discovered in himself a powerful desire to belong. That desire had made him follow Valerian back to this place. But this was a community, not a cheery scrum of mess-mates; since there could be no family without women, he needed his own woman to become part of the whole. Now, after one futile attempt to break away, he wished to settle.

The village women had not changed, would never change, and he was as repelled as he always had been by their cruelty and superstition; but now he would have embraced the stringiest *baba* the region had to offer rather than the opulent girl who was presently making him undergo such misery.

They had tried once. Afterwards, she said: "Well? Is that all?"

For her? How could he tell her that he didn't think so but didn't really know? He had hoped she knew more, knew how, and at one point felt that she must by the way she clawed at his back. The truth sounded like deceit: "To begin with, *dushichka*, only to begin with." An apology wouldn't have gone amiss. With that tongue stuck out of the corner of her mouth and those sightless eyes, she had been preparing to squander herself at the merest hint of him staying. How could he explain that those years of self-denial had quickened him?

Polly twisted aside. He saw her slim white legs. "Is that all you can do? I thought you were a man."

"Now, my dear, you mustn't take it so seriously . . ."

"Seriously? You don't know what you're saying. I mean, why on earth d'you think I let you . . . I let *this* happen in the first place?"

Belyakov took a little while before producing the only reason which could account for the situation.

"*Love! You!* Lord above, you're quite mad. Don't you realise that I only consented because I'd never have to hear that sort of crawly talk again? You can't believe I wanted to be courted, all that rot?"

He honestly thought she had, but had left it till now, obviously far, far too late, to say so.

His admission amazed her. How on earth did he think he could compete in that line? Was he really any good at pretty speeches, compliments, telling thundering fibs to get his own way? No, he wasn't.

Suddenly, jumping upright, she snatched down the ikon over the bed and blew out the little red lamp. "I know what it is. I expect you need a blessing."

His beliefs were crudely sincere, especially after drink, and this act of impiety made his anger rise. "You blasphemous little . . ."

"Devil?" said Polly relaxing her hold on the ikon, just enough to allow him to take it without her appearing to have given in. "Go on, say, tell me what you think of a girl who can do that. Papa did. Once I heard about him and that French governess, years ago, all about their words. Tell them to me."

Belyakov replaced the ikon of Mother and Child on the triangular shelf and carefully wasted time by pretending to re-light the lamp. He had no idea what this so-called wife of his intended except in some way to build a marriage on their mutual and total unsuitability. To be fair, difference was what had attracted him in the first place but he had expected that his taking the initiative natural to a man would have brought them to terms. Instead, the reverse had happened. She was leading him, God alone knew where, and every move he

made was some kind of pitfall. If she'd wanted him to be himself –
whatever that meant – Apollonya Dmitryevna had not given a hint
about it until this evening.

It was late. He was weary. "How should I know what your father
got up to? Never talked to the likes of me about his goings-on, did
he? You forget, *barishnya*, I was never allowed in your house."

This was said with enough sullenness for Polly to clasp her hands
in applause. "There, you see, that's what I wanted – a new beginning
– an attitude." Belyakov grunted. "Poor Vlady, did we treat you
simply too cruelly?"

"Not a bit of it. Most of you didn't notice when I was there, that
I existed." It was less of a grumble, more of a recollection of fact,
too familiar to be provoking, even if old Laskorin had been a hard
bastard at times.

She was kneeling by his side, her thighs slightly parted. "Look,"
she said. The expression of her voice was so strange that Belyakov
stared into her eyes. "Look," she said again, almost piteously, and
he let himself follow the rowing movement of her arms as she bent
her back to touch him. A feral scent of rust and iodine issued from
the contact of her hands with the sweat of his body where she had
imprinted two outlines of her wet, pink palms and fingers on the
expanse of smooth flesh below his breast. "Look at what you have
done," she murmured. The accusation was not meant to invite
remorse but was a plea to resume what had already been begun, only
this time with his fore-knowledge that her desire lay in being forced
to overcome, not her own, but the man's resistance.

"Remember your life, remember the suffering, is this enough to
make up?" She fell back onto the covers and wriggled forward so
that her legs overhung the squat brown bed. "You must want to do
more."

He sought to detach himself from memory. Suffering? He would
be dishonest to claim it. His calling had been reputable, a source of
pride, and her people had honoured him. And even if that had all
been different, and he had been one of Valerian's true malcontents,
what pleasure could it be to exact revenge on a woman who, as a
little girl, he'd trapped goldhawks for and walked by the hand round
his traps?

He did not understand her. That must be normal with a new wife.
She did not understand him, and that was probably normal too.

So, to hell with soul-sharing, the time had come to stop making
efforts.

"Well?" she said, reverting to the style of banter with which she
had previously treated Belyakov's fits of moroseness. "Are you going

to sit out for the rest of the evening?" Not a twitch. It was grotesque, this steadfast glumness. What had she done? Her feet found the discarded nightdress on the floor and she began to play with it, catching the neckline between her toes, opening it out. "A good thing this isn't public. I mean, fancy having to account for one's own performance, like after a play. Imagine – the notices . . ."

"Shut your mouth, woman."

Polly kicked up the nightgown and, snatching it by the hem, slid her arms through the apertures, covering her breasts. "You beast," she gasped. "How dare you. What right do you think you have?"

"Every right to every part of you. Like you said: marriage gives people that."

The words were scarcely audible as he stood over her once again, kneeing her apart until the evidence of his former, brief success spread in a glisten still sleeking her thighs. When she tried to fling back his hands from her waist he wondered if, at last, he had excited her, but the momentary pleasure only fuelled his anger at the thought of his previous humiliation.

She would know what it was to be had by a man. He would teach her, disgrace her, terrify her.

Belyakov fell to his bride like a woodman splitting a log. She grunted under the dead weight, twisted, flopping her delicately pointed chin from side to side, enduring him. And she would have gone on, inarticulate, waiting, imprisoned, longing for the quick release which had freed her before. Then she had thought it easy but then there had been only discomfort. Now there was pain and she felt the source of it within herself, harsh and ungiving.

Belyakov felt it too, as a sore, unlessening difficulty which turned in upon itself, excluding him; and he tore at the nightgown with which Polly had sought to cover her breasts. Into the heat of his anger came an unbidden but appropriate memory of that day, a few months ago, when he had pulled up Natalya Igoryevna's shirt in order to shame her. Until that moment he had never admitted even to himself that it was not the body of a woman which left him cold but the entire tedious pantomime required to invade and enjoy it. His movements slackened. Beneath him Polly grew limply passive, closed up, breathing slowly, eyes shut, glad that, in the end, it was still no good.

In full view of her incipient smile, Belyakov sat astride and did what, until today, he had always done alone. As he stuttered on the edge, unrestrained, his back thrown out in a powerless curve, Polly opened her eyes.

So that was how it was with men. When Loulou had said that they had no need of you, could come into existence like this, at will, outside a woman, she had intended a warning. Now the fact was before her, Polly revelled in the sight of a man possessing himself; seeing him overcome exactly in the way she had wanted herself to be overcome, by sheer, unconciliating desire. Loulou was wrong; he needed the stillness of himself and of her beneath, warm and inciting. Long after, she would marvel in front of the mirror at the familiar, neutral line of her body which a man had impugned so deliciously, flecking throat and cheeks and hair in bloodwarm jets the colour of breast-milk.

"There. Now is that my duty done?" Her voice was small, tight, the tone self-congratulatory.

In one movement he was off the bed, his back to her, pulling his old hunting clothes from a wicker chest by the far wall.

"Mummy thought she had prepared me for anything. But that . . ."

She was lying, of course. Mimi Laskorina had been far too inhibited ever to broach such topics with a daughter but Polly was constructing romance, and the figment of her sophisticated mother was as necessary to the plot of her future marriage as the ice-cold beauty in French novels married against her will to a libertine whose florid debaucheries left her inviolate.

Unmoved submission, that was the means of holding permanent sway over a man.

Dreamily, she went on: "I shall never object . . ."

He could not have spoken, had he known what to say, but only dressed himself in silence and anguish. At the moment he could not tell which was the worse: her indulgence or that act which had required it.

"I should have realised, naturally, a man of your habits, set apart by the nature of your calling . . ."

He poked the tang of his soft leather belt into its notch. Silence would be the groundswell of their married life. He would never need to ask what she wanted or intended because she would make herself plain without reference to him.

"But even so, a certain kind of woman might have found that just now quite despicable, demeaning . . ." Perfectly true, she was convinced, but as for herself, it could be a source of pride. "But, naturally, if that is the way you wish our relations to continue, then I shall be content." The sheer effectiveness of her body had been intoxicating.

"You can't be . . . not after, I mean, not after what you've been saying."

"I am, absolutely," said Polly, thrilled by the pretext of high-flown sacrifice. "I swore to be obedient and I shall do exactly what you require of me."

"This is a game," he said. "You've had this at the back of your mind all along."

In attributing calculation to her behaviour, he was wrong. Polly had genuinely wanted and expected some new experience, but now that the promise of intense pleasure at being subject to this dark man with the spare, splendid body and passionate speech had been deferred, she would make do, *pro tem.*, with the unphysical. It was better that he should feel guilt since when she was again faced with the grossness of his needs (which was how she had determined to describe them for any purpose to do with him) it would be simple to adopt a position of moral superiority while retaining the simultaneous hint of unspoken reproach at the way he had failed her.

The role was assumed.

"Well, if you *are* to go out, be sure to close the door behind you. I don't wish to freeze to death."

For a moment he hesitated, surveying the floor strewn with discarded wedding clothes.

"If you are intent on being as you were, then so shall I," came the voice from the bed. "Even after this night." Already she felt grandly above him. Married four hours and already strangers. A heroine. Should she weep? No, that would only make him a martyr. Instead, Polly allowed him to linger over the collapsed little body stretched so composedly nude and desirable full length across the bed-coverings in cool, unwelcome subjection.

Nothing would change now. It would always be his blasted, irreparable fault.

Belyakov turned away at last, relinquishing the unequal struggle by lifting the latch and stepping into the dark.

Beyond the hut, night gleamed under a hunter's moon, mist rising shoulder high in the willows. He set off at a trot, barefoot, sucking in the moist, chill air, suddenly purposeful. At the river bank, the old exhilaration came back. This was how a doctor must feel, shutting the door on a sickroom.

His boat was wedged among the reeds, the blade of one oar shadowed against the blue seas of the moon. In a little tonneau at the stern he found his soft gamebag with a flask inside. Above the creak and slash of the oars as he rowed for the midstream current, Belyakov found himself draining the silence for every slightest noise. Here and there a night bird fumbled, rocked by his wake, but the stillness was dense over the outline of the great Laskorin house. After what seemed a very long time, he shipped his oars, took a long drink from the flask, and huddled down in the waist of the boat, continuing to listen unexpectantly until he fell asleep.

IV

NATALYA

September 1917–end of May 1918

22

Kostya. It must have been. Kostya had been in. Tonight, moments ago. Left her to bleed in the dark. He had struck her again, that way, making the blood leach inside like fire gravitating to her eyes. Flame bulged them in their sockets, too swollen for the lids to part.

She had done as he asked and he had done what he always came to do and what he wanted; and now, as always, she was on fire and bleeding. She had desired him but he had abused her and struck out. That was how it must have been. She had turned over to him, face to face, was smiling when the blow came across her mouth. Hard as the uncushiony horsehair bolster which numbed her belly when he sank upon her. Big. A splendid fellow, a fine figure of a man. A man's man. She held herself raised, still proffered over the hard arm of the ottoman, specks of green malachite from the footrule which he had slashed at her lips gritting her outspread hair. The posture must have seemed unreluctant. He wanted resistance, to be chafed. To use her where she puffballed, bloodied and strait. Salt gruel in the lacerated mucus like iodine flashing into split cuticle. Then a perfume of mushroom tilth, dank and friable, percolating her teeth. She coughed out droplets which clung to threads of her hair like seed-pearls.

A first time for everything. Something you could get used to; something, even, that you could like, enjoy, want, beg for. Eventually, it might have been just so. Just what the doctor, had there ever been such a doctor, would have ordered for Kostya's complaint. But Kostya was a man of attack. What was his had to be stormed, not surrendered. He needed the uncompliant to be put to the sword.

Her eyes opened. She had not gone blind. It was a room, and very dark. The air was dense from the reek of snuffed candles.

White flames blobbed somewhere beyond reach. The filmy texture over her pupils swam as she blinked, then cleared. A candelabrum with seven branches stood on a gate-legged table, the two wings of which were folded down. On a table she saw a copper-gilt samovar, a suite of glasses with sugar-twist stems and blue-clouded bowls, two bottles of white burgundy and a portable looking-glass from a travelling case. The silverplate tray on which they all stood had been over-rubbed and the metal beneath stood out the colour of tea.

The effect was perplexing. On the table, on the tray, nothing looked good or well-made. Kostya would never have tolerated this shabbiness. Shielding the sofa on which she had come to, was a canvas screen, the work of serf craftsmen. Languidly she examined the pressed grasses and flowers, sea-shells and feathers smothering its panels. All colour had long gone. By candlelight the bits appeared skeletally white, sticking out from a ground of mutton fat.

Behind the screen must be the entrance to the room. Loulou turned in the opposite direction and stared round.

Shuttered windows ran the length of one wall. A wrought-iron catwalk showed above where books were stacked in open-fronted presses. The knotty grain of wood and dark leathers of the bindings had the solid, uncared-for feel of saddlery. Kostya would have hated it.

She felt someone approaching. The floor juddered under the screen. Had he not gone after all? Was he returning for another bout? She licked her bruised underlip and stared, paralysed with fear, at the blank windows. Not Kostya. Another. A light-footed man with the step of a dancer.

The room seemed to stretch, the objects in it deliquesce. "Martin," she whispered and slid to the floor.

Someone was raising her head to a cushion. Her throat burned. She wanted to be sick. "Martin," she said again. The sound came out oblique and blurred.

A man's hands caressed her face from the bridge of the nose. The nails were hard and oval. Beneath, Loulou relaxed. With Martin she was safe. Safe as in his apartment on the Fontanka where it was so immaculately bare and the waterway mist hung in the air like voile. Fastidious hands, the hands of a masseur. Unstained, scented with the Latakia from his cigarettes.

"Forgive me," he said. The voice had deepened and was younger, slightly derisive. "Forgive me," it repeated. "I should have prevented him."

She shook herself free and the man sat back on his haunches like a small child surprised by the misbehaviour of one of its toys. His hair was paler than Martin's gold, the beard rougher, rather unkempt. The resemblance of the face was that of the voice: youthful, unstrained. Martin in ensign's uniform that day she had met him on the steps of the Mariinsky brilliantly cockaded in Life Guard colours. But this face was flawed from some care inappropriate to youth: two lines above the nose jutted deep into the forehead. Martin never worried. This man was not Martin but Martin as he might have become.

Little by little she unpanicked, fighting down images of dream: dark faces across tables; Polly fraught by her huntsman with desire and alarm; stair-treads slippy with blood; the twist of Kostya's smile beneath leaves; the face of Schmidt, bending over her, sputum winking on his teeth.

The man rose and stood up straight. By this decisive movement of his long limbs she identified him.

The man who maketh the rain to come, the walker in the sun, as the peasants said, he whose touch made the canes fruit. Damn and blast, it would *have* to be him when she was in such a tizz. Valerian. Of course. He came through walls like Jesus. Very well. Just as long as she didn't have to put her hand in his side.

She sat up with a jerk and pushed at his topboots, rejecting his aid. There was a blodge of crusting blood on the cuff of her blouse. Damn, you never could get it off. Her nose and mouth swelled out like tree-fungus, her chin was numb. A copper bowl containing water appeared on a stool beside her, a sponge floating on top. A towel lay on the floor. He had thought of everything. It was the last bloody straw.

Only one question to ask: "What happened?"

He put a hand against the small of her back as if she were a flopping infant, and reached for the sponge. "You fell down the marble staircase."

Loulou protested to herself, feebly. Liar. This was men's work. She knew that. The smell of them was on her. She dabbed at the wet places of her body.

"I'm bleeding."

The blood was less shocking than the pathos of the fear trembling in her voice.

His left hand tremored at her thigh. He is lying and because he lies he is afraid of me. Behind those grave eyes the truth crumps in his brain to trigger spasm. In his body he fears me. Look at him, my husband's murderer, the sheet-gold coronal of his hair bobbing from a guilty tic. Liar. Killer. She might have smiled if her lips obeyed her.

"And how did I fall – on this staircase?"

He gave a wisp of a sigh and dropped the sponge back into the ewer. "Certain persons discovered who you really were. A woman has been here, telling strange tales of you." Out of sight he was rubbing his hands together as if to restore the circulation but in fact, she guessed, trying to subdue their involuntary flexions.

By "certain persons" he meant Schmidt. Now Schmidt was vile but

Schmidt was sane. And by this time he would have told his master all about her; perhaps, even, showed Valerian the photograph.

"How can those be reasons?" she asked without hope of a sensible reply but feeling a little better since things began to add up.

He shrugged, seeming overcome by detachment. "Sufficient unto them."

Oh Lord, thought Loulou. Easy, girl. If he convulses you'll be the one handing out water and soap.

". . . The envious . . . the greedy . . ." It sounded like that but his head was bowed and she was unconcerned to listen hard. Another moment and he'd be ranting like a fair pedlar.

"I find you really quite astonishing," she said over the slur in her voice. "Have you no sense of responsibility at all? Why blame them if they only think that they do your bidding? Besides," she added in her best high-born tone, "it's undignified for a man to ask a woman to forgive him."

His eyes rested on the squalid serf screen. "I have puffed them up with pride and stolen away their humility and love." In this mood he would preach for hours, lathering himself up for murder or fits.

"Oh, do shut up, do!" Loulou opened her mouth as loud as she dared. "Churchiness is all right if you're not aching all over like me. Be a dear and get off your horse."

His voice shifted to the straightforwardly audible in a rapid change of mood which she was coming to recognise as part of his nature. "Forgive me . . ."

"No, no, *no!*" she shouted. "*Tu vas de nouveau enfourcher ton dada.* I loathe men who beg forgiveness."

"*Mademoiselle,*" he said. "*Voulez-vous prendre un verre avec moi?*"

The accent was grating, but the sound of the foreign language seemed to please him and Loulou congratulated herself.

"Madame, actually," she said. "And I wouldn't mind one bit."

Valerian draped the towel over his arm and scurried about like a waiter. Soon they were side by side on the floor, glasses in hand. The wine was thin and over-aged, rising in the throat almost to choke her. He noticed nothing, owlishly quaffing the burgundy in sacramental swigs. "Nice," he said at length. "Nice."

His indiscriminateness piqued her. Her men had known about wine. "Maid's water. Ugh, how can you?" she exclaimed and emptied her glass into the basin.

Still, she was glad to remember that Kostya was dead, even though midnight feasting with his murderer could be seen as rather tasteless.

But thank God there was an end to some fine tastes now that Kostya was out of the way.

Was she obliged to hate him, this boy, for what he had done, or be grateful for what he had ended? On balance she could allow herself some sentiment towards this odd creature. Not because he was gloriously handsome – looks had hardly ever appealed to her, except in women – but because he radiated a vulgar energy by which she had never been previously touched.

Shrewdly she eyed him. Innocent, like Yasha, he wouldn't know what to do. No sense of advantage. A virgin? A silly word for a man. It happens to them automatically, doesn't it, at night? At a certain age, she had been told, it comes out of them in dreams. How unlucky girls were to be incapable of anticipating their own pleasure.

What would it be like with a murderer? A common criminal, to enjoy herself with him before he was hanged? Fulfil his last wish. You needed a villain for that, one steeped, dyed in the wool; a monster shuddering into you. With this boy it would be dishwater wine. "Nice." Just nice.

His hand was beginning to quiver again. How clean he would be in all his secret places. How would he like my mouthing them? She found herself more aware of the pain in her body and breathing fast. A boy. Whatever he did to her it would be over too quickly. No technique as ravisher or murderer – or, for that matter, drinker. One of the bottles was empty and he was pulling out the cork of the other. Time to take a hand.

"Tell me," she said. "You head a mob of killers, you yourself have killed. What is it like to have the power of life and death?"

He drained his glass with a look of genuine grief. "I saved you," he said.

"*Saved* me?" screeched Loulou. "They're in the palm of your hand, that rabble downstairs. They jump when you cough. Now," she said. "Now you're telling me that you're as trapped by them as I was. No, they do what you say, and believe what you tell them. What other choice do they have?"

Valerian's cheeks were flushed but instead of inflaming him the wine made him sheepish. "Well," he began haltingly. "It's difficult. They become restless."

Loulou got to her feet, hobbled round the screen and listened at the door. Somewhere, below, women squealed and there was hearty male laughter. "Restless?" she repeated. "That's them just stretching their legs, is it?" The screen fell over as she hit out with her arm and tipped over the basin of water. Valerian scrambled out of the way. Loulou pursued him, kicking over glasses and bottles. "Come along, young man," she gasped. "They're frolicking down there – it's a stew, *a nasty little dirty communard stew* and they're all diving into one another because *somebody's* said that Jesus has decided piggishness is – what was your word? – Nice! Now open that door this minute and go downstairs and stop them!"

Valerian trod on the sponge and almost slipped. He shook his head, as much from drink as in refusal. "I can't," he said. It came out like a grumble. "I can't."

Loulou warmed to her own sobriety. "For my safety?" she sneered. "Or yours?"

"It's not that." Valerian was running his hands over his blouse.

"Then you won't go? You won't free me? You'll let them broil in the swill down there and keep me locked up a prisoner because, because, because you're not Jesus but *Judas*!"

"You're not a prisoner," he said bemusedly. "You aren't locked in. Well, you are, but that's just temporary."

"*Temporary?*" she screamed. "How long is temporary?"

Valerian plucked distractedly at his hair. "I don't know exactly . . ."

"Till God whispers in your ear?"

He giggled. Loulou stood before him, her nose at his collarbone, and raved: "Well? Well? Well?"

"Till I've found the key," he said stupidly. "I seem to have mislaid . . ."

She stared at him disbelieving, and then burst into tears.

"Well, look at it this way," he said, after righting the screen and mopping the floor with his long Cossack *burka*. "You may be locked in, but they're locked out."

He seemed to think this funny and laughed a great deal, and then became drowsy.

"Oh God," sobbed Loulou. "This vile, vile house. I'm a child locked up in a cupboard for something I never did. Wretch! I thought you promised me protection."

He edged forward sleepily and tried to take her hand. Rushing from him she began to hammer at the door.

"So I did," said Valerian remembering. "And you shall have it."

She had given up banging and shouting and fallen to a heap on the floor. These outbursts were exhausting and she had taken nothing since the wedding feast when she had been too distraught to eat properly. The sip of wine had not affected her. She lay down like a sleeping dog behind its master's door.

Hours after, it seemed, she heard a thud. Looking round she noticed that five fresh candles had been placed in the candelabrum. Another thud, an exasperated curse, then a wave of crashes. Valerian was nowhere to be seen. Perhaps his congregation had been annoyed by her screams and found another way in.

"Mademoiselle! Mademoiselle!" His voice was entreating, compliant. "Come to me!"

High above, in the glow from two candles stuck in bottles, Valerian was clawing great folios from one of the presses, throwing them over his shoulder, two or three at a time, his drowsiness quite shaken off.

"Come up," he said again, flapping with his hands at the dust. Inquisitive, Loulou mounted the silvered ladder to the walkway. At the top, by Valerian's end of the catwalk stood a recessed arch cloaked by drapery. Behind the curtain was a door opening into a little room. The walls and ceiling were lined with cedarwood, open-grained and soft to the touch. Fibres glistened in the candlelight. A solitary window sat high under the eaves. Loulou liked the feel of the cedar. The door fitted snugly and another smaller door faced it across the floor timbers. Loulou sniffed. Every surface was impregnated with the faint sweetish tang of plum-pudding.

"What is it?" asked Loulou, meaning the smell.

"Your quarters, your safe-hole," said Valerian, smiling pleasantly. "For you and the little man."

"But there's . . . nothing," said Loulou aghast. The smell was making her giddy.

"Oh, there's decency thought of," he said. "The other room can be his – smaller, but then he doesn't take up so much space. A wash-place, too. I shall see that you have all you may need in the way of furniture and provisions." He looked down on the books scattered below. "And since you read tongues there should be no shortage of entertainment."

Loulou shut her eyes. A home from home. Except for the smell this would be little different from the five unbearable months she had spent on her own estate. "You're quite mad," she said almost reverentially. "This is a box."

Valerian gently brushed her split lips with his thumb, and made as if to kiss them. When Loulou opened her eyes, he stopped. "How did you guess?" he said, still gentle, still smiling. "This is where Laskorin kept his cigars, mountains of them, in boxes from floor to ceiling."

This is my destiny, thought Loulou, to be wrapped up like a leaf and crammed into a long box stamped *Romeo y Julieta*. "It's a coffin," she stammered.

"No, no," said Valerian earnestly. "A humidor. Aren't you going to thank me? It's the only dry room in the house."

Oh God, how tired I am. It was true. At that point she could almost have longed for Kostya. The mute stones of this house seemed more evil. A line from a magazine story came into her mouth: "I know I shall die of this confinement."

She sensed as soon as she had spoken that this was too much for Valerian. Complexity of any kind was foreign to his undivided nature. By now she knew that he had some affection for her – there could be no other reason for his devising this method of safe-keeping – but in accordance with some queer childishness he refused to consider the illogicality of what he was doing for her and for his people. Poor creature, she thought. He must feel the onset of reason as one senses a headache. And it was reason, she had long ago deduced, which drove him to violence. It would be prudent to appear to be gratified. He was a murderous simpleton offering her sweets.

His manner confirmed her judgement. In reply he seemed to shrug off something of his tenderness and reverted to public brusqueness. "If you die you shall die of my people who love me and will devour you."

She wanted to ask "Why?" But she knew the answer already. Had known it all her life, from the earliest time of memory. It was simple: if she had been one of them – a nurse, a maid, a groom, let alone one of the peasants who shuffled up to bless her in her baby-carriage – she would have killed her then, this Natalya Igoryevna, *knyazhna*, princess, landed-lady, who sucked on an ivory comforter and kicked up her creamy buckskin shoes. Stabbed her in her round, proprietorialising eyes.

Her kind had never flinched. Why should theirs?

He broke into her thoughts: "Have no fears. I shall bid Gerasim and Fedya to stand guard over you. They have my trust and dare not disobey."

Fedya was unknown to her. If he was as decrepit as Gerasim both she and Yasha would be lost in no time. "But he is so old," she said. "Incapable . . ."

"Of bearing arms? Exactly so."

There it was, the soldier's response, *yest, tochno tak*. Talking with him, isolated, feeling near, she had forgotten his past. He seemed then to be hardly a man, but as a boy he had been recruited and seen and committed acts no boy should know of. There was a hard shadow within him that darkened his gaze when he spoke. He had been commanded and could himself command. You felt the authority like spirits in the belly.

Glad to divert him from concentrating on her fate, she pressed him: "You once said that we would soon be cut off here?"

"Exactly so," he repeated in this new, efficient manner. "That is why Gerasim and the boy are all that can be allotted you. Unhardened men need time to become adept under fire but our time is almost upon us and will be brief."

He was sombre, like a woman contemplating her first labour. Loulou could only envisage Galicia where troops swarmed on snow-clad peaks, immeasurably distant.

"But has it come to us, the war?" How could she know? For months it had been locked away from her and she imagined the war as going on eternally, as much a fact of nature as the phases of the moon.

Valerian gestured towards the blind walls. "It has come."

She was seized by images of ransack. It was worse, the rapine of a foreign army. They looted totally, including you. "My God," she moaned. "Germans with inventories and timetables. We will be picked clean."

Valerian smiled down on her. "Not only Prussians and Austrians, Mademoiselle, but Russians, too. Our own."

She could neither believe nor disbelieve him. One part of her knew what bastards *they* were: the inhabitants of this house could be the average levy from any rural conscription point. But that couldn't be the whole picture. She had lived her young life cheek to cheek with valorous men. Martin. Kostya. They wouldn't have fled. "You mean to say they have turned on – *us*?" she whispered, then realised her mistake.

Valerian strode out onto the catwalk and gripped the hand-rail. Loulou felt her knees shake as the familiar mystical speech which she had prided herself on making him abandon, flowered out of him, swashing the dark with its bloom. "I have been in the fire and was unconsumed. At the cutting-place my arm has cleaved the bones of men. I have seen battle. I have seen death."

Loulou was at her wits' end. It was both terrifying to hear him like this, and infuriating that he ceased to give precise information. She went out and stroked his rigid fingers. "There," she soothed. "There. You have suffered." The language was catching. She had nearly added "mightily".

"Of suffering there shall be an end," went on Valerian less stridently. It was for Loulou to deduce what kind of end he had in mind. "The last battle is upon us," he said, quieter and quieter under her caress, "when the earth shall touch sun and they shall burn upwards like flax."

Loulou had already counted herself and her kind as one constituent of "they". Who else? "The great ones?" she prompted, feeling as craven as Schmidt.

"And the least," he said almost normally.

She felt puzzled. "Yes?"

"That trench scum who preached atheistical paradise to the unlettered and envious, weakening their wills, unmanning them for the labour of Christ."

Oh dear, thought Loulou. No wonder the battle is going to be his last. Red, white and blue. Tsar and anti-tsar, with the Lord's children squashed in between. They were finished.

She almost wished she could take him seriously. The principal feeling which he aroused in her, and which she could not entirely control, was sheer pleasure in his adolescence, a gawkiness deriving from his unmanageable beauty. Yet no boy in her own young life had ever engendered such effect. Martin had always been fully sprung to manhood and Kostya, however perverse, had only adult inclinations. To contemplate Valerian was to watch a work of art, fearful of its destruction, but more afraid that it may come to life and harm her.

He told her of his plans. From the late summer there had been skirmishes which had not been difficult to counter. Deserters, unorganised and demoralised, had drifted back from the line and were marauding for food within fifty miles of the estate. At first there had been no heart to them and they fled at the first brush with Schmidt's patrols. Like the gentry before them they seemed leaderless. But as the autumn came on Valerian had sensed a new cohesion: they had allegiance, they were disciplined, they were led. Two weeks ago, three of his best horsemen, foraging for grain in the sacked villages thirty miles to the west, had been captured and taken to a unit commander who gave out rum and tea and conversed with them for half a day before releasing them. His two squadrons of cavalry were sweeping the river country for those landed proprietors who had barricaded their great houses and were set against yielding to anyone: the new order, unbelievers, the landless or the renegades. To help them was the commander's mission. As for Valerian's men, they were an irrelevance: not troublesome but useful since they had done part of the work for him. But their views rendered him helpless with laughter. They were not alone, he roared. This whole region was riddled with communities just as crackbrained. "My old NCO asked why, in that case, he was letting them go? 'To cut one another's throats first,' he said. 'To make it easier for us to pick off the survivors. But you're all doomed. I shall bury you! With full military honours and a church service, of course!' And he sent them off each with a Mass-bell and a saddle-pack of vodka and bread."

"Will they come?" asked Loulou.

"They will come. Either they or their enemies will come."

She looked round her. "And what will they do?"

He laughed very loudly. "Level us to stubble and then plough us in."

"Can you do nothing?"

"Delay," he said. "Long enough to make a pretty fight. The railway line has been destroyed, the house is fortified. They will have to come overland or down river and we have prepared for that."

She looked him over wonderingly. He could be a bare-back rider in a circus, a wrestler, a gladiatorial something-or-other with that great back stretching out the white stuff of his shirt. What a splendid combatant he will make, this murderer of my husband, fresh-linened and cap-à-pie for the last throw. He will rise to it truly, while the rest of us scrabble for life. The yokels' Hamlet but one with real poison on his repertory sword.

The wonder was that not every woman had long ago given herself to him.

23

When she complained of the closeness of the room he went down the metal stairs, unbolted the shutters and opened the casements. A cool breeze flowed in, extinguishing the candles. Outside it was still not dark.

He stood at the side of the middle window and ran his fingers through his hair like a woman at her dressing-table. The fading light tinged the curls on the nape of his neck. Loulou scented autumn on the wind.

"Winter soon," he observed banally as she followed him down the steps. "At least you will be warm in your rooms. I shall see to it you are made comfortable."

Loulou was becoming accustomed to his habit of switching from the lofty to the conversational. It was like chatting to a hall porter who suddenly dropped your bags to go into a trance. She moved away from him to an armchair embroidered with game birds and sank back, drinking in the air. By now her body felt one total ache. He knew how to stand, to gesture and to move, this young man. He was used to audiences *en masse*. It was part of his trade to look good, but she wished he would stop performing for her.

"Cigarette?" he asked, cool as an interloper at a ball, handing her a silver box engraved with old Laskorin's initials.

Loulou waved it away. "It may surprise you to know," she said, trying to assert some dignity in the face of a man whom she recognised now as her captor and gaoler, "I have simply given up caring about my comfort. Or even my survival. One can only endure apathetically, hopelessly, without feeling. And you expect me to be grateful for furniture! I am snared like a wild thing but at least the squirrel does not have to thank the schoolboy for its wheel. At first I thought you mad, but now I know you are at the mercy of enthusiasms. You keep me out of whim. And if you choose not to turn and put me to death, others will when you are gone. Why not you, why not now?"

"You please me," said Valerian, luminously pale against the thickening twilight.

On the side table a posy of wild flowers had been jammed into a

206

vase several sizes too small. She felt embarrassment adding to her anger and resignation. In some queer fashion he was paying court to her. Ashamed, she remembered how far she had allowed herself to be wooed. But there was no danger, he was too unpolished. With her, as with the flowers, he was all execution but lacked finish. Still, better to leave him less room to manoeuvre.

After a pointed silence she asked: "Where are we?" The curiosity was real: she could remember nothing like these strange rooms on her previous visits to the Laskorins.

"Smoking rooms . . . private . . . the old fellow's . . ." said Valerian between puffs on a fat monogrammed cigarette. "Natalya Igoryevna, if I thought there was a chance . . ."

"Of course, of course, strictly out of bounds to us as children. Heaven knows why. When I was a little girl I loved the smell of tobacco. Not cigarettes, though, except for Turkish. That's quite a pleasant one you are smoking, but not Turkish, Egyptian I would say. There's a distinct tang . . ." She gabbled on for some minutes, her mind racing. These were *his* rooms. He had installed himself.

Valerian continued to smoke, waiting for her realisation to become explicit.

"Such a lot of book cupboards," rambled Loulou. "What on earth did he need them for? Not a reader, old Daddy Laskorin. Quite a different sort of man. I hardly ever saw him without a gun in his hand. He used to come to table smelling of gunpowder . . ."

She had got up and was flitting about the room, talking the whole time. "See," she said lifting a copy of the *Illustrated London News*, many years out of date, from an ornate magazine rack. "This is the sort of thing he used to doze over. Advertisements for corsets, arsenical hand-whiteners and bust-enlarging creams."

The real world of beautifully-engraved hangings and bomb plots where the rabid Valerian would be shot on sight so as not to flutter the ladies who creamed their breasts nightly until they jutted out like porcelain wash-stands. Did it work?

"Yes, a horrid man. We kept out of his way. He looked at one as if . . ."

"Appropriate," said Valerian.

"What is?"

"Not reading. I don't much, either."

"Well, not everyone has . . ."

"The same tastes? I imagine not, but his have come to fit me like slippers. A little snip here and there, and I made myself very snug."

"You mean that these are your apartments?" said Loulou, round-eyed.

"Exactly so." He threw the gold tip of his cigarette out of the window.

Loulou could not face him when he turned. "Oh no, no, no. Polly may be a certain kind of person, but I am different, quite different." Her voice trailed away.

His stride was very long. She remembered how tall he was. "I know nothing of the love of women," he said, close to her.

Oh God, he was so appallingly naïve she could have smiled. Instead she contrived hysterics. "Keep away, you brute. Don't come any nearer. You may think you're strong but I shall fight, believe me. I'm wiry, I shall fight, scratch and fight, in my sleep and wake up still fighting."

Without any need she backed away. Valerian knelt down and held out his arms imploringly. "I wish to heaven you were not so afraid."

Loulou closed her eyes and tried to remember where the empty wine bottles were. With one of those in each hand she might feel safer.

"I am only a man as other men."

Exactly so, thought Loulou. As other men. If she found the bottles she must remember to hit him hard but not too hard. Men were so unpredictable under attack. But kneeling there like some infatuated girl he looked foolishly harmless. A slap might do it if he activated himself.

"I don't know how you can do this," she exclaimed, trying to make out that she was on the point of breakdown. "I once loved someone and now that someone is dead." This mixture of truth and downright lies struck her as an excellent ploy. The mad were always sentimental. "And it was you who killed him, murdered him. Dear God in heaven, what right do you think that gives you over me?"

Had Valerian been in a condition to work this out, he would have seen that it gave him the only indisputable right, the right of conquest, but instead he succumbed to delicacy.

"Grieve not for your husband," he said. "He was a man of honour, a gallant man, an officer who died nobly." The sheer unreasonableness of this panegyric stunned Loulou. Valerian saw no more connection between his own actions and Kostya's death than the wheels of a train which had run over someone's head. "But that has finished. The world has revolved to a different place now. We are all free."

"Free?" cried Loulou. "This is what you call free – locking me up, terrifying me?"

Valerian shook off the exclamation with impatience. "Free! Free! Now there is no marriage or giving in marriage."

"What then, if you please, was that business down there with Polly and her awful man?"

"That was no marriage."

"Ha!" cried Loulou. "I am glad we agree."

"No, no," said Valerian. "Not marriage but *union*."

The word gave her a sharp pang of the illicit, as when Martin had once jokingly called her his "mistress". Valerian, pleading an old-fashioned suit, nevertheless, appeared to be following the church rule that no woman could re-marry while her first husband lived. In that sense Loulou was legitimately open to offers. If union was farce, marriage, as far as she was concerned, had been travesty. And the best couplings fitted exactly so, front to front, in the field, under the bush. The rest was priest's jabber.

This wildwood insanity could grow upon one. Why should I go on telling lies about Kostya?

"That sort of thing is no longer important to me. Nowadays, the only quality I prize is honesty. Truth alone is what matters."

She enjoyed working up such elevated sentiments in order to bewilder him, but his eyes were guileless, and he went on gazing at her in that dumbstruck way which made her want to laugh again. The tucks of his spotless shirt were loose over his belt. His knees must be hurting him. Did they pound his washing at the brook, his Mashas and Praskovyas?

"Hear me," he urged. "I know nothing of women. Not in any way at all."

Oh dear. Union. There was no diverting him. In her world a man's confession of virginity would have made him a laughing-stock to his fellows and an object of fear to women. "You have been in the Army, miles from home. You cannot expect me to believe that."

"Truth must declare itself," he said. "You yourself have spoken so."

"That is the truthfulness of a child," said Loulou. "You are a man and men need to hide certain truths in order to be men."

It was Valerian's turn to be scornful. "I was never a child, Natalya Igoryevna. The only childishness in me is fear of the dark. When I was a small boy they sent me to an anchorite near Kazan. His cell was lightless except at dawn and I became very afraid. He dismissed me saying: 'Be not apart, love the world in God.'"

"He was wrong, your holy man," said Loulou. "Or you were mistaken. It should have been: 'Love God in the world.'" She reached out a hand to his shoulder. "Here, come to me."

Under the shirt he was cold.

"I cannot love," he said, "for I am without a sense of sin. The war

came to me. I was fearless and untouched, then I killed someone —
not directly, but they told me the thing which had happened was
terrible, that many had been killed and that I was responsible. My
colonel disowned me."

"What happened?"

"I remember nothing."

"I mean afterwards."

"Ah, they withdrew me from the line and kept me under close
confinement for five months. When the enemy cut off the salient we
were overrun and Belyakov found me half-dead on the Kiev highway.
I had been wandering for days. He got me back. That was the time
everyone was going home."

He was becoming agitated and she doubted her ability to soothe
him again. Whatever lurked within she had no desire to unspring.
Her own nightmares were hell enough.

"At night I think I shall die without knowing what it is to ask
forgiveness." He looked straight at her. "Once I paid a girl to sit
beside me while I slept."

Cheaper than candles, apparently, thought Loulou. But did she
shed light?

"I remember some things," he said. Loulou's fears were returning.
And her spite.

"A storm lantern," she said. "You need a patent storm lantern."

"If anything is to light me through the night, Natalya Igoryevna, I
wish it to be you," he murmured.

For an instant she was tempted to put her lips to his forehead, just
once; throw her arms round his neck; let him sweep her off to a hard
bed in the bare little room upstairs, and strip her to the skin. Yesterday
she would have swooned like a nun. But there was Kostya. Not that
his memory was worth a fig: if this semi-literate bombardier with the
superb eyes had run him through in front of her she would have cast
herself at his feet in gratitude. The boy was right for once. That was
no sin, that act.

Her mouth wettened. The openings of her body crept aside recep-
tively like the corollas of flowers. *No, no.* Under Kostya's careful
fingers she had split at every seam, like a ripe boll of cotton. She longed
to be impenetrable: dry, ribbed, harsh, tearing, closed, anything to
shut him out. But no, no, this violable body allows no respite.

And she had lain there, skinned as an eel in the litter of mucilage
while he bestrode her mouth. Seeing him there, all drawn up and
opening the line of her lips and smiling into her frenzied eyes, she
knew that the shame lay not in what he did but in what she wanted
him to do; and his knowing that in spite of herself she wanted this:

the unbound mouth of the fish snapping at the hook. And what the girl did below, the impress of her blunt peasant thumbs palpable on the flesh of the open-legged Natalya Igoryevna Alekseyeva, her mistress and owner, parting an ingress for her tongue, heading up from there to mark the spot and dart in and out, snake-headed. What the girl did was unendurable. Under that, Natalya Igoryevna begged with her eyes to swallow him whole. He watched as she watched, and they fed one another, voraciously. What the girl did was perfection, but for her it was like whitewashing a fence. One last feathery dab and she fell back, stilling the sway of her breasts as Kostya began: "Slut, slut, slut, slut," faster and faster, whipping Loulou to cream. "No, no, no, no." Her legs jerking she flailed at the knotted muscles of his back. "Bastard, bastard, don't, don't make me." But he did. He always could. And when it happened he could have murdered her. When it happened she drank him like the poison cup of a condemned queen. She would have clung on, mollusc-mouthed to the dregs. No, no. They flayed you and pegged you out. Clove you to the breastbone. Not again, never again. This downy boy would demand no less. Not now, perhaps, but soon. Upon her he would instruct himself. Never again to be touched by complex desire: to want to give and not want to be taken, almost dying from the pleasures of contradiction.

She pictured herself in the peasant girl's eyes, a girl who upped her skirts and rubbed herself languorously while Kostya used her mistress. Used her advantageously, amused himself by marking her silk and satin skin. Loulou remembered. The girl stood, always stood, to watch. Stumpy, spread legs, hair like black wire half-way up her belly, she strummed away four-fingered on a pin-head in the slush of red coral, while Kostya set to on her lady, her *grafinya*, who knelt upraised on a chair, the bland patina of her haunches criss-crossed from his bath-house switch. The humiliation came in tingling freshets. The girl squirmed out in acclamation at every sucking in of her lady's breath. He stopped, inspected her, drew his hand between and, satisfied that she was flooding, snapped his fingers at the peasant girl.

Only a long time afterwards did Loulou realise that something was wrong. Then she knew nothing. Conception was a mystery she broached with Mama. Mama was tight-lipped. She knew Kostya's preferences, had submitted too (must have done) but never gave out a word. To withhold a child was well within Kostya's nature. Loulou had brought him no money, only her father's estate: what did she expect?

Not that.

Valerian suddenly took her hand in his. He was talking: "See, I have had them bring flowers for you, and wine. Bridal tributes. Today . . ."

"Stop it!" screamed Loulou, snatching her hand away and covering her ears. "You are all foul, despicable, revolting. Preaching death and torment to those heathen animals out there because it panders to your conceit, and now, just because you have a woman at your mercy, you moon like a lovesick half-wit and twitter about wine, love and the miracle of life. Brute, bastard, brute!"

He blinked, as if a tree branch had flicked back into his eyes.

Loulou was possessed. "Oh, our dear sweet Polly succumbed, didn't she? Our tripping little maid pure as a starched pinafore, she shook herself down to swagger with jailbirds and rebel criminal scum and undergo that death's-head charade you call a 'union'. But he'll take it out on her skin, won't he? Humble her, won't he? Won't he enjoy it, won't he glory in it? Wouldn't you? Honest bullying isn't enough! You have to degrade and despise. Have a woman on the end of *you* like a monkey on a stick!"

Her coarseness disturbed him and he stared along the line of his boots. "But I have never looked on a woman impurely, without respect . . ."

"Hypocrite," she panted. "Tormentor. You lie in your teeth. You have shut me up here for your pleasure. I would prefer that mob to tear me to pieces. Skirt-snuffer, woman-taker, hateful, morbid charlatan!"

He turned away from her helplessly and got up, stretching his long legs. "I have promised you safety and you shall be safe."

"We shall see, O protector mine. But I tell you this – if ever you dare appear inside those rooms again, I shall kill myself in front of you. Understand? And don't think that you are so hallowed that death cannot strike you because I swear, my mealy-mouthed agitator, that when I go I shall take you with me to whatever wimbly-wambly Paradise your doddering Jesus has reserved for us." She paused. He said nothing. "I intend to drink your wine, wash you off me, sleep for two days. I am indifferent to your confessions, your vanity, flattery and love-lies-a-bleeding lust. I have not one jot of interest in you except that one day, I hope, you will be brought to justice and bricked up in a tower until they escort you to the scaffold."

She raced up the steps to the gallery and into the room that was to be Yasha's. Slamming both doors she waited for him to disobey but when he did not come she fell deeply asleep where she sat.

24

Two days into the New Year Frossya fell ill. For a while no one knew. After a week the news percolated to Schmidt. There was no priest to be had, no doctor, and, in any case, the woman was too crazy and old to benefit from the ministry of either. Nothing, he decided, could be done.

The old nurse was abandoned to the care of Asya, the deaf-mute girl who made preparations for the death in the only way she knew. The straw mattress from the little room behind the kitchen was dragged outside to be burnt in case of infection. Asya then made a bed on the floor out of wolf-skin rugs from old Laskorin's dressing-room, heaping them over the clothes she had found scattered around the pillaged bedrooms. Before his death Asya's father had maintained the hothouse boilers and she knew all the places where he had hidden away stores of fuel to re-sell to his village cronies. So now the stove burned day and night, and when Frossya heaved herself down to die on Mimi Laskorina's *amazonka* riding-habit, she had no need of covering but lay vividly exposed in her red and yellow calicoes.

Twice a day the girl fed her, crouching down between the dying woman and the stove to spoon up milk from a bowl. On the third day Frossya turned away. Asya sat back cross-legged under her skirt and began to wait.

The only visitors were curious children, mostly boys. Death was much talked of in the house but they had rarely seen it, and waited with Asya, in an abashed and giggly row, enjoying the warmth and their anticipation of an event which they sensed ought to be private but which was too good to miss. They remembered the old *babushka*, everyone did, but in dying she made herself strange. Their parents knew her death would be a portent for Valerian's new order, and they stayed away, ill at ease, waiting for the short winter's day to end.

Two floors above, in a corner of the wrecked library screened off by makeshift walls run up from the biggest books, sat Valerian's three most senior lieutenants. The room was unlit. In the glow from a brazier set high on a grey-stone slab, they had talked away the pale winter afternoon, drinking tea and smoking black tobacco. Now there was a pause while Titus, an amiable Siberian, topped up their glasses from a can kept simmering at the edge of the fire. As the men hunched forward from the shade of deep armchairs, their faces glimmered briefly before once again being overwhelmed by the dark. Between sips at the China tea Solomon and Osip drew hard on their pipes, respectfully waiting for Titus to resume his theme.

"No, this isn't the first time I've heard that kind of talk. It took my father in, and his father, and here I am, just like them, listening to the same story with hardly a rag to my back."

Titus's family had emigrated to the north when the railway came. They had not prospered.

"My old man thought it'd be different from what happened to his old man. But it wasn't – he still had to pay."

"Land is precious," said Osip in his sing-song whine. "In those days someone always had to pay."

Titus stabbed at the ash with the toe of his fine-grain leather boot. "Do you think I didn't tell him that? But he took no more notice than his father did when he told him the same. It won't *belong* to you, Dad, not as long as there's breath in your body."

Solomon scrolled up the paper cover of a Tauschnitz novel and bent to the fire. The embers clicked and slipped as the flames leapt into the bowl of his pipe.

"Land has to be taken," said Osip.

Titus swilled round the dregs of his tea before emptying his glass on the fire. Osip had the mind of a brigand: take what you could grab today, even if you swung for it tomorrow. "That's just where you go ahead of yourself, Osip Nikolayevich. There's more than one way of getting what you want."

"Your father, then, what did he get?"

"Land," said Titus. "Tsar offered him land, like a Tsar before him offered his dad land, land and freedom."

The fire was dying and there was no more wood. Osip crouched nearer to the brazier, poked Solomon's knee with the stem of his pipe and gave him a cheery wink. "At a price," he said. "You said yourself, at a price."

Titus took up the point. "Very well. At a price. But make no mistake about it, my father had eight sons and two girls and he was lucky, the government land was good. He could have paid the price, paid it off in twenty years. But being the son of his father, he left work to the women and taught his sons to do the same. In six seasons his land was desert from not manuring, cropping at the wrong time, letting the boys quarrel and drink. You know our people here, Osip Nik. Let up for a minute and they'd see the wheat rot in the earth."

Titus had become uncharacteristically excited. Although Osip enjoyed provoking him, he knew the Siberian's temper and left off. Besides, what he had said about the community was true, and applied to him also, as Titus well knew. Osip had charge of the eastern reaches of the estate, mostly rich arable, flat to the plough, but he was a soldier not a farmer, got drunk with the men and slept with their women. Facts which, so far, had not come to the ear of Valerian.

In the silence that followed Solomon brooded. He had learned from his Scriptures that Osip was sinful in his doings with women but did not hold that against him. Osip was a stranger who had lived a wild man's life among the Orenburg Cossacks where guns were esteemed more than horses and the worth of women was counted in sheep. Such values were foreign to Solomon who loved land above all. But if he ever took a wife he knew he would love her more than his gun. None of this could be said directly. They would take him down for his presumption. So, as usual, he stroked the great shaven dome of his skull and felt stupid listening to his own voice. "I hear you're a separate breed of man – Titus" – no one ever gave the Siberian his patronymic – "in those parts."

Titus kicked at the brazier. "Separate? What's that supposed to mean?"

Solomon shrugged. Inevitably his questions caused people to fly off the handle but he only spoke because you couldn't act dumb all the time.

"Different, he means," said Osip. "Different from him, that's all he's saying. There's scope for differences between brothers."

"Difference is another matter," said the Siberian. "I'm no steppe-Kirghiz in a fox-trimmed hat because my father tried his luck in Streitinsk. I'm a Russian born and bred and lived Russian, even out there, among the heathens."

"Tell him about the theatre, the one at Tomsk," said Osip.

Titus exploded. "The Opera House, the Club House, what use had I for them when every Sunday in Blagovastchensk I could brush against the finest ladies you ever saw outside Petrograd? Imagine that, Solomon, you old stick-in-the-mud. What woman of that sort has ever stumbled down your street?"

Solomon knocked out his pipe on the claw-foot brazier. "I've heard tales. Rife immorality."

"You know why that is?" shouted Titus. "It's because where there's immorality, there's money, and where there's money there's a chance to be had. That's the difference we're talking about."

Osip's whine became silkier. "A miner, see, he was a miner. Gold towns . . ."

Solomon pondered, unable to decide whether by persuading him from his beliefs they wanted to include him in some secret, or only to decry his stupidity in holding to them, as they knew all along he would. "Property is the devil," he said at last. "That way, praise be, we've ordered life differently in this community."

Osip turned away with a laugh at such simplicity. "Saying prayers and conceiving bastards to while away the time until Judgement Day. I gave you back your word, Solomon, this is *separation* here, in this stinking tabernacle. How long will it last without a strong man to rule and defend it?" Before Solomon could say the name, Osip opened up: "*Valerian?* Don't tell me. Like you, I've heard more faith stuck on that mad boy than grease on a priest's frock."

"Faith is enough," said Solomon.

Titus stood up. "Leave him, Osip Nik. Drop by drop is the way to let it sink in." He stretched his thick short arms. "This fire's a miserable sight, we need more kindling. Keep your seats warm, lads, I'm for a stroll to get the blood up."

The others sat in silence listening to the rattle of the wind on the loose shutters and the stamp of Titus's footfalls as he paced the boards from one end of the library to the other. When, after half a dozen turns, the Siberian gave no sign of rejoining his companions, Osip half-rose and dragged his chair nearer to Solomon's. "They say three of Vissarion's men made a run for it," he whispered.

Solomon did not catch the words. "What's that?"

Osip removed his pipe from his mouth and articulated slowly: "*Viss-ar-ion's.*"

Vissarion was quartermaster to the southern district, a man with a reputation for ferocious discipline. Solomon was not surprised and said so, but very quietly, following the Cossack's lead.

Osip nodded. "Queer thing, though – their horses found their way back, day after, fresh as flowers and unsaddled, without a rein or stirrup between them, and not a mark of hard riding."

"Ambush?" said Solomon.

"Use your head, man, Vissarion patrols thirty miles south every second day. There's not a bird in that country as sings without him hearing it."

"What then?"

"Even queerer. Next morning they turned up themselves not a mile beyond the river."

"Change of heart?"

"Change of everything," said Osip, tapping his forehead with the pipe-bowl. "Naked as the day they were born, lashed to each other with their own horse harness."

Solomon gave a sharp intake of breath. "Thirty below, night-times . . . all month. How was they?"

"An image of perfect peace," said Osip with a grin.

"The Lord help them who did it when Vissarion catches them, that's all I can say."

"Then you can say on, brother, because Vissarion knows who."

Solomon gave thanks to justice before asking for names.

"Let a man ask his master," said Osip solemnly. Before the Georgian could digest the significance of this reply, Titus had approached unnoticed.

"Well, preacher, we need more coals to heap on our fire. Tell me now, Solomon – what will burn best in this den of iniquity – Bible books?"

Although Solomon was a peaceable man he believed in force. This belief was both instinctual and reasoned. He was sure from the exhilaration he had felt in battle that the quickness of hand and eye which always came to him then were in fulfilment of the purposes of God. At the same time he knew that keeping check on the temptations of force was part of a spiritual exercise which ought never to be lost sight of, however brutal the mêlée. This had made him a good soldier, had taken him up through the non-commissioned ranks of the Army, and now made him a commander excellent in the handling of troops. In this respect, Valerian's behaviour in summarily executing three fugitives deeply aggrieved him; the more so since he had taken Valerian as his superior in every moral and secular matter. There was a time when he would have died for Valerian and his visions, but now he realised that if Osip's allegation proved to be true the time was already past.

While Solomon reflected Titus raked ash from the brazier with a gunrod before piling on several thick volumes of the writings of St Chrysostom. The wedges of old rag-paper caught very slowly until Titus poked them about, the whites of his eyes turning yellow in the rising flame.

Still Solomon kept silent. He was already aware of discontent in the community: the farming was in a poor way, most of the autumn preparations not having been done. Sickness had spread among the herds, owing to neglectful husbandry and lack of fodder; there was idleness and quarrelling amongst the people. But a far-seeing man should be ready for such setbacks. In the beginning it was bound to be slow: folk clung to old notions of the here and now, unable to see beyond themselves to their children and their children's children.

Valerian had known this all along. What had caused him suddenly to become so brutally impatient?

"How do you come to know these things with such certainty?" he asked without looking at his fellow-lieutenants but staring at the leaves curling on their bed of fire.

"Because I lay awake nights, not praying but exercising my brains. What, I ask myself, should we make of Hermann?"

He well knew that Solomon detested the Volga German for his slyness and the fact that these days he scarcely ever left Valerian's side. Titus pressed home this advantage. "A fine writer, our Hermann. If any man lingers too long, or answers too quick or speaks out of turn in his master's company, Hermann takes a note of his name."

"For what reason?" asked the Georgian.

Titus cleared his throat and spat into the fire. "Well asked, brother. I too asked of him myself and back came the answer, spick and span: 'For future reference.'"

Rancour crept into Solomon's voice. "A busy man, a ferreting man who counts heads, does no work but blames others for his neglect."

"Don't you see, brother?" urged Osip. "That *is* his work."

Titus had always marked Schmidt down for a shrewd and unscrupulous man. In his view the German had a long-term plan, details of which were still obscure but involving some kind of usurpation of power within the community. According to Titus, Schmidt had long ago defected in spirit from the common enterprise, was biding his time, and his total control over the stock of munitions in the cellars was alarming. Osip and Titus had even approached Valerian with the suggestion of rostering Schmidt's duty-picket alternately with trusted men from their own ranks in order to secure access to the stores. When Valerian refused out of hand they had begun to realise the extent of Schmidt's power.

Solomon shuddered and stretched out his hands to the fire. The way ahead seemed clear. "Then kill him."

"And the boy?" said Osip. "The boy is the one who matters; can he be allowed to survive?"

Solomon might have accommodated Valerian's emergent cruelty, talked him away from Schmidt, appealed to his innate sense of right, but a sudden recollection combined with Valerian's new strangeness to precipitate his doubts into a decisive act of will.

"Did I hear right?" he said slowly. "That he has taken a woman who is not one among us?"

Eagerly Osip grasped his chance. "You heard right, brother."

Solomon gave a shout. "Then you know what to do – kill her, and after her, kill him."

An uncertain voice called from the shadows beyond the circle of light: "I say – is there anyone there?"

With one shove Titus broke through the wall of books, wielding the gunrod above his head.

"Gosh," said Polly. "Don't be so cross. It's only me."

She had been blundering round the house for nearly an hour following the smallest of Frossya's boys. Ten minutes before he had disappeared completely so she had made for the only light she could see.

Confronted by the diminutive figure in skirts Titus felt foolish but Osip was threatening. "How long have you been spying back there, eh, missie?"

Polly did not cringe but stepped over the books into the firelight, the lenses of her spectacles silvery in the flames. "I don't know what you mean, *molodoy chelovek*. I am rather short-sighted, you know. I was told someone was looking for me. I should not like to think that I had kept anyone important waiting."

Beneath the girlish pique was a whimpery note. She had crossed the library soundlessly in stockinged feet and caught Solomon's last words: "her", then "him". That could mean any couple including herself and Belyakov. But she stared back, apparently guileless. "Gosh," she said again. "How many times have I told you people that I hardly understand a word you say?" This was barefaced cheek, but taken with her flattery – all three were gratified to be called important – it had the desired effect.

Titus thickened his dialect. "Just a pert kid," he said to Osip, returning to his seat. "Let her prattle." He patted the arm of his chair. Polly sat down at his elbow and adjusted the trim of her spectacles. The fire had dimmed once more.

"Child," said Solomon, "who were you wanting?"

First her, then him. Perhaps it meant Vlady, then Loulou. Or Valerian and Frossya. Asya even. One had to be loyal and keep mum. Solomon's growly voice sounded kind so Polly did what she did when in trouble at school. The girls called it gabbing. "I don't exactly recall. Everyone seems to want somebody in this house. It must be the weather; it makes one so nervous this time of year. Then this little boy appeared from nowhere and said I was needed. Isn't it awful to be shut in for week after week? Of course, men like you can brave the elements, but imagine what it's like to be stuck with one's husband the livelong day."

When Titus wound a curl of her hair round his little finger Polly did not flinch. "Why, I know you from your wedding day, *sudarinya*," said Solomon. "Isn't Vladimir Ivanovich your man?"

"Vlady, yes," faltered Polly. "But I don't know where he is. In fact, I haven't seen him for ages. He keeps talking about making a long trip, perhaps he's gone already. It's awful the way he never tells me anything."

But there was no need for her to go on. Whatever she had heard she would tell her husband, of course, each man knew that; but Belyakov was an outcast. Not a soul would believe a word he said. He had failed to escape, withdrawn from Valerian into marriage with this absurd female and was useless, even at that (so it was said). A spent man, no threat.

Titus relaxed, passing into gold-field slang which was impenetrable to Polly but caused Osip to glance over her figure and laugh good-naturedly. "If you can't do a woman's work in bed," he said eventually in more comprehensible speech, "perhaps you'd be useful at the side of one. There's a *baba* dying in this house."

Osip clasped his hands behind his neck and stared at Polly's ankles. "Go ward off her evil spirits and do us all some good."

Solomon escorted her to the door and gave out directions to Frossya's kitchen quarters.

"You mean I can go?"

He smiled. "Of course you can, my dear. What did you think we were going to do – murder you?"

"*Nyanya*, at *last*," breathed Polly.

The little boy she had lost poked his head round the stovepipe and gave a titter. Frossya lay on the floor swathed in rags. A sweet smell of lamp-oil, bodies and shavings suffused the low room, reminding Polly of funerals when she knelt to take the old woman's hand.

"*Nyanya, dushyenka*, is something the matter?"

The boy let out a snigger, Frossya coughed and stared at the ceiling. Polly instantly rebuked him, then, inwardly, herself. Sick people made one so nervous, one invariably said or did the wrong thing.

Acutely embarrassed at her theatrical pose in front of the boy and the sinister Asya huddled in a corner beyond the range of the oil lamp, Polly followed the old woman's gaze to the cratered plaster. From that angle of vision the room appeared much larger, barer and quite horribly sordid.

"Apollonya Dmitryevna . . ."

Polly did not want to come too close but the old woman clamped on her hand, drawing her nearer. The rags were not rags at all but old-fashioned clothes and recognisably Laskorin property.

"My little one . . ."

The reversible scarlet lining of the cloak must once have been really nice.

As she whispered, the tracery of lines around Frossya's lips throbbed like a fish's mouth. "*Barishnya*, kiss me."

In the old context Polly was used not to kissing but to being kissed; and certainly not on the face. But she overcame her distaste and placed her cheek cautiously against Frossya's. Although used to the old dear's ways, one never knew. She might bite like a snake.

"*Nyanya, nyanya*, can I get you anything?"

Polly's manner was sympathetic, but the appropriate words would not come. Across the silver-fox collar of the opera cloak she caught sight of the boy relaying her phraseology to Asya in hugely-distorted mimicry.

Suddenly Frossya asserted herself: "This is my last night on earth. A good thing, too. It's time I was taken."

"Now come along, Granny, that's no way to talk, I simply won't hear of it. Why, there's years ahead of you." Her own encouragement made Polly efficient. She felt at the stuff of the cloak beneath the old woman before turning up the folds to cover her shoulders. "Be a good Christian and stop moping, *nyanya*, it's quite morbid to hear you."

It might have been more bearable if she had loved the old woman, just a little, as people did in story books, but that sort of thing hardly ever featured in real life. Frossya had always been in league with Mummy to make Polly's childhood a torment of unrequited affection. They had claimed to care for her by being strict and remote. No woman had ever offered Polly the unmerited affection she craved.

Still, since Frossya had gone on mending her clothes, almost to the end, it seemed right to Polly to offer some service in return.

"Now, *nyanya*, I am a busy woman but I want to be useful – tell me, dear, is there anything or anyone I can bring you?" But Frossya had relapsed into stupor. Eventually Polly rose. "Here you, boy." The lad gawped at the snap in her voice. "Did *nyanya* say anything before I came?"

"Asked for you, *barishnya*."

"Obviously, or I wouldn't be here. Anything else?"

The boy squirmed. "Said she was bad . . ."

Polly stamped her stockinged foot on the flagged floor. From her corner Asya threw a chock of firewood at the boy's shins. Having thus attracted his attention, she made scissors of her fingers and wild snipping passes at her hair.

The boy's eyes swivelled from one woman to the other. "You're not her," he said.

Polly squealed. "Who am I then?"

Asya's motions became frantic.

"Not her," repeated the boy. "*Nyanya* wanted the short-haired one."

"The one who lives with the dwarf?" mouthed Polly to the deaf girl. Asya stopped waving and retreated into her shawl. The boy began to weep. Polly rocked on her heels, infected by similar self-pity. Dash it all, Loulou at every turn, cutting her out. It was perfectly beastly to be made a fool of like this. At the door she turned. "Stop snivelling, boy, and tell me your name."

He sobbed it out: "Vitya."

"Well, Vitya, you can tell *nyanya* that I shall see what I can do. As for you, my lad, I shall report you to Mr Schmidt for insolence." She had no intention of doing any such thing, or even knew if it were possible, but on reaching the first floor, Polly was gratified to hear the boy still howling uncontrollably at the bottom of the stairs.

Solomon had left soon after Polly to mount up his night patrol. Osip and Titus congratulated themselves on their afternoon's work. Now it was evens – three against three. Three against two on the military side for Schmidt, they reckoned, was no soldier and Makar was getting on, not the man he used to be. As for Vissarion he was all cut and slash, audacious but unbrainy. Time was on their side, too, food was running short. They would make their move in the late spring after the rains. Until then only Solomon had to be kept on the leash. Like all obtuse men he could be impulsive but they would manage him.

After arriving at this settlement of the future Titus and Osip left off constraint, worked up a blaze with more books, and drank Finnish schnapps in honourable memory of campaigns endured, long-dead commanders-in-chief and each and every woman they had ever had.

25

"When Brett Mackenzie hit Laredo it was summer and the trail was cold. That dawn the Spokane twins had ridden out to the high Sierra, leaving three men dead on Main Street and a saloon full of scare-eyed cowpokes chewing their lips . . ."

"Not *again*," groaned Loulou, burrowing under her sables. "Not *him*, the Territory's most incompetent lawman, always riding in just after the cut-throats have fled into the sunrise. I mean, didn't he find it a tiny bit galling?"

Scowling, Yasha stamped on the bare boards and blew on his fingers. "Find what?"

"Oh," snapped Loulou, "I don't know – being caked with dust, having a tongue as black and dry as bootleather, his horses continually dropping dead from exhaustion, but never wreaking vengeance on the malefactors because he's missed them by a whisker. It's tedious."

"It's the story," said Yasha. "I mean, there wouldn't be a story would there, not much of one, not if he chimed in with them right first time and gunned them down straight off?"

"It's always the same with your stories," said Loulou. "It's the way you tell them – like a piece of string. Tell them like beads."

She was right: his stories were all middles. It was now January and so far he hadn't finished one. Brett Mackenzie was still downing his whisky at the poker table while Lucy Austin, kidnapped from the homestead, was still lashed to a wagon wheel at the Spokane hideout, becalmed at the pre-rape stage. They were all pictures to Yasha which he loved to contemplate again and again. Telling them aloud made him blush and although he stammered through the scenes to entertain Loulou, she had become increasingly tetchy at the absence of suspense.

He glared at the hazelnut shells and rinds of dried apricots scattered on the floor, then shut his eyes, trying to form up the runs of printed letters on the first page of *Adventures of Brett Mackenzie, Ranger.* "Give us a minute, think I've got it: 'As the chestnut mare arched back her neck, a cloud of red dust fell from her mane . . .'" Blinking rapidly and taking deep breaths he was ecstatic; the image was sublime.

Loulou itched under the fur, beads of sweat swelling into globules and gliding along the inside of her thighs. She shifted, opening her legs to the cooler air flowing under the skirts of the sable, but the moisture still prickled. She thought of lice. They flee to seams, burrowing there like quicksilver droplets. "That girl, that Lucy Austin you seem to be so fond of, the one who simpers over cats, did she keep her stockings on?"

Yasha was furious. "Why do you do that kind of thing all the time? Always the same with you, wanting something else, never satisfied. That's disgusting, you know that, disgusting."

"Well, it's what I want to know, it's what anyone wants to know – the details in a story. They're the bits that count."

She didn't need to know; that side of it she could well imagine. What she wanted was that he should tell her what she knew so that she could luxuriate in the sound and shapes of it. Big Matt Spokane unpeeling Lucy's stockings from the tops, two hands at a time, scuffling hands, grimy hands, and his leering, wall-eyed twin scratching himself and spitting into the sand. A story that got somewhere. Loulou began to enjoy herself. "Well, they hadn't taken her on to wash pots or do the cooking, had they? They must have had a reason for tying her up."

Reasons did not concern Yasha as long as an event took place spectacularly. Before and after were irrelevancies. Not that he couldn't remember what happened next, he knew every word in the book: Lucy was rescued by a gold prospector who married her and set up as a boarding-house keeper in Butte, Montana. That was no good, not for Natalya Igoryevna. She wanted literature. Lies. He flung out his arms. "Of course they did – they staked her out for the Apaches."

Loulou wriggled and poked her head out from the deep collar of the coat. "Yashichka," she began softly. "Tell me about that, tell me about Red Indians. What did they do to white women? Is it true that they, you know, one at a time, that the whole band does . . . ?"

This was too much for Yasha. "Your place is down there," he screamed, stabbing his thumbs at the floor, "with all that tribe of alley-cat messers that can't think of nothing else. And I'm stuck here, day after day, trying to give you some decent entertainment."

She sighed and clutched the sables closer. The fur smelt of mothballs and dog-biscuits. The wind softened the clatter of feet and reduced Yasha's voice to a growl. The room darkened. A single window, imperfectly shuttered, allowed in a finger of bluish light. Against the outside walls snow whirled and built up, rubbing and pressing at the house like a great cat. Soon the very timbers would be set creaking.

"Sage-brush stood as high as his saddle pommel by the time Mackenzie's bloodhorse reached the edge of the salt flats. Brett screwed up his eyes at the blazing sun . . ." Yasha had reverted to the actuality of the book and his voice droned along in a chant while Loulou shut her eyes and tried to summon up pictures of deserts.

Dying on a salt bed under the sun was a delicious prospect. It might not even be disfiguring. Perhaps the dry heat preserved you when all the fluids burnt off and you went crackly and liver-red like the strips of bison Buffalo Bill delivered to the rail-gangers. Yasha, high-voiced now above the wind, told of wild animals, buffalo hunters and murder while she waggled her toes. In the cold you die part by part, literally: fingers, toes, nose, ears. Tips and ends, the outermost reaches first. You don't notice, not at once, and if it overtakes the whole of you, little by little, there's no pain. And she remembered her terror when Papa had flung himself at her after she'd ridden too long in the snow; he knew the signs and slapped until the blood came trickling back to her frostbitten cheeks, stinging and blazing. It's only coming back that hurts. To freeze whole like a carcase, full of vodka in a drift, that was to preserve one's integrity. And dignity – the cold was undistorting. You succumbed all of a piece. She'd read of an entire village discovered with everyone dead but intact, solid frozen. In the grainy-brown magazine print they were unmolested by death, caught in an attitude from life: elders stooped over a card game, children stock-still in a heap, thin fingers locked in the spiked fur of puppies; babies rigid at the breast. Wholly at their ease.

A violent thud came from below followed by a roar from Belyakov. Polly set up a nagging squeal from the stairwell. They'd fallen out again. Abruptly the voices ceased and Loulou heard something heavy scraping along the floor.

"It's that white-faced loon stuck in the chimney again," she groaned hopelessly. "He'll never get to the top. He's arthritic. He'll never manage to repair Valerian's stove. We might as well make up our minds to it. Quite shortly we shall all simply freeze to death."

"Not if milady Belyakova is still rough-riding her husband, grafinya." Yasha smirked deferentially, abandoning his frontier tale for their next favourite pastime of mimicking Polly and, in particular, the huntsman, whom he had come to detest for his spineless fury at his new wife's nagging.

In November Polly and the huntsman had moved up to the great house for the winter and the bride was applying her feminine touch to their new quarters: a room by the entrance to Valerian's apartments, in which Laskorin's body-servant had once squatted amidst a

plethora of bandboxes and split trunks. Now there was an enormous
bed, a carpet, two cane chairs and a commode.

Belyakov had been forbidden to drink. Male sweat brought on
Polly's asthma so she made him wash night and morning. No baby
came. His arrogance had evaporated. "Too good for him," giggled
the peasant women smoothing the bedsheets. "Never lets him get up
to her mark."

Inside, the cold made Yasha want to sleep. Yet if he disciplined
himself, wrapped up and hopped across the icy boards for a peek,
the world which met his gaze had precisely the same effect. Nothing
moved, nothing changed outside in the white waste which had once
been a park. The monotony was numbing. After a blizzard the light
would play tricks, tilting up the entire landscape as in a child's
painting, so that distant trees, even village huts wide to the outskirts
of the estate, appeared to be growing from the snow which lay thick
on the topmost sash of the outer window.

For almost a month it had snowed every day. After the first couple
of falls Yasha had still ventured into open country. But soon, even
the moderate snowdrifts in the Laskorin rose garden had built high
enough to drown him. No longer could he lie up in his den by the
railway anticipating that moment when the law-enforcement officers
detrained to bring his confinement to an end with the blast of an
official whistle. He had the names all ready, nevertheless. That
Schmidt, he was top of the list.

"They'll be here," Loulou kept on saying. "The whole country
cannot be like this. With the first thaw they'll be here."

That was all very well – she had some freedom of movement – but
he was trapped by his size. Day by day fresh layers of snow made
him more dependent on the goodwill of Valerian. Yasha began to
feel sorry for himself. On the ornate brass bedstead he burrowed
nearer to Loulou in unselfconscious intimacy. Over the past few
weeks closeness had become part of the nature of their lives: refugees
clung together waiting for the sky to lift along their route. Until
the end came they would remain outsiders confronting that wider
intimacy which flourished all around them in Valerian's strange
community.

Yasha had tried to make the room more feminine but when Loulou
seemed not to notice he had given up, and his posies of autumn wild
flowers whispered drily in the draught which seeped through the
shutter slats. Behind her head the yellow wall was sheeted in lace-frost.
One of Mimi Laskorina's improvements had been to rip out many
of the old blue-and-white tiled stoves and replace them with a new

patent heating system. In spite of her money the layout of pipes and boilers had never worked properly, leaving the upper storeys practically freezing while thawing out the walls of the kitchen and cellars. Mimi had pretended not to mind. Now when the temperature on the second floor was almost intolerable Loulou cursed her and longed for firewood, and flames you could see.

For two days she had been tormented by the sound of hammering. In the apartment below her little room Schmidt, Georgii Ivanov and an ancient carpenter were fitting up a stove for Valerian. The irony was the boy did not seem to feel the cold, and while Loulou and Yasha shivered he would go riding without a topcoat or stalk through the house at night half-naked, breath smoking in the pitiless frost.

"Am I never to have any peace?"

Yasha chafed up the blood to her numbed fingers. Touch was more comforting than answers and performing small services like this eased his sense of all-round inadequacy.

"We *shall* die, I swear it, if we don't . . ."

Escape? Not that again. Hours they'd wasted, scheming, planning. He'd drawn up timetables, maps, but she kept changing her mind out of terror of Schmidt who was always slinking about, going through their stuff, then framing tall stories about how the countess must be doing it with the dwarf since they shared the same sleeping quarters. Tickled the women no end that sort of sauce, but they hated her for it too because she was supposed to be Valerian's and for all that they resented her they could have strung her up for besmirching his honour with a lapdog dwarf deformity.

Trying to escape had started the trouble in the first place. Why did he bring her back? the women asked Schmidt who only winked and returned the question. But Matryona and her daughter were jealous as well as shrewd and Yasha wondered if Schmidt sensed the widening gap between master and community which eventually Valerian might not be able to bridge. Perhaps Schmidt was in some deep play against Valerian himself. You'd never know with that sort of sharper until he trounced your best hand.

At the clop of heels on the iron walkway outside Loulou withdrew her fingers from Yasha's clasp.

"It's all right," he said. "Don't get flustered. We ought to know that step by now; Belyakova's come calling, God help us all."

Polly burst in without knocking. "I heard that, you unmannerly pig. Loulou, why do you tolerate him?"

Polly was never called by her new name without the implication that, somehow, she was not a properly married woman. Yasha was especially fond of this slur which now, as ever, brought on temper and tears in rapid succession. Yet this time Loulou, who normally abetted him in his ragging, was struck by the violence of her cousin's loss of control, and frowned Yasha down. The girl was in a bad way, shaking and sobbing. It must be the man.

"Really, Apollonya Dmitryevna, you were a silly child to have given yourself to that wretched person. I am very sorry for you, but you wouldn't listen at the time." She could not say that she had no intention of letting the girl upset her own delicate balance of mind. "And now I can do nothing."

Polly stopped back the tears at her underlids with a polished flick of her little fingers and replaced her spectacles. "Oh gosh, you don't imagine I'm in this state about *him*, do you! Or *him*," she added with a baleful giggle at Yasha. "When one's life throws up so many fateful encounters as mine, husbands rank very low indeed."

"Well, that's Vladimir Ivanovich fixed." Yasha made himself comfortable under the furs, his interest awakening. "Now she's going to get something off her chest."

Loulou patted a place for Polly by her side. "Sit down, my dear, and tell me all about it."

The note of patronage annoyed the girl who stood her ground at some distance from the bed, but dropped her voice. "I surprised three of your Valerian's generals in our library . . ."

"Lieutenants," said Yasha.

"What?"

"Not generals. Lieutenants. Generals are higher."

"For mercy's sake," whispered Polly, "call them how you like, does it matter when you heard what I heard?"

For a week or two Yasha had had an itch that something was cooking. "So go and tell your husband," he said, hoping she would too and stop frightening Natalya Igoryevna who was a bag of nerves already.

"I did," wailed the girl. "I begged him to listen, but he had his nose in a stove and he's always so grumpy these days that he wouldn't believe a word I say."

Yasha took charge. "Which ones?"

Polly was nonplussed. "Which ones?"

"Which *generals* said what you heard?"

"Oh, they were all so big, so *ferocious* . . ."

"A bald one?"

"How did you guess?" Polly slipped her hands through the front of the bed-rail. "A horribly bald one. I think he'd done it on purpose, you know, his face was quite young."

"What did he say?"

"Well, he said – not to me, you understand, I wasn't supposed to be there, of course – but I heard him, it must have been him, the voice went with the head . . ."

"Yes," said Yasha.

"Yes. Well. The bald one said: 'First her, then him.'"

Loulou shivered inside the sables. "Is that all?"

Yasha pinched the flesh over Polly's collarbone.

"Nothing else?"

"That hurts, you hateful little toad."

Yasha nipped deeper. "Nothing?"

Polly hopped away. "Yes, there was, if you must know. 'Kill them,' he said. 'Kill them both.'"

Yasha uncurled himself and sprang off the bed. Putting out a restraining arm to Loulou, he began to stalk the girl around the sparse furniture. "And what did he mean, the shaven one, our Solomon? What do you think he meant? What came straight into that sweetbread brain of yours, Madame Belyakova, when that bald voice spoke?"

"I don't know." Polly glared back over the marble wash-stand. "One understands so few people here. It's a matter of interpretation."

"I can translate easy." With a jiggle of his neck he signified Loulou. "You thought it meant *her*." He thrust out his hand and dislodged Loulou's pile of hairbrushes. "Her and me."

"What if I did? It's disgusting this so-called partnership of yours, disgusting to people with moral standards. I admire them for speaking out . . ."

"So do I," hissed Yasha. "Speak plain and make known, that's the style. Well, I did, the day before yesterday, to that straw-backed husband of yours. A heart-to-heart, man to man."

Polly clutched at the porcelain ewer, furious with anticipation of what he might have heard from Belyakov; from the house-women, from any passer-by who could have peeped in at the window of the little house by the river. Yasha scavenged around for one more big lie with which to scare off this trouble-making, interloping little cat who never passed up a chance of making Natalya Igoryevna's life that shade more unendurable. "I told him – another breath of scandal about your domestic arrangements and the brotherhood'll chop the pair of you."

Polly went white with relief at his absence of detail.

"So that's likely what he meant, the bald general, him and her – *you* and *him*, missie – see?"

* * *

There was something else. Frossya was dying and insisted on a last meeting with the countess.

"You must go, Loulou. Perhaps she knows who is going to be murdered."

Paradoxically, while Loulou hated her imprisonment, she also resented leaving her room to be stared at and pointed out wherever she went. Valerian had ordered that she was not to walk unattended and before the snow her only exercise had been an occasional stroll on the terrace with Gerasim. Even there her captivity was too public and she felt like simpering Lucy, staked out for the Apaches.

Besides, she did not trust Polly. "It might be a trap. Tell me what to do, Yasha, for heaven's sake. You are free but I can go nowhere alone."

Yasha had no doubt in his mind that Solomon's death sentence was intended for her, but who was the man? Him? Valerian? That might be the old woman's secret. "Up you get," he said. "We can't afford to miss a trick. Tell you what: I'll get the kids along for company so you won't be lonely."

Valerian's apartments were always full of children who, eager for diversion, would come to Yasha's call, swarming up the steps, surging into Loulou's cosy room to listen to her stories, play noisy games and pull her red curls. When Yasha whistled down from the catwalk Belyakov was tinkering with the stove which still refused to draw, surrounded by a milling throng of a dozen or so little boys and girls. At Becky's answering screech-owl hoot he raised himself heavily, the look on his face sullen and hard. His woman had been gossiping. He knew it.

"Won't catch without shavings," Becky called. "I keep telling him, but he won't listen."

"You're wanted," said Yasha. Before he could stop them a good half of the children had shot past him into the room.

Becky stood aside, hand in hand with a tiny barefoot boy whose cropped head barely came up to her waist. "I can't," said the girl. "I know those games – the littlest one gets squashed and I'm in my best." The small boy burst into tears when she let go his hand to show off her black shiny frock and blue velvet hat trimmed with osprey feathers. The child stopped crying and buried his head in the front of her skirts. "Shy, you see," she said. "Tell him a story."

Yasha came down the stairs and lifted the boy onto his knee. "When Brett Mackenzie hit Laredo," he began, "it was high summer and the trail was cold . . ."

26

Valerian straightened his back, gave a sigh and began to make the sign of the cross. Frossya watched, unconvinced. "In the name of the Father . . ." Valerian's long arm stretched like an insect limb from head to heart. "The Son . . ." Under its death sweat, the old woman's face twitched with expectant glee. Valerian stopped, coughed, thought for a moment, and made a truncated movement with his right hand, then his left, as if trying to distinguish the right direction. "And the Holy Ghost," he said abruptly, dotting both forearms with his fingertips.

Frossya jerked herself up and would have rolled off the mattress had he not caught her fall. "There," she gasped ungratefully. "There's the heathenism of him revealed – in ordeal. Satan stands at the sinner's side bothering him out of his godly wits."

The deaf-mute girl wiped the old woman's face with her unwashed hair and glared at Valerian who was smiling peaceably. His equanimity seemed to give rise to another spasm of coughing in Frossya. Afterwards she jabbed the girl savagely with her elbow and dragged herself up on the pillow. "Dying I may be," she said, still out of breath. "But it's no holy fool's chrism I want for my last anointment. Asya, Asya!" The girl had turned away and was making low, unimpassioned grunts to the wall. "Be silent. Have you no seemliness?"

Valerian stretched out and touched Asya's wrist. The girl looked from under her hair and grinned at him flirtatiously, showing her bad teeth. The noise ceased but the action enraged Frossya.

"There you are, you see," she spluttered, looking from one to the other as if appealing to both to arbitrate on a shameful deed not performed by either. "Unregenerate! Interfering with cripples as Satan wrestles for my immortal soul! When the Lord was to snatch me all I ever prayed for was to be taken from the bosom of gentlefolk which nurtured me fifty years. Now my God hath forsaken me to the mercies of Pagan Jack, this Ivanushka, brazen-faced fornicator, cut-throat, plumed in stolen feathers of his masters. Hoy, take heed lest thy blasphemies so hang on the air that the quality eavesdrops and flays them out of your back."

She began to weep.

Schmidt stood behind the chair of his prophet, braying a lengthy prayer no word of which anyone present could understand. From time to time, he shook a silk-knobbed rosary in Frossya's direction and broke into an impromptu beseechment which was the only intelligible part of his drone: "Rejoice! Rejoice! For the Lord taketh His own." Tears ran down his cheeks and a smile played at his lips. The contradiction was only apparent: the onset of death induced in him a sheer havoc of feeling which in itself was the revelation of God's mysterious workings.

"Damnation." Loulou swore, tripping over the bottom step, overcome by vertigo after being raced down the kitchen stairs by the crush behind her. Yasha and the children burst in before she had time to get to her feet, tumbling about her like the lamefoot retinue of a village queen-for-a-day. With a flourish Schmidt warded them off to a respectful distance from the bed where Asya sat at Frossya's weeping head, playing cat's cradle and kissing the tips of her fingers. When the children snuggled up to him Valerian did not move.

"This is she," wept Frossya, without opening her eyes. "Let her stand forth and be known to all as she is known to me."

Not realising who she could mean but swiftly taking in the solemnity of the occasion, everyone kept silent.

Discomfited by the quiet, Schmidt was about to resume his chant when Gerasim came clattering down the stairs. Under his arm was the large wheel from a child's perambulator. Nodding amicably to the visitors he began to pass pencil-thin candles from the top pocket of his carpenter's apron into his mouth before fixing them, two at a time, all round the rim of the wheel. Becky tilted back her hat and hugged the small boy, marvelling at the old man's adeptness. So did they all, like children before a magician. When the wheel was fully studded Gerasim lit a first candle, then kindled the remainder by blowing around the circle, inclining the fire so that each taper blazed up from the touch of flame. Wax pooled on the deal table and shadows scattered up the walls.

Twisting a funnel shape from a paper ikon of the Christ-child, Gerasim inserted the pointed end into the wheel hub. The mezzotints of flesh and halo glared pastily amid the steel spokes.

Loulou watched Valerian. His brow and cheekbones were ivory in the chiaroscuro, his eyes hidden.

Gerasim doubled at the waist in obeisance to the ikon, crossed himself elaborately and, with a simpleton's grin, shuffled backwards, turning only at the stairway to clatter up as noisily as he had come down.

"Oh God," groaned Loulou aloud.

Once upon a time this sort of thing was male obligation. Many a foul hut had been sweetened by her father's presence at the last eventide of drunken coachmen, pensioned-off wood-fellers and other down-and-out retainers. While they consumed their final hours in weepy argy-bargy about the solace to be found in the next world, his daughter went without her good-night kiss. Later, when she was older, she too had been included in the rigmarole and couldn't stand any of it: the crackbrained philosophy, the smell; above all, the touch of the near-dead.

The old woman's hands were shrivelling to the yellow of crystallised orange. Besides, she really did stink. "Now," said Loulou, brisk as a shop-girl. "How can I be of service to you?"

Schmidt sniggered complacently at the fall from *bon ton*. "Lord love us," he said, loud enough for Frossya to hear. "You'd think she was selling lace drawers on the Nevsky. 'How can I be of service . . . ?'"

"Soft, Hermann," said Valerian, rising. "You will go no further. At these times all speak as they must." He loomed over the mattress at the German, his eyes opaque, his voice a thick rustle. Becky peered at him, anticipating a seizure, but instead Valerian seemed to recover himself and gave Schmidt's ear a genial clip. "Out, out, my Teuton bullock, let the heifer suckle her dam."

"And the demented one, *sudarinya*," panted Frossya, rolling up the whites of her eyes on Loulou. "With his roustabout beastliness of tongue. Christ spurn his soul."

"But, Master," protested the German, "now she stands at the threshold of the great secret, there is fear on her lips, she has truths to tell, I know it."

Frossya began to gurgle: "Bedbug . . . Prussian bloatbag, gravefly . . . scum of the night hag . . . eater of grass . . . scale-hoof swine of the pit . . . uncleave thyself from the clean . . ."

Valerian caressed the broad base of Schmidt's neck and led him away, murmuring in his ear: "Truth is the salt of the prince's dish, my dearest friend. How can there be relish in it for thee?"

Having interpreted the signal in Valerian's alteration of mood, Yasha and the children scrambled to their feet and were already half-way up the stairs.

Loulou sat heavily on the end of the mattress and wrinkled up her nose at Asya. It was true. They all smelt. A phrase from one of Yasha's favourite stories came to her: "Alone at last," she said, and gave a giggle.

Frossya looked up, one bony eyebrow raised in faint reproof, and

Loulou's mirth evaporated. She fidgeted with the edge of the make-shift coverlid, nervous that the moment had come. Frossya was not afraid of death but the bravado with which she had heaped abuse on the men melted away once she and Natalya Igoryevna were alone.

The countess bent forward and kissed the old woman's hand. "Well, Granny?"

There was no reply.

Loulou was dying to smoke. Instead, for no reason, except that circumstances seemed to dictate it, she asked for Frossya's blessing. Although her tone was low and sympathetic the old woman still did not respond. Wandered away, poor old dear, thoughts concentrating upon last things. Finding half a Turkish cigarette uncrushed at the bottom of her pocket, Loulou put the unlit stub between her lips. If she could somehow attract Asya's attention the girl could light her a spill from the stove.

But before she could make a sign Frossya was scrabbling herself into a sitting position once more, trance broken, her eyes darting round the room. "Names, secrets," she muttered in a queer abrupt way. "I'm weary of the burden, *sudarinya*. Stay with me. Where is he hiding, that long-haired blasphemer?" Loulou assured her that Valerian had gone but the old woman refused to be comforted. "Don't dare say his name aloud, will you, dearie, in case the word comes between us."

All the time Asya was looking away, at the floor, at the fringes of her shawl, anywhere rather than at the two women mouthing in silent dialogue. Loulou put the cigarette back in her pocket. "He's not a devil, *nyanya*, he can't hear you now."

"Worse than a devil," whispered Frossya. "A restless perverted soul."

At this Asya smiled and nodded, raising her pale brown eyes to Loulou. The moment after, she had withdrawn again, pleating the folds of the shawl round her head with astute fingers. Loulou shivered. Being mute must be like being buried alive in a transparent coffin.

"I said he would bring trouble. I gave them due warning." Frossya was rambling again, stroking Loulou's hand, gripping the wrist and pinching the soft skin on the underside at the end of each word. "When the boy came they should have taken him to their hearts."

The history of little drowned Petya was a poignant commonplace amongst the Laskorin servants. Loulou felt a stab of pain. Hunger and the tension of not being able to smoke while trying to follow the old woman's disjointed testimony had brought up bile to the base of her throat. When she leaned forward to ease the pain her face came closer to Frossya's lips and the shallow exhalations beat frailly on her cheek.

"Rejected him, turned upon him, bundled them both away like beggars . . ." The old woman must be approaching her crisis. Nothing made sense.

"Hush, dear, these are old, old stories."

Frossya's hand squeezed surprisingly hard. "Will you learn nothing, girl?"

Loulou cried out in pain and exasperation: "What is it you think I don't know, *nyanya?*"

"The girl from France. The governess." For a while Frossya lay back, apparently satisfied with the extent of her revelation, without having persuaded Loulou that anything of importance had been disclosed. No doubt some poor wretched girl had actually suffered at the hands of the Laskorins. Governesses were invariably victims in such families.

"Nothing matters now, *nyanya*, and it's not decent, you know, telling other people's secrets."

The priggish remark seemed to bring the old woman into last full spate, her memory intact from twenty years back.

Evidently the paradox of very good looks and a remarkable piety in young Mademoiselle Brancas from Limoges had caused quite a stir. Frossya suspected the church-going: the girl was in a foreign country without a word of the language yet she spent as much time on her soul as a soldier's widow.

Millie, who was only twelve at the time, fell for her, bag and baggage, and the house was soon full of Bible tracts which Frossya burned whenever she found one. It was unhealthy, all that missionary talk in stuffy rooms. Eventually Mimi put a stop to it, but not before her husband had been drawn in by her complaints. Of course, he didn't take Mademoiselle's side; she had no right to do priest's work with his daughters. But he was calmer with her than expected, questioned her beliefs coolly, gentleman-like, and the Brancas had replied just as cool back as she always did, sure of herself in looking so lovely with that heart-shaped face peeping out from her fairy-princess, story-book hair.

Loulou began to take an interest. "So the *barinya* sent her packing?"

She had to wait while Frossya gave in to a fit of coughing which would have sounded more like a prurient chuckle had not the old woman been so ill. Her contempt for Mimi had outlasted her mistress. "No, miss. She *encouraged* him." The cough erupted again. When Frossya snuffled back to comprehensible speech her voice was fainter and raw from hoarseness.

One winter afternoon Millie had come upon them in her father's study, the floor strewn with discarded pamphlets and Mademoiselle's stockinette camisole. It had been going on for months. He locked himself away, but no amount of begging and pleading could save her, nor the child she had in her. Madame herself took a steel comb and scraped back that wonderful hair before they whipped her.

Loulou spoke to herself: "*Damn Mimi, damn them, damn you all to hell.*"

And at that moment she was glad that Petya had drowned and that Millie with her tweeds and worse than sentimental affinities for women had gone to the bad before her death hand in hand with her horrible mother.

Whether or not there was any more to Frossya's story, Loulou no longer cared. She could finish it herself: Mademoiselle Brancas had given birth to a son; the son had survived and returned to the house of his father.

"Served them right," said the righteous servant. Mimi was punished, so was her husband; their children were taken; it would go on until nothing was left. "Served them right."

Briefly Loulou rested the edge of her hand on the old woman's brow. She was nearly gone. Already the eyes were filming up, milk-blue above the tight inveterate mouth. Soon, soon. The earth was too hard for digging. Let her burn. No one would mourn except perhaps the girl-mute, another relic.

Later, alone in her cedarwood room, Loulou thought of duty. As the only remaining Laskorin child, should not Polly be told? Frossya had made a shrewd choice of confidante, knowing that Loulou was close to the boy, "Boxed up like his pet" was the word that went round. Where Polly would have detected pure innuendo – disgusting but typically spiteful on the woman's part – Loulou could find basis for comparisons. Both shared that carefree excitability of temperament which, in the boy, precluded any sense of conscience, and in the girl such dismissal of her past that now she appeared determined to re-create herself on impulse from moment to moment.

Neither belonged, neither had any sense of their continuity from past to present to future; a blindness to self-nature which had been the principal irritant in her relations with both. Long since, Loulou had pondered other resemblances: *her* self-righteous bossiness; *his* unthinking arrogance, that kind of sexual transmutation of trait – but did this sum up to a twinning of souls? Their colouring clashed, it was true; but his fairness from his mother was the positive of Polly's dark, relaying a common structure nevertheless which originated in the father's black waving hair. They had, too, his grace, a peculiarly direct manner with the eyes, and that fastidious ease with their bodies which tempted one to touch. But brother and sister? Loulou imagined Polly's impatience (when she was told): "old crone's pi-jaw".

If Frossya had speculated correctly about his origins was she also right about the boy's motives?

"He was family. Why else d'you think he led them here, this band of cut-throats?"

27

Instead of following Loulou all the way downstairs, Polly had stopped before the open double doors of the grand salon which Valerian's people had now turned over to winter quartering for farm animals. The last time she had been here was for her own wedding nearly five months ago. Then it had seemed merely a little dilapidated. Now it was chaos.

With sudden bitterness she recalled the exotic gifts heaped upon her and Belyakov, only to be summarily removed a few days afterwards, and the thought crossed her mind that here, amidst the destruction and filth, was the perfect place to have hidden them: in the chopped straw, perhaps, piled over the ruined furniture; or secretly nestled into the cratch of loose fodder where the overstrung Blüthner had once stood.

A start had been made on clearing the salon of furniture in order to make space for the beasts, but evidently the effort was half-hearted. Only two sides of the room had been stripped of the low Empire sofas which stood by the walls beneath the pictures. They lay upended, partially blocking the light from the windows in the furthest corner. Someone had tried to tip them through the casement and down onto the terrace below because the white brocade hangings had been ripped away to give access to the glass. Now these lay soaked in urine leaking from the animals' pens. But while the panes were shattered, the thick oak frames had only splintered under the shock and had become impaled on the horse-hair stuffing of the underside of the seats.

Recognising her mother's property Polly instinctively raised her skirts from the ordure filming the maple-strip floor, but dropped them back almost immediately. The dirt was limitless and, as her practical sense told her, by now inescapable. If there were something she wanted she had better plunge in with both hands free to root it out.

In the thin glare of a hurricane lamp a horned ram was nuzzling its testicles. As the head moved between light and shadow Polly's eye caught a glint of metallic yellow protruding from the floor. The ram was tame. Judging by her approach that she was about to feed him he butted up to her playfully, then fixed her with golden-lozenge eyes.

She was no good with animals. "Chuck, chuck, chuck," she wavered nervously and stepped back.

The sheep stood four-square, watching for her to fetch out the pig-nuts and dry fern which the women gathered under the drifts by the orchard and brought for him in their aprons. His interest stimulated the harem of ewes to abandon their lambs and push their bony noses through the hurdles of his pen. The bleats unsettled Polly even more, but she returned the ram's stare and slid a hand into her pocket for the fragment of loaf-sugar which she had been saving for tea. The ram smelt it for he suddenly twisted his head and nipped at the bulge made by her hand. Polly squealed, stepped back and missed her footing on the wet floor.

An arm caught her. It lay like a bar across the small of her back, fingers pinching hard under her ribs. "Only our Zhuzha," said a woman's voice. "Don't let the old charlatan intimidate you, *knyazhna*."

At the deep, easy tone the ram shuffled back, gave a toss to his horns and began to lick the ears of the nearest ewe.

"Don't be afraid, Princess." The voice was educated, almost elegant, but the hands which righted Polly were powerful. With one twirl at her waist they had her round.

The girl found herself confronting a woman with soot-black hair streaked with white. If it had not been for the gold she could have been a lady's maid. Companion, even. The face did not belie the voice. There was refinement in the nose and mouth; but the woman jingled, positively rigid with gold. At the throat of her open-work bodice hung a Circassian gorgelet of coins formed like a triangular bunch of grapes, the apex of which fell low into her bosom. Loops of gold wire encircled her arms and each of her fingers carried at least one ring.

The woman was short. Imperial portraits rose and fell under Polly's chin. "You know me?" she asked, feeling that if the woman drew her any closer her eyes would lose focus on the glow of the massed coin.

Instead of an answer the woman inserted her fingertips under the whalebone of Polly's stays, making them dig painfully under her breasts. "Remember the lake," came the rapid whisper. Her breath smelt of olives. "The long-haired boy who played there alone, skimming pebbles on the wave-scuds?"

Polly was not clever, only shrewdly sensitive to language. The form of the question gave her ground for instant decision. "You're one of *them*, aren't you?"

The woman smiled. Her left front tooth had been chipped at an odd angle and the effect was to make her beam crookedly, like a tortoise.

"You all live in a world of words, talking shocking bad poetry and trying to frighten people. I'm not afraid of old women's jabber. Take your hands away from me, this minute."

Uttered with such vehemence Polly's last remark caused the ram to bellow and lock his horns under the topmost hurdle. But the woman held tight.

"Under the ice, *knyazhna*, a naked white fish upturned, azure eyes to the sun . . ."

Polly shuddered and untensed her flesh bunched under the woman's fingers. "You know nothing, you riddle-makers. I know your kind, cast your net wide enough . . ."

"Not him, not him," went on the woman relentlessly.

Polly was near to tears. "There was no one else. Papa found Petya in the morning."

It was true. Her father had found his son on his back in the evergreen sedge of the lakeside, clutching a lead soldier of the Preobrazhensky regiment, the barkless twig arrows he had made for his bow sticking up straight through the ice floe which covered him, solid as a millstone. He had gone out to fish through the ice like the Eskimos, and the floe had capsized. That was twelve years ago.

"There were two," said the woman. "Two, red and gold from the sun."

"Let . . . me . . . go!" screamed Polly. "You're mad. You're all mad! Murder and death aren't enough. You want to torment us now, poison our minds with your lies."

Without letting go the woman caressed her brow against Polly's bosom. Her hair reeked with a vegetal odour. "Hush, my little one. I tell you things you could not dream, restore your kindred to the living, give you your desire, give back the son to your father and the father to the son."

Polly shrieked. For a moment the beasts broke off their ceaseless nudging and fidgeting in the mutilated salon and the only noise came from the high-stepping click of the wild does' hooves as they moved round their circular enclosure. But when the vibrations of Polly's cry fell away, the unpolled steers began to jostle and rear onto each other's backs, at the same time setting up a lowing call which quickly widened into a bellow.

As if in answer, the woman gave howl after howl, wrestling with the struggling Polly, dragging at her clothes, tearing and wrenching the terrified girl through the slops of wet straw and droppings across to the long window which gave a clear view of terrace and park beyond. Most of the glass was still intact, but the bitter air from the outside was palpable, taking Polly's breath away.

"See there!" screamed the woman against the wailing of the livestock. "Isn't this your longings made flesh?"

The night was clear but moonless. Little was discernible beyond the yellow aura given off by lights from the rooms below where Valerian held his winter gatherings. The lying snow was heaped like grain slashed by greenish shadow from the starlit beeches. Nothing stirred except for snow trails winnowing off the drifts in the wind.

"Well? Nothing to be afraid of," shouted Polly, recovering some of her pertness.

"Not a night to be abroad," the woman called back.

Polly felt better. Except for the deep-throated gurglings at her back, they could have been exchanging pleasantries on a spa promenade. She began to laugh. This was a mistake for, without relinquishing her grasp, the woman suddenly squatted on her haunches, and mewed like a wounded mole, the sweet, harmonious trill cutting across the boom from the animals. The note carried. Out of the park came a call, not in echo but reply.

On the house side two days and nights of blizzard had drifted up snow into a curving mass which overtopped the balustrade from one end of the terrace to the other. On the very same spot where, the summer before, Loulou had her first close glimpse of Valerian, came a noise like that of sand being crunched. The snow on the balustrade began to fall back in long strands ruffling the upward line of the drift.

"Ah," breathed the woman, evidently in recognition. "Look upon him."

Just beyond the reach of the glare from the house-lights below, something shook and scraped on the coping of the balustrade. It rose jerkily up, freed of snow, brown and dry, crackling like a thorn bush. The woman's body slackened, aghast at some weird interior pleasure.

"I know, I know," hissed Polly, suddenly quite unafraid. She knew every item of furniture and ornament in the house. "That was Papa's."

Etched against the snow was the magnificent boss of an oryx which had once hung at the foot of the marble stairs. The horns curled out over the white like enormous moustaches.

"Swine," she called out over the park. "Thieving swine!"

"Swine!" repeated the woman joyously. "Swine! In season they come!"

The horns twitched and suddenly came aloft. Beneath them, scald-pink from the frost, was the figure of a naked man.

Sensing Polly's body fall, slack and full, the woman relinquished her hold and scrambled up to the inner sill of the casement. Her head touched the girl's as they both scanned the man from head to toe. As if expectant of their gaze and relishing it, he stared up, then threw back his head, the muscles of his throat pulsing like a song-bird's. A stream of vibrant falsetto notes issued from his mouth.

Polly was enchanted. "Ooooh," she whispered, tracking the span of the man's chest with the awe of a child inspecting the underside of a musical box to see how it worked. "A serenade!"

The woman did not respond but raised her arm to her mouth and bit into the soft inner side until the blood came. Oblivious to everything except the rhythms of the bird-song, Polly abandoned herself to curiosity and prepossession. However much she had pried, rarely before had she seen a man entirely naked. Belyakov's modesty had dismayed and afflicted her. This man was proud. She saw him as geometry: inverted triangle above, dwindling to a point of near hairlessness over the belly where, just touching the apex of the triangle below, it burst into a flare of curls at the base. Beneath the gingham underskirt of her robe, Polly cocked her hips one way and another. Narrower there, slenderer, tighter, like a woman stood on her head, the woman's spread of thigh matching his depth of chest, his hips the counterpart of her own sloping shoulders. Plucking Eve out of Adam. So easy, sleight of hand, done with mirrors, turn him one hundred and eighty degrees and there you were: a mate from mismatch.

And as the man stood there before her, out of him reared what she had also rarely seen and never even imagined as separate, but only known within herself.

Another figure hopped over the terrace, similarly muscular, male, graceful and nude. Over his head was a pasteboard mask with protuberant snout and line of teeth painted along the cheekbones. While the first man had panache, this one was crude. His fox-face was slipping when he gambolled up to the man with the horns and fell on his knees, the warmth of his flesh misting the air. Then they all began to come, swarming over the coping, old, young, male, female, pummelling and scratching, dotting the bed of snow like ripe plums in their eagerness to catch up with the outrunner.

Some strange confrontation was about to begin because the women, none of whom was masked but whose hair was swept identically in bands across their faces, leaving only their mouths visible, kept back to the line of the balustrade, huddling some distance from the men.

Polly looked from one group to the other. "Oh Lord," she murmured, putting a fist to her mouth and lisping as she always did at moments of pent-up emotion. "This is going to be *dith-guthting*."

This was put to her companion, as much in question as remark. Polly was used from girlhood on to being dragged away from spectacle the moment promise teetered on the brink of fulfilment. But when she turned the black-haired woman seemed to have lost all thought of her, and was staring at a flaxen-haired girl whose body shone against the snow. A cry went up from the women: "Katya, Katinka!" and fell to a drone as they circled round with the girl pinned waist-high between their shoulders. "Katya, Katya, Katya, Katya." The chant seemed to steady them. Letting her arms drop straight to her sides, the girl turned up her face to the night sky.

Polly was intrigued by Katya's hair. Under the waxy blonde was a sheen which now and again caught the light from the torch-lit windows and glowed soft red. Each time she passed into full view Katya, although blinded by the bands looped tightly below her eyebrows and held fast at her ear by an amber bodkin, arched her spine inwards, as if aware of the movements of the men. Her low breasts tautened and jerked back, revealing the warm tint of her true colour against the purplish mottling which flecked the rest of her skin.

Too low, thought Polly, gratified. Hunching, she relaxed the weight of her own breasts and felt the insect-like stabs of her roughening nipples. At that moment she had no interest in the men. Their effect was all transparent in the woman. And Polly watched enviously, hungrily, seeing herself laid open in the same way.

She remembered the smiles of the laundry girls when she questioned them. How they brought up their eyes, glitteringly, and said that before she knew herself, she could never understand what there was to know. But marriage had not taught her. Not really. Was it because she had no child? Katya had had a child, that was plain from the droop of her breasts. A baby's fingers and mouth had dragged at her so that now you could have slipped a hand beneath them to the topmost knuckles. She knew the meaning and fruit of desire, that much was obvious, even to Polly.

Without warning the chanting stopped. The women fell to the snow as one body and the girl was thrust up like a standard. The fox-headed man leant in, snatched her up from the ruck by her knees and twisted her round his head. Polly gloated, imagining herself helpless in the grip of another. Fair as fair, split deep and open, an invitation to part. If this was a clear-cut incitement to her as a woman, what must it be for the man? The girl slithered through his hands, brushed the snow with her toes and with a gasp flung herself backwards onto the hard-packed mound.

Polly unsmeared the glass with the sleeve of her frock. This was how you looked, this was how it looked, this was what made them so harsh when they did things to you. They did them severely, without constraint. In silence, but listening to you, taking in your noises, feeding themselves off you, swollen up from what must seem to them a one-sided transaction. Your tenderness made them cruel; for that you must be more tender so that they will be crueller and you must want that more and more and more. You cannot gape without desiring to be filled.

Polly now understood what was wrong with her marriage.

They were unsparing with Katya. Oryx-horns came first. Then, with only the briefest of remissions between, the masked men came up, planted their feet astride in the hollows of snow warm and deep from the imprints of their predecessors and fell to, backsides dimpling from strain.

Polly lost count. At the seventh or eighth, she couldn't remember exactly, Katya began to slither cross-wise over the mound. But the man only crooked one knee and followed the slide, catching her arms at the wrists. He did not stop. Not even when, at a whistled summons from a gaunt, hollow-shouldered man who had already taken Katya, two of the oldest women with long flat breasts and swollen ankles were led up. Less blind than the rest from the sparseness of their white hair and evidently knowing what to do, they seized hold and held fast like midwives with Katya's wavering legs buried up to the shin in their armpits. With lowered heads they stood their ground facing the man, whispering to him brokenly, gutturally. When he came on, quicker and quicker, the corded musculature of his shoulders stringing his back into the shape of a bow, the whispers became cries.

To Polly no word was discernible. It was a language of sounds both human and inhuman, an animal noise to be instinctually comprehended. She longed to see his face and the face of the girl. The smack of their thighs brought out yells from the two old women who wobbled and slipped in the slush. Polly squeezed against the projecting edge of the marble sill and put her fingers lightly to her ears. Streaming into the night flowed the plainest, most strident, filthiest words she had ever heard. Words that pictured themselves at the very moment of utterance. Words that signified only parts, and the action of parts, in isolation. Nothing whole or complete with any kind of human content, simply things which did their work discreetly in the dark.

It was exciting to her, this naming. Her vision was sated. She had seen another as she herself wanted to be seen. As man after man had rolled away from Katya, she had sensed in herself that widening which seemed to cut into the girl, laying the fine hair apart at the squiggle of the stiffened lip-lines. And Polly had seen what had done this, and shivered for it to be done to her. She ached for it to go on being done and for it to stop, and resume. To be on it and want to get away and not to be suffered to move under it but to hold it within her like the bull holds his ring in the moist recesses of his snout, and wrenches, powerless when the pole is clipped to. With no barrier between them, no past, no status, no fear of compromise or ridicule, she could have stripped herself naked, and cast herself wide to the herd.

The man faltered, relaxing the curve of his back. The mass of his shoulders seemed to loose into a weight which drove down making him buckle through the hips. The women's ranting became fiercer. They would have him to the end. And their cries flickered about him like whip-thongs on a pony which was dropping in the shafts. Because of his one failure they were calling out to the man, challenging him with obscene jeers to rise again to the shackles and drag them, himself and Katya to the stopping place.

Gleaming with a sweat made lurid by the sulphurous haze from the windows, his body quivered with the effort to rise. It seemed to collapse and then straighten. Polly exulted, triumphing over him in pity and contempt. Too soon, for the old women redoubled their screams, and with the practised twist of surgeons re-snapping a badly-set fracture, pulled forward and slammed Katya's thighs vertically at his chest.

Polly felt lost in a complexity of desires: wanting the man's victory, hating the women's collusion, but hating herself also because she would have similarly connived. Had she been Katya, long before, and without aid, she would have dangled her legs down the man's back and slid under to take him entirely. It should have been her, it should be her; it would be. She stamped her foot. She could do it, she could *make* him, take him off-guard by her intuitive response. This girl was no good. She was a sacrifice, an offering. To expect her to respond was to expect the communion wafer to twitch in your mouth and resist dissolution. This girl just lay in the slush and melted, unvociferous. You needed push, Daddy said, push to get on. Push and pull, like his gunrod, fluffing up in the barrel, damp and lubricant, making it gleam.

When Polly came round from her intensity of pleasure, she was trembling. Outside the snow was dirtied and churned but they had gone, the people, all of them.

What had been done to her? Afterwards, Pelagya was nowhere to be seen, the jewellery had disappeared and the goldy-yellow thing. The hands that had explored Polly's body had also been busy proprie-torialising elsewhere.

While the excitement of what she had experienced persisted, the girl no longer cared for the things she had lost. In the depths of the salon where the light from the hurricane lamp cast huge shadows the animals stood mute at her presence, curious and attentive in the ramshackle pens of dismantled furniture; the passive stares of the ewes kindling the fire in Polly's brain. Yes, she had seen them together, the men and women, seen what Loulou, the dwarf, her father, Vlady and any of the host of people alive or dead, who talked down to her so impudently and treated her like a child, had hinted at to make her feel stupid. Each one had his or her own improper story, more luscious, more enjoyable, more daring than anything recountable to silly Polly. But after this she could outbid every one of them. Let Natalya Igoryevna dare to condescend in future: she had no lover, she had no husband, she had no child. She tore herself apart while beautiful creatures frolicked around her in the soft snow.

Under the dark glass dome of the stair-well Polly giggled aloud.

Early next morning she encountered Loulou on the upper galleries between their rooms.

"I have just come from Frossya, dear — where were you? We were searching . . ."

The concerned, embracing tone enraged Polly: "Out, away, in the snow, whatever you like, minding my own business."

Wrapped from head to foot in sables Loulou looked as if she had been on a long journey. "Frossya is dead, darling. This is a very serious matter . . ." She had placed herself in danger by moving round the house alone while Yasha slept and Valerian stayed with Asya at the dead woman's bedside.

"Frossya? A serious matter? How on earth do you make that out? Whenever anything *really* serious happens, you make yourself scarce. Last night, for instance . . ."

"Apollonya Dmitryevna, Frossya has told me about Mademoiselle Brancas."

"And Daddy?"

"And your father."

Polly's shriek was in pure delight. "Pooh, is that all? If Papa had had a brick for every woman who tried to foist her bastard on him the poor old chap would have been able to build a first-rate lying-in hospital. But at least that means he was a real man, not like those idiots you used to admire so much, Natalya Igoryevna. And there are other men, proper men, not so far from where we stand now."

This struck Loulou as an odd way to characterise the huntsman. Although the gallery was wide Polly seemed purposely to jostle her as she sauntered past to the head of the stairs.

"You stupid girl, can't you understand that if it's true you are related to Valerian?"

Thoroughly unmoved, Polly raised her eyebrows. "Don't be childish, my dear, that sort of thing doesn't count. Not," she went on, beginning to take pleasure in the status which might be conferred on her were the boy really to be her half-brother, "not that I hadn't already noticed an inclination, a preference, though . . ."

"But Polly, sweetie, Frossya was positive. Doesn't this change everything?"

"I expect he just assumed the relationship when he assumed so much else. But, now you choose to mention it, we're certainly different from the rest of you, more assured, wouldn't you say?"

Peculiarly, inexplicably so at this moment, thought Loulou, as if the girl had experienced some precious revelation.

"That's why I am allowed to go anywhere quite unmolested, while he keeps you out of sight, Loulou dear. Free spirits, you see, with natural affinity." Polly frowned, working it out. "It's more than the artistic leaning. A sort of natural authority we share." She paused with her hand on the gilded pineapple of the newel. "I can't pretend it's a shock, Loulou; you've never really understood either of us, have you?"

Speechless at her cousin's airiness, Loulou watched Polly trip down the stairs.

Half-way to the next landing the girl called back very loudly: "I know you suffer from a nervous disposition. But since you are convinced that he's family we might all benefit if you could bring yourself to treat him as such. I mean, couldn't you manage, my dear, to be a little more *approachable*?"

28

I fatten. My breasts overfill. The hair on my head is glossy from meat. I am become a great sow.

From the round stool before the three-quarter-length mirror set into the wall Loulou glared at her naked reflection. Her curls had inched out into a floss of miniature ringlets which tickled her scalp and the nape of her neck.

I grow. My body asserts itself, makes me again according to its own inscrutable rule, the beat of the pulse in my throat renewing the turn of thigh and arm, distributing the excess of nourishment and a whole winter's languor into the whites and reds of throat and lip to regenerate my open and secret places. A health cure. A pampering become flesh, a feast for the eye in the hard spring light.

Every day there had been gifts.

Yasha brought her ribbons: long velvety tongues of black and green in ruffled silk envelopes with the grand haberdasher's name along the undersides. And embroidery scissors, bluntish and gilt, the tang of each blade fitted over with ivory through which rippled the line of the living bone. He had found them on the floor of an empty room, as if someone had just buffed up the blades before laying them down to glint, and to be found.

She teased up a single ringlet with the heartfinger of her left hand and slipped her thumb through one eye of the scissors. *Coques de cheveux, Madame?* Or shall we bunch them, these folderols, exquisitely, *à la Japonaise?* Better shave you for the dead house, or for the travail to come, Madame. Better be on the safe side where the lice do not leap from crown to crown; where you can see and not be seen. Lop them off, mutilate the outgrowth that can be stinted but never stopped. Plough in the stubble. It will fire again and again. In effect, Madame, are you once more to save your alabaster neck by shearing yourself down to a boy and taking off like a beardless holy man with a bag beneath your unshaven underarm?

Yasha wants to. Yasha wants you to.

The scissors twinkled against the sun. The room crackled with light. The surfeit of objects oppressed her. At the beginning she had space for the disposition of simple things: a geometrically-patterned rug, the unadorned dressing-table, a wash-stand, a wide-brimmed pitcher and bowl, the bentwood towel rack, a set of mezzotints of Byron's beauties, and (Fedya's touch) the crêpe-paper fans along the cornice; all reminiscent of school. But Valerian had begun to fuss her vital space with inessentials. With all those neatly-sewn, fashionable clothes which the women were given to make and which they brought her with the contempt of sempstresses who had pricked their fingers to embroider the satin *culottes* of a *poule-de-luxe*. Once they had sewn man's things for a man; now they were reduced to fripperies for a tart. They said nothing but their silence was enough. He had made them serve her and she was hated. He would kill her, this boy, whom she hardly ever saw but whose voice rang every night through the rooms below, the boy whose gifts came daily, some days hourly, boxing her in with excess.

The austere lines of her room had become fudged as Valerian bore in upon her by proxy with the sumptuous and over-sweet: apricot-toned dessert wines, a silk eiderdown; a container the size of a coal-box full of long, slim ladies' cheroots, tipped with rose-petal; the lid played a tune when raised: *La Donna è mobile*. Men's conventional pleasantries, always whorish and sentimental.

All of a piece with the ribbons and scissors; trumpery for a *cocotte* Nanou from the *corps de ballet*.

She fondled the ribbons, let the longest unravel between her knees and clasped it between her thighs. Taking the other end in her teeth, she tautened the whole length and began to rock to and fro, anatomising those parts of her body laid bare in the mirror-glass, with words she had never before said aloud but only heard from a man. They had an appropriateness to her present mood which irritated and excited her. Only half an hour before she had silently cursed Yasha using exactly similar words, but with an inner voice which she realised afterwards was not hers at all, but that of another creature which resided within her and for the first time had found full-throat. It was the voice of a man urging on a flagging horse but its clamour so intensified and wilful that, as Kostya used to say, laughing at her embarrassment, it could separate a pair of copulating dogs. Under that voice the nature of the woman she had never doubted she knew in all its aspects laid back its ears like a mare and succumbed. It was a discovery. And more than that, an almost infinitely repeatable discovery.

In the glass she took pleasure in scarcely recognising herself: the face set in a mask, a flush dipping into the throat.

Yasha had noticed her mood, found fault with himself and left.

But there was no blame to be attributed. He had exasperated her to silent fury, and the interior voice had spoken. Now she needed no one. She was articulate, she was wholly, narcissistically herself.

Afterwards she wanted to weep: Yashichka, Yashichka, nothing ails me. You cannot understand and I cannot tell you. The breasts concentrate and tower. You see only the outside of the cage, the barb, the whip and the flail, the keeper's wherewithal; within, the animal rounds upon itself and whiles away the small hours in its own torment.

She bit her underlip and tasted salt. This will come to me now, and in the night and whenever I choose. Soundless and unperplexing. They may wear themselves out upon me, but I am intact. They have taken my husband, my freedom and my friendships, but I am alone and indestructible.

Calling aloud the night words to the swaying figure in the glass, she fluctuated between two narratives, marking the periods of this interior soliloquy with more and more violent expletives, cursing every ingress to her body and delighting in this new way of classifying her every openness as a seduction and an avenue. The ribbon twisted to an edge, separating her from mouth to mouth.

Polly would be outside in the sunshine with Belyakov. He too had the look of a caged animal. He should be caged with her, Natalya Igoryevna. Animal should dwell with animal. He was hers. They were all hers, the men with that look, hers, to listen, argue, to protect. To couple. When she railed he would have fought back. Combat, coupling, congress. There was a truth between them as there was a truth between herself and Valerian. Kill or be killed, eat or be eaten.

With the heels of her hands she churned her newly-thickened breasts and tugged on the ribbon like a dog savaging its leash. She felt the marrow of her bones being sucked up and squirted back as honeyed jam; and Valerian standing over her, smiling and her being unable to stop; and the sweetness rising like syrup and his gorging himself upon the taste of her, and the sight and sound of her.

When she screamed, the noise of the scream came out as his name.

Fedya was on the other side of the door, trembling.

"It is finished," she shouted, leaping from the stool. "I have come to the end."

Fedya was a lanky, nervous boy of sixteen whom Schmidt had deemed useless for anything beyond guard duty. They had tested him at the firing butts but he had wept uncontrollably at the report of his own gun. Prone to self-pity, Fedya sulked until given the job of watching over Loulou's door. This he did enthusiastically and with aplomb: day and night he kept to his post, sleeping little, smoking

thick green cigars, reading Lermontov and day-dreaming of duels.
They had given him an unloaded pistol which he kept cocked at the
ready in his left hand. At precisely the same moment in the long
hushed afternoons it would clatter to the floor as he nodded off
over his book. At such times Loulou had peeped round the door,
maternally, and watched him sleeping, feet propped up on a folio
Bible, the extinct cigar lolling from his fine mouth. It seemed typical
of his general inadequacy that his careless smoking never caused a
fire.

Now he was pretending. Loulou took the cigar and blew on the
embers. He did not stir. She waved it under his nose. The smoke
caught his nostrils but he would not come to.

She wondered if he were really asleep and envied his childish
dreams. If he were a child, if anyone had ever been or could be a
child in the terrible world of this house. She put the cigar to his face,
sizzling the down on his cheek. Fedya's feet shot from the Bible. He
was upright in a flash, waggling his pistol. He opened one eye and
shut it again.

"God preserve us!" he mumbled. "Woman in her nakedness."

"I am a dream," she said replacing the cigar in his mouth. "Bring
me the man who can put his hand in my side."

The tiny hairs stood up on Fedya's newly-shaven skull. "The man
who . . . ?"

Loulou leant over him, the heavy warmth of her drifting through
his military *blouson*. "Fetch me," she bawled an inch from his ear.
"Fetch me that dis-gusting young man you call your master. Tell him,
boy, tell him that her ladyship has need of him."

Fedya's spidery limbs crumpled as she weighed him down. Even
the sweat of her was sweet. "Mastersatthediggings," he managed to
get out, lips brushing the slope of her breasts.

The armless chair slid from under him as he fell slowly backwards.
He took in this naked Ishtar, running his eyes over her from top to
toe, then gave a high-pitched giggle.

Loulou flung her arms wide and screamed: "Then I shall go to him
as I am."

"Yes, miss, no miss, as your miss pleases. What business do I say?"
said Fedya slithering from under her and making off, all whirling
arms and legs, down the metal staircase.

Loulou leaned against the mahogany doorpost, nakedly insolent.
"You can tell him that his mistress is out of her mind."

Valerian was a long time in coming. When eventually he tapped at
her door and entered without waiting, she was once more before the

mirror, swivelling on the round seat and hissing gently through her teeth. Only her feet were bare now. The salmon-pink kimono knotted with white embroidered chrysanthemums was one of Valerian's presents.

"Natalya Igoryevna," he said closing the door without a sound. "I am told you are infirm."

This Old Testament sick-room tone grated and she turned her back on him. With the closed-up scissors she began to stab at a bombe-fronted chest below the mirror until white clawmarks stood out in the veneer.

Valerian glided forward. The hue of her eyes was ashen. "My dear," he said sepulchrally. "You are unwell."

He was so close that in the two-dimensional image of the glass his head appeared to be grown from her shoulders, and when she spoke it was as if to herself. In the wood a five-pointed star was emerging from the glaze.

"On the contrary," she said. "I am filled to overbrimming with myself." The blunt ends of the scissors ground a hole in the centre of the star. "I have matters to relate."

Valerian's eyes travelled the length of her profiled neck. "In the Lord's good time," he said. "Now you must rest."

Loulou flung the scissors at the mirror where they clattered harmlessly off the thick bevelled glass. "Rest! Rest! I am swollen like an Arab wife from rest! Rest, dark, offals. Sleep. Night. More bloating. Listen to me when I speak to you. I have something to say."

Valerian sighed and stood back, a childlike smile spreading over his face. "A story?" he said, conscious of a weakness in himself in submitting, but anxious to soothe her.

"With a moral," said Loulou.

Valerian settled at her side. "Perfect. A fable. You may begin."

"There were once two boys," said Loulou. "One dark, one fair. The dark boy was a servant, but not just a servant."

"More of a friend?" suggested Valerian. "I know the kind of thing."

"He performed a great service for a lady, but before he performed it the lady scarcely noticed his existence. At the beginning she was not a very nice person, but the dark boy . . . became like a younger brother to her and they were happy . . ."

Valerian chuckled. "I know – *Until* . . ."

Loulou's voice rose. "Until the fair boy who was neither true, nor patient, nor kind, nor strong came along . . ."

Valerian opened his eyes and frowned. "One moment, Natalya Igoryevna . . ."

Loulou kicked out at his midriff and shouted very loudly: "And because he was jealous, he played dirty tricks, obscene tricks, to destroy the dark boy by making him repulsive in the lady's eyes."

By now he was on his feet, nervously flicking at his long black mantle and glaring at Loulou's image in bewilderment. The exorcising gesture infuriated her. Opening the lowest drawer in the chest she seized a bundle of loose sheets torn from artists' watercolour sketch-pads and tossed them at his open sandals. The papers were rag-made, expensive, some as thick as card.

"Look at your filth!" she screamed. "There is what your angels and shepherds really mean. After your little art sessions shoulder to shoulder with Polly Laskorina comes your real inspiration, your true versatility!"

Without a word he picked up the longest sheet, scanned it briefly, winced, dropped it before doing the same with half a dozen others. Except for that one relaxation his face revealed no shock, disbelief or even surprise.

Loulou rose and stalked round him. "How graphic is your style, how adaptable to the matter in hand! A line here, a dash there and behold – the preoccupations of real men! Not a dwarf, not a tumble-legged freak without a thought in his head except for six-shooters and bows and arrows, but a full-grown man who wants to use himself on a helpless persecuted woman!"

He waited until she was spent. "These are the scrawls of children," he said simply. "There is no knowledge in them."

Loulou first became afraid, then more adamant and more violent. "Then what is this? And this? And this?" The papers wheeled through the air as she cast them at him.

"To see is not to know," he said. "Children watch as the ox offers his neck to the stall, seeing but uncomprehending."

Loulou was aghast. "Watch whom?"

"All of us. There is no exclusivity here. Life is open. Once those children saw in the dark what is now done in the light."

She paused breathless and he ignored her, dispassionately collecting up the drawings, assembling them into a neat pile according to their dimensions and securing them with one of her ribbons.

"Is that all, Natalya Igoryevna, you have to relate?" he said at last.

"Hypocrite-Jesus!" she exploded. "I know what you do! Every night you crawl up my stairs and push these things under the door. Little tales told in pictures. The whore under the naked dwarf, pinioned like a white tarantula. Every night I suffer this indignity. Who else would do this?" Her voice passed into hysteria. "And who else can move freely when all else are guarded and asleep? Who else but the *master*." The word dragged in her mouth. "The *ma-aster*."

Valerian contemplated her in silence. By now she knew that she had been mistaken but his presumption of superiority in the face of her wrongs was insufferable and unnerving. Her final resort was to abuse.

"My skin crawls in the mere presence of you," she sobbed, pulling the kimono tightly round her. "You batten upon the helpless like a grave-fly, intimidating the innocent." Appalled at her own stridency she kept his image in the glass before her, warily, in case the scandalous injustice of her fishwife talk should provoke a catastrophe and he fell upon her in a paroxysm of righteousness. "You canting, unclean, maniacal debaucher of children! Madman, murderer, insane seducer! I shall persecute you, drive you to the last gasp, ram your maggoty cant down that throat . . ." Repeatedly she laid back the folds of pink satin across her breasts only to adjust them again with a prim, demonic smirk. "Dirty, dirty, dirty," she whined.

With a gesture of profound weariness Valerian sank down onto her overstuffed bed and twisted his gangling adolescent legs under his chin. "Soon you will be free. The enemy is almost at the gates. There is no time for hatred."

This was perfect. "Hatred?" she said carefully. "For someone like you? Oh no, you presume too much, young man." Had Valerian been merely an over-zealous suitor and not a homicidal lunatic she might, at this point, have tossed her head. "I barely notice you, except as a peep-show monster, a straw-bellied puppet, totally a figure of fun." Lying and enjoying the lies because pain was pleasurable to return, she floundered deeper and deeper, unaware that even a far more experienced man would have found her contempt amusingly, ridiculously and touchingly encouraging, since what she said she herself took deeply to heart. "What on earth do you think you look like," she went on, "in those frightful clothes? And, my God, the way you talk! Praise-the-Lord this and Hosanna-that, St Paul's horse never heard the like."

Suddenly she put a hand up to the glass, and spoke as a girl might speak to a friend who was wearing some unsuitable trinket. "I mean, could you ever imagine an educated woman taking you seriously? With all that *ghastly* hair?"

Valerian wriggled up on the bed and peered at himself in the glass as if his face were that of an alien being. For a moment she marvelled that someone who looked so beautiful could be brought to regard himself as strange by the feeble spite of a woman. She felt contemptible but powerful and safe.

Valerian pondered. "You could cut it," he said. In his hand were
the little scissors.

In the main room of Valerian's apartments there were more dogs,
children and stink than in a gipsy encampment. Clustered by the
metal stairway, conversing in low voices, was a knot of men, among
them several of Valerian's chief lieutenants.

When they saw Yasha one of them pointed. Normally they gave
him a wide berth, but this time they blocked his way, silent and
hostile. As he stood there, feeling more foolish than afraid, Becky
trotted up, eyebrows shaggy with wet charcoal, pastel crayon plastering her cheeks and lips. Her stock of cosmetics having run out, she
was now driven to using artists' materials. She looked horrible and
had grown. Yasha was now half a head shorter. She gave him a
nudge. "No entrance."

"Oh, clever," said Yasha. "I wouldn't have believed it if genius
hadn't told me."

A squat man with a moustache blew Becky a kiss. She pouted and
stroked her neck. "I can see that," she said. "You're bright for a daft
bugger. Know what's going on?"

Yasha shrugged. "Competition? See how far you can chuck a
Bible?"

"Naw, better'n that – what *they* call," she primped her scarlet
mouth at Valerian's councillors, "a confabulation."

"You don't say."

"I do an' all," said Becky. "And so does our Debs. She says
Valerian's up there with your brother, only your brother ain't your
brother but your sister, and Valerian's gone up there to get up your
sister."

She nearly fell over at her own joke. "Still," she said when Yasha
failed to laugh. "No use spitting against the wind, now she's spoken
for there's always you, ain't there?" She planted a kiss on Yasha's
forehead.

Before Yasha could work out what had happened to Natalya
Igoryevna the biggest man in the crowd hopped down the stairway,
grabbed him by the shoulders and began to curse in a queer dialect,
not much of which Yasha could decipher except for "shit-eating
runt". At the constant repetition of this the other men broke into
loud laughter. Yasha gathered this had something to do with his
relationship with Natalya Igoryevna.

Becky pulled the hair of the dialect man. "Siberian snot-gob," she
observed. "The master don't like indecency. You'll catch it, you will.
He'll fry your chitterlings for the yard dogs, Pig's-arse."

The man relinquished Yasha with a snarl and rejoined his mates.

"He don't, you know," whispered the girl. "He told Debbie when she started making drawings of mum-and-dad-whatsits. Bide your time, he says to her. He doesn't know the half, not Father Valerian."

"Getting to now, though, looks like, doesn't it – the other half?" said Yasha bitterly.

"My half," said Becky, wetting her eyebrows. "Lawks! Makes you proud to be a woman."

Yasha tousled his hair, suddenly dumb. Natalya Igoryevna had drawn him out, made him a different person, but this morning she herself had seemed different. Now he knew why.

Becky's blue eyes wandered over the troupe of silent roughnecks with an elderly, unamazed look. At least she'd never be let down.

From behind the closed door they all heard Loulou's sprightly laughter. It seemed a long way off.

"That's a bloody swindle," said Becky. "I thought they groaned."

29

With the gravity of a schoolboy swapping birds' eggs under the desk Valerian slipped the scissors into her palm, folding over her fingers so that their tips pressed into the warm ivory. He did nothing else except to lay the hand against his cheek. It was at this point that Loulou laughed, and this laugh, high, coltish and brilliant, penetrated Yasha's soul. The laugh was girlish, virginal even in its self-conscious ring, but Yasha had never heard such unrestraint in the laughter of Natalya Igoryevna, and he was afraid.

Valerian's brief touch tantalised Loulou with the sense of her absolute nudity beneath the kimono. How gorgeously violable she must seem within this flimsy wrapper. How enviable were men to recognise their desires at sight. At her laugh his hand trembled and fell away. When the fit passed from her, he reached out again. She froze and forced him not to dare. To prolong the intense delight these rejections called up within her, she remembered Kostya who could spin out his need for her endlessly.

"Forgive me," said Valerian, and she smiled.

In dreams he had come to her, this broad-handed boy, and taken her by the throat till the blood darkened to pitch behind her eyes and she had cried out, expelling his night spirit through her open mouth like afterbirth. He had ridden her in sleep, abducted her, raced her into a creamy sweat. Now she had him at full stretch, clean as a whistle, under pressure, under the lash – gentle, bred to excel and straining every sinew of heart to make home and to please.

"When I touch you," he said, "I can forget."

Had he rehearsed his part? Was he prepared? Within, she dilated like the pupil of an eye. This was not going to be easy. Out of the face of a boy he looks at me with the regard of a man. Anything could happen. One never knew. In a week we may all be dead.

Think of Kostya. Think and go on.

"My husband, you know," she said brightly, "could be so quiet and gentle. As quiet and gentle as you. I felt safe with innocence."

He looked at her straitly, unadmonished. "Had I been your husband, Natalya Igoryevna, you would always have been safe."

Loulou shouted: "Ah, there speaks the man. That is what *he* claimed. But I was obliged to learn from him, that what men claim they intend to discard."

Again Valerian was unmortified. Only his mouth narrowed. His persistence almost made her want to laugh.

Deliberately she adopted a vulgar breeziness: "You can give me looks like that, my boy," she said tapping his brow with the scissors. "As long as you like. But I know your mind. Trust given is trust lost."

For a moment she wondered if he might cry.

"I refuse to hair-dress for you. You are forgetting yourself, young man."

He showed not the slightest sign of any such thing. His self-control was so ludicrous she wanted to slap him.

His forehead wrinkled. "You mistake me, Natalya Igoryevna. I want it as a submission. An offering of peace."

Loulou thought of Yasha and Big Chief Brokenbrow's corn-cob pipes of peace. This was terrible. She was going to burst into helpless giggles. He so obviously meant it. Not even one stolen kiss. Would he even know how to kiss? Unlikely. In this house the three-year-olds were better practised.

Clasping the kimono tight at her throat she suddenly jumped up and put a hand to his hair. The thick, coarse locks sprouted from his scalp like golden water-lily fronds. Out of the citronella yellows of the unsunned roots the summer had tipped each strand wood-ash white. When she spread it between her palms the hair smelt of fur-felt and civet.

"I cannot cut this," she said. "I am not capable." The kimono swung open.

Valerian made no answer except to pull the black robe over his head, lay it across her pillow, and sit like a corpse upright in its shroud, fingers meekly protruding from the lacy, overlong cuffs of his white shirt.

"I am in your hands," he said. "Allow me to trust you."

"You must promise," said Loulou. What he should promise she had no idea but he nodded and drew back from her a little way.

Her calm was all but lost and she trembled. The weight of her unloose breasts was pleasant. He did not stare but smiled fleetingly, and for the first time she was frightened, and longed for some asperity in his voice or look to make her angry again. But none came. Before snipping at the long front curls, she had to clench her teeth. Below, Valerian shifted very slightly.

The slipper satin hissed along her shoulders when she pushed his head down and flared the short curls at the back with the dull side of her scissors.

"Imagine me," he murmured. "Helpless . . . Imagine yourself powerful and then you may teach me. Teach me as you were taught."

He made no movement, his eyes were uncompassionate. If he knew what she was going through he betrayed it by no sign. She felt herself as a girl again; but this time not the eavesdropper on a filthy story but a fascinated participant in it.

He watches me, dotes on my ineptness, pities me. Kostya instructed me, made me. I knew only him. For Martin I was too much and too little. That last time he told me: "I can do nothing for you; to be naked and bound is your body's whole initiative; you can proffer only to be taken, not give."

Yasha's green and black ribbons lay at her feet partly drifted over by clippings from Valerian's head. "A little here," she said, checking the new length of his hair against the scissor-blades. "A little there, and we shall be *un beau garçon tout à fait soigné.*"

Valerian suddenly gripped her round the waist, the pressure of his hands so great that she sensed the contour of her hipbones. The scissors fell to the floor. To retrieve them without losing either the touch or the look of him Loulou curtsied down and blindly felt about her. The ribbons caught in the open scissors and came up on the blades.

"My husband," she said, "was a skilled instructor. He had insight into nature. The strong are born to immolate the weak. That is the only secret worth discovering. Women tremble from it as you shall tremble."

When, she could not tell, because under the dishevelled hair his face was blank and he seemed barely to breathe and there was no tremor to his grip. Only his eyes moved.

Her inflection became harsh. "We shall make sport, young man. We shall have a play. And you shall be unrecognisable, even to yourself."

Businesslike as a tailor Loulou shook out the ribbons, placed the scissors between her teeth, looped round his right wrist in a green velvet knot and then tied the left with the black. Tugging fiercely at both ribbons she jerked his hands from her waist and simultaneously heaved him backwards onto the bed with the full weight of her body. If he were taken unawares Valerian did not show it; nor did he move or protest or speak when Loulou stretched across to wrap the loose streamers of green and black round and round the ornate cross-struts of the bedhead. She shoved him, she pummelled him until his limbs adopted the position she wanted. Then she tied his feet.

"Now," she began. His unresistant heaviness made her pant and she stood at the foot of the bed breathing hard. "Now would they recognise you, your people? Is this really their precious Jesus disposed upon his cross?"

The kimono hung apart. At right angles to the bed a broad stripe of her lay white to his eyes. All the time watching him, Loulou inched back until three-quarters of her figure was within his perspective.

"Men do this," she said softly, widening the kimono so that her downward-pointing breasts gaped across the unfolding satin. "And this," she murmured looking beyond him to the wall. "This. And this. And this." At each word she bit thumbnail and forefinger into the orangey aura of her nipples, sucked the air against her teeth and wavered, swayed, almost buckled at the knees. Valerian lay meek, unspeaking, following the rhythm of her twisting fingers. As if dissatisfied she stopped, met his eyes, then with a half-swallowed scream, gave a savage pull which dragged each breast from its unblemished lines, roughening them both into cones of violently unnatural sharpness. For a moment she held herself there, stretched out and still, eyes shut, face averted, the tension of her flesh straining against the arc of her neck.

Just as suddenly she released herself, breasts slipping back into their familiar contours.

"First I kissed him here," she said, touching her own forehead. "A pure kiss for the bridegroom. Then like this." The tips of her fingers were in her mouth. "Then here, then here, then here." A silvery line glistened further and further down the middle of her body where she was dabbling wetted fingers on the skin. "How dry he always was, how cool, reticent even with his sweat. Women stream, women cannot help themselves, women gluttonise on their own voluptuousness! That's what he said, my husband, when I was on my knees before him, catlicking that fine dry skin."

She spat into her cupped hands and caressed the air. "Like this, like this I shaped him. Long, long strokes, down, down, down. 'An essential preliminary,' he would say. 'A foretaste.' And all the while I wondered: What would it be like to be so, to be him, to have that done, to be able to be so open, so exposed?" The outer edges of her two smallest fingers resting in her groin, she teased against the fine hair with her thumbnails. "But how could I compare, what could I bring forth?" Crossing over her thumbs like a child playing cat's cradle she ploughed the neat scar-line until it reddened and split.

Valerian's face seemed to have shrunk to the leanness of an ikon's; the eyes large, old and, for the first time, apprehensive.

"It is the end," he said in a low voice. "Your time has come."

Loulou was trembling violently. "For me and for you. Together. *Nous commencerons une vie nouvelle.*"

Apparently overcome by that orderly sense of practicalities which had marked her binding of him, Loulou wiped her hands on the wrap and shrugged it off. "And we shall begin with these."

The buttons of Valerian's shirt were wooden pegs pierced by four holes. As she began to undo them, her tongue protruding from the corner of her mouth, the audacity of what she was doing shocked her; but that he should allow her to do it made the shock immeasurably sweet. Close up, her eye magnified: prickly creamish thread amateurishly carded and spun from strands of unequal length, loosewoven, patchily sun-bleached, sewn at a bias; thick fastenings, clumsily hand-whittled. Everything hand-cut, hand-washed, hand-stretched, all as home-made as a peasant's footrags on a brickstove.

His wretched people even toiled over his folk-buttons, sacrificing themselves to perpetuate their master's unkemptness in the sight of God. It was a paradox. This sack-linen served only to concentrate his beauty. And he did not notice. He was not vain. He allowed them to clothe him because they needed him to concede something that gave them knowledge, a contact of intimacy.

Her eye followed the fragile curve of his jaw, the gold unshaven stubble, the broad flat eyebrows and strong-boned cheeks of an Antique boxer, the grave lashes which swept up overlong for a boy with a man's face. The image was impregnable. It could be transformed, never spoiled. Underneath, the line lay good and true. A virgin so intact that all which was perfect within him was undebauchable, even by death.

She ripped the shirt across the seam, carefully. No maid-of-all-work could repair it now. Cheap stuff, anyhow, *muzhik* shoddy, made only to last and last. On your back forever. They gave him what they had, his followers, instead of what was due to him.

Her violence had no effect. She cut back the sleeves to his armpits, but he did nothing except shudder his bluish-white chest. The last time she saw him so naked he had been unconscious. Now he was maddeningly, unflinchingly alert. She cooed filthy words in his ear, the mirror-words which had so excited her. He smiled. She wept enragedly but no tears stood in his eyes. Was he afraid? Was he disturbed? Did he pity her? Did he desire her? With this kind of creature who could tell?

When she straddled him, his waist was warm on her skin.

In the tatters of his clothing he was as radiant as the Son of Man. She wanted to weep again. Nothing moved him.

She infuriated herself. This angelic listlessness was a fraud. She shuffled heavily down his clamped legs and began tearing at the rest of his clothes. The material was dense and unyielding, taking her scratches unimpaired.

"With this you feel in command," she said, panting from the unaccustomed exercise and tugging at the solid brass buckle of his belt.

"My man, my Kostya, would have removed it first. Without it he could not love me."

The spike was fixed deep into the oxhide. Loulou crouched over Valerian's thighs and began to work it loose.

"As to that point he was very, very particular," she murmured in a strange, self-mocking sing-song. "Very particular indeed. Not to say strict, not to say *severe*."

The unoiled leather so bruised her fingers that she felt sick; in the end she wanted to fail. But just when she was about to give up Valerian breathed in deeply and gave her play enough to wrench out the brass pin. It was his first sign. She waited on further movement, but when none came she slid out the whole length of the belt, blind from excitement.

"Damn you, damn you, damn you . . ." The words blurted out, addressed to no one outside her clouded mind, but applying there to everyone who had ever touched her and anything that had ever broken her skin. Keeping the belt at arm's length she doubled it over to the shape of a rifle-sling and raised up the higher end where the buckle glowed sullenly. "Damn you, damn you all to hell." The unstitched edges slit the fold between her thumb and finger, dampening the untanned side of the leather. The scent of hide and wet frictioning aroused her to paroxysms. The buckle veered aslant, its pin wiggling like a strangulated tongue as she held it an inch from her mouth. She crooned over the blank lozenges left in the metal like emptied eye-sockets. "Copperhead . . . Reptile . . . Crawl-belly . . ." Choctaw-talk, Yasha-talk, swimming in the light of a dry-sunned mesa where creeping things were done to death with a twist and a crunch. "Blood-on-tooth, sting-in-the-tail . . ."

For no reason her speech suddenly became normal. "Oh, Kostya, you were always so correct, so efficient." Bracing herself astride Valerian's hips she switched hands on the belt, paid out two or three feet of the buckleless end and half-rose on her knees. "Only a game," she whispered. "It was not meant to hurt, the Scourging. Only to be a mockery in order to make him ready." A thin whine parted the air above Valerian's sternum before Loulou came down on him two-handed with all the force of her slender arms.

On the white body between her knees no mark sprang up. Again.
At the rounded shoulders. Again and again. The damnable sloth of
flesh. The excruciating slowness. God is not mocked. Man cannot be
laid open. Again and again, thrown back in a headsman's swing, her
arms wrenched up her breasts; in her shadowy armpits sweat clung
to the saffron hair. *Kostya, I am no good.* The lash was broad, the
stroke unangled. No cut came.

She shrieked at the mute figure. "Cry out, damn you . . . Beg me.
Supplicate. Speak. Kostya adored me. Kostya worshipped me. He
was riven by my screams: *Nathalie, Natalinka, Natashenka*, beg me,
implore more, scream, scream, scream. God never speaks but with a
loud voice."

The dun leather snaked transversely, here and there, dulling the
white of his skin with tiny blood-blisters. Shortly there would be no
power to her blows. Once more, before that. Again. "Bitch, whore,
slut. Open up. Oh, how the air swam from my mouth. Flog the milk
from your breasts, the skin from your womb. Scream, Kostya, swine,
scream for me, for me, for me."

Down and down again on the same spot, she whipped clumsily,
frantic to break into him. At last the welts came, broad and lumpy
as hives; then blood, pursed and scarlet, burst into a trickle.

She knelt down and put her lips to the place.

Becky was at the window, drawing on the steamed-up panes. She
drew a man and a woman. The man wore a stove-pipe hat, the
woman a tiara. They were holding hands.

Yasha sat in a basket-work invalid chair, idly banging the wheeled
steering-arm from side to side. Valerian's lieutenants drooped over
the stair-rail like disconsolate ape-men waiting to be fed. The air was
blue from shag tobacco.

Yasha started to unpick the straw: Yup, a wise-guy like he wasn't
could have told him the end at the beginning. No female could keep
herself to herself. Didn't matter what age or what looks, they just
steamed on, flaunting. They never got off the topic of their miraculous
selves. Becky's tart in the crown — another sucker in the female
chain-gang that clanks up its collective arm for a primp and a pat
as the silk-hatted captain parades along the ranks, holding himself
out like an executioner's fag they'd kiss any old boots to get a drag
of.

Women. A bunch of asthmatics dying for air. And no wonder: men
step into the sun to die, lit up; but that lot would even flirt with
Death, hoping he'd split a grin and let them off in return for a feel.
Even Him, the fastest draw in town. Anything to uncurl the trigger

finger round your throat that'll squeeze you off quicker than a .357 Smith and Wesson.

Thank Christ the last detective is a ball-less man, all wised up.

"'Ere, wassername!" shouted Becky, blodging stick arms onto her couple. "That's heathen goings-on, you know, with your brother. Somebody oughter to tell her. Says it in the Scriptures, it's not right. There's rules, like cut your beard on the square."

Yasha chewed on a long, unwinding straw. "Who says?"

"That Leviticus. 'E says."

Yasha did not reply.

"Don't know who he is, do yer? I always guessed you was a real 'eathen."

From behind the little door at the end of the gallery came a high gabbling sound in which no word was distinct, but whose pitch slowly heightened. Becky put her thumb in her mouth and carried on drawing while Yasha, in common with everyone else in the room, stopped what he was doing and listened. The voice squealed vibratingly upwards to a moment of silent hesitation before crashing down upon them all in a frenzy of vicious discords.

Yasha covered his head as if the ceiling was about to fall in.

In the ensuing silence, robust, brigandish men stamped their boots, coughed and rolled fresh cigarettes.

"Ooooh," said Becky, standing back to view her finished picture. "Get away with her – she's pretending."

The bed was narrow. When she collapsed over him, weeping luxuriously, covering his body with tears and kisses, Valerian tried to edge her aside and lie awkwardly, face to face, but she pinioned his body, encircling him, cushioning him to her, lapping him round the impress his flat, hard chest made upon her breast.

"All over," he said gravely, with one concerted movement tearing the ribbons from his feet and hands. "No more."

Unprotesting, she allowed him his wish and they lay on their sides, face to face, each independent of the crush of the other's body. Now he could not keep still but explored her; the flow of the back into her waist, the hour-glass swell of her above and below. Under his hand, like the hair-bones of a fish, were hundreds of seamed lines. As he stroked they ribbed into a network outwards and downwards from the centre of her spine to the backs of her knees.

"Finer work than yours," he said, thumbing the ridges and touching her hair with his mouth. "But why only there?"

Loulou pressed her temple up to his lips. "Ah, you see, Kostya was an artist. Haven't you ever turned over a canvas to know how the picture has been made? With a woman you can make the alteration simultaneous. Criss-cross, from glaze to blemish, immaculate to maculate, reach the grain under the paint, all held for you, accessible, within the frame."

"He hurt you," said Valerian.

"He could not help himself. I incited him. I do not mean encouraged – my being as I was incited him, but I was complicit with him in the sheer fact of my body."

"He hurt you."

Smiling at his insistence, she switched into schoolgirl chat. "Oooh, yes. And how. Awfully. Split cane . . ."

He winced and took his hand from her back.

"I healed but I don't think he ever did."

"Thank God he is dead."

This was the closest Valerian had ever been to confirming Schmidt's story and she was uneasy both at the reminder of Kostya's death and Valerian's deviousness even at a moment like this in not taking the responsibility for it upon himself.

"God, always God," she cried out in sudden embarrassment at the nakedness of her unmindful relaxation with this Christ-boy. "Curse him, curse me, curse us all for flaying and allowing ourselves to be flayed, but leave God to His own neutrality. God made to set before Him what could be made, not to be thanked, not to have creation drop the knee. What kind of thanks is that? Who can thank his father for his existence?"

For a while they were both silent. Then he startled her. "Well now, Natalya Igoryevna, if you cannot instruct me in theology, please teach me something else." He whispered in her ear.

"Teach you what to do! Am I the scullery maid for the boy of the house to practise on?"

She hit out at him but for the first time he exercised his strength, pulling her to him, spreadeagled, squeezing her.

She felt trapped, powerless, unfrightened, and very annoyed. "You young idiot. Men don't ask questions like that, men are supposed to be born knowing. What kind of man are you?"

But the abuse had no force. Before the last word was out she had the sensation that something had been decided. Without losing hold of her he heaved them both up and wriggled out of the rest of his clothes. The scratchy homespuns grazed her belly.

"Here," she cried. "Don't be so rough. That hurts."

"Like these and these," he said, rearing her up, caressing the scars on her back and making her breasts hang heavy on the weals on his chest. As she was borne up he pitched and rolled her above him like a child's plaything. The motion made her queasy and she began to cry out, her head wobbling, her tapered nails slashing at his neck where snippets of hair and thread still clung.

He shouted back: "Is this how, Natalya Igoryevna? Tell me, show me, is this how?"

Her voice fell to a whine: "Don't ask, don't ask."

For a moment he held her above him smiling as she scrabbled, and kicked the air. "But I shall, I shall, I shall until you give me my answer."

He dropped her down gently straddled across his upraised knee and Loulou leant away, head lolling, hands still at his neck. She wept but he would not attend to her tears. Her self-preserving anger dissolved. He had caught up with her as her body itself had finally caught up. Open, liquid and frail she rocked back and forth on his knee, the breath whistling violently in her throat. She did not know what he would do to her; if he knew what to do; or how it would be if he did. She knew nothing. She would not look. She could not speak. Now words were no more than sounds. What she did not know and what possessed a terrible fear and what she wanted more than anything else she had ever wanted, were about to come together.

Valerian unflexed his knee and she slid over his hips. Reaching out, she kissed his eyelids and felt beneath her. The touch was astounding. Softly, blindly, she separated but held back, bore down and closed over, forcing him down to curve along the open line of her. This was as far as she knew. Here she wanted him to be still. But from that very first moment, captivated by impulse, he moved. He went on, eyes large in a pale astonished face:

"I shall injure you . . ."

Loulou swept the uneven fringe back from his forehead. She had found a quiet voice: "Do you want to?"

"No. Yes. I want to . . ."

"Then you must."

"But I should not."

"Where we are nothing is higher. You are as you are, are as you must be."

"What must I do?"

Closing her eyes, Loulou inclined her head upwards and with her hands at the hollow of her back pressed gently down.

"I cannot tell you," she murmured. "I can't tell you because I don't know."

Valerian was not listening. The rocking movement had an irritant rhythm which was sufficiently pleasant to Loulou and one which she well knew. But after a while he became discontented and began to push violently, interrupting her deepening concentration, and she bumped above him like an inelegant horsewoman. Without warning or foreknowledge, he suddenly splayed his long legs and matched her fall with a heave of his thighs. A whimper was the only sign she gave that she was pierced, but it was enough.

Instantly Valerian froze, wild with remorse. "What have I done? Oh God, you will die . . ."

She patted his mouth and eyes with her lips, sweating from the sharp, deepening ache. "Not enough, my love. Here, let me take you."

And with a grimace she clasped her fingers round him only to snatch them away as she relaxed and engulfed the whole of him in her own long, searing, unique pain.

For one as innocent as he, the shock was too much. Once, twice he shifted within her before all his movement became involuntary. She watched fascinated. He thrashed under her like a gaffed pike, filmy-eyed, baring his teeth, fluttering in a kind of helpless rage, and from the back of his throat came a cry of an animal baying in despair and triumph. Except for the rigid, fiery line inside her which blazed, stinging and tight as the raised skin on a burn, she felt nothing. When it was over she came away from him calmly, and with tact, and the pain flared more invasively. Blood was on her hands, clotting the hair on his belly, spreading over the sheet. She dabbled it at his lips and on her own.

"Kiss me," she said.

He opened his eyes at the taste and clutched her. "Natalya Igoryevna, I have never kissed a woman."

She wanted to laugh but instead took a deep breath. "Then how clever you must be. You don't say the right things, you are very awkward and clumsy, very sudden . . . but look what you have done. Aren't you pleased?"

"Was this me?"

"Really you," she said smearing his lips. "And me."

It is true, thought Loulou, God forgive me for making it happen with him. The irony of her defloration's being the act of a virginal maniac who had never kissed her would have made Kostya ecstatic. But she was glad at last to be known since the irony was far richer for her: her husband was ousted at last, supplanted by his own executioner. It was wonderful. Never in her life had she been so happy. She knew now what Kostya had kept from her; was known by the boy; and knew herself.

"Do you belong to me?" asked Valerian, croaky from his scream.

She rubbed his face between her breasts. "I thought you people had reservations about private property."

He sat up, very earnest. "But I have possessed you once."

"So you must learn what those with possessions have always known – that you must fight to preserve what you think is your own."

"Then you belong to me," said Valerian staring at the topmost window-pane which yellowed in the dusk light. His blue eyes were unhazed by joy. "The sun flowed through me, Natalya Igoryevna, and God is in the sun."

This was the worst part and she stayed utterly quiet for he was very, very serious.

"I look at you now and say: from Him I have taken what was intended for me, and what is mine shall not be taken from me."

This time he had no need of her help.

Held above him again she tried to protest that it was too quick, that she hurt, that his strength was too much, that in any case, one couldn't so soon after. But he was young and the evidence of his youth was there, at the simple warmth of her.

Soon it will be over, he is a boy, it cannot last, he cannot for long be hard with me, I am cut, I am in ribbons. God make him fast. Let me hold him, keep him fast, tear me red, rub me raw. Christ, oh Christ, swell into every cut, get at me. Finish. I am grovelling. Finish, finish, finish. I am dying. Finish, finish me . . .

She snatched his hand and placed it where Kostya or his woman had always placed theirs. Valerian's breath came in great swoops: "Ah, ah, quicker, quicker . . ."

As his upper lip curled back a slow, silver thread sparkled in her womb.

Don't stir. Wait, wait. One last tumultuous judder and he was thrown from side to side, screaming, calling all the names of God. Mercilessly she rode him, burning out the dark with wolfish, rending cries: "There is . . . There is no . . . There is no *God* . . ."

Yasha did not wait for the end but slipped away, unobserved. The passage was empty but as he raced between the cool walls Loulou's final agonised screech broke over his back and swept ahead of him jaggering the air he breathed. He felt terror at her inhuman exultancy, grief for himself at having to bear the pain of it, and gladness beyond words that soon he would be beyond it all, outside and out of reach.

On the staircase he slowed. He felt like a thief who had stolen a great diamond, cut and re-set it, only to wake one morning to find that he had lost it and he could not even remember what it had looked like.

V

MARTIN

June 1918

30

At the edge of the cypress plantation bordering on the Laskorin maze, Yasha waited.

A stone-chat was pecking at the sprigs of a shrivelled broom-bush, making it crackle and sway. After the bird flew off, the swaying persisted. From the slope, the upper branches of the trees leaned into the wind, muffling its howl. Hardly a breath disturbed the undergrowth but the dry bracken crisped again and shivered.

It was enough.

Yasha did not wait to see what kind of beast followed behind. From the top of a hugely overgrown boulder, once a decorative marker between wilderness and plantation, he clambered down into a hollow which snaked along a boggy overflow from the main river. Again he waited.

Free of trees the wind squalled through the little valley allowing no other sound to carry above it but on the wildest gusts came a scent: an unaccountable scent that cloyed the back of his throat like sweet mouthwash. He loosened his coat and sniffed his own sweat. The scent seemed to exude from his pores, hang on the wind, envelop his whole body.

Someone could have tainted him, marking him out as the drag for a secret hunt.

After the spring thaw the river had backed up into its feeder stream and formed a shallow lagoon in the tributary bottom. From the edges of fine gravel he knew that the far shore must be on a gentle slope. Above it, the steep incline was dotted with useful-looking clumps of thick dock. With these handholds he could make the gradient and get a vantage point from the top.

He waded until the brown water came up to his armpits then dived like a cormorant, head-first at the bed of the stream. Three times he shot under, wriggling and twisting, trying to rinse the pervasive scent from his hair, nostrils and skin.

Once ashore he breathed deep. The smell was still there, hanging above and about him, saccharine and gluey.

He struck out for the rise and made it to the crest in one mad scramble. At the top was a knoll thickly planted with dwarf birches. From their cover he surveyed the country through which he had come.

Beyond the open parkland to the north-east of the house were terraced shrubberies, now tangled and intertwined from neglect. Down there he had chopped out tunnels through the saplings into the murk of weeds. Weeks it had taken to clear each run, days to connect them up. Now he had a network leading to the cypress grove. He could have gone straight through to the safety of the river but someone or something had spotted him. Probably in the park where he must have showed up in the grass like a ferret on a rug. Lying up on the high ground, camouflaged, he was safe: every quiver in the bush would be the signal of a pursuer's approach.

Even for him it had been abominable ground for speed but for one less familiar and nimble an hour or two could pass before he got the hang of the system. Warming his back in the sun, Yasha listened as the rush of wind swung to the opposite quarter and flowed back again, dizzying the leaves of the birches.

Yah to you, Makar, you old moledigger, I'll have you. Rooted out your bag of tricks already, see if I don't skin you proper yet. Men is hard to fool, a man bites back.

On instructions from the Committee of Safety over which Valerian presided, Makar had seeded the land with traps: silk trip wires connected to scatterguns, pits under leaf-covered nets, mines as small as saucers; all stowed under earth like squirrel nuts. Over the weeks Yasha had burrowed them out, one by one. It was a question of patience, like life; taking things to bits slowly, and pondering connections.

He'd had plenty of practice.

Without warning the sun came clear through the haze and suddenly it was hot. Yasha slid back towards the trunk of the nearest tree and shaded his eyes. The brush was blindingly green. He blinked, leaving tawny patches on his retina. The vegetation undulated beneath the clash of winds. The continuous waving and noise began to irritate him in this stark light. His sight was fuzzing. You couldn't see a blasted thing. And the smell had come back.

A shadow fell smack on the birch bark, wobbled up the bole and spread out to the quivering leaves. Yasha's right shoulder froze. That side? The weapon side? A quick snatch, a roll to the left and he could be up, knife in hand. He dug his elbow into the leaf-mould to give him spring.

A man began to laugh.

Behind. Lie doggo. Little brave him pretend dead.

The laugh died away to a chuckle. "Game's up, sonny Jim," said a languid voice.

Slow as a trigger-pull Yasha twisted his head and looked back along the ground. Level with his eyes was a pair of muddy dancing pumps fastened over by gaiters which once had been white.

Spats. Eight hundred miles from Petrograd. Spats. Yasha didn't believe it.

The stranger squatted on his heels and smiled into Yasha's face. His peaked cap looked blurry in the sun. Under it the long fine mouth puckered at one corner, then straightened across stubbly jaws. Only later did Yasha discover that the spasm was uncontrollable and took place once a minute with the regularity of a metronome. The boy cringed. At this moment it scared him stiff.

"Relax, old chap, I won't eat you." The voice was gentle but to Yasha's ear too refined for comfort. You never knew where you were with well-bred drawls. To his intense chagrin the man complimented him on his scouting. "Most impressive I found you, young fellow, a real shikari in the making. But insufficiently devious. Unhappily we were forced to profit from your mistakes."

We?

Another voice joined in: coarse, expectorant, angry, harsh and hideously accented. The voice of home: "I'll do for that sodding kid . . ."

The educated gentleman took out a revolver with a chain loop at the butt. The grey bullets looked fat in the ports of the chamberings. Instead of increasing his terror the move gave Yasha a kind of ease. His captor had authority. His prize was a prisoner of war, not a scalp. Yasha's head began to clear and his heartbeat slowed. He dropped any thought of escape.

"That'll do, Corporal, if you please," said the man in spats. The coarse voice was chumbling on, its accent unidentifiable.

Between the skewings of his facial muscles, the gentleman attempted another grin. "Take no notice of Myelnikov. An intemperate soul, comparatively new to the game but with a heart of gold. Classes all boys as 'the hooligan element'. A deprived upbringing, I should say, has made him censorious." He bent lower as if Yasha were his long-lost friend and gossiped: "Between you and me, that sort can be really quite excruciating. Plucked from the absolute bottom of the barrel."

Yasha rolled over and sat up.

Corporal Myelnikov had either not heard this last remark or did not dispute its truth. Seated on a knapsack he was picking his teeth with the quill end of a feather. Yasha didn't need to sniff the corporal

– his was the smell. He was aromatised. It came off him in invisible puffs: from his infantry blouse, straw-stuffed boots, the balaclava rolled up on his forehead like a turban, and his craggy pop-eyed face caked with the muck they slapped on for moonlight patrol. What a turnout! One whiff of him would clear a tenement quicker than the Fire Brigade.

"Get on with it," said Myelnikov. "Do it proper like the rules of war says. Interrogate the little bugger, and then I'll shoot his arse off."

"Haven't you forgotten something, Corporal?" said the gentleman.

"Then I'll shoot his arse off, *sir*, " said Myelnikov.

From the knees upwards, Yasha began to shake. They were like murderers-cum-music-hall-artistes: Stinker, Spats and the Dwarf. Play up, Yasha, be a straight man, do your turn. Remember what Pa used to say: "He may scare the jugs off the dresser, but he's all the world to his Ma-a-a!" Say the next thing that comes into your head.

"I done nothing, sir," said Yasha, addressing them both. "I'm the deformed son of a rural factor."

Myelnikov tried to connect these two pieces of information but failed.

"You can blame the parents, sir, for breeding this tiny monstrosity, but as for habits, sir, habits is not bred; evil leanings grows out natural like teeth. Permission to deform further, sir, by re-arranging his limbs?"

"For God's sake, shut up, Corporal," drawled Spats.

"For His sake, sir, taking the fact of His existence as un-arg-uable, I will shut my non-commissioned gob, sir, while the defective person is de-briefed according to the Rules and Ordinances of the Military Code. Sir."

"Why were you in a place of concealment?" asked Spats kindly.

"I wasn't, sir."

"He wasn't, sir," mimicked Myelnikov polishing his bayonet with a fistful of grass. "I know, sir – he was tossing off in the bushes."

"I was looking for my kite," said Yasha.

The corporal slid off his knapsack with a loud guffaw. "So that's what dwarves piss with. Kite-shite – he's a plant from up there." Myelnikov brandished at the serene frontage of the house. The gentleman frowned between twitches. His knuckles were bloodless on the revolver grip.

Now he'll do it. Hullo Ma, hullo Pa. Here I am. This is me. Yasha, come home.

Myelnikov read the indecision on his superior's face. "Can't do it here, sir, can we? About as private as B company's shit-house. One bang and we'll be neck-high in nutters from the God-factory."

"Too visible," said Spats. "Quite right. I don't want corpses marring the prospect. Dead men chatter."

Myelnikov sighed and wagged a finger at Yasha. "There's decency for you, Kiteflier. Saved your knob to rise another day. At the double! March!"

As they trotted in a threesome down the slope of the knoll, hidden from the house, the gentleman resumed his friendly expressiveness. "Don't take it too hard," he said. "Strange times make strange bedfellows."

They were half-lifting, half-dragging Yasha. From time to time they dropped him, juddering his short legs before resuming their hold. He felt mortified and helpless.

"Doesn't mean it literal," said Myelnikov. "We don't kip down together in nighties. Think I'm a crude bastard, don't you?"

They wheeled right onto a narrow track. Yasha was twisted round, thrust forward and they continued on their way, bobbing him up and down along their chests.

"Think I stink, don't you?" continued the corporal.

The stench was indescribable. Yasha feigned idiocy. "No," he said as the crown of his head clunked on the corporal's jaw.

"Well, I do," came the triumphant reply. "And I am. See these eyes?"

Yasha had to wait for the upswing. When it came Myelnikov helped by yanking his hair. "Have a good cry. There's corpses looking at you, peering out of these. A bleeding walking mortuary I am. Know what I am?"

"A bleeding . . ."

"An animal, that's what I am. Ask him."

"He's quite right in all particulars," puffed Spats with a touch of resignation.

"A belching hyena," said the corporal whom the exercise seemed not to affect in the slightest. "A jackal with thigh-crunching teeth . . ." He reeled off a litany of increasingly disgusting animals.

"That's enough, Corporal," grunted the gentleman. "We're here."

"Here" meant a sand-strewn glade littered with snail-cases, and set around with mature standing timber. The high spread of trees was magnificent. Squirrels leapt from bough to bough.

"Nature," said Myelnikov dreamily. "Ain't it lovely?" He gave Yasha a playful kick. "Whose are you, little laddie-o? Makes me nervous, not knowing." He threw back his head and laughed. "One of them Jesus jitter-bags, are you? From over there?"

The house was obscured. Only the tops of the pilasters were visible through the dancing leaves, their capitals flashing gilt in the sun. An answer was required, as the gentleman might say. But the gentleman had had his say and was smoking a thin cigar, looking moodily at his spats.

"I was a mascot," said Yasha. "I got taken along."

"Ah," said the corporal. "A kidnapped marmoset. We'll have to get you a red bolero. And did they tweak your organ to make you hop, the gracious ladies?"

Mother of Christ, Moses, Samson in the mill-house, the holy bones of all the saints, Kabala, the Torah, get me out of this. Spirit me up, assumpt me.

"I read tea-leaves."

Snail-shells parted into fragments under his behind. Snails had it easy. No chat. One dumb peck and your vitals were de-housed.

"Another fucking drawing-room fortune teller. The country's crawling with them. Know what I'd do?" Myelnikov put out a heavy hand. Trapped fragrance volatilised from the outspread fingers. "String them up, a dozen at a time, like the old days."

"The only language they understand?" broke in Spats, flicking his cigar-butt at the squirrels.

"That's it," said Myelnikov. "We've lost the art of punishing. I look at it this way, sir," he went on, relinquishing his hold on Yasha's neck. "The people has a squalid progeny. It's not their fault. I can't blame them for what lurks in their bones, but when it emerges and is allowed to walk the earth unhindered like this rune-casting dog's breakfast, I say to the parents, a whack on the bum in good time would have saved him from the lime-pit."

"Finished, Corporal?"

"Sir."

"Then bundle him up. You know the routine."

Myelnikov snapped to. "Here we are," he said to Yasha, a black bag in his hands. "All over in the piddle of a dick."

Before Yasha could think he was jerked backwards. The end of a sack came down over his head and his arms were pinioned to his sides. Through the tight weave of the canvas Myelnikov still stank.

At first he had screamed; and continued to scream as he felt himself being raised from the ground. But instead of the neck-cracking drop which so terrified him in anticipation there came a hefty blow to his stomach. Although winded and gasping for breath he sensed from the flow of blood to his head that he was being slung like a carcase over somebody's shoulder.

"*Tishye yedesh dalshye budyesh,*" chuckled Myelnikov. "Keep your trap shut and you'll arrive in one piece."

Yasha stopped screaming. By the time they shot him out of the sack he had lost his sense of balance and sprawled at the corporal's feet. He tried to stand but fell again and vomited.

"Seventeen minutes," said Spats. "Our best time yet."

"I like to keep myself in trim," said the corporal. "Gives a man self-respect."

They spoke over Yasha's head, congratulating each other in his presence as if he had been a gun limber that they had slung over a ditch on a block and tackle. There was something so horribly efficient and impersonal about the pair of them that Yasha realised they hadn't spared him for mercy's sake. They were up to something. They had plans for him.

He held his head between clammy hands and looked round. Another clearing, smaller, grassier. Overhead a dense web of branches and foliage formed a roof. Slivers of white shavings and wood-chips littered the grass. The trees stood close, the gaps between them choked over with the unrestricted growth of spindly trunk shoots. At ground level a stockade of rough palings from severed boughs was being built, its chinks packed with bark strips and dead bracken. Yasha saw no way in or out. It was almost cosy – like being in a leaf-lined basket.

Myelnikov yawned, hopped from leg to leg and, with a sigh of contentment, pissed through a hole in the stockade. "I'll take a look at the Madsen," he said. "But I reckon she'll give no more than two hundred a minute with the magazine quadrant out of true."

Spats was seated on a tree-stump, his long legs thrust out and almost touching Yasha's. He made no answer but went on unhurriedly itemising the contents of Yasha's bag. Loaf, boots and blanket had already been tossed to one side.

"Suit yourself," said Myelnikov swinging back the lid of a long steel case camouflaged under brushwood. "I'll put her on semi. She's a beauty when there's no hiccups." From the case he withdrew a pair of gun barrels almost two feet long, fitted one to a bipod and rest, inserted a magazine quadrant into the fairings and lay full-length squinting along the sights at Yasha.

"Da-da-da-da-da-da-da-da-da-da-da," he chanted. "Da-da-da-da-da-da."

Yasha squirmed helplessly. Spats weighed Dushan's watch on the palm of his hand before slipping it into the top pocket of his tunic.

"Know what this is?" said Myelnikov chattily. "Better than a rip-saw. One burst at the waist and a man's hands is permanently suspended from doing up his flies. Da-da-da-da-da-da."

Yasha knew what it was. They had them in the cellars in packing cases stencilled *Musketen Bataillione*. German issue for special units: Madsen machine-rifles, forty-round magazines, replaceable barrels, five hundred rounds a minute. The specification was stamped on the boxes but Myelnikov couldn't read German.

"You've done it up wrong," said Yasha. "The barrel's on a reverse thread."

Lying side by side on Spats's knee were the small calibre pistol Yasha had taken from the Laskorin cellars and a lock of Natalya Igoryevna's hair done up in a twist of paper. He was scrutinising both as if for messages in a secret code.

"Shit," exclaimed Myelnikov revolving the spare barrel. "He's got something, that midget."

The gentleman smiled his tortured smile. "Well, my little Chinese snapdragon kite-fancier. I'd say you had a story to tell. Chekhov, A. P., needed only one object of the most mundane kind to start him off on a story, but you have several, and quite exotic. I look forward to an amusing *récit*. A strong constitution is needed for a walk in this wind. Not the sort of day to choose for a hike. Tiring, don't you find? But good for kites, I would agree. A perfect day, in fact, for flying them."

Overhead the spring breeze roared. Myelnikov dismantled the machine rifle and brushed himself down. "Never seen equipment like that in our mob," he grumbled. "Could have done a lot with one of them."

"They were issued," said Spats.

"Not to us, they wasn't."

"Delicate mechanisms, Corporal, demand delicate attentions. Your mob, as you so elegantly term the flower of the Russian Imperial Army, your mob was defeated by intricacy. Show you a thoroughbred and you'd butcher it for pie-filling."

"Still," said Myelnikov. "I ask myself – all that clever-bugger stuff – what does it do for a man? Then, quick as a flash, I answer myself – It wins wars!" He laughed loudly.

"Corporal."

"Your hon . . . Sir . . . Sod this . . . Comrade Captain?"

"Today we are messing together. Prepare a meal." The gentleman, his rank now disclosed, bowed in Yasha's direction. "You'll allow me to offer you some refreshment?"

Yasha swallowed. "I ought to be getting along . . ."

"He ought to be getting along," screeched Myelnikov in hideous mirth. "What's it this time? A country ramble? Flower picking? You heard the officer. It's eats-time. Compulsory."

The captain tapped the side of his nose. "Corporal," he drawled. "Bugger off."

Myelnikov shot upwards and grabbed an overhanging branch, twisted under it, four-footed, and made off for the trunk like a galvanised sloth. With curses and grunts and slitherings he disappeared into the greenery. For a while there was silence, then more curses and a clatter of tins.

31

The captain and Yasha regarded one another.

With Myelnikov out of the way the boy felt almost calm. "Asked for it, didn't I?" he said without rancour. "Walked straight into the cage. No trouble. Just like that. With all the experience behind me I should have known, but it was the others. I was on the look-out for Schmidt and that lot. Never thought there'd be you."

The captain put his head on one side and quizzed Yasha judiciously. "You did well for a novice on his first two-front war. We had you in the field-glasses when you broke cover by the lake. Easy enough to stalk you after that." He nodded, as if confirming something to himself. "Still, you're basically sound on fieldwork, if a little impetuous. They're fortunate to have you. To be perfectly frank, I could do with a second string to my own team. Myelnikov is not the best of beasts, and at the moment he's in agony with his teeth." He spoke about the corporal with the irritable tenderness of a mother whose infant was cutting its first molars.

Yasha seized on the officer's candour: "But, we're mates," he stammered. "We're on the same side. I mean, I'll play anybody's way who's not mixed up with *them*." He had not intended to go so far. The captain might be an honourable man, and that type had principles about letting sides down. "Try me out," he ended limply. "I could do a few odd jobs."

"Decent of you to offer and all that," said Spats, spreading his hands in a gesture of helplessness. "But where can I keep you?"

"I don't take up much room." Yasha tried to retrieve the situation by eagerness. But the officer stared him down and made him wait before resuming.

"We can hardly sustain our own position. We've been living off the land and our hard tack for the last few weeks. Myelnikov needs a tooth-puller, I could do with a square meal, and our reliefs have gone down with dysentery. Consequently, although I am conspicuously undermanned, you, my dear fellow, are surplus to requirements, not wanted on voyage, a luxury, that sort of style."

The bastard talks like a swell standing down his butler. So he thinks he's marked your card. Careful. Play the ace in your boot.

"I got it all up here," said Yasha. "The lay-out, what you in the military call their dispositions. I've been everywhere."

The captain looked hard at the trees behind Yasha, took an enamelled snuff-box from his map pocket, brought out two very short cigarettes, lit both and tossed one to the boy. The paper had print on it.

"Machine-guns?" he barked.

Yasha sucked in the smoke. Pay it out a bit at a time. "Three Vickers, two Hotchkiss. Vickers all with spare barrels and one thousand rounds apiece ready belted."

"Main armament?"

Yasha thanked God he had spent so many hours in the cellars. "Four *Granatwerfer*."

"Bugger little bomb-throwing contraptions." The officer spat. "Ordnance, Mr Kiteflier, the big stuff."

"One piece," said Yasha. "An old German seventy-seven – pre-war."

The officer took off his white-topped cap, removed his mittens with his teeth and ran broad-fingered hands through short, grey-speckled hair. "Well, that seems a fairly comprehensive survey. A bite to eat, and then we can consider your long-term prospects."

"Listen, there's more." Yasha was desperate not to have exhausted his usefulness. "Won't make sense to bump me off before you've got all the goods. I know what I'm talking about. I know the whole story."

"Know it all, do you?" said the officer, picking at a ragged patch on the green band of his cap where the regimental cipher had obviously once been. "Good at stories, I expect."

"You don't believe a bloody word," said the boy.

The captain looked up and met his eyes. "I wouldn't say that, my dear old chap. I wouldn't go quite that far." He smiled and the smile sparked off his tic.

From Yasha the words tumbled out pell-mell. "I been there, I lived with them, I know every rathole. There's enough rooms there to billet half a brigade and you could squeeze another into the cellars. That's some place. It only looks as if it's falling apart because they've gutted the inside, shored up the load-bearing walls with debris and made it a fortress. They're not just pie-eyed saints. There's sappers there, siege-artists, they know how to fit up a block house. You might think it's going to be a bleeding stroll but wait till high-explosive shells start crumping round your tree-trunk den. I nearly went crazy, watching and waiting and nobody to tell me after she . . ." He broke off, then gabbled faster and faster. "Stick with me and I won't split. I know their hides, their tricks, where the guards are, how they think."

He wasn't saying the right things, he knew he wasn't from the look on the officer's face, but he knew no other way. Whine? Fall to his knees? What the hell then? This guy was chipped out of rock.

"You're no little bare-arsed refugee, are you, laddie-o?" said Spats, drawing on a fresh cigarette and closing the box with a snap. "You're a missionary amongst the heathen. You're the kite and they're the fliers. When the preaching's done you'll pop back and tell all, leaving us here to be skinned for idolaters." He laughed through the smoke. "You appear to have fallen into your own trap, Mr Kiteflier. It's missionaries who end up in the pot, not cannibals."

Contemptuous, indifferent. Hard. Topped by a different hat and in another place that mug would have been twitching over a long-barrelled forty-four.

You're looking at your last deal, boy. Him or you for Dead Man's hand? Silence came between them and in the silence Yasha could think no more but was aware only of the stillness that had descended on the trees.

Out of the blue with no whirring, tick-tock or other mechanical prelude, a perfectly-tuned C sharp broke on the air, and the ceremonial quick march of the Preobrazhenskii Regiment tinkled out from the officer's own pocket.

Dushan's watch, God Almighty.

"Hear that?" said Yasha.

"I hear it," said the officer.

"Know what it is?"

"I know what it is."

"No, no, what it means."

"It means what it plays – a death-knell."

Imperturbably, the officer withdrew a handful of cartridges from his belt-pouch and broke his revolver at the barrel-housing.

This was Yasha's last throw. "I kept something back, something that'll mean curtains for you too."

The officer raised his eyebrows and rolled the gun-chamber along his cheek. "Is that right, old chap? Well, I never."

With great deliberation he fed in three rounds, spun the empty chambers to the top and prepared to insert the remainder. He was slow. He might be interested.

"That stuff you found in my sack, it belongs to someone, to someone like you."

Yasha knew the officer knew what that meant – the "like you". *Oh God, is it love that keeps them together?*

"How did you come to possess them? Keepsakes? Mementoes?" The swine was too polished to hint at stolen goods, but his expression did indicate a greater interest in Yasha's property than in Yasha himself. As if already the boy should have given himself up for dead.

He licked his lips. "More. Sort of tokens. Like messages from prisoners. I got out with them this morning because . . ."

"Because you're as weavy as a ferret and so small nobody spotted you."

Yasha was surprised. That was how it was. Almost. "All winter they've been there. I was sent out for help."

The officer's hauteur slackened, but the last rounds went in. "Ransom?"

Yasha's extempore could not cover this one. "Dunno."

"How many?"

"A lot, a lot."

"Numbers, boy, numbers," said the officer, locking back his gun with a flick of the wrist.

Twenty? Valerian's mob had probably murdered twenty. "Twenty-six," he said and tried to believe in himself. "Including women, of course." Romance had appeal for debonair souls or so his novelettes had said. There was still no response. No souls, no hearts, no nothing now except what they had on their backs, inside their hands. Poker-faced brag was the only game left for officers who'd ripped off their badges of rank, and countesses who slept with the boot-boy.

Yasha tried coolness and nodded towards the hidden watch. "Belonged to a major, that. He sent me because of the women, on account of – how did he put it? – 'Increasing indignities to which they are subject.' They were lucky. Most families round here got picked off last year. But I expect you knew that already – judging by your cap."

The officer shook off his indolent stare. "What do you know about my headgear, little man?"

"Pavlovskii, wasn't it? First Guards Corps, I know the uniform, I had this book . . ."

"This major – what regiment?"

Yasha hedged. "He had quite a wardrobe . . ."

"Don't bugger me about, sonny."

"Empress Marya Fyodorovna's Own . . ."

A chancer, fired from the hip, but it went home. The officer sniffed the muzzle of his revolver before replacing it in the holster. Then the old languor seemed to afflict him and he yawned broadly. "The families round here, and round there," he said, embracing all the Russias with a sweep of his arm, "deserved what they got."

Carefully pinching out the stub of his cigarette he crumbled the remnants of unburnt tobacco and swept it into his tin. "Unbelievable," he said, "how the concept of luxury alters. Look at me, old chap – thirty-four years old, the best of educations, once a rising star, the terror of the Austro–Hungarian *Kommandatur* for my operations behind the lines – short of a roll-up. See where I am. And who with. Why do I do it? Myelnikov barely understands his own language. He learned to read from the Psalm Book. He was an Anarchist bomb-thrower before the war. Just an ignorant peasant. He survived three field courts martial for striking his superior officer. Now he has a future and my future is in the past. When a creature like that leaves off his sheepskin and boots, underneath he's the same brainless rascal whatever uniform they find for him. Millions like him, different features but the same brute mug staring out, greedy for an enemy to bite back at. Then you happen along, and I like you, with your smidgin of intellect and queer twisty independence." The tired brown face twitched violently. "And I'm going to have to shoot you. In the end I shall simply have to. No. I'm sorry, old fellow."

Yeah. Yasha gave up and chewed on a leaf. It was just his luck to end up plugged by a gunman in a state of psychic distress.

"Your story doesn't make sense."

Best I could do on the hop.

"You're suggesting I risk what's left of my life to save some fat old ladies who've been asking for this kind of trouble for fifty years."

One young lady, thin as a branch. The fat ones got squared up long since.

"And what do you offer in return?"

Nix.

"Help me to storm the house?"

Do me in and you'll never make the front steps.

"Do you think I need you? Preposterous."

Need you? Nobody needed, needs, will need you. Dwarf. Blackie. Hook-nose. Night-soil bagman. Pre-sodding-posterous.

"My dear chap, let me give you a piece of advice: never exaggerate."

Never raise your voice or your eyes from your plate; never cheek Ma; do the dishes, doff your cap and the kind gentleman won't dunk you in the sewage pit.

"Had you not mentioned the major I might have believed you."

How do, Major, will death love me as much as he loved you?

"There is no major inside that house."

Once it stood larger than life, that spectral presence between her and me.

Yasha was on his feet, backing off, casting about. The officer put a hand to his gun but Yasha was quicker. On one of the sappy timber baulks which formed the main-frame of the hide was a row of hooks. Suspended from the nearest was a Verey light pistol. He wrenched it off, hook and all. There was a flare already in the barrel.

"Oh yes there is, there fucking is!" he screamed. "He'd be more than gold to you, he's a warrior."

The officer swung his gun arm loose, concentrated on the monstrous round in the Verey pistol and screamed back: "Warrior! Warrior! Bogged up so long in that freakhouse and not a slash out of him! That's not my man, that's not my Martya."

Martya, Martyushka. Kabalyevskii, Martin Aleksandrovich, was realler to Yasha now than the skin on his back. *God come down in a cloud; my darling snow-baby, lending me life.*

"Yours and mine," breathed the boy. "Kabalyevskii, warrior-prince."

"Suzerain, viceroy, *conquistador*," whispered the officer. "The glory-man."

Yasha shook at the knees in blessed relief. "I told you, I told you. Big, isn't he? Corn-colour hair?"

The officer's gaze was dogged, receptive, drawing out every fleeting reminiscence from Yasha's memory of those conversations with Natalya Igoryevna. "Attached to the Fifth Army in Galicia. Before the war – some kind of painter. Mad about snow, snow and trains."

At each scrap of recall the officer clenched and unclenched his hands, as if the man were before him in the palpable flesh. When eventually he found words his voice was low: "Martin, Martin, what more shall I learn of thee? What did you bring, boy, that was his?"

Yasha watched the officer draw out the watch from his pocket and silently flip it open.

"Odd," said the captain.

Yasha knew what he meant. The flowers were a bit dandyish. "A love-gift," he said. He was so deep in his own lie that he could have sworn to it. "You know what ladies are like."

The captain seemed reassured.

"Slipped it to me on his way out for his daily exercise, and begged me to get help. 'The only way,' he said. He'd tried everything but the place is as tight as a drum. He couldn't break out and you'll never break in, not without a siege-train. But you've got better than that, Captain, haven't you – you've got me."

"No prison house could hold him. He is a giant among men."

God help us. This one was as stable as a yard of sand. He's on the wrong side of the wall.

Yasha's voice wheedled: "You're forgetting. Know someone well and you overlook his little weaknesses." What were they? Was he a drunk? Yasha watched for reaction.

Dew sparkled in the captain's eyes. "Women. With Martin it was women."

The boy struck out now, sure of his story. "Come on, you can guess why he couldn't."

The suggestion did its work slowly. "You tell me, old chap. You tell me, why was that?" said the captain at last.

Yasha was ready. "Because of *her*," he exclaimed, pointing theatrically to the lock of Natalya Igoryevna's hair which had become tangled up with the watch chain. "He came for her. She'd been waiting for him and knew he would."

"Who?"

"Who what?"

"Who knew and waited?"

Yasha took a deep breath. "A countess-woman. She's in a jam." Further explanation was needed but he opted for incidentals, seeking colour for his tale by waving Natalya Igoryevna's love-lock under the captain's nose. "That's bits of hair," he said.

The captain reached out and fondled the silk ribbons of Bengal indigo blue. "Not straws in the wind?" he said.

Yasha bent over the little package. You never knew with women – she might have done him. "Nope. Genuine article, right off the head."

"I recognise hair and know where it comes from," said the captain dreamily.

"Course you do." Yasha felt unsure.

"The tint is unique, unmistakable, and she barely noticed me. A sprite, an evangelical sprite." His kissed the thin tress. For a long while neither spoke.

Yasha was out of his depth. "What colour would you say it was, then? Chestnut? Auburn? Looks sort of ginger to me."

"It would," said the captain. "To you."

"Ah." Yasha relaxed. This was worse than the God-farm. His life still hung by a thread and all of a sudden he was talking hairdressing. "Bit beside the point, isn't it? Fact is, he gave it to me, your friend. A fine girl she was once, he said, before the monk got to her."

"Monk?"

"In a way of speaking, you understand. Their leader, he's a kind of monkish person."

Or was. The monkishness must have fallen off lately, judging by those screams. *Best to sit tight on all that.*

At this the captain's old good-humour appeared to revive. "Valerian. A rather special individual, I gather. Not what you'd call a monk's monk."

"More of an individualist. Seen him in action, have you?" said Yasha, glad that no further account of Valerian was required of him.

"It's my vocation, old chap, to know. My line of country. Twice I have met him: once before and once during the war. He has accomplished much for one so young. An eccentric, not without charm, but unhappily this is no age for the individualist."

It was a magic circle: they all kept bumping into each other like toy-trains on a loop line and whistling how-de-do's.

"Charm" stuck in Yasha's throat. "Have a heart, Captain, he's got more notches on his gun than Wild Bill Hickok."

The captain grinned at the strange reference. "We don't live in the same world, old fellow, do we? Or do you imagine that my being his acquaintance or his friend or even his admirer will give me a moment's pause when my time comes to kill him?"

"No, sir," said Yasha very positively. "And his gang of bugaboos?"

"Down to the last single solitary one."

At last they were getting somewhere.

The captain tucked Natalya Igoryevna's posied hair into his field tunic and regarded Yasha with a new, invigorated expression. "You've earned yourself a respite, Mr Kiteflier. Keep it up and you may live to terrify your grandchildren with stories about me. Tell me more. Tell me about the bugaboos. We're within striking distance and the unit is moving up. How scattered is the work-force in the fields? How quickly can they be assembled? How many men with military experience? Any NCOs? Can the women re-load small-arms ammunition? Have they got guncotton? Is there a well?"

He went on and on. Yasha could not answer all the questions, so he made up some things, fudged others, kept a lot back and tried to sound convincing. Once pumped dry he knew he'd be thrown to the Myelnikov jackal. The captain was shrewd and, Yasha reckoned, didn't entirely trust him. But for the moment he was comparatively safe. No matter how much he told about the lieutenant system and the chain of command, the captain and Myelnikov would hang onto him until the very last moment because they knew that in the last resort (i.e. with a pistol to his head) he'd negotiate them up to the front gates with fewer casualties than otherwise they'd take from mines and concealed gun-points. He knew the way, and as long as he didn't reach the end of it, he was going to be all right.

Eventually the captain stopped. "We shall need a detailed map."
He called up into the tree: "Corporal, stand by!"

A moment later, winding down through the branches came a thick
rope, knotted with handholds.

"After you," said the officer, lifting Yasha to within reach of the
nearest.

32

With the spring thaw came unusually heavy rain. Storms rolled down from the north making a quagmire of the soil. Then a bitter wind whipped the mud into hard-ridged peaks. In May, frosts set the edges as hard as glass, burning the black fields to wasteland. By early June the community knew that their crops had failed.

From beyond the estate there was no news. Makar had mounted up with three of the other lieutenants and they rode for two days. To the east, tracts of frost-burned wheat darkened the horizon. In the north and south the land was trampled flat from the movements of troops and heavy artillery. No one knew to which side they belonged. In villages fired by armies they gaped at the emptiness.

Lacking fodder, they dared not push the horses too far. Occasionally intelligence was received: a holy man at a cross-roads told them the Germans had killed the Tsar and now ruled the country, burning churches and stealing women. Makar offered to take him pillion but the man only peered up at the wide-snouted cob and said he preferred pilgrimage to rest. They let him go.

In one hut they found a family. A gaunt mother and daughter insisted that the Germans were in retreat, and grain had been promised. It was all a question of waiting. Yes, their food was gone. No, they would stay; if they didn't, when they came back, their land would have been stolen.

Osip, the raw-boned lieutenant with the yellow bandana, spat on the ground and reared his horse against the wind from the north which reeked of burnt palliasses, amatol and rotting barley. "V bolotye i tikho, da zhit tam likho," he shouted. "If you want a quiet life stay in the bog, it stinks but it's your own."

Makar gave out some millet with a blessing.

When the riders straggled back the women streamed down to greet them, wailing, abusive, shouting at each other, at the dogs which barked cheerfully, ruffling their coats in the crisp breeze, and at the children who kicked pebbles up and down the great Laskorin carriage-way.

Mismanagement, ignorance and greed meant that last year's harvest had hardly covered the stones of Laskorin's threshing floors. Now his barns contained nothing except two hoppers a quarter-full with musty grains that might be enough for a week, a fortnight even, if eked out, but no more. Valerian had become a recluse. The women had begun to steal for their children. Discipline was needed, order and system.

Schmidt called an emergency council.

Everyone demanded to know where Valerian was. Schmidt could not say. "Presently, the master will come. Presently." In fact he had not seen the boy for three days.

Exhausted from his ride Makar cat-called in broken German until the meeting threatened uproar, whereupon he fell fast asleep, the rowels of his spurs embedding themselves in the earthen floor.

Far into the night the sitting went on. They heard that soon it would be every man for himself. Men, women and children were grubbing on their knees for green shoots. Already fighting had broken out. Valerian did not come. Leaderless and afraid the lieutenants screwed up their eyes and smoked, trying to divine the future, trying to sound business-like, trying not to lose face in front of the women. But when morning broke they had found no comfort and no plan.

In the days that followed Valerian ceased his attendance at services. When the women went to his room on their daily rounds he could occasionally be surprised in the act of staring out of the window, smiling to himself and then frowning; starting suddenly at their appearance as if about to speak, but thinking better of it. The stupidest or most cowardly assumed that his wits had gone, since he no longer talked of God but of wedding clothes. The children noticed nothing and sang to him his favourite song of Graf Sheremetyev and his serf-wife, the ill-fated Praskovya, while he drank wine, alone, before clanking up the iron staircase and disappearing behind the door of the little room.

There was no comfort to be found anywhere. Matryona summoned a meeting which lasted a whole day. Makar dropped out of the rota for patrol-duty. Schmidt became desperate. Valerian and the woman were unapproachable. He could no longer count on his being Valerian's deputy to pacify the people. Soon they would be looking for victims and he was an obvious offering to be burnt. But if the best and strongest lieutenants kept together they could carry their troops with them and impose their will on the rest.

Consequently the people had to be told: someone had sinned. And to expiate that sin, the sinner must be sacrificed. Only after that could the threat from outside be prepared against.

* * *

A great scarecrow of a man towered above the cream chaise-longue, fresh-faced from the storm rain. At the loops of his gas-cape hung Mills bombs, their castings bright in the wet. Loose over one shoulder was a webbing bandolier containing 7-mm. ammunition for the German automatic carbine slung butt-down across his chest. He had not removed his peakless cap and stood insolently aware of the rainwater dripping from his high waders onto the polished floor.

In his presence the shrivelled flowers on the bedside table seemed even more like thistle-dry claws, and the room tawdry and shrunken.

The man spoke witheringly, pushing out his lower lip at the end of each phrase. "Smoke, I'm saying, Valerian. Smoke. Black powder smoke in the birch glade and dead shrike hit on the wing. Hermann has deputed me since he won't meet you here." At the last word he jerked a thumb at the fans on the wall and smiled broadly. "But he asks for me to say that some of the troops is unregenerate superstitious and need a sight of their commander to boost theirselves. I say they better say their prayers because they ain't fit for nothing except to be butchered, Lord or no Lord, but Hermann thinks different, so here I stand."

Before Valerian could reply Loulou came in from the dressing-room wearing a morning-gown of sprigged muslin. Her hair was up and intertwined with silvered lace.

Vissarion pulled himself to attention, and slammed his heels together à la Prusse. "Ma'am," he said refinedly. When she moved away without reply he regarded her with no malice or desire, only with a rude curiosity.

Valerian ran his fingers down the doorframe and dust collected under his nails. "Hermann is an old woman."

"God's truth, I'm telling you. Children got into the tunnels and saw two men. Strangers, Hermann thinks . . ."

Valerian shouted: "I've told you before – keep children away from the fortified places!"

This was no answer, or advice, and Vissarion knew it, but obediently he took up the factitious point. "You know how it is, Valerian, with the women busy at the munitions . . ."

"You may leave me," said Valerian turning his back.

As he wheeled smartly Vissarion winked at Loulou but she stared away, head down. Long after the lieutenant had gone she remained motionless and silent, trying to control her trembling fingers by squeezing back the skin from the half-moon nails. It was too late. The man had seen her fear. Soon they would all know of it. She could hear them: why was she so afraid? Had she really bewitched their

commander, their leader, stolen their Vicar of Christ? What was she
– witch or fool? Had the master defected for the sake of a school-girl
ninny who vapoured at the first whiff of gunshot?

As if having decided something, Valerian strode to the door, opened
it with a tremendous rattle and barked out an order which sent the
watchmen, Fedya and Gerasim, scuttling down the iron steps. Kicking
the door to again he faced Natalya Igoryevna. The new short hair
bristled as he rubbed his temples.

"Why did you insist that I gave credence to that idiot's views by
granting him a hearing? The man is a fool. I chose him and his fellows
precisely because they were fools. Now, because of your interference
he imagines he is a man of affairs, capable of decision."

She broke into a plea: "You cannot keep yourself apart or they
will start to hate you as they hate me. That way we will both be
destroyed. They are leaderless and see enemies everywhere. Restore
their faith in you, and in their own lives, and in the terrible things
they have done in your name."

In any other man Valerian's behaviour this last week would have
seemed to Loulou entirely a tribute, earned and deserved. Of course,
he had deserted his responsibilities, but what lover would not?
Besides, unlike other men she had known, he was not subject to
higher powers. (From the start she had instinctively rejected his
supernatural pretensions.) Her ordinary female vanity had been more
than satisfied by his desire to take her, then to bathe her, clothe her,
dress her hair, feed her, never leave her side without hurrying back a
moment later, obsessed, greedy for her, enchanted. His appetite for
the most intimate proximity had shocked her at first, but she analysed
it logically and submitted: to a man of his mind possession was
nothing if not total.

Quite soon she had become assertive – there seemed nothing he
would not do – and she tested him by pretending that she was too
languid to choose what to wear.

He had thrown open the drawers of the press and riffled through
her clothes. "How shall we have you today – village *baba* in her thick
stuffs, or the cambric afternoon frock or the coming-out dress?"

The game continued pleasantly enough but she soon tired of her
affectation and made her own choice. He noticed, smiled and said
nothing. Later there were callers at the door. Instructions were
requested, even commands – since the community, for all its egali-
tarian aspect was, in fact, an autocracy. Valerian procrastinated,
acceding to nothing. Eventually Fedya and Gerasim had to be posted
outside to turn away more petitioners.

Loulou was amused, then touched, then afraid. On the seventh day, after Vissarion had been denied access on four occasions she demanded that he be heard.

"Faith . . . faith . . . lives, terror," Valerian muttered stamping along the boards. "As if it could save, as if grace would come . . ."

"But you must, Valerian, you must try . . ."

He stopped her with a glare and swung open the tall doors of the cupboard press where her clothes lay shelved in neat piles. "So, on the seventh day the lady becomes the peasant wife who ceases to fawn and becomes strident . . . and hectoring . . . and starts on her wifely business . . ." At each pause he threw aside a heap of her clothing. "Well, your *muzhik* has a will to retaliate. Stand up, woman, when your peasant husband commands you to put on more suitable dress."

Peeling off the morning-gown he lowered a new frock over her unresisting head. She held out her arms to the sleeves like a baby. For the time it took to light a cigarette he looked her over almost casually. "Turn round, woman." She did as she was told and felt his eyes on her naked back. "Up straight," he ordered, and she sat up, waiting for his hands. "Gladden the hearts of those you claim to love so much by wearing the bridal gown they sewed for you. Or is the honourable life not to your taste? Or any woman's?"

She would not answer and could not weep.

Valerian stooped to do up the hook-and-eye fasteners running down the back. She smelt smoke from his cigarette as he laid the edges together along her spine and tugged. The bodice was uncomfortably tight. Catching sight of herself in the glass she gasped. The dress, cut from wrinkly white cotton, was hideous. When Matryona, bowing respectfully, had brought it to her one day, Loulou had cast it aside in a sulk saying that white did not suit her. But now it was more than the colour: the narrow sleeves, pinched-in waist and hobbling skirt constrained her slightest movement. Even the tall collar rubbed under her chin.

"Behold," said Valerian. "The true measure of their love."

Before she had time to penetrate the meaning of this remark he had crossed into the room that had been Yasha's and shut the door behind him. She dropped stiffly onto the bed. The boy was hopeless. The imperative mood was so exclusively his: *should, must, ought* were words rarely to be found in her mouth. Press him and he metamorphosed into the brute that must have spawned him.

Papa Laskorin? Something else. *Canaille*. Bully, dark man, stir-ruped and spurred above her, looking down.

The near door clattered and Valerian stood legs astride in the centre of the room. It was a sight she had not witnessed since childhood,

years before the war. In place of the loose blouse he habitually wore
was a dark red tunic with stripes at collar and cuffs. Guard stripes.
It was uniform but not all of a piece for beneath the jacket was a
white waistcoat. Slung over one shoulder he carried a scarlet *burka*,
a caftan edged with gold braid; on the other she saw ciphers of rank
on the gold-laced broadcloth of an epaulette. Dark blue trousers
bagged into short riding boots; spurs *and* a whip. The ensemble was
heterogenous – a cross; part Guards, part *Konvoi* Cossack. But for
action somehow dated, old fashioned.

She pressed her fingers so hard under her hair her eyes ached.
"Valerian . . . ? Why . . . ?"

At any other time her tone was such that he might have made a
short answer but he laughed as he made for the door. "You in your
glory, I in mine. Dressed each for his fate. Out there," he said carefully
setting the astrakan cap so that only a narrow stripe of his forehead
was visible, "you say I am desired. I shall go to them a feast for the
eye, so shall they all, my lieutenants, to outdazzle the face of the sun.
Let the enemy bask in me for I am what I was and what I am – their
fit adversary and victim."

The storm had passed. From the window of their room on the west
front Polly and her husband watched the muster in the great court.
The horses were brought up, restless and snorting, their hindlegs
slithering in the mushy gravel. Each mount was saddled up and
equipped: short carbine, holster to the right of the pommel; water-
bottle to the left; and behind the rear lip of the high-standing saddle
a long blanket roll across the hindquarters, containing bivouac, spare
ammunition and entrenching tools.

The sun flashed at bit-ring and hoof; four blood mares, three
stallions and Schmidt's pony circled prick-eared, chopping their yellow teeth at the leading reins.

"Trouble," said Belyakov and lit a cigarette.

At any other time this might have provoked a scene but Polly said
nothing. From the tone of his voice she had come to read her
husband's moods. He had always said that their hour would come,
and had always known that when it came there would be no need to
speak out what they both knew. Was it now? She was uncertain and
silent.

Once Belyakov had been Valerian's nearest friend and Schmidt's
best comrade. That was in the old days, a past as inexplicable to her,
now, as her own. Once he had saved her life and that she recalled
without gratitude, merely as an event. No obligation was entailed,
no favour conferred because the huntsman had become hers and

when a man was yours you owed him nothing from the past. He had to keep you day-to-day, and you him. Marriage was like that.

But amongst men things were different. Polly carried with her from the world she had lost – lost without regret but it still kept a hold upon her – that men were never free of obligations which, at any time, they could be called on to fulfil. She did not imagine that Belyakov thought of his life in this way, but recognised from his behaviour that it must be so.

His attempt the previous year to escape from the community with her; their marriage; his cultivation of the subsequent estrangement between himself and Valerian, all those things were done in the knowledge that once he, Schmidt and Valerian were brethren in heart and mind, and he had betrayed and forsaken them out of weakness, and for her. That was why he drank, why he raged, why he swore.

In front of her Valerian's wedding-gift, a broad-backed Orloff stallion, careered in the sun, snatching at his Arab mane, all blue-blood and temperament, scenting the humid mares and impatient for the saddle to creak over him, weighted and full.

When Schmidt's adjutant hammered on the door demanding Belyakov's presence in the courtyard, Polly went out and said that her husband had a fever and could not leave his bed.

When she returned Belyakov had not moved and continued to watch through the window, his back to her. She had no idea of what he would do.

After Valerian left without a backward glance, Loulou flung herself on the bed and lay back exhausted. For the first time in seven days she was alone but the isolation only made her more restless. She wanted to sleep but could not settle. In the mirror the high stock of the dress set off the rounded line of her chin, and her skin creamed above the rigid brocade, deepening the copper tint of her hair.

"Such frightful taste," she said aloud, and made herself comfortable.

Voices shrilled beyond the door, then died away on a surge of wind which fluttered Fedya's paper fans. Behind her the door swung open but no one came in.

On the bed Loulou floundered, the raised seams of the wedding-frock chafing on her bare skin. As she reached for the floor, the skirt-train caught at her heels and she fell to her knees.

"Too grand you look, *knyazhna*," said a woman's voice, "to be curtseying to me."

Matryona was standing above her, draped from head to toe in a dark brown cloak. Her arm was outstretched but her hand concealed.

The voice had been so unironic, so polite, even, that Loulou, imagining Matryona had brought a message from Valerian, gave a half-smile, grasped the woman's arm and swayed upwards in the tubular skirt. Before she could take a step back to loosen the hem, the woman had dropped her arm and moved swiftly to the open door of Yasha's room, peered inside, then slammed it shut.

As if at a signal, one behind the other, two more women entered Loulou's room. The first, a small thin creature with nervous brown eyes and cheeks purpled from broken veins, was carrying a square-lidded laundry basket. Without a glance at the astounded Loulou and at devastating speed, she swept every object off the dressing-table and into her basket. She had begun on the drawers when Matryona came right up to the countess and punched her hard between the breasts. The blow was so agonising that Loulou collapsed on the bed without a word or sound and Matryona dived on top of her, clawing with wide fingers. For a second Loulou tasted oil and sweat. Then a rope straightened across her teeth, tightened, and jerked between her lips.

"Gag her neat," said the hare-eyed woman. "Walls have ears."

Matryona jerked Loulou upright by tugging on the rope and the second woman, middle-aged with a beaky face from which a pair of kindly eyes peered at the prisoner through little round spectacles, helped Matryona to place her straight on the bed by setting a cushion at her back. The rope bit into her arms as both women wove around her. When they finally came to rest, she was trussed like a hog.

More women crowded in, among them the carpenter's wife, beautiful blonde Katya, and Matryona's daughter, Masha, both visibly pregnant. Katya plucked one of Loulou's fans from the wall, turning it over several times to gaze at the birds painted on the panels, while the other girl snatched the satin kimono from behind the door and slid it over her peasant blouse.

"Shame on you, Masha," shouted the bespectacled matron. "Unseemly it is to rob the dying."

Masha opened wide her pale blue eyes and twirled defiantly in a flurry of pink. "I knelt all night before the ikon of the Blessed Virgin and much good came from my entreaties – he still went to *her*."

"I could do with a nip," said the little hare-faced woman. "There's been no generosity in this place, not since the old one's time."

"Not since the war," said Katya. "Not even at my wedding."

"Not since *she* came," declared Masha, glaring at the figure on the bed and crossing herself with difficulty in the narrow kimono.

Loulou's arms were becoming numb. The high white collar scraped at her throat. The bespectacled woman took pity on her, caressing her face as she struggled. "Ah, darling, you were born blest," she crooned in a long, deep voice. "A fine-boned, well-attended woman. Girls, look at these nails. Not like yours, not like mine. Hands and fingers such as these were made to be desired, bred for the joy of a man, soft to his touch."

Matryona was rooting under the bed. Three corkless wine bottles rolled out. "Consumed in heartless disregard," she said gloomily. "Not a drop left for God's faithful."

"What do you expect?" said the lovely Katya. "It's hard enough to descend to the level of beasts when you're *not* laying together in sin."

"What would you know of men, girl, with that shrimp of a husband?" said Matryona.

Katya cradled her bulge. "This," she said. "This comes of the evils of liquor."

The older women laughed and wiped their eyes but the girls, closer in spirit to the one on the bed, regarded Loulou with a grim, maleficent envy.

"Brazen whore," muttered Masha. "Making herself the talk of the place."

Katya folded her arms and stared reverentially. "Witchery. He ransomed his soul for her rich limbs. Didn't eat, didn't sleep, tiptoed in and out of this room like a shade, not a man."

There was a general shudder.

Under the gag Loulou howled like a bitch. The noise came out baffled and gurgly but it was enough of a protest to incense the younger women. Dunya, the smallest, a girl with a long black fringe, who up till now had taken no part in the pillaging, went up to the bed and thrust her wrist under Natalya Igoryevna's nose. An intricately-stranded silver and gilt bangle slid along the thin, hairy arm.

"See that?" she snarled. "I'm sick of waiting. I've selected my own reward for sewing your trousseau silks."

It was the gift Valerian had made Loulou after their first day and night entirely together. Dunya knew this. Every woman knew it. Not a single passage of Valerian's courtship had gone unnoticed by any of them. To Katya, a woman who inspired such unwonted show was a creation of story-book fantasy. But what appeared in her as awe and well-founded respect caused in the others an unnameable dread which they enjoyed but longed to extinguish.

Matryona blew the dust off a miniature carriage clock before popping it into her bosom. "Have we taken our due? Time passes, women."

In her terror Loulou could have wept at the bare laconic tone. Perhaps their business was with her goods, not with her. What could it profit them to murder her now?

By now the room was almost bare. Even the curtains had been taken down. Nothing was damaged. All that was left were myriads of dust specks tumbling in the noonday sun.

Loulou rehearsed her argument in case the moment came when the gag was relaxed and she could say: "Valerian has returned to you. He was unwilling but I made him. It was my wish and I persuaded him. Go out to your men where you will find him. He is there in your defence."

But as she ran over these words, a new fear came: a reasoned fear; the kind of fear a victim feels when he pleads for his life. These women knew what Valerian was capable of, what he would do to them if they so much as bruised the tip of her finger. The image formed of her kneeling to him in intercession while they stood in line with ropes around their necks.

They were not here upon impulse. Matryona was not stupid. She must have a plan.

The woman with the spectacles put her hand on Loulou's knee. "Poor dearheart," she murmured. Tears stood in her eyes. "So young."

"She'd have done it to you, Marya, you old fool, only not in a snatch but slow, slow, like they did it to the old folk," exclaimed Masha. "Or has it slipped your mind, the time when hardly a year passed without a laying-out for one of the tribe of kids at your skirt?"

"This is no way," moaned old Marya. "No one comes back. What are we doing?"

"Seeing there's a finish to it, that's what we're doing." For a moment Loulou flinched in anticipation of a blow from Masha. "So our crops won't die, our land don't shrivel and we don't peer down the guns of strangers. Doing what Valerian couldn't bring himself to do."

Matryona brought her daughter down to earth: "Whisht, girl," she boomed. "Valerian may look like a boy but he's a man and a man was always a mystery to you, my lass. Valerian's no different from the rest of men, when a woman allows him his ease with her. Guilt is their flaw, guilt at their weakness. Today we must do what soon he would have done himself. Afterwards he will weep but who knows better than a woman how to console a man who longs to be comforted?"

With one hand she wrenched Natalya Igoryevna to her feet and bundled her upright across the floor. Dunya threw open the door.

The gallery was packed with silent women, their faces shimmering in the sudden light. "Sisters," she cried. "All is not lost."

A clamorous babble filled the air in which prayers and obscenities mixed.

Becky squirmed to the front of the crowd. In her hands was a thick halter plaited from wheatstraw. Her face quivered with glee: "Lord love-a-duck, 'is brother," she murmured, standing tiptoe and pushing the knot of the halter under Loulou's left ear. "Who's been a naughty boy, then? What've you been up to with our master, all dressed up in little girlie's clothes?" She turned to the mass of chattering women and silenced them with a shout: "Each to his own, sisters! What do we teach her?"

"Each to his own!" came the response, repeated and repeated, blocking any other sound from Loulou's ears.

But inside her head the countess attended to another voice, remote, yet clear, chanting the beginning of a story over and over: "When daybreak came the lynch-mob was already out of hand . . . When daybreak came . . ."

Yasha. Yes. They will have killed him. Of course. That was from where his voice came – the preliminary place of murder.

They had been clever, but over her they could no longer contain themselves. The kind old bespectacled Marya with the *babushka* endearments, languorous Katya with a child in her womb, the gross Masha, they had all conspired in ignorance and dread to incite Matryona to tighten this murderous noose; how they will have babbled and plotted while she and Valerian had frittered away their idyll under the eaves of a desolate house.

Each to his own; and never meeting. That was the irony of closeness. These women coveted the man without understanding. Vengeance or love, there was no communion even in the sweetest of life's gifts.

33

Myelnikov tore at the bread, making soft moans. The officer ate nothing but drank a great deal. His good-humour recovered, he went on and on about the corporal:

"Finds it hard to masticate. Wisdom teeth, would you believe? Now he has this dependency problem with oil of cloves. Helps the pain."

"Not as good as some things, though," said Myelnikov spitting crumbs down through the leaves. He gave a thump to Yasha's back which made the boy splutter. "Such as a bullet in the head."

"Wouldn't make you stink, neither," said Yasha.

Myelnikov chewed on morosely. "Cheeky little sod. I'll crucify you."

The threat was made in good part, almost affectionately, and Yasha relaxed as he ate, looking round the tree hide and allowing the officer's words to drift over him.

"Lord, Nature is so boring. Omnipresent, fructifying and dull, quite without variety. Trees, trees, trees."

"Hark at him," said Myelnikov. "What kind of words is that? Trees is his fructifying bread and butter, even I know that. Mother, father and wife they are. Where would we be without his fructifying trees?"

In the green shade the officer looked older; the springy tufts of hair were almost grey, the deep lines at the sides of his mouth a vivid black.

"Now, the corporal here is an oak, a solid, dependable oak, roots outspread in the black earth, immovable. Ah, the majesty of the People!"

Myelnikov snorted. "You know nothing, you know you know nothing." He tweaked Yasha's face round by the ear. "I have to put up with this twanging day in day out, worse than toothache. The People is what the People always was for the likes of him: it's either the veneerings for the marquetry commodes they plops their arses on or dead wood lying about to be planked into coffins when it suits their turn." His taut belly loosened with laughter and he stripped one of the red apples to the core with plunging movements of his front teeth.

The officer smiled as if pleased at Myelnikov's violence and wanting to respond in kind but content that the corporal took the smile as an inferior would accept a blow, mutely, contemptuously and with hatred.

Yasha was embarrassed. "They live longer than us, trees," he said. "In California. Redwoods . . ."

Myelnikov tossed the apple core into the air and caught it on the bridge of his nose. "They will here," he said triumphantly. "When we've thinned out the underbrush and given them a chance to breathe."

Yasha had not eaten since the night before and although the bread was very black and very hard, and the cheese rather dry, he munched happily. Must have his wits about him, this Myelnikov, to come up with provender like he did, stuck up a tree half the time. And there was beef-strips to come, floating in a kind of jellied fat, and little pyramids of russet apples each wrapped in a beech leaf. As he ate, Yasha considered the partnership: sinister but homely. That about covered it. When Spats passed over his bottle, Yasha felt appreciation and a certain mellowness. Perhaps, in the end, they'd let him join.

"Right, gentlemen," said the captain, corking his bottle. "Business."

On the plank table slung between two branches was a sketch map, rather artistically done out with cotton-woolly trees and hatched scarps. An outline plan of the great house was at the top, near the compass-rose. The officer smoothed down the crinkly paper with the flat of his hand.

"The Laskorin property, or what we could make of it from our reconnoitring and a pair of duff field-glasses."

"Waste of time," said Myelnikov. "My peepers is better than any Kraut optics." He filled his mouth from a stone jar and began to gargle.

"Inadequate, you see, without the benefit of inside knowledge," continued Spats, smiling at Yasha. "We need you, my dear chap, to illuminate the obscurer parts."

Yasha leaned over the map. They'd done well on the vegetation, but not so good on checking what it covered. A couple of right townees, that was obvious. Gun-pits they'd missed; the echeloned trenching; and the small-arms ammunition cache. But every flower-bed was inked in.

"Not bad," said Yasha carefully. "Nice penmanship."

Evidently gratified, the captain re-opened his bottle. "Have another nip," he said. "The fire may only be fitful, but one needs all the beauty one can get in life. The passion and the yearning die but beauty lives forever."

Yasha noticed with surprise that the officer could not take his drink. Things were looking up.

"Bollocks," said Myelnikov rubbing his little finger up and down his gums. "He's a squit." He took a long swig from the bottle. "Eyes like baby-rabbit's shits. He's tickling you up, your honour. I seen 'em, boys! Cunning as warty toads. Pick one up and he pisses into your hand." Drink made him vocal but quite un-angry.

The captain's mild blue eyes beamed upon Yasha unsentimentally. "He makes his point, Mr Kiteflier, you must admit. Inelegant as a garotte but he says his say with style."

"Give him to me," said Myelnikov. "Half an hour of re-decorating his interior and he'd give me the works, right down to the colour of the underfootman's second cousin's drawers."

Yasha looked from one to the other like a cripple whose cap had been snitched by two bullies. The bastards were having a game. His legs were giving way.

"Where's your compassion for this waif?" said Spats to his subordinate. "He was driven away – weren't you, old chum? Cruelly, all his dutiful service forgotten. He saved someone's life, you know."

"Scab deserted," said Myelnikov. "Fast as his crook legs could wag."

"Ah, but that was *feeling*. Now, we can't help our feelings, can we, Mr Kiteflier? She'd fallen, hadn't she, old chap, head over heels?"

They weren't questioning Yasha. They knew what they knew and they were going to let him know exactly how much, bit by bit, so that he was scared half to death. If he had wanted to speak his tongue would not have worked.

"For that pansy-haired God-flopper in the vicar's frock."

"Cassock," said the captain, pulling Yasha's ear.

"Cossack-cassock," said the corporal. "He tittupped her skirts like a raddling yeasty pig-boar."

Not for a moment had the captain lost his suave reasonableness. "Truth is, it's a poor look-out for honour these days. Progress has to be eased along by a modicum of treachery." His tone was one of complete understanding. "We're all tainted." Pausing, he looked at his nails.

"None the worse for it, neither," said Myelnikov. "Specks of corruption is the salt of life. Cough up and you'll feel a new man. Clean slate and all that."

It was a trick: they wanted him to grab at the philosophical straw:
confession was so good for the soul that you didn't mind digging
your own grave. They had him down for a mug. He wasn't, but they
sure scared the hell out of him.

Yasha found his voice. "Yes," he said. There was a long silence.

Myelnikov lost patience first. "Yes? What scum-bag foolery you
telling, boy? We want particulars."

"Yes. Yes. Yes," said the officer, rolling the word in his mouth as
if it were an abstruse candy which refused to melt. "Can you elaborate,
old fellow?"

Confirmation or information? A few secrets should help him live
longer. Until they actually had the noose round his neck he was
keeping mum as to hitherto undisclosed facts.

"Yes. That's how it was, with her and him."

"Strewth!" cried Myelnikov admiringly, clapping his officer on the
shoulder. "Works like a hammerless cocking piece, Captain, your
brain, blasting away at its – what d'ye call them?"

"Intuitions," said the captain. "Based upon principle. In this instance the principle being: Criminals often hold a specious charm for
women."

Myelnikov tapped the phrase out on Yasha's head: "'Criminals-
often-hold-a-specious-charm-for-women.' Knew that did you, my
rancid little polecat? Only tells me now, though, don't he, out here
in Mother Nature's bosom where women is as frequently encountered
as chandeliers in a doss-house. Blinded I was all those years, blinded
by the beauty of women." For a moment he dwelt upon the memory
dreamy-eyed. "When all I had to do was show 'em evidence of my
horrible misconduct."

Yasha was nettled. The old love was still in his blood. "She's no
moll, I know she's not."

"Moll?" the captain asked Myelnikov.

"The unchurched helpmeet of one of your specious rapscallions.
Isn't that so?" said the corporal. Yasha nodded miserably.

"A young blade's trugging block, all gossamers and silk hankies to
look at, but underneath a ripe piece of stew-meat."

Yasha leapt at Myelnikov butting with his over-size skull. Before
he could do damage the corporal had him by the loose neck of his
blouse and was swinging him round.

"She's seen murders, she's seen pillaging, and she's been and heard
the last trumpet that calls up the end of the world and she's still over
there, dabbing the brow of a mad young bugger who'd stake us all
out on a rock for the buzzards to dip their beaks in our eyes."

When Myelnikov let go Yasha hit his head on a branch, sprawled and almost fell through the tree. He was dizzy but out of his mind with rage: "You bastard jail-piss – I'll swing for you yet."

While the corporal grinned and clapped his hands, the captain scraped mud off his spats. "Your loyalty is admirable," he said lazily before taking another drink. "But the gallows is our department and priorities must be observed."

After his outburst, Myelnikov became glum, distancing himself from his officer as if a bond between himself and Yasha came suddenly to mind. "Bloody class with him," he murmured. "Always a question of bloody class. Who's first, who's next? Who brings up the tail? One! Two! Three! And Christ take the hindmost."

He banged his forehead with Yasha's discarded loaf. "I'm sick of him, I'm mewling, puking sick of him and his sort. He's a bleeding Hindenburg with a red star on his cap. Scratch one, scratch all, underneath they're frock-coated effing stock-jobbers."

"Ignore him," said Spats, his tic flickering wildly. "He reads books. Now, about your distressed lady. In twelve hours unit HQ will issue orders. Corporal Myelnikov is acting courier. All we need now is to establish contact by signal."

Yasha was distraught. "Twelve hours? I know that lot . . . They'll have strung her up for a witch before then. I shouldn't have left. I heard them talking about it . . ."

The officer unlooped the field-glasses and snapped his fingers. Yasha scrambled up. "That break in the branches, do you see?"

The boy rammed the binoculars against his eye-sockets. The left lens was blank, leaving the other without depth of field, and the gap looked like it was at the end of his nose. "Nothing," he said.

"Raise Mr Kiteflier's sights a little higher, Corporal, if you don't mind."

Myelnikov stood the boy on his shoulders and gripped him round the waist. The captain guided Yasha's hands. Suddenly the blurred greenery parted and the great house sprang into focus. There was the terrace; the ha-ha; the windows. Everything was yellow at the edges from refracted light, visible as pretty roundelled views. Even the overgrown shrubbery looked neatly picturesque.

"Peaceful?" asked Spats.

"Lovely," said Yasha.

Myelnikov chortled. "Quiet as the grave?"

"Almost," muttered the boy, tracking the façade inch by inch with the one good lens. There was something queer. "Steer me round a couple of points," he said to the corporal, who shuffled obediently northwards. Out of the first-floor window farthest from the side entrance to the house protruded something long and black, which

Yasha recognised as quite out of place. It was a lifting beam from the granary complete with rope and pulley. With a wriggle he slid down Myelnikov's back and tossed over the field-glasses. "Twelve hours is half a day late. If you want my advice, Captain, I'd call up reinforcements now before that lot does for your mates."

Cursing at the glasses Spats eventually spotted the beam. "Lifting tackle?" he said. "What are they up to – swinging in a field-piece to cover the park approach?"

"Gawn!" sneered Myelnikov. "First recoil from that and they'd be through the floorboards."

"It's not for lifting," said Yasha. "That tackle, it's for dropping."

The captain whistled. "Settling God's scores for Him already by advancing Judgement Day." He let the glasses fall and looked into the boy's eyes. "Surely not for your Natalya Igoryevna?"

The corporal was twisting round his head to bring the beam into relief. "What they do with lead-swingers, then, your babes of Jesus – make 'em walk the plank?"

At that moment a figure in military uniform emerged from the glass doors of the main entrance on the north front, followed in quick succession by four others in exactly similar dress. They bunched at the top step. One stooped to flick his boots with a riding whip.

"Christ!" exclaimed the corporal. "They're a long way from home."

Each was in the trooper's tall cap and long cape of the *Konvoi*, the Imperial Cossack bodyguard. Hatless in the afternoon sun a blond man, resplendent in officer's uniform, strode into their midst, shouted a command, and the whole party stood to, their backs to the observers in the hide.

"Well, I'll be damned," muttered the captain. "Last time I saw that scrubby golden head was in . . . Here, Corporal, hand me the glasses."

Myelnikov yanked on the boy's legs and Yasha threw over the binoculars. For a full minute the officer scrutinised the group on the steps while the corporal worked over their accoutrements with the naked eye.

"*Stavka* Cossack bastards," he said loudly. "Did in my mates at Moghilyov rail-head. Said they was mu-tin-eers, the dog-whipping swine . . ."

"Stands like him, struts like him, by God, it *must* be . . . Mr Kiteflier, and I took you for a liar."

"Blob of officerial fluff," shouted Myelnikov, jogging Yasha up and down. "Give me half a chance and I'll stuff that ramswool *schlyapa* right up his swanking backside . . ."

"Do control yourself, Corporal. You're peeping at a hero."

"Ooh," said Myelnikov. "Is that what I'm doing? A pal of yours, I take it, sir, one poured from the same mould as Your Honour, as it were?"

"You might say so," said Spats. "That gallant gentleman happens to be my friend whom I thought had perished long ago. A distinguished soldier, *Graf . . .*"

"Bugger me," sighed Myelnikov. "Amazing how they find each other, his lot. Middle of the desert and their camels'd be making introductions: *Count* Sod meet *Prince* Gob . . ."

"Major in Her Imperial Majesty Aleksandra Fyodorovna's Uhlans, Kabalyevskii, Martin."

At the mention of this name a grave-shudder passed over Yasha. He'd heard it too often. As soon as the captain spoke that name Yasha was back on the leads with Natalya Igoryevna in the swelter of last year's heat and intimacy. Kabalyevskii. *Knyaz, Graf* or what have you, wasn't in any condition to render services to his lady love. That boy was dead meat, long gone. Gone even before Ma and Pa.

Who'd believe the truth? If the captain heard it, he'd kill Yasha for listening and doing nothing when he eavesdropped that night on the deserters who'd bumped off the captain's school chum, hoppo, or whatever.

Sir-Kaba-bloody-lyevskii was under the greening sod with his painted snowscapes and chuffer trains and cock-and-bull tales for daft ladies. Skeletalised already. Jumped, by the scum he'd called scum once too often and thought he'd left behind to finish off his war for him.

Still, he must have had something about him, foot-slogging half-way back to the Alekseyev estate. All for a blasted woman.

Spats had liked that. "Character," he called it. "The grand gesture."

The epitaph of a fool, long on chivalry, short on life. The captain saw only what he wanted to see. But there was no Martin in this place. Natalya Igoryevna had finally run out of men.

A high-pitched whistle came from the direction of the house. The party on the steps conferred for a second or two while the officer put on his cap, then descended, dropping completely out of sight. Myelnikov was about to speak when two women appeared on the terrace dragging a tall step-ladder.

The captain came up from behind and stroked the back of Yasha's neck. "If I do this," he said, "will you hold nothing back?"

The boy's bravado had deserted him. "Nothing."

"The map?"

"The map too. Only do it now, before they do."

For the first time the captain shouted at Myelnikov with the authority of command: "Lights, Corporal." To Yasha he spoke softly: "We will put a fire above them, boy, to match the fire below."

34

Polly ran in little bursts which became shorter and shorter as the ascent steepened. Though not a soul was about she felt embarrassed at the wobble of her unstayed breasts under the loose blouse. If only she had had time to change more than her shoes. But the sight of Loulou being hauled away, roped like a heifer, had driven out all thoughts of what was *comme il faut* for a country spin. Temporarily, of course. The most damnable thing about being a woman was that you'd catch yourself worrying about flabby thighs on a desert island.

Still, she had dispatched her Vlady after those harridans. In spite of husbandly ums and ahs, he'd loaded that awful double-barrelled gun that scared birds and set off through the house to do battle with the hags.

She stopped short of the summit, slid flat to the earth and worked up the last few yards in a stalker's crawl. Looking for Valerian and rescue, she saw at first only a flock of brown and scarlet animals pirouetting in a fog at the shiny waterside. Lungs rasping, she wiped her spectacles and pressed the lenses closer to her eyes. Horses, thoroughbreds, those fine-legged creatures she had watched in the cobbled yard. But the riders? Such riders she had not seen; had never seen before except at parades. And now, as then, they flittered around a central figure, cap brasses and silver-lace shouldertabs splashing bright amidst their fleeces and serge. Was it the old times come back? At last, at last, the bad dream was broken: the once-upon-a-time men had returned, pelisse and sabretaches wondrously pristine.

Polly scrabbled to her feet and waved. She jumped up and down, a long-lost mad daughter shrieking against the wind in ecstasy of disbelief: they *couldn't* be. They *must* be. It was them, her own, come back to her, come home. Close, so close, a mile distant. From the heights she felt she could reach out and touch them. But they heard and saw nothing, continuing to swirl in a vortex of russet and gold, absorbed in the play of lunges and caracoles.

The handkerchief at her neck was too small, her skirt too dark.

With a great yowl of freedom she tore off the birch-white peasant blouse. As the linen flick-flacked above her head in the breeze, Polly wept undeniable tears.

Schmidt saw her first. He knew the swing of those breasts. He recognised her – that daft one. And he guessed her game. Out of range, and the angle was too oblique, the wind too gusty for the side-arm which was the only weapon he carried. Makar had a Schneider. Makar could take the shot.

A horseman broke from the group, trotted to the foot of the slope, halted and leaned to one side of the saddle. Polly noticed the long gun. She huzza-ed at him, anticipating a shot in the air to signal that he had seen her. Instead, he thrust his arm through the sling in a peculiar way, forcing the point of his elbow against it as if his arm were an arrow and the sling a bent bow.

At the ford Valerian had reined in. His horse smelt the water and became springy. He calmed it in the habitual way with words and with tickling at the roots of its mane. To his surprise Solomon splashed ahead into the shallows, then turned, the chest of his grey barrelling against the current. Without removing his hand from the horse's neck Valerian swivelled his eyes left, then right. He was not flanked. He had a split second to repose.

All his life he had been anticipating this moment. How it would come. And how he would be when it came. Across the dark river the horizon shimmered peaceably through the line of trees. Before, he had expected a sign, some shift of nature to clinch the recognition that he had come to the place of reckoning; but now he knew that the world held him, as it held everyone, securely, mutely, indifferently until the last moment of time.

Satisfied, utterly sure of himself and in what he was about to do, Valerian breathed in hard, tensed the muscles of his legs, then let out a yell which on its own would have shot his horse forward without the accompanying savage drive from his heels. The mare was a steeplechaser. She did not breast the river but leapt and plunged as if the water were an obstacle to be swooped over. When she cannoned obliquely into Solomon's mount both animals thrashed and rolled, searching for footing in the loose shale of the river bed.

Valerian let go the reins, stood in the stirrups and slashed deep with his sabre into the bone above the eyes of Solomon's horse. The animal screamed, bucking and sheering away before sinking onto its twisted hindlegs with such violence that the man was bucketed backwards over the rump, carbine in hand. Under water the weapon discharged itself into the belly of the horse, ripping it from end to end. And an instant later the shining head of the Georgian lieutenant shot up amidst a tangle of harness and black and pink gouts of animal flesh and blood. Waist-high in the stream Solomon did not flinch when Valerian veered at him, tilting to the right to gain free-play for a two-handed blow with his Cossack sword. When horse touched man, foreleg to shoulder, Valerian held the pose and spoke only one word again and again: "Why ? Why? Why?"

Solomon swept the bloodied water from his bald crown, steadied his legs against the current and shouted wide to the sky: "'Being the chief man amongst his people he shall not take a wife that is a whore . . .'"

Before the admonition was complete Valerian's sabre had severed his windpipe, and Solomon's round head bobbed back on the supporting water connected to his body by no more than the topmost bone of his spine.

Wavering on a pair of low step-ladders, Georgii Ivanov, his lumpy face pink from embarrassment, was squinting at the text of a pocket Bible.

"Too close, I'm telling you," he complained. "The lines is too close. And there's some queer letters."

Becky sat on the bottom step, prompting him from memory. "'And the woman, the woman that committeth . . .'"

"Ah . . . ah . . ." said Georgii tracing the words with his forefinger. "That's a dear girl . . . 'The woman that committeth . . . ad . . . ad . . .'"

"Ad-ult-er-y," said Becky slowly, jogging his elbow.

"I know, I do know . . ."

"Betcha do," sniggered the girl and began in a low voice to chant the obscene words of a soldier's jingle: "'And the man goes Oh and the woman goes Ah . . .'"

Facing her was another step-ladder, three times taller than Georgii's, which in the Laskorins' day had been used by the gardeners to head the trusses of the south front vine. At the top was a platform wide enough for two men to work from. Now it supported two women: Loulou and Matryona.

"'Shall surely,'" went on Georgii more confidently. "'Be put to . . .'" Then he stopped and tried to hand down his Bible. "Here, missie, my eyes ain't so young as yours."

"'Death'," said Becky without taking the book.

Shakily Georgii sat down on the top step. "That can't be right," he said, staring up at the figures opposite.

"Course it's right, you old fossil," shouted Becky. "In the Bible, ain't it?"

There was a burst of laughter from the women clustered on the terrace. As the only man available (and Matryona had insisted that only a man had sufficient authority – such being the rule in the community) and as one who was literate, Georgii had been dragged straight from the bath-house to preside over Loulou's impromptu trial. Now the fact of the sentence was coming home to him.

"He shall not defile himself," Masha called out. "It is written."

"Why then it should be Valerian too paying the same price," said Georgii frantically leafing through the Old Testament for evidence. "Why do the likes of you trulls have to set on her alone? She loved him, like we all do."

Well-rehearsed in scriptural text, Masha and Katya stroked their bellies. "'For she may be got with child and the child will be the son of a sorceress, the seed of an adulterer and a whore.'"

"''Sright," said Becky. "Top 'er."

The horseman at the foot of the hill snuggled his cheek against the rifle stock. Suddenly Polly felt ashamed and covered herself. The barrel rose, foreshortened; then stopped. For one hesitant moment Polly remained upright. In the silence a wounded animal screamed, the rifleman's horse whinnied and danced its forehooves, and at the flare of her left hip Polly felt and heard a winging, irritated *zizz*. The sound of the report came as she was heading down into the grass.

Incredible. The unspeakable cad was firing at her.

She watched a beetle rambling in the shoots, and squeezed herself in, anticipating the shock of the next bullet. Hoofbeats vibrated in the earth.

He could ride up and take her leisurely, like they spear otters from on high. Where had they gone, the lovely men?

A wooden beam projected from the third window of the long drawing-room. Loulou stood in its shadow, her hair gently lifting in the breeze. Around her neck the horse collar from Lola Laskorina's Shetland was attached to the thick sailrope. They had removed her gag but Matryona held her by the shoulders.

Below the women argued, their faces upturned, intent on her demeanour. Acid welled in her throat. The flutterings of her heart strung out into a pitter-patter chain. She was expected to behave. She could and would behave. All endings were rubbishy. There was nothing left finally except comportment.

Beneath her there was none.

Haphazard, Georgii conducted her unexultant defence. He had tracked down the Decalogue: "'Thou shalt not kill,'" he shouted from his ladder.

The women were contemptuous. Everyone, the round-eyed girls, the emaciated old women with senile mouths, everyone, including Georgii himself, knew this. "Now he tells us! No talk of Moses when there was work to be done. The cellars, women, remember the cellars!"

Matryona and Masha had killed men with their bare hands. From their shawls and headscarves the women thrust out their lips, smiling and nodding as though at an Easter fair, their malice ostentatious; the reality of past actions had come alive again in the prospect of Loulou's sacrifice.

The biblical colloquy resumed: "'He shall take a virgin of his own people to wife'," said Masha. A hush followed this while Georgii sought a text. Schooled by many meetings where the drama was high from the capping of citation by citation, the women allowed the man his moment.

Georgii pleaded his justification: "'A widow or divorced woman or profane or an harlot, these he shall not take.' I have spoken with this woman. She is none of these things – neither widow nor put away by her husband, nor profane . . ."

"Not 'arf," came the voice of Becky. "She's only a bleeding tart."

The air crackled with rifle shot. Polly lingered, very afraid. But no thud or whizz came her way. The noise retreated. Daring herself, she lifted slightly and parted a tuft.

The riders had bolted, scattering outwards in a star-formation, the nearest hallooing at a band of men coming up on foot from the direction of the house. Carried past the drop to the ford, to deeper water where one could not wade, the dapple-grey carcase of a horse twitched in the current, bleeding. The stain was softly pink, and out of its centre swaggered a bare-headed rider on an Isabella chestnut, his golden hair sheened strawberry in the red water-light.

His mount rose under him at the bank, kicked itself free of the river and hurtled into a gallop straight at the rider who had given the halloo. The men he had called barred the way, and he twisted and turned searching for a gap until the golden man unseated him with a blow from his whip, then rode at him in side-steps and cut him like a hunter cuts down a wolf.

By the time that Schmidt had grabbed her by the hair from behind and clamped a powder-burnt hand over her mouth, Polly had forgotten that she too was a huntsman's prize.

* * *

312

The women were becoming restive. Mad old Pelagya was strewing rose-petals at the foot of the makeshift scaffold. She looked from Loulou to Georgii and croaked ingratiatingly: "I knew her by her eyes. Let the deed be done, Master."

At any other time she would have been shouted down, but this new voice broke the tension. "In the name of Christ, you crippled perverter of Holy Scripture, heed the call and finish," shouted Matryona, digging her fingers into Loulou's shoulders. Loulou stumbled and the women thrilled to her gasp.

Georgii menaced them with his Bible. "'And he that blasphemeth the name of the Lord shall be . . .'"

"Eaten alive?" queried a new voice from the tall window. "Chopped for the hounds? Roasted by virgins? Because we all know, don't we, Georgii dear, that God's Almightiness can't do his business without conniving scamps and crones like her."

Belyakov clambered onto the outer sill and sat astride the beam, kicking his heels against the crumbly stucco and aligning the foresight of his Manton express rifle at Matryona's white brow. Loulou did not budge and prayed that for once he was sober. Beneath her the women hushed. "Vlady," she murmured into the silence. "I knew you would come." In fact she had expected no one; and if she had it would have been him least of all. God, she'd been so *rude* to the man, and made fun of his wife. Was heartfelt insincerity sufficient at such a moment?

The women heard, and at a nod from Masha stood as one body, closed around the legs of the tallest step-ladder and laid their hands on the struts. Both pregnant girls lined up in front, hand in hand.

Matryona was unmoved. "Who first, Vladimir Ivanovich?" she sneered. "The dam or the kid? Whichever – the whore shall still swing."

A noise of gunshot sounded from the park. Isolated on his ladder, deprived of a role, Georgii began to intone from Leviticus: "'The children of Israel shall abide many days without a king, without a prince and without a sacrifice and without an image . . .'"

Only Becky escaped from the crush, crawling through the women's skirts to a safer place at the far end of the terrace where Pelagya was fiddling with her roseheads. "Dry up, why don't you?" she shouted disconsolately. "Fun's over."

For a long time Belyakov studied Matryona along the barrel of his Manton, still playful with his feet, whistling a Little Russian country jig. When eventually he rested the gun across his knees, Loulou knew that she must be lost, and the old contempt which she had always felt for him whipped up to a surge.

"Kill me," she shrilled. "Kill me and you kill the child."

Georgii stopped reading.

"How now, milady," grunted Matryona into her ear. "Then reasons are doubled. This end I take upon myself alone."

The heavy bullet of the express rifle, capable of splintering the horn-boss of a buffalo, struck Matryona at waist-level. It did not stagger her, or fell her, or neatly pick her off as every person present including Belyakov expected it to do. Instead it carried her backwards in a good ten feet of horizontal flight above their heads before depositing the body in three irregular fragments at arm's length from where Pelagya sat replenishing her basket of petals from an earthenware pot. Loulou teetered above, the noose still round her neck, as useless to help herself as a sandbag dummy the hangman uses to test the drop.

Masha was the first to shake off her awe. Her bulk seemed to shrink to that of a lithe unburdened girl as, billhook in hand, she leapt into the press of women around the bottom steps of the ladder, sprawling and clawing at their stunned faces in order to slash through the cord which kept the legs upright.

The two shots which killed Masha, one upwards at the nape of the neck, the other in her spine, came from a less booming gun than Belyakov's; but had they been as loud as cannon-fire, no one would have heard; for before she dropped, in what the other women took to be a faint, the detonation of a signal rocket careered into the frontage of the house and swelled richly along the sounding façade before dying out in a stinging buzz which remained in the ear long after.

Belyakov walked the beam like a tightrope, dropped down to Loulou's side and drew back the knot, enabling her to slip her neck from the noose.

A gust of hot wind blew down from the leads. When they smelled the smoke and saw the fire nobody on the terrace screamed. Pelagya alone moved, her face lit up, fingering the stem of a single blue flower.

Only later did Loulou remember the details: Polly and Schmidt had appeared on the terrace, driven like cattle by Valerian who had shot Masha. He was unscathed, as immaculate in his uniform as he had been in the little room hours before. Polly's upper lip was bleeding; but she too, seemed absurdly like her old self. Only Schmidt was affected by the carnage, quite unmanned by it. His performance in front of the women was riveting.

"Master," he had cried out. "I loved you too much." And he fell to his knees, weeping openly, before the dry-eyed congregation. Horrible, horrible, he even clutched at Valerian's legs.

Loulou averted her gaze.

"Master, yesterday you turned me from your door when I came with warnings. You disregarded me because of that wicked woman . . . and I wanted her dead, but only her, never you. They forced me into this" – here the women hissed – "and I only agreed because I thought you were abandoning those who loved you . . ." Schmidt's forehead was almost touching the flagstones. "Master, I thought you had betrayed us. Now the enemy is come and Vissarion is arming the men."

Loulou had believed every word that he said.

35

In the old shrubbery Fedya was asleep over his book.
That morning Lieutenant Solomon had given the boy a repeater
rifle, ordered him to lie low and keep watch on the old road a mile
to the north-east of the house. Gerasim had been sent down river to
guard the southern approaches. Neither was performing any serious
military role, but as Loulou's former guardians they were not above
suspicion of sentimental attachment to their charge. At such distance
they would have little time to act once she was seized. One might be
old, the other might be daft, but to the last Solomon had been a
cautious man and had issued his commands accordingly.

Fedya was told that the enemy was on the march, raging for
Valerian's blood and, of course, his lady's. As their father and
leader, Valerian was naturally in jeopardy, but Natalya Igoryevna, the
renegade doyenne of aristocratic line, would also attract no mercy.
In their defence sacrifice might be called for.

All this was calculated to inflame Fedya's adolescent nobility.
Alone he would have to guard the coach road which ran along the
north-eastern edge of the park before disintegrating into the mud of
the village street two miles away. Alone, Fedya would have to watch
over that road as it wound from the village, across the marsh, to the
plain beyond the railway line where there was so little cover that a
scouting patrol would show up five miles distant.

Fedya was ecstatic at Solomon's trust and had great hopes of the
repeater rifle. Unlike other weapons given him, this one was fully
operational. He spent most of the morning making the bullets fly
harmlessly from the extractor mechanism as he worked the lever
below the trigger-guard. When no enemy appeared by midday he
began to read, yells from house and terrace passing over his head like
bird calls. From that side, Solomon had said, no danger would come.
Besides, houses were always noisy. Having been brought up in a
one-roomed hut, full of squalling brothers and sisters, but taught to
read by his mother, Fedya knew the value of a book in silencing any
racket around him. And the Laskorin house had a library. Out here
he could be a warrior-poet among savages, reading *David Copperfield*

in Russian translation, every so often pausing to slit the uncut pages
with the brass magazine rod from his rifle. It was a hard book, with
many fine words he did not know. He wondered where London was
and if they had prisons there. Even if they did he thought the London
people hadn't much to complain about. Someone would be bound to
rescue you.

As far as Schmidt and the lieutenants knew, there was no enemy
beyond the marshes; the only killing would take place inside the
house and out in the park by the river; the only conflict would be
with Valerian. But none of this was known to Fedya who rubbed the
bead sight of the antique Winchester against his ear-lobe, enraptured
at the charity which one Englishman could extend to another.

Corporal Myelnikov hopped down from the rump of a blind stone
lion whose haunches were encrusted with orange lichen flowers.
Leaning back against the plinth he winked at its mate across the
drive-way and looked up. In the late afternoon sky violet was succeed-
ing storm-blue.

He fished a notebook from his ammunition pouch, swung out his
brass pocket watch and checked. 4.45. *Typhoon, monsoon, hurricane*, he wrote; at four forty-five approx. about to bucket on the
unwaterproofed head of an old soldier. Bugger all.

Tucking back the watch, he found his pencil and groaned. The
captain had demanded a record. In case things went wrong. In case
the fish-brained dwarf was on the go for both sides. Masterly, that.
If he was, notes of his squitting double-doings would be triumphant
proof of the officer's deep mind. Get it down, Corporal, black and
white, irrefutable. Had eyes, hadn't he? Had a mouth, wasn't crippled.
What's wrong with your verbals, especially when he wasn't exactly
a writing man? In chimed the dwarf like music: 'case they corpse you,
Corporal; 'case they drops you dead; on paper you'll be there to life.

Ha bloody ha. Here goes: 4.47 *p.m.: Hanging*. After studying the
entry for a while he added: *in progress*. Then read it through several
times, savouring his new-found professionalism.

Wholly guesswork but it looked good.

Not a squawk from the inside of the house now the cavalcade was
gone. Maybe they'd hanged the female already. Save a lot of trouble.
He hated non-combatants. His orders were: observe and note; but
the two objectives weren't necessarily connected, and he could make
a guess about the inside of the place. Re-furbishing intelligence was
an old hobby with him. As long as it gratified the authorities you'd
got your first stripe up. Endeavour to give satisfaction, that was the
motto.

Captain and dwarflet, out of sight now, but he knew where they were: about four hundred yards up that slope. Having a drag beside the fish pool, judging by the smoke. All that dodging down the old road, scouting from hedge to ditch, and there they was, as unsightly revealed as bull's bollocks on a silver tray.

Cloud was piling helter-skelter in the north-west quarter. He stroked the knob of the lion's tail wondering if he might advance his report by a sentence or two about the weather. When his left calf twitched he dropped the notebook and lay flat. The stick-bomb shrapnel in his leg bone was better than an extra ear. One twinge and he could triangulate a sniper at three hundred yards. So he wasn't solo in this bastard hell-furrow.

Half a mile? He had time to resume the scribbling business: 4.55 *hoof beats NNW approaching*. Do it slow. Don't panic because you can't join up the letters.

When the full-stop was coming up the two riders were almost upon him. He should have written: "two". He could have written: bloody prig off your illustriousness; flesh may be grass but hoof shoes is steelier than steel to the lettered or unlettered.

Two? Two beasts for sure, strung out in line, leader making pace. Across the pommel was a broad pack which slouched from side to side, untrimming the gait of the shaggy pony. A lively animal thing, so close entwined with the rider that at first Myelnikov thought a dead man must be strapped to his chest. The pony twisted like an artillery mule searching for footing, splaying its hindlegs, wheeling in gavotte round and round the clumps of hawthorn at the edge of the carriage way.

The rider was evidently steering it free of tumps in the ground by his knees, for Myelnikov had spotted the reins bunched high out of reach on the pony's mane. Between rider and reins was a woman. The corporal observed her silk-stockings. Face to face she sat obscuring the rider, legs sticking out, astride. It could have been a circus turn or horseback rape.

The trio wrestled past him in dumb-show, the pony too well-schooled to whinny, the man too cautious to disclose his position by shouting. Even though the woman had sunk her teeth in his bridle hand, up to the gums.

Bitch, thought the corporal dispassionately.

Bursts from a light automatic carbine fluffed up ash and sand inches from the pony's right forequarter. When the animal slewed to the opposite, another tight grouping of shots flopped below its upraised hoof.

The corporal hunched. Diabolical musketry, true as an eye-beam.

Right bias, left bias, straddle fire, splitting the degree. Doesn't want to hit them. Could. Take 'em off with a single, straight through the pair, belly to belly. Oh you could, dead-eye magic shooting man.

The second rider had fired twice on the gallop. Now he reined in his horse two hundred yards back and was watching the pony which had come to a dead stop, champing free of the bit. Myelnikov studied the magnificently-accoutred figure. It was him all right, short-sworded and daggered, festooned on his cuff braids and swaggering scarlet cape, Mr Astrakhan shako in gold-knot lace, stirruped straight on a brutish big mare, my captain's glory-boy with the undeflectable eye. Major Wonderful, the my-dear-fellow-slap-you-on-the-back-splendid-chappery, resplendent in the calm with which he levelled the barrel of his German aviator's carbine at the guts of the lower ranks.

Another squeeze. Seven millimetre ball sang overhead. Myelnikov sagged behind his lion. Let some other erk catch a packet. This bugger was a shot. A principled bugger, though. Had qualms about hitting women, that was plain. Always have, that type. Me, I'd do them both, indiscriminate as to sex. Guns in garters, Goldilocks. Watch it.

A stone's throw from the corporal the man urged forward with his knees but the pony was rigid from dread and whirled back its ungirt mane. Fleshy, nearly bald. No uniform but a kind of skirt. Priest's issue. Familiar, seen before, more than once. Got him: uncle from the loon-hatch, the big one, the black one, the murdering sacred heart of Jesus.

Myelnikov prayed enragedly to the major on the short-nosed chestnut: *Go on, why don't you?* Forget chivalry, forget animal welfare. For Christ's sake, while they're still – shoot the effing horse.

At that moment it seemed to occur to the bald man that he was literally a sitting target and he butted the woman in the mouth. With a howl she collapsed backwards along the length of the pony's neck and the animal skidded sideways before beginning a maddened, circular canter.

Dragging his chestnut's mouth round so hard that the animal snorted in fear, the blond major bent into gallop and was upon the couple in a moment. Clouds of sand rose under the horse's hind hooves as he reared up in a dressage arc to stab its forelegs in the pony's eyes.

With astonishing grace the bald man slithered to the ground over the pony's haunches, pulling the woman with him. Myelnikov saw her white face, her spectacles askew and the full line of her upper lip, vertically split.

"Shoot one, shoot both," shrieked the bald man, laying his 7.63

Borchardt pistol along the woman's jawline. "One jerk and she'll crack like a pot."

He backed down the driveway. The woman had closed her eyes. The horseman watched, cradling his weapon, still as night. Foot by foot the couple retreated to the stairway. The bald man took the steps in reverse, dragging up the woman to cover his chest. At the last but three, he leapt backwards, still hanging onto her, and the pair of them rolled over and over to some safe place beyond the corporal's line of vision.

But the major saw, and fired high. Chips of tracery flew off the stone arch of the doorway. Then the chestnut ambled forward at his soft-spoken geeing and the drape of the rider's cloak brushed the lion's paws.

Myelnikov watched his progress, expecting return fire from the house; but no shot came. At the foot of the steps the major dismounted, hitched his rein around the tub of jessamine at the right balustrade and leisurely climbed the flight holding up his sabre at the point of the curve.

All the time that took, Corporal Myelnikov had him square on the foresight of his long rifle. Cocky big bastard. Ice-cold. Shall I, shan't I? Drop him. Let him fraternise for the only time in his life with the dust beneath his feet. The captain didn't say nothing about his cheek, about his insulting su-sodding-perbness. A man is not a machine but is born to be tempted by the easy shot.

The corporal mastered himself and brought out his notebook. *5.15 p.m.*, he wrote. *Hostage taken. Unknown female. Riders in house.*

Good riddance. Here's hoping they'd hang the lot.

Left by itself the pony shivered and bent its head. "Easy now," muttered the corporal. "Horses is more useful than people at the end of a rope."

"Quite a decent show," said the captain, cocking the Verey pistol.

Yasha wriggled on the saturated moss. His wet jacket itched. "Glad someone's cheerful."

"The corporal has his thinking side and St George is not his favourite saint."

"Tough on girls, is he?"

The captain took Yasha's scorn unaffectedly. "Simply obeys orders."

For a long silent minute man and boy lay together, head to head.

"Captain," whispered Yasha eventually.

"Private?"

"Get a move on."

"All in good time."

The captain grasped the pistol butt with both hands almost at right-angles to the earth and at arm's length. Yasha ground his teeth. A man to whom he owed no allegiance, this stranger beside him had become his master. It would be easy to betray him, yet he obeyed his orders. The captain knew this, and he would betray Yasha if it suited his book. The very possibility of their both being capable of treachery when their lives depended on one another darkened the boy's mind.

Nothing was as it seemed: who now was Natalya Igoryevna? Would he save her or would she save him? Who were the riders with whips? And their tall commandant who gave chase to Polly Laskorina and Schmidt?

He was losing track. His world had spun into cloud.

"And she cut off their tails . . . with . . . a . . . carving . . ." chanted the captain. "*Knife.*" And pulled the trigger.

The blast detonated in the vacuum of Yasha's inner ear so that a moment afterwards he was deaf to the noise of the second rocket. When he looked up, hanging over the house were two trails, one draggily grey from the dud, the other powder-puff white. The boy watched them cross, his head seething. A whiplash electric crackle, then an airburst of stars, cochineal and indigo, strung out in a tail shuddering two hundred feet above the highest leads of the great Laskorin pile.

The captain clung to him, joyous in the scarlet light, shouting out his exultation: "Wet primer in number one, so we lost the white, but what about that, Mr Kiteflier, what about *that* – a dead marker if ever I saw one."

They were truly lovely, those stars, the incandescent wheels they made on the twilight, but what did he want, this gaunt elated man? More than excitement? Yes. More than the onset of battle. The transfiguration of nature, his and the world's. A clean burning out, just like Valerian had said. The last torch to the last rag and remnant. When it goes I go with it, but I want to go up like an air-bomb flare, in supervisory light, watching over the frazzle of the final illumination.

At the burst of the second rocket the horsemen became visible on the slope above the house. They had whirled round below the crest and were now moving back at a trot towards the Laskorin mansion shouting and pointing at the sky. The shock must have been terrific. They stood out, black on scarlet in their Cossack *burkas*. For a moment nothing seemed to move in the brightness until the leading rider stretched out his whip to the north-eastern quarter of the sky beyond the railway spur.

Yasha turned his head. From about three thousand feet a dazzling white flame was slowly descending to the horizon. Its sound came to him as a crack and a hiss. The riders watched as Yasha watched, transfixed, the landscape printing itself lightning white.

"Ah, tophole," said the captain rubbing his hands. "*Starshina* Volkov is letting us know how near he is."

Yasha did not know whether or not to be relieved. "What's that thing?"

"Parachute flare," said the captain. "You watch – it'll hang around longer than them."

He meant the riders. And he was right, thought Yasha: beneath the fragmentation of the star shell they now were skedaddling like mice in a grain silo, down the slope and back to the house.

The boy comforted himself in the blaze. At that spot from where Sergeant Volkov was route-marching his plug-uglies, four or five miles along the railway, last summer, Natalya Igoryevna had pulled off her man-sized gardener's boots and stretched out, tired and hungry, to watch the sunrise. With remorse he remembered her need to marvel at the world. Had she time now to admire the wonder of this metallic burn-out? She would have despised the riders, wheeling beneath the fire. She would have laughed.

The captain was evidently thinking of her too. "If these people believe in angels, we can hope they accept messages from heaven," he said. "And Martin might get to her now, while they're taken unawares."

The horsemen were reining in, disappearing one by one round the house to the hitch rein in the great courtyard on the west front, hidden from Yasha's gaze.

Martin?

Fedya was sick of the road. He had been watching it all day, on and off, and nothing had happened.

His book had dropped to the ground. Solomon had given him no rations. The others had bread and full water-bottles. He wanted to creep across to the distant river bank and drink but he remembered Solomon's fearsome eyes and did not desert his post.

Had he been alert that afternoon he would not have missed Corporal Myelnikov prone at the lion's side, or Yasha and the captain working their way along the road verge a hundred yards away from his observation point. But Fedya was not cut out for action; his mind wandered and he dreamed. He saw nothing that afternoon and, even now, although cooler and more attentive as the heat lessened, he was entranced by the churnings of the dark river. Fedya could not know how fortunate he had been. He slept deeply, unmoving. That and his lassitude had kept him alive. Against Myelnikov, the captain or Yasha he would not have stood a chance; any one of them would have killed him on the spot rather than have their position revealed.

As the river slid by unmonotonously, Fedya followed its course back stream, round the oxbow and into the wide strait five miles to the north-west. Now the banks were flooded over the river-side forest, but something moved on the water at the far tree-line, stopped and did not move again. Probably cut lumber floating off from the woods. But the movement dispelled his pleasure, and his senses sharpened. He could smell smoke.

The smoke seemed to be coming from the river, from that opaque mass under the trees which came nearer without moving. Fedya did not know if he should be afraid. Valerian would know what it was, the smoking thing on the water; natural and supernatural were all one to him.

But if anyone had asked Fedya's opinion he would have said it was an omen.

Myelnikov shambled up the gully on the bald man's pony. He sat side-saddle, guiding the beast by flopping the reins on its neck this way and that.

"Hornets," he grinned sliding off at the captain's feet. "Got me in the sit-upon. Oh my, the hazards of war."

Yasha lay on the grass poking his fingers in his ears. The corporal looked at him. "Sonny's first big bang-bangs, is it?"

"Our chum has no stomach for the waiting," said the captain. "Wants to be up and at them singlehanded."

Myelnikov chuckled and backed the pony into a hazel bush, soothing it with clicking noises. "What — peevish for medals are you, my little scutlegs?" Seating himself carefully on the ground he removed his right boot. "Where's your sling, then, Davidovich? Or was it the jawbone of an ass?" Several flints rolled out of his upturned boot. Replacing it on his foot, he began to unlace the other. "Oughter have chipped an eye on him close to, that major-feller. He'd crop the curlies off you with one twinkle of his auto and no boo-hoo. A bastard shot, my lights, a bloody bastard shot."

In desperation Yasha appealed to the captain: "I told you, there's cold-blooded murderers in there that scare each other, never mind him . . ."

"Give Old Nick the runs," said Myelnikov equably poking around in his remaining boot. "That marksman gent."

"You both seem to be forgetting," said the captain languidly. "The gent is on our side."

Myelnikov clapped his hands above his head. "Course he is. Another honour like your honour. Sometimes I forgets from sheer decrepitude of non-commissioned soldiering – officers is pals."

Yasha abandoned the effort, perplexed by his own deceit. How could these two know the real facts? He had chosen to tell them lies and the captain had chosen to believe him. Oddly, his stock seemed to have gone up with the corporal.

"He's right, you know," said Myelnikov to the captain. "I seen your blond bugger like I see you now a whisker away from this boot and I tell you straight, commander mine, I wouldn't have stopped to ask what way he did up his longjohns without a fistful of certificates to prove he was partial to enquiries about his underwear. That sort shoots for himself first, then works out sides."

The captain smiled. "That's my Martin."

At its tether amidst the hazel wands the pony laid back its velvet lips in a whinny. The corporal soothed it with handfuls of grass.

"Not that I could swear as to his stopping the hangings," he went on, with a leer at Yasha.

"Which hangings?" said the captain.

"Search me which. But there was more than one customer, I can tell you that."

"I told you," shouted Yasha. "They're devils. I keep trying to make you understand."

"Notebook, Corporal."

Myelnikov threw across his little oilskin book and went back to stroking the underside of the pony's neck. "All there," he said. "I'm no better than a dumb beast, of course. Don't ask me. Read the book."

The captain found the page, glanced over the entries and tore it up. "Cryptic, Corporal, bald to the point of mannerism."

"A proper timetable as requested. What else do you expect from an old sweat – landscapes? Any case – you saw what happened. You was in range."

The captain lost his temper. "Your mission was to get *inside*, Corporal."

"So it was, your honour," said Myelnikov, saluting smartly.

"Not a word of it there, man," shouted the captain, kicking away the book.

"No, sir. That was before the accident, sir."

"Accident?"

"Deep regrets, your honour, but this animal," said Myelnikov tickling the pony's ears, "consumed my writing implement. Little perisher eats pencils."

The captain sank to the earth. "We'd better do it your way, Corporal. Tell us the story."

Myelnikov sat down between the pony's legs and prepared to enjoy himself. "Well, after he slicks up the steps like a lizard, your major, I hears a door close and then nothing. Then the horse-wasp stings me." That much was true. "Being a restless soul I casts about to do my duty, so I tethers the animal and sets off on an infantry crawl up the avenue. Not a squeak from the house, not even when I gets up to the window casements. Exercising due caution, I proceed to have a squint through."

Yasha was biting his nails savagely. "I'm going down there," he cried. "*Now.*"

The captain caught him by the hair and shook him still.

"Black as your hat inside. At first, until you get your focals working and then it sort of clears . . . lifts a bit, like mist . . ."

"Sod it, Myelnikov," swore the captain quietly. "Leave out the art."

"As you please, sir. So I sees them, naked as babes."

"See who?"

"Why, the ladies. Two of 'em laid flat out like indecent monuments on one truckle bed."

Yasha beat his fists into his eyes.

"Didn't you do something?"

"I did, sir, and very fitting it was. I ran all the way back to this horse."

"But they could have been . . ."

Myelnikov waved away the interjection. "Could have been drying off all cosy after the bath-house, could have been waiting for God to drop out of the ceiling, but they wasn't."

Yasha gave a heart-rending yell and made a dive for the corporal's throat but the captain swooped on his legs and held him down. "How d'you know, Wormgut, what d'you know . . . ?"

"Oh, I know," said Myelnikov stretching himself. "It's like the writing. You goes by the marks. And they had them, very striking – right round their pretty little necks."

Rifle shots sounded from the house. In a flash the corporal had unslung his weapon. A lull. Then four figures emerged. With a twist of the bolt Myelnikov brought a round into the breech of his Putilov. He whispered into Yasha's ear: "Lift up your heart, Rat's-piss. Quick, before I pops them like lice – name us some names."

* * *

325

Above the shrubbery the sky reverberated blue-black against the electric red of the exploding rocket. Under its fire the plantation shimmered and bulged outwards carrying the glow across the water.

Fedya tried to scream but no sound came. He wanted to race to safe cover, back to the house, but his brain refused to impel him. In the star-trails hanging smoke and glitter over his head, Fedya saw bearded comets, meteors; his sky was steep with precursory light. The time was at hand.

Words came to him as he fell to his knees: "And he was clothed with a vesture dipped in blood." When the white lights came he stretched out his arm to the riders side-stepping their horses down the hill and broke out in a loud voice against the drifting powder-smoke: "I saw the beast and the kings of the earth, and their armies gathered together to make war against him that sat on the horse, and against his army. *Valerian, Valerian, Val-er-i-an!*"

As he dropped to the earth in a frenzy of anticipation, Fedya accidentally banged against the cocked hammer of his Winchester. It went off, making a hole the size of a silver rouble through the five hundred and twenty-two pages of his *David Copperfield*.

"Bastard," said Yasha.

Myelnikov kissed the pony's nose. "How the hell was I to know?"

"You knew . . ."

"Oh yes? Naked from the womb and I'm called upon to discriminate? Maybe I oughter have turned them over. Maybe they had monograms tattooed on parts the eye isn't supposed to rest on . . ."

The pony whickered, its teeth greeny with foam, and snapped ferociously on the coarse grass which the corporal held out. Every so often it spat out a messy cud with a kind of grin.

"Humourist," said Myelnikov. "Another bloody card."

Yasha's roll-call had petered out almost as soon as it started.

"Effing ladies of the bedchamber," Myelnikov had said. "Where's their varlets? Let like save like. I'm done up."

There had been a moment when the faces of the fugitives had glimmered roundly against the stone of the north front before more firing was heard and they had bobbed away like ducks in a shooting gallery. Long enough for Yasha to recognise the women, and to realise that Myelnikov had been lying.

Now the captain had stripped off his greatcoat and was buckling on an extra pistol belt diagonally over his service tunic. He sang under his breath.

Myelnikov began again to the pony: "Well, I ask you. Tsar's types have had a slice out of my life, I can . . ."

"Don't be so bloody censorious, Corporal," said the captain stiffly. "You're a snob." He looked down on Yasha, straightening his chest under the thick bandolier, gave him an almost affectionate clip round the ear and tossed over his cigarette tin. "Keep that close to your little person, Mr Kiteflier. The corporal consumes shag like nobody's business and we can't survive here without a gasper between us."

"Here, Cap," said the boy, trying to appear nonchalant. "That Martin-bloke – mightn't recognise you, might he? Bit off his rocker, they said in the house . . . shell-shock or something . . ."

Seized by the prospect of action, the captain was not listening. Myelnikov had led up the pony. The saddle was felt, and instead of stirrups plain loops of squashy leather sat high on the animal's flanks.

"What fun," he smiled, hopping onto the child's-size saddle with scarcely a bend of the knee. "A nursery charger." He sat hunched up like a jockey.

"He might shoot you before the introductions," Yasha went on, grabbing the bridle rein. "Who knows who in this murk?"

"Won't get nowhere," grumbled Myelnikov who was half under the pony, adjusting its girths. "Not on this poncey gymkhana number."

"Such tender-hearted comrades man and horse never had," said the captain. "But there's work to be done before we call it a day, lads, and I'm still in command." With his cap tilted over one eye and a cigarette drooping from the corner of his mouth he might have looked rakish but the fat little pony robbed him of style. "I shall create a diversion, Corporal."

"Not half," agreed Myelnikov.

"Give me covering fire."

Yasha clung to the bridle. Sporadic shots came from the park. It was dark amongst the trees. This couldn't be allowed to go on. Perhaps, after all, the captain was a decent bloke. Besides, he didn't fancy being left alone with Myelnikov. The knowledge of his deceit made Yasha panicky. "He might not be who you think, Captain. People change."

"Piffle," exclaimed the captain excitedly, kicking his heels into the pony's flanks. "Get away, I'm missing the fun."

He was so convinced, so determined, that Yasha felt himself drowning in a muddle of contrition, fear, bewilderment and exhaustion. Myelnikov snatched the rein from his hand and gave the pony's rump a ringing spank. Momentarily the captain seemed to take to the air as the pony leapt, before bolting off in a zig-zag. Down, down he went, out of the trees, dancing into the wind as inelegant as a grizzly cascading down an ice-slope.

"Oh my God," muttered Yasha when they disappeared from view. "I knew I'd be the death of someone, telling tales . . ."

Myelnikov fiddled with the leaf-sight of his rifle, making no move to give his commanding-officer covering fire. There was no knowing with Myelnikov. He was one of those people who seem to make themselves up as they go along. He might shoot the captain, Yasha, or himself. You'd never know why. But he was apparently in no mood to exert himself. He continued to flip the sights back and forth, all the while sucking his teeth in a melancholy whistle. "*Nynye polkovnik, zavtra nokoynik,*" he said at last. "Cocksure today, corpse tomorrow. The whole bleeding fusillade of colonels, captains and other mouthers of instruction."

"I didn't do anything," Yasha began in self-disgust.

"Course you did."

The boy looked up gratefully.

"Course you did," said Myelnikov. "Saved your skin, that's what you did. Now it may be a horrible skin, all pocky with impurities of one kind and another, a dwarf's skin, but when all's said and done, my lad – it is your very own, and at this moment be grateful that it is holding together that bodged sausage what you call a body."

Yasha peered into the trees. Now the firing from the direction of the house was less ragged. Someone was being targeted. "Aren't you going to help him?"

Myelnikov slung the rifle across his back and looked round, preparatory to moving off.

"Listen, sonny," said the corporal as they paced briskly down the hill. "First thing you learn in this game is: some orders you obey, some you don't and some you give yourself. Command reverts to me on desertion of my officer and I issue the orders now – Hop it double quick."

Yasha had to run to keep up. "You're bloody deserting *him,*" he shouted. "That's mutiny."

Myelnikov trotted on serenely. In a clearing half a mile further on he stopped and looked back at the house which blazed with lights. "Know something, midget balls? That captain of ours whose baccy you're clutching to your heart, he's a prodigy of nature."

Out of breath, Yasha was thankful for the break. "Brave as a lion," he gasped in genuine admiration.

"Wrong animal," said Myelnikov. "More your leopard. Well-versed in spot-changing. Already swapped his badges and his silver buttons once."

"What for?"

"What for?" shouted Myelnikov. "To command men the likes of me, that's what for."

Yasha cringed. After a while he reasserted himself. "I don't get it," he said. "Isn't the likes of you what most armies are made of?"

The corporal slapped him on the back. "That's just it, my little piddler in the sun. It is. But most of 'em are unaware of a most salient fact."

"What fact?"

"That there's more of us than there is of them — your captain and his sort — and when we gets it into our heads to obey or disobey orders, they'd better string along with historical in-evit-ability."

The wind had got up. It was cold in the open.

"Any case," the corporal went on, "with any luck my captain and his major'll pot each other off and save us the bother. Where you hiding that tin?"

Reluctantly Yasha brought the box out of his left boot.

"Right," said Myelnikov. "Roll us a couple each. Spoils of war, Kiteflier, spoils of war."

36

"Vladimir! Vladimir Ivanovich!"

Osip's barrack-room voice rolled into the twilight.

"Vlady, old son. Come out and play with the big boys."

On the steps there was laughter and the fire-cracker snapping of automatic fire. "Aw, little wifey doesn't want um to . . ."

"For Christ's sake, Valerian," whispered Belyakov. "It's only two to one, we can take them. Cover me."

Crouched among the cucumber frames of a walled vegetable garden at the north-eastern corner of the house, Belyakov felt stupid in front of the women. For all the response shown by the boy, he might have been speaking to an idiot child. Valerian stared back, wordlessly, his face languid and clumsy. Belyakov knew that look of fatigue: some time soon, out here in the open, on this quiet summer night, Valerian was going to convulse and the whole bloody pack would sick them out like rats.

"A man of your age, Vladimir Ivanovich, ought to know better," called Makar, "than letting a female make a poodle dog out of you."

Raucous voices took over the theme in part-song *chestushka*: "Should have stuck to your bottle . . ." ". . . .Could have stuck it in his bottle. Had it both ways then and no nagging . . ."

No longer subject to Valerian's rule Osip and Makar and two of their men were making free with the remnants of the Laskorin cellars, both ammunition and wines. Spent bullets tinkled on the glass of the cold frames around Belyakov's feet.

"Go to buggery!" shouted the huntsman.

"Oh God," groaned Polly. "You're such an impetuous creature — they'll spot us."

The men on the steps made no move but shouted back into the house. A clatter of boots on stone reached the fugitives, followed by the voice of Schmidt. "Where are you?" It was a stupid question but like his comrades Schmidt seemed only to want to establish contact, not to seek them out. His voice was quavery as if from weeping. "Blasphemer!"

Behind him, Osip and Makar roared with delight. "Give it to him,

Hermann!'' Osip cupped his hands and gave a cock-a-doodle-doo. "Once, twice, deny him thrice!"

Loulou pressed against Valerian. She wanted to kneel and hide her head between his hands but after a touch at her eyes he shrank away.

Schmidt tried to shout but his voice cracked. "Traitor!" he blubbed in self-disgust and humiliation.

Valerian looked away eastwards to the line of firs on the horizon where the sky was clear and dark.

"Judas!" shrieked the voice. "You'll not escape us this time. Your horses are slaughtered. The dead souls of Masha, Solomon and Titus cry out for vengeance. Give yourself up."

To Loulou the way ahead seemed as clear as the sky. That dead girl had been pregnant. "You must go," she said gently, and turned up her face to kiss him, but he was gazing past her, perplexed, muttering under his breath.

Had he never felt guilt?

It was Polly who protested. Since her discovery that Valerian was her own flesh and blood – well, half, Papa's half – and that she had this strange brother, Polly had viewed him in a new light. Indulgently, as became any well-bred girl who knew a thing or two about adventurous fathers. The same indulgence extended to his liaison with Loulou. Not in the least bit shocking. How could it be with persons of rank? Similarly, it was perfectly understandable that her half-brother (dressed suitably at last) should be the commander of this gang of oafs. And the thing to remember was that one never entered into discussion with oafs. They always took advantage. It was in their blood. She ought to know.

"It's really very dangerous to treat with such boors," she said. "Take a firm line. Don't take any notice of her, my dear. Only you can control them."

"Darling Hermann isn't greedy," bawled Osip. "He only wants his little turncoat Jesus."

Belyakov dragged his wife away from the silent Valerian and shook her by the arm. "State your terms, Hermann," he called.

"Give him up to us, disarmed, and the women go free."

"And me?"

"Come home to us." Osip waved his bandana. "And we'll feast you and forgive."

"You must go," repeated Loulou to Valerian in the same gentle voice.

"Natalya Igoryevna," exclaimed Polly. "You're quite the most contemptible person I have ever known. You are driving him onto the guns."

High in the house a child whimpered. Valerian strode to Polly across the broken glass, and kissed her on the mouth. "Sister," he said. "Leave me."

Night was coming to the cloudless sky.

Whether it was for reasons of sentiment, or family or a terrible fear, to Belyakov's amazement, she clung to the boy's arm, murmuring endearments. "*Brat moy*, my brother, my love, how can I let them take you from me?"

"You love me, *dushichka*?" asked the boy.

She gazed at him, unaffronted at this "darling". The question meant nothing to him but he could not tell his sister that.

"I love you," she said quickly, wondering at the subdued face before her.

"Then go," he said and moved out of the shadow of the wall into the declining light. "Hermann," he called out. "Safe conduct. Two women, one man, all unarmed."

"Safe conduct," came the unanimous cry. "Three civilians. *Laissez-passer*."

As so often before, Loulou was rapt at Valerian's performance. He stood apart, watching them as a dog watches sheep into hurdles, his energies narrowed to cautious oversight.

Huddled together stiffly the three figures stumbled away, following the line of the wall to the iron gate, then into the open where they were visible and still within firing-range. Loulou caught her foot in the hem of the impossible frock and nearly tripped.

Belyakov put out a hand to her. "Where the hell do we think we're going?" They paused. The house was silent.

"On, on," shouted Valerian. "Before your lives slip away forever."

Soon they were within the dark of the trees, out of the line of fire.

Without shifting position Valerian tracked their progress, finally twisting half-round to face their place of safety and presenting his back to the watchers from the house. For the whole of that time – three minutes, four minutes – his hands were working accurately inside the voluminous *burka*. The order he knew blind, off by heart, could follow neck-deep in a marsh or buried alive:

From hand-loading to automatic – are you listening, Private? – is accomplished on your *Flieger-Selbstlader Karabiner* in the following steps – One: slip catch on bolt-handle to engage gas piston; two: open gas port on barrel; three: fit your thirty-round magazine, vulgarly known as the Lüger Snail.

For the second time that day he relaxed, waiting for a sign. The moment of death would not be the culmination, for he had lived his life in a series of discontinuous moments, every one of which he had spent making himself ready for its end; and when it came, making preparations for the next. In imagination he dug his fingers into the necklace line of bone stranding his dead mare from tail-end to mane, each part strung, but to the touch, individuated and discrete. He could see how it was with the lives of others: the sense of their being who they were depended on a piecing together of apparently unconnectable events, as the animal mass of his Isabella articulated grace and vivacity at the twitch of her spine. The fancy made him smile: what, then, did that make him – a tumble of unthreaded pearls, a creature without backbone?

Not in the face of death. Under fire, at rest, commanding or commanded, with or without the solace of others, he had bowed to the truth of death as a revelation of absolute Nature. The mistake he had made was to seek elsewhere for such constancy. The only truth possible to know was not on the lips of a virgin and the Mother of God but in the ushering smile of their double who took you back to the place before the beginning, and withdrew. *Stabat mater*.

He eased the sling of his carbine and gripped it stock and barrel under the *burka*. A slow breeze chilled his face. The drawing away of the stars would be forever imperceptible. No sign would come.

Bargaining voices floated across from the steps beside the portico: "Dead or alive? I've got him, spot on the cross hairs." That was Makar with his pride and joy, a sniper's rifle.

"He's mine!" roared Osip. "He's mine. Let me split him for old times' sake."

"Keep him fresh, alive alive-o. We've not started on him yet, and when we have it'll be the women's turn." They were making merry in anticipation.

"Come on slow, Master," called Schmidt. "Hands on head and one pace at a time."

Valerian concentrated, rippling body and limbs in a shrug like that of an athlete before a race, then slowly began to do as he was told. When the line of his arms and trunk formed an arrow-head shape, he stopped, the butt-plate of the downward-pointing carbine projecting through the opening of his *burka*. Osip saw the glint, hesitated, then fractionally raised his head for a better look.

As he did so a sliver of metal the size of an inch-thick pocket watch – fragmented casing from a Mgebrov rodded rifle grenade – took off his left ear.

Since the grenade had fallen well short of the steps, exploding on the patchily-gravelled driveway, Osip was particularly unlucky. Unluckier still when, in reflex, he squeezed off one round and kept his finger on the trigger of his carbine which blazed away automatically at the wall of the kitchen garden. At the angle of the wall, tucked amidst the bean-poles, Valerian smiled. His moment was not yet.

In the thickening twilight someone far up the slope, beyond the trees which sheltered Loulou, Polly and Belyakov, was pin-pointing the figures on the steps by the flashes from Osip's gun. Before the lieutenants had time to recover from the blast of the first, another grenade sailed down, grazed the stonework, and lay on the bottom step as quiet as a fruit. Valerian guessed the type, guessed that Osip, Makar and Schmidt knew the type too. Inside the little catches no longer bit on the detonator pellet *which is now free, you lot, to dash its cap onto the needle and thus explode the mun-ition.*

No one attempted to throw it back. When the casing burst the old soldiers were already prone and no damage was done except to the lace of Makar's right shoulder tab.

Hard on the explosion came a shadow blacker than the tree-trunks, a shadow bounding and leaping, cutting into the bitter green of the darkening turf; a rider, crouched low over a toy-like horse, was sweeping upon the house, bawling obscenities and whirling his cap. Valerian watched but did not move. As the horseman skidded the last few yards the lieutenants found his range but he was careering so wildly that their aim was distracted, and he disappeared, unscathed, behind the far wall of the garden. A second later a dull crack carried over, there was a *phut*, and a fat brown cylinder with lighted fuse plopped among the cucumbers and erupted. Then another, and another until in the confines of the garden Valerian was smothered in a dense cloud of white smoke. Kicking his way blindly through compost and scattered tools he leapt at the wall, finding easy holds in the soft brick. At the top he glanced back: below the first-floor level of the house all was hidden in a swansdown mist which continued to billow from the canister. He dropped heavily and stood still, bewildered about which direction to take.

The captain was a hundred yards away side-on to the slope, cradling his rifle with one arm, the other stretched out towards him. "Stirrup! Stirrup!" he shouted, his undersized mount nattering restlessly, whinnying at the smoke fumes.

Firing began once more from the house.

Valerian zig-zagged up the incline, impeded by his heavy cape. The captain leaned out of the saddle and called again and again, his voice encouraging, beseeching. Under the chatter of rapid small-arms fire Valerian could not distinguish the words, but they sounded like one and the same thing, being repeated over and over.

* * *

"Martin . . . Martin . . . Martin Kabalyevskii . . . Over here!"

Oblivious of the threat of snipers, Loulou scrambled from the wayside ditch where she had taken cover with Belyakov and Polly along the old village road.

"Kabalyevskii . . . Martin . . . Martin . . ."

There was no mistaking the name. Him, him, it *was* him. A fresh burst of energy swept through her. "Merciful God. At last . . ."

Neither Polly's gasp of anger nor Belyakov's out-thrust arm could restrain her and she raced away into the park, tripping once again on the wedding-dress skirt, scarcely pausing to fold it round her knees before flying on, back to him, back to the house, white legs exposed against the yellowed grasses of the out-of-heart pasture, bare feet twinkling over kingcups and daisies, her breath coming in gulps, her eyes alight and searching; searching out the original of that voice, the bearer of that magic name.

Vividly clear in the June night, rider and pony bunched before the wheeling clouds of smoke. Fedya, sunk beside a solitary holm-oak, roused himself as he saw his former charge flash past, unseeing, obsessed, shouting; and he leapt up, heroic again, eager to defend her.

From a pallid gap between the shadows of trees Loulou gave out a piercing bawl. When the pony checked, slithered round and came charging directly at her, she ran to meet it, head-on. At the last moment the horseman veered and caught her round the shoulders, laughing as if it were a game. "Natalya Igoryevna, well I'll be damned! What a place to meet!"

Damn, damn. Only him, after all. Only him, Aleksei, the comedian, the charmer, smiling and leaning out of the saddle as he used to in the steeple-chase ring; not Martin but Martin's inseparable companion, the lion to his lamb; merely a disappointment then, now a cruel joke.

When she could speak she could not greet him by name. "You here, you . . . Where is Martin?"

He pointed the pony in the direction of the house. Silhouetted against the thinning smoke was a tall figure. "Where else should he be, my dear, except with me?"

But before Aleksei could finish a calcium flare shot up from the maze suddenly illuminating the figure which sprinted towards them, face brilliantly white, and Aleksei touched her neck and she turned to him, bewildered, and saw that he was wearing the cap and tunic of some drab uniform quite unknown to her. He had become a stranger, as the man making speed for them was a stranger, and the light revealed this.

335

Then a boy came between her and the man who was running, a boy with a rifle, as long and awkward as his legs, and she found the sight so *outré* that she inwardly smiled.

The pony took fright, twisting its hindquarters to one side, snorted against its tightening bridle-rein and blundered into a fledgy mass of saxifrage bush where the captain fought it to a standstill in a shower of unripe berries. His face was deathly stiff as Valerian braked his run by skidding to one knee and rolling over twice until his head found contact with the warm underbelly of the little pony.

"Oh God," murmured the captain. "There's been some terrible mistake. Oh no, surely not, not you, tell me it's not *you* that I've saved."

When Fedya rose to the offside, honking like some flightless goose, and fired blind from the waist, the pony screamed once as the second bullet splintered the cannonbone of the left foreleg, then tottered half-round on sinking haunches to present itself broadside on to the boy with the gun who fired as she tumbled, and continued to fire when both she and her rider sprawled to an indiscriminate tangle.

Before the captain knew he was hit he felt the horse go suddenly soft beneath him. He opened wide his mouth to cry out but to his astonishment no cry came and it occurred to him that for some reason he must have gone deaf. And during everything that followed, he sought for similar explanation of why his mouth refused to unslacken, why he had become so heavy, why he swayed and what he was doing on the ground unable to move his legs.

By then Valerian was flung out across the twitch and fuss of the dying pony's neck, taking the calmest of aims at the gangly boy who cartwheeled in triumph while the voice of the woman rang in his ears: "*No, no, no, no!*"

Because Fedya took no conscious aim but fired instinctively, unsighted, at the outline of the strange horseman who had accosted Natalya Igoryevna, the captain was the first target he had ever hit, and the match of impulse and action which felled man and beast came to him as an intervention so beautiful in its accomplishment that for a moment the boy felt himself to be in unique accord with the world of cause and effect. But the act which seemed to him so wholly perfect only came about with the captain's compliance, for the horseman had sat too long fronted to the light, unmoving, trying to discern the features of the man who came pounding towards the brightness of his rifle and the starry jingle of his pony's bridle rings. Had the flame hung higher or burst whiter he might have obtained a clear view, had a shorter time to distinguish truth from appearances, to ponder the lies of the dwarf-boy and the confusion of the woman, had a moment left in which to be decided and turn away, immune from deceit. But the time he took was given to the boy, and the boy gave it back to Valerian who raked him with a five-shot burst down from the sternum.

The shootings in the park were observed by a three-man patrol scouting the inner perimeter of the maze. By the time the message had been passed to Sergeant Volkov at the rear, over half the men in the company knew that they were now without an officer, and the news was greeted with a clamour for action. When Volkov hesitated, having made no provision for a night attack, the cavalry troopers selected a detachment of their best riders which, by stampeding loose horses before them at the lowest hedge wall to the north-east of the maze, reduced the thickets to a height that their heavily-accoutred mounts could safely leap. Once in the parkland they roamed at free will to give vent to their desire for revenge at the loss of their captain, retaining a profound disbelief that a bunch of peasant women and deserters without artillery could pose them any threat. They were a minority, hotheaded and unrepresentative; no one but the captain could have stopped them that night; Sergeant Volkov did not even try. Such men were the cream of his troops, but they had ridden too far and too long to be held in check.

That night, in effect, two field promotions took place: Sergeant Volkov became acting commander, on sufferance, by relinquishing the initiative to his men. While, on the opposing side, Vissarion made his bid for undivided control. With Valerian outlawed, Solomon and Titus dead, Osip wounded, Schmidt losing his grip and Makar nearly drunk, his moment had come. Never given to humility, Vissarion now saw himself as an elect, the chosen, and by dint of strutting and bullying he had swiftly activated the first line of defence the moment the flares had soared above the park. Since the house was surrounded by few naturally defensible positions, he could expect attack from the three landward sides; but in case of night assault he guessed that the enemy would concentrate on the south and north approaches where mounted troops could manoeuvre more freely. Accordingly, he brought down two of the four machine-guns from the old road lying to the north-east.

At the pre-arranged signal – one round from the antiquated seventy-seven – the outlying troops picketed on marshes and wood-land along the railway would draw in to take the attackers in the rear. Vissarion contributed nothing new to this plan which Solomon had drawn up months ago, but he supplied the energy and ambition required for its fulfilment.

The community had been in-dwelling, obsessed with a leader who had betrayed it, and become consequently neglectful of military duty. That was the reason for the enemy's closeness – not his superior skill or equipment. Now Vissarion had determined to redress this dereliction by a show of resistance which would convince the brotherhood, once and for all, that he was the one last saviour they need ever seek for.

After the field-piece boomed its solitary shell harmlessly into the river, Valerian knew at once what to expect. The plan had been of his making too, and he believed now, as he had then, that it would work.

Yasha wept.

"Shut your noise. When I say down, you go down," hissed the corporal, ramming the butt-plate of his rifle into the back of the boy's neck.

Flat on his face among thistles and darnel Yasha continued to agonise: Natalya Igoryevna's shrieks, the captain calling out at the top of his voice, a *pock-pock* of semi-automatic fire; more screams; then a brief silence before a hideous explosion and clatter of church bells from the distant village. Something terrible had happened. Myelnikov had seen it, the bastard had seen it, and run as he'd never run before. Something more terrible was about to happen, any moment, and Myelnikov still said nothing.

Clenching his teeth against the pain Yasha began to crush the thistle stalks by rolling his head from side to side until the spines drove into his cheeks, but he persevered, unnoticed by Myelnikov, and at last succeeded in clearing a narrow funnel of sight. From the ribbons of mist streaming out of the hollow which meandered among outcrops of rock before debouching into the river a mile or so more to the west, he could fix the approximate position: they were lying within a slight depression which on their left rolled up into parkland at the eastern flank of the maze. Also to the left, at a distance of one hundred yards or less, stood the thickset blue-beech hedge towards which Volkov's cavalrymen were stampeding the riderless horses.

At first Yasha felt comforted by the shouts and cracking of whips, and assumed that this turmoil was a nightly event which a cavalry squadron had to perform before turning in. At first, while the spasm of hooves was unmenacing, he did not feel afraid, and tried to rouse Myelnikov but the corporal stayed mute, one bullying obdurate arm across the boy's shoulders, squeezing him rigid.

It was then that the noise began in a uniform steady thrum, so remote that Yasha could still hear the chirrup of pine-siskins along the hedge-brake and he suddenly recalled Myelnikov's talk about shells, how some kind of sounds could come up gently, without advertisement, catching you out: *carpet-slippered buggers*. And the massed gallop was like this at the beginning, but before the leading rank of horses became aware of the obstacle a dozen strides ahead, their thunderous sound had engulfed him, and he could hardly subdue his longing for the crash to come.

A pair of roans, black and silver, leapt clean over the winnowy topgrowth, neck-and-neck. At their tails a mare, big with foal, cleared her forehooves, seemed to slip from behind and fall on her flank, bridging the hedge top. Yasha caught the flash of terror in her Brazilian ruby eyes as a following mare struck her and they both went down together on the hard-grain spikes in the heart of the hedge.

Scarcely had the blowing screeches of the stricken mares died away when he spotted the riders, cap-peaks blobbing against the faint stars. Was this whole company following upon some signal, invisible to him and Myelnikov, riding out of the dark to effect a great victory?

He could not believe that they were so stupid as to act without plan or foresight; only when the first man reared his mount over the fallen horses did he begin to understand that they were recklessly unafraid, and must be bent on some ferocious purpose which was racing them on to the distant guns.

The last trooper had not reached the park side when a putter of massed rifle fire broke out along the house front three-quarters of a mile away. The man hesitated, adjusted the set of his khaki-clothed helmet, then turned and spurred back.

Myelnikov relaxed his hold on Yasha to prop himself up on his elbows and watched horse and rider disappear into the gloom of the maze. "There's a canny lad," he said, "who knows a stupid-sod enterprise when he sees one."

"What's happening? Are they coming back?"

The corporal clapped Yasha on the back with an inclusive gesture. "We will be – like him. As for the rest – well, in my book, suicide's no sin but I wouldn't recommend it for the health."

"Does that mean they're not after us and we can clear off?"

The volleys from the house tightened into a smart co-ordinated rap, coming slowly closer from the south-west. Further off heavy machine-guns had started to bicker.

"Please yourself," said the corporal. "I don't have no moral objections to your arse being jaggered by shrapnel."

Yasha remembered the mines. In this low-intensity light he wouldn't have a chance to thread through them. Neither would the blokes on the horses. And, as if to confirm his intuition, a series of flashes vented among the oak timberlings on the inner edge of the park, and above the ripple of quick-fire he began to hear moans and cries.

"Where's their back-up?"

"Bloody warming itself by the brazier, where we ought to be."

"But it'll be a massacre up there. The place is a blockhouse."

"That's right." Myelnikov unfastened his haversack and brought out a zinc ramekin wrapped round with a rag in which were four little biscuits. "It's what the sergeant calls paying the penalty for being over-zealous. They took off too soon, see, thought they'd carry the day without him. He'll learn 'em. Here, boy, have a Revolutionary biscuit."

When Yasha choked on the desiccated garibaldi the corporal handed over his canteen. The water was tangy, iron-red, but Yasha gulped it gratefully.

"Now that's down satisfactorily, say your prayers because we've got a long night to live through."

With that the corporal secured his rifle to his wrist by a strip of bandage, rolled over and fell fast asleep.

Yasha never forgot the loneliness of that night. While the corporal snored he searched out every spurt of light which might signify that the action was advancing towards him; and he tried to interpret the brawl of shouts and explosions from the house. But had he been closer, been actually present in the cobbled courtyard where five of Volkov's cavalry men were trapped in the eastern pound among the stable blocks hardly able to swing round under the fire that poured on them from roof-top and windows, he would not have understood any more than they did how it was happening. Volkov could have forecast the outcome from the very start: without artillery support they didn't stand a chance against the overwhelming number of defenders in the house; but no one had listened to him, or even remembered that he existed during that last furious quarter of an hour when every single trooper was unhorsed and pursued to his death on foot by hordes of boys and women armed only with staves.

Towards the end of the first hour Yasha identified two more machine-guns opening up a mile or so to the rear and he guessed that a second raiding party had split off from the first and ridden round in an effort to flank the house from the south-east. The day before when he and the captain had scouted the road the machine-guns had been unmanned, but now they were fully crewed, as Yasha had always known they would be in case of imminent attack, and he cursed his ill-luck at not having had the chance to put his knowledge at the disposal of Sergeant Volkov.

What kind of a sergeant must he be, though, to have permitted such a shambles to begin?

Before dawn, Myelnikov snorted twice and sat up rubbing his face. No sound of fighting had been heard for some time and the corporal, who had slept through explosions, gunfire and screams, seemed to have been shaken into life by the profound stillness which now hung over the park and house. Although Yasha's eyes prickled, he had not been able to sleep, not even when the action fizzled out. Glad that at last his companion was awake, he wanted to talk but kept silent when confronted by Myelnikov's ill-at-ease, malignant smile.

"Nice morning for waking up dead." He kicked his boot into Yasha's side. "Not so chirpy, are we, son?"

"Get off me." The boy shifted round. "You knew all along what was going on and you wallowed off to sleep like a pig. I want to know what's been happening out there. All of it. From the beginning. I've got a right after all the hours of watching and listening I've done alone. You've had your rest-up. Now, what about it?"

The corporal looked straight at him and breathed deep. "What took place, boy, can be explained in one go – love. Love at last sight. Because my lot was witness to his final act, d'you see? Saw him punch his ticket, cop it, greet his fate, all ringed round with diabolical lights."

Eastwards the sky was lightening ahead of the sun. Yasha still did not understand.

"The captain, stupid – mine, yours, theirs, hers. Shot, shot down in his prime. There, look for yourself," shouted Myelnikov at the shadowed front of the house. "There she stood, your lady, drooping over him like the hangings on a whore's bed. And if your darling major hadn't happened along with his fancy shooter she'd have joined him."

Although he realised that the captain had made his bid to rescue Valerian with even finer disregard for consequences than was shown by the troopers who had charged headlong into the park over the carcases of their own reserve mounts, Yasha found it hard to reconcile himself to the officer's fate.

To hell with that kind of person, and the way they played on your feelings. And if Natalya Igoryevna hadn't been enough, now he was stifling sobs for her male counterpart who had worked the same trick of arousing an affection that so easily could become outright love, then decamping all of a sudden, leaving you totally unreciprocated. Disgusted at his own lack of control under Myelnikov's impassive glare, he dabbed at the tears with the back of his hand. At least he'd chosen better than pike-face opposite who'd never fall for any of them, let alone the worst, the golden boy, Valerian. Well, even Yasha hadn't stooped that low, at least he'd been sensible about *him*. One look at Myelnikov and you'd know that love could never cloud those piss-coloured eyes.

"Well, carry me out and bury me decent," said the corporal when Yasha's brief tears were done. "I never seen such a wake. Catch any bleeding officer making a mug out of me, or my mates."

"He already did," said Yasha. "And what d'you think you can do about it – redeem the situation?"

But the corporal was above sarcasm; he was thinking hard. After a bout of strenuous hawking he produced the rag in which the biscuits had been wrapped and blew his nose. "You, boy, are now in hock to me, seeing as I have safeguarded your miserable dogskin."

"You don't do favours."

"That's just how your type always goes wrong. I'm all soul, me, don't you know?" The phrase was the captain's. "I mean, who else would have stopped you walloping on last night, right up death's jaws, haring to the rescue, when a cartful of heroes couldn't have pulled back my captain or one single one of those dead men and horses down there. All set, they was, on bravado, just like you. What d'you think of them now, little laddie? Sorry they're missing your company?"

Yasha gazed at the sorrel mare still spiked on the hedge, wondering who would come to drag her away and if they would dig the same hole for the horses and the bodies of their riders which dotted the park together like so much huge rubbish. "All right," he said. "What do you want?"

"It's like this – the mates of my mates that's dead here" – Myelnikov swept an arm over the park – "is over there," he went on, indicating the whole maze. "And they've lost their captain, lost a heap of themselves, most of the ground previously gained, and all they've got in exchange is the rule of one blinkered sergeant that no one respects. Now they're going to have to take that house, and they're facing professionals who don't give quarter. So it's up to you, lad, to rectify things, as it were."

"Me?"

"You."

"But I've never been in the Army. I was too short."

The corporal advanced upon Yasha with feline grace and slid to the earth before him, his eyes uncomfortably close. "It's not your experience we're calling for, old soldier."

"No?"

"No, it's your specialised knowledge. And as of this moment that's the only thing worth having, when our mounts must be down by half, we're low on ammunition and without a proper commander."

This last was repeated with such soft, unusual insistence that Yasha tried to wriggle back. "I told you once, I'm no leader . . ."

Myelnikov made up the gap between them and carried on with the same fluid emphases: "No commander, see, no one in charge, and we need one, we must have one, otherwise we're done."

"Stop looking at me," said the boy. "You bloody volunteer yourself if it's that touch-and-go. I only know . . ."

"A major!" interrupted the corporal so violently that Yasha shrank down into the grass. "That's who you know, that's all you know, and that knowledge is what you're going to effing *ut-il-ise* for the benefit of the common good."

"Aw, no, not him, not that one, he's missing half the rungs on his ladder," shouted the boy, devastated at this hint of Myelnikov's intentions. "I'm off," he whined, leaping upright. "I'd rather get dead on my own without him, he's . . ."

The corporal shot out his arm and yanked the boy back by his jacket, regarding him in triumph. "He's lovely, that's what he is. I had my eye on him last night, when he got his dander up and snipped out that locust-legged kid, the moment my captain fell. Didn't think twice. Toothy as an eel for the slaughter and cool about it, too, accurate and cool. Know him, don't you? Been one of his familiars in that mass-house over the way? Well, we have need of his services this minute, and you can tell him that from me."

"I'm not going back there," said Yasha. "You can whistle for him. He does murders."

"By God, he does, and it's beautiful to see, that's why you're going to heave him aboard for us. I mean, can I do it?" Myelnikov's voice was fraught with appeal. "Course not – he doesn't know me, might not take it too kindly from the sergeant, neither, seeing as we've not had the pleasure, but you, now, you're his friend, his last friend since the captain's passed on. What d'you say?"

Yasha began to cry again. Myelnikov was relentless. "I thought you'd see my point. Now, this is what you do. I want you crawling after him, smelling the ground he treads on. And when you locate a suitable venue for a head-to-head, I want you telling him, pouring out your little heart, all grace and flattery. God shall rejoice when he steps into our officer's boots and rejoins the world. See what I mean?"

"I see it," whimpered Yasha. "But I can't, I can't, and you can't make me."

The corporal drew his pistol. "Oh yes, you can," he said. "And with this behind you, you will. It's him or me, lad, and like I told you, no bugger in braid makes a monkey out of me."

37

At dawn Sergeant Volkov made up his lists. Out of a company already under strength seven were dead, not counting the CO. More serious was the lack of remounts: fifteen horses dead, blown or crippled and no back-up in sight. Ammunition inadequate if it was to be a long do. Small-arms ditto. Plus side: more than enough fodder in a captured outbuilding where some fly bugger had a secret store. And one neutral fact: the two prisoners who had crossed into his lines, one woman and her husband. Maybe useful, maybe not.

And *Barbara*, of course, the 210-mm. siege howitzer installed amidship the old grain barge moored up-river, they still had her.

Having completed his damage assessments Volkov harangued the survivors. Under the stress of command his voice became squeaky. Among themselves the men used to mimic him but by now they were too dispirited and only the prisoners took an interest.

"Just look at you – call yourselves soldiers?" he shouted.

No man summoned up the energy even for this. Sergeant Volkov's abuse was uneasy and bland. There was no fire.

"Society has commandeered your services, society has laid duties upon you. Society depends upon the fulfilment of those duties. Why? Because that society is *yours*, it is *entitled* . . ."

The circle of troops around him settled into the bracken and rested. None of this stuff ever made sense. With the captain you knew where you were: he said, you did. But with Volkov you had to give orders to yourself, and Christ help you if you got the instructions wrong.

"You all know what we call a man who shirks his duty, a man who refuses the call of his brother, a man who shows no solidarity . . ."

They all knew. Each man could have repeated it from memory. Already had at similar moments. With a few bits thrown in.

"No society ought to allow people like you in its ranks."

No fucking fear, mate. Fucking so-ciety ought to pick its own bleeding scabs.

"Know what you are?"

Dontcha know? Dontcha know?

345

"Traitors who have betrayed our great land. A plague . . ."
Clap in camouflage.
"You're dead . . ."
Bed. Dead. And nothing in between.

The matter was simpler than Volkov thought: his men despised him. They listened because listening was what they did to people put over them, but they stopped at that, short of orders. The captain, now, the captain was different: a rum sod but on your side, the proper side, against the pen-and-paper men. After he was killed they had gone berserk and charged in without plan or orders. They got a mauling on account of their *indiscipline*. That was why Volkov was having a tantrum.

Indiscipline had been the captain's style. He'd just ridden off, neglecting to forward Sergeant Volkov's finicking map of this finicking estate with its scale, its legend and exact dimensions of every cattle pound and septic tank; omitting entirely to direct it to the proper quarters – Battalion HQ could whistle for it: they didn't have to turn over the cowpats looking for mines. And any man would have gone with him but he took his own recruit in Myelnikov – one mad bugger less.

Sergeant Volkov breathed in, pushed out his pigeon chest and tried to talk from his diaphragm. Time to ease up on the men.

"I used to know this region of the country," he said conversationally. "Had friends in these parts. Artisans setting up communal workshops, readers, thinkers, salt of the earth, sound as bells . . ." He basked in the warmth of recall.

Before the war Filip Sergeyevich Volkov had been head clerk at the office of an auctioneer who had prized him for his talent at clear succinct exposition. Now his knowledge of local real estate was a boon to HQ, where his reports were much studied for their detail on location, extent and naturally defensible features of the great demesne houses and parks in the south-west of the government. Volkov had only one word for the owners: "Vermin," he would say lovingly, tapping his teeth with a stylus used for etching contours on Staff maps. "Insanitary."

Wherever representatives of the old order might be secreting themselves, there was the sergeant with his swagger stick and signaller's notepad thieved from the kit of an English RSM in Odessa, taking names. Hangings, shootings, burnings were jotted down in longhand; the more colourful but less efficient techniques, such as herding the inhabitants of one country house into a rowboat then sinking it with mortar fire, he recorded in private shorthand for elaboration into morale-boosting lectures for the men. Each incident was as meticulously set out as the cheerful red flags on the map pinned to the tailboard of his Commissariat wagon. For some reason the captain took to the idea and issued notebooks to his company, but they never caught on.

"Vermin," he now said aloud to the troops, characterising past masters. "Filthy vermin."

The tall dark prisoner passed his tobacco-pouch to a broken-nosed Kalmuk who had been whispering at him from the front row. "I don't appreciate that kind of talk," said the stranger. "And neither does my missis."

Volkov was astonished. But the men were not. Several turned and grinned at the man and wife. They were glad someone had spoken up. Anything was better than Volkov's bull. The sergeant knew this, but prided himself on his handling of men: the breed under him was indoctrinated with superstition. Wagging a finger in the direction of the house, he spoke in sorrow: "No wiving or shriving in that place you come from, or so I'm informed. That grand house, it stinks of sin and the women in it are all polluted."

Presumptuous too, he could have added. Before sunrise he had been along the river and heard their Mass-chants, laughter, and the chink of their bottles. Did all right in there for women. And the rest. Better off than this lot. And him, for that matter.

"Come off it, Sarge," said Viktor the mulemaster. "Just 'cause you haven't dripped your liniment for a couple of months, don't crack on it's wickedness for them as has."

There was a wide murmur of agreement, except for Polly who sat up very prim and said: "Mr Volkov is quite right. *Un-imagin-able* things have gone on over there."

By now the men were thoroughly alert. Belyakov tried to shush her.

"Ha!" exclaimed Volkov. "Now we have the beast by the tail."

At dawn Yasha found them in the hollow where he and the captain had spent most of the previous day. The man was straggled out, flat on his back, as nude as a starfish. She stood over him sifting the browned cracknels of beech-leaves into a dust which spiralled down through the mist onto his naked thighs.

"My dove, you came to me at last. Awake. Remember me."
The voice had led him to her. The voice had not changed.

Yasha gave a butcher-boy whistle. An answering yodel came from a clump of sycamores and Myelnikov emerged, his balaclava festooned with ragwort. Natalya Igoryevna gave no sign of having heard, and they both watched.

"Settled his hash, I expect," whispered the corporal. "And now she's tidying him up to fool the creepy-crawlies."

The boy wagged a frantic hand at his companion who sank down again noiselessly. Yasha wanted to catch her in this private moment. He wanted to know how it was with her and the man. The scornful beauty he had harried and safeguarded for so long was garbling like a thrush. Either she was mad, or on the point of going mad, or had been mad all along. It didn't make much difference now, but she was a sight to behold, this fine-boned ragged creature snarling, then drooling, then dragging at something between the man's teeth, and all the while that lovely, lovely, lovely hair, fox-throat yellow in the morning haze.

"Cut too tight. One must be free . . . Martin . . . Your body never knew me. But Martin has come to inhabit this body. And my lovers fight bone for bone. Kostya has no place to rest and Aleksei bleeds . . ."

In the pit of his stomach Yasha went cold. The man had been gagged. Webby streamers of blood and spittle dribbled from the scarlet rags in his mouth. She lifted the head gently from behind. "He has gone," she said to the open eyes.

At once Yasha recognised their mad glaze. No such luck. The figure on the ground was only temporarily incognito. Before she could rise he was across the hollow, leaping at her shoulders, pulling her off the man. "Skip it, lady," he growled. "He's gone to no limbo he won't come back from. Stop fooling around. While he's like that you're safe."

There was no resistance; he tried soothing: "All over now, all over," and disengaged her fingers from the gag as she wailed: "Martin, Martin . . ."

"All gone, Martin, lady, all gone."

While the nursery rhythm lulled her, Yasha was thoroughly scared. Valerian must have foamed and fallen in the night battle and she must have dragged him here, alone in the dark, watching him tear at himself and trying to stop his teeth severing his own tongue. Who would wake first from the dream – him or her – was less vital than what Valerian might do next, but Yasha, for the moment, ignored him after covering the body with the captain's discarded greatcoat, and attended to her. Hers had been the vigil, hers was the need.

He tried her with tepid river-water from his belt flask but she dribbled it down her chin. He sat her down, arranged her frock – what was left of it – over the florid mark round her throat and across her bare knees. The skirt was torn apart and giving at the seams.

"Listen." *Listen?* By the look of her she hadn't even recognised him. She shuddered and twisted a lock of hair behind her ear. It might be a trick; she might have plotted with the man: she'd pretend to go hysterical and Valerian would shoot up, whirling a cutlass. Yasha whistled, watching the body out of the corner of one eye. Not a twitch of the coverlet. No Myelnikov either. The swine was probably pigging for truffles, nut-hunting among the corpses dotted in the bush.

He began again, riding his "Listen, listen" over the snuffly gasps Loulou made through her nose. "There's been a misunderstanding." Christ, a moment like this, and he was talking like a waiter. After a cough he redoubled his enunciation. "*I* told them he was Martin." He jerked his head towards Valerian. "So they wouldn't kill him, see? The soldiers – remember? The soldiers?" All teeth, scales, and eyes, voracious as pikes, how could he forget? But, shredding her curls and staring ahead, she managed, she forgot. "So when he comes round, for God's sake tell him who he is. I mean, who he's meant to be. Martin, that's who he is . . . Well, who he will be, if you take my meaning. Looks like him – even fooled the captain."

He heard himself sounding insane. No wonder she wasn't taking any of it in when he just about grasped it himself. How much more could she take?

Sappy twigs squealed underfoot. Yasha cringed, but it was only Myelnikov loping up at the double, rifle unslung. "Still barmy?" he said after a spectacular grimace at Natalya Igoryevna. "Guess what, midglet, our Captain Devil-may-care has been aided and abetted into keeping his skin whole."

"What kind of disease makes you lie quicker than decent people breathe?" Yasha burst out.

"On my honour." Myelnikov gave a grin. "Caught a packet, that's all, his eminence. Know who stuffed back his particulars?" Yasha stared incredulously at the countess. "You got it – that witless miss. On the trot all night she must have been, from one to t'other, bandaging, watering. A right sister of mercy." On his blackened face was an expression almost of respect.

Yasha let out a moan. It was going to be a sticky day. Already Loulou had thrown back her shoulders and raised her eyes to the corporal, recognition flickering on her lips.

"Well then," she said smartly. "Where are they?"

This was too much for Myelnikov who was prepared only for dumb madness. Women brought out the worst in him. And the timbre of authority in the voice of this one was grit in the eye of his soul. He scowled back, unrolled the rim of his balaclava. "Expecting company, missis?"

She showed her teeth. "Your comrades-in-arms, soldier, or have they deserted too?"

Myelnikov cocked his head to one side, deciding to play up to this madam who was obviously so far out of her head that next minute she'd be requesting brass-bands and nosegays to distribute to the troops. "Why," he said, "this here's your soldiery, ma'am, numbering from the right, Myelnikov, Pavel Aleksandrovich, corporal, twice decorated, four times wounded, on detachment, under orders from temporary field CO Volkov, a sergeant and man of doggish evil eye." He paused and doffed his balaclava engagingly. "This unpersonable hump," he continued, indicating Yasha, "slavering to lick the crumbs off your feminine person is not stupid enough to be a soldier, but is what we call *hors de combat* – the brains of the outfit." He leered up to her in the stiff-legged gait of a child learning to walk. "And as for commanding officers, blind me, milady, if we don't have one each: one stretcher-case captain with more holes in him than a piss-bucket, and this other Martin-come-lately who's lost his breeches. Soldiers, ma'am?" he jeered, twisting up his chin. "You've got what you've always had: the whole crook-backed Russian Imperial Army hobbling behind the bare arses of the bleeding High Command."

As Myelnikov's voice rose in the silent clearing, Valerian groaned, coughed and looked around.

Natalya Igoryevna ignored the corporal swaggering in the bracken and fell across the chest of the man on the ground. "I thought you had gone, I thought you were dead," she sobbed again and again.

Valerian tried to push her away while Myelnikov stormed on: "No word of a lie. The complete modern turn-out at your service – brains, brawn and Volkov, the man whose pencil is mightier than munitions." When Valerian stiffened and began to draw himself up, the corporal stood to attention. "Sir," he called out. "Myelnikov, sir, reporting. Mission: to liaise with friendly auxiliaries such as your sirship. In consequence, therefore, and owing to the unfortunate indisposition of my superior officer, Major Martin Kabalyevskii, I place myself under your command."

Yasha gawped at this turnabout.

Polly spoke for some time, unabashed at the sex of her audience. She liked indelicate men. They did not dissimulate their pleasures. At the end they gave a little cheer, glad that she had not missed experiences which they would have traded their boots for.

Thumbs in the slant pockets of his riding-breeches, Sergeant Volkov continued to pace up and down. "We-ell," he said. "This *is* a fine how-de-do. What are we going to do with you, eh?"

This remark was addressed more to the troops than to Polly, in the expectation that some wag would come up with a suggestion so obvious and obscene that Volkov could take credit for allowing it to be made. When no one spoke or sniggered the sergeant was at a loss and fell back on property-surveyor's patter in a characteristic misplacement of identity.

"Beggars belief," he said, looking across to the house. "And I expect he was very particular."

Polly raised an eyebrow: "Who exactly do you mean?"

"Why the gentleman, my dear, who owns this desirable gentleman's residence."

"Hey, *starshina*," said the Kalmuk morosely. "You're forgetting." He turned to the men on either side. "What's he forgetting?"

"Forget his dick if it wasn't fastened to him," mumbled the man on his right.

"With a red star," said another.

"Forgetting what, my man?" Volkov asked, very flushed.

"*Owned*, Sarge. Owned. Been a change of landlord since, or so you keep telling us. Ours now, ain't it? Not no gent's."

"Ah," said the sergeant, relaxing the swell of his chest. "It is, it is – in a manner of speaking."

"Bugger manners," said Viktor to his hinnies. "Instead of oats he gives us poetry."

"Oh, absolutely!" cried Polly, having been so carried away by the novel sensation of public speaking that she had not followed the exchange. "I should jolly well think it was. Frozen poetry! Landscaped gardens, bathrooms galore, English plumbing . . ."

Volkov's eyes became dreamy. "Tip-top appurtenances," he murmured. "Inside and out, furbished to the highest specifications. Extensive modern amenities, bang up-to-date."

Polly jumped to her feet, skipped up to the sergeant and clapped him on the shoulder. "You don't mind if I take up that particular point? I mean, people ought to be told about such things."

Volkov gazed at his crew of deadbeat ragamuffins, unsure that they counted as people. This was turning into a committee meeting with speakers from the floor. Still, the men were alert for the first time in weeks. Nothing like a bit of skirt.

Polly turned to the soldiers, her voice ringing with outrage: "And you know what more they did, don't you? They stabled farmyard beasts in the white drawing-room."

There was disappointment at this. Only Viktor expressed interest. "How'd they get them in, missis?"

"Two by two," someone guffawed. "Religious, you see, packing in an Arkful before the deluge."

"What deluge?" asked Belyakov absently, picking tobacco shreds from his teeth.

"Us, mate," said Viktor, grinning at the sergeant. "This fucking great big shower."

Polly pressed on, determined to expose a raw nerve: "They even turned the tennis lawn into . . . into a *conventicle*."

The soldiers threw out cries of mock horror: "Gosh! Dearie me! In the open, just like that — awfully rude!"

The sergeant forgot his military inhibitions. "Good God," he murmured as if apprised of some devastating truth. "A desecration. Some folk are no better than animals."

"There you are," said Polly resuming her place in triumph. "I knew all along that a dim view would be taken by the proper authorities."

At the mention of officialdom good-humour ceased, and Volkov was able to re-assert himself. "This is all very well, of course, and nobody enjoys a joke more than yours truly, especially after a hard action, but we have serious matters in hand, lads." If he had had a gavel this would have been the time to bang it. "As you know, operational objective number one is to take particulars of selected properties. Number two is to enter into possession on receipt of instructions. Heretofore you have rushed at it like pigs over a cliff. This must stop. Understand?"

A Zaporozhye Cossack with coachman's earrings sprawled back onto the grass and gave a howl. "You seen it lately, Sarge, you done a whatsermacallem . . . ?"

"Survey, Igor?" interposed Volkov. "Let's have some professionalism, if you please."

"Survey, Sarge, you done one? Like eyeball to eyeball with that fucking heap of masonry? Waggle your theodolite at them till the cows come home but those walls are as thick as elephant shit. It'd take a Krupp howitzer to open the front door."

"Worse than that monastery," said Viktor. "Had to burn that in the end. And not before we lost a round dozen extracting monks from the wainscot – remember? That's expensive on men, that kind of hand-to-hand stuff. And this lot's not monks . . ."

"Or nuns," said Igor, winking at Polly. But the matter was serious and nobody smiled.

"Stucco," said Volkov. He looked at the faces in front of him, secure in his specialised knowledge.

"What's stucco?" asked the Kalmuk.

The men's mood had changed. "Fucking shut your Asiatic gob, Hadzhii." "Get back on your magic carpet."

"Crap and sticks all bunged together," explained Viktor. "Could push an apple through it – or a dumb Mongol's head – right, Sarge?"

"Very apt," said Volkov.

The circle of men wavered cheerily at this news. They had artillery support for the unit: four Rumanian field guns, rather ancient but Krupp-made and lovingly serviced. The 2.85 inch-calibre was small, and since they had little high explosive the gunners had not reckoned they could make much impression on solid stone with shrapnel shell. But stucco was like people and with fourteen pounds of shrapnel per round you could make a lot of holes in a lot of persons.

"Good old Sarge," shouted one of the Cossacks. "We'll have their surplices in tatters!"

"Under modern tactical conditions," began Volkov. "A deep zone of shrapnel effect is most desirable . . ."

"Bloody tatters," went the word from man to man. "Wonderful engineering," the sergeant continued. "The rifling goes from one turn in fifty calibres at the breech to one turn in twenty-five at the muzzle. Mathematically, the development of the groove is a parabola . . ."

"I think I am going to have a headache," said Polly with a theatrical touch at her brow.

"Not your cup of tea, missis," said Viktor politely. "Bit on the intellectual side, I expect, all this witter about trunnions and wedge breech action."

"Thank you, young man. I can see you are one of nature's gentlemen." She was having her doubts about the sergeant – the way he *truckled* to them. Positively reptilian.

Dragging Belyakov's sleeve, she stood up amidst a ruckus of sympathetic jeers, but before teasing came into full flow a pair of artillery wagons appeared round the bend half a mile down the track, racing and bumping along the ruts in close order. Volkov placed himself in their path, his arms akimbo, but neither slowed down till the leading wagon was nearly upon him and he had jumped to one side.

Viktor leaped at the first wagon's trace horse, dragging down its head until both carts wobbled then slewed into a mud pool. The horses of the second had been roped up to the tailboard of the first, and bringing up the rear was a trio of wretchedly lathered mules tethered in a string. The driver of this makeshift convoy was a lad who looked about sixteen.

A consultation took place between him and Viktor, ended by the mulemaster wiping his face and calling across to the sergeant. "The little bugger says he's seen a ghost."

"He'll see his Maker if I fetch my stick to him," shouted Volkov. "He's six hours late. The men are ravenous. We'll all be suffering from apparitions if the rations aren't broken out double quick."

The Cossack rolled over and made munching noises at his fingers. A few soldiers piled their rifles and drifted over to the second cart, hopped over the tailboard and began to throw out round black loaves from under the tarpaulins. There was no rush. Most of their mates were too tired even to eat and curled up under their capes for a nap. Polly remained on her feet, feeling silly among these unconcernedly exhausted men, but noticed the bread and her hunger, and she and Belyakov joined the queue at the tailboard.

Viktor and the sergeant were arguing with the boy driver: "Don't be such a stupid sod, Mischa; you were tired, that's all."

"And frightened," said Volkov severely.

"That, too," conceded the mulemaster. "You were shit-scared stupid, Mischenka, but nobody minds."

"That road was sealed off after mopping-up operations," said Volkov. "As per instructions, tight as a drum."

The morose Kalmuk strolled over, skinning a bratwurst. "Sort of long coat did it have, your bogey?"

Mischa spoke normally for the first time. "Now you come to mention it . . ."

"'S one of them," said the Kalmuk indistinctly, a chunk of sausage in his mouth.

Volkov became testy. "One of what?"

"Them sodding monks we skewered. Dropped from heaven. Come calling."

Volkov twitched his swagger stick and placed his back between Mischa and the Kalmuk. "Now, boy," he said avuncularly. "Tell me what you saw."

Mischa began to cry. "There were two of them. The big one spoke." He gave a sob. "In Russian."

"That was handy," said Viktor. "What did he say?"

"I didn't catch it. He was all muffled up in a coat, our captain's greatcoat . . ." The words came higher and higher in a penetrating wail. "It was his coat . . . And the little one, he was our captain's corporal – you know, Sergeant, the one who . . ."

"Gawd," breathed Viktor. "I hoped we'd seen the last of that stinking pongo."

Volkov poked the boy with his cane. "You're useless, there's bats in your attic. They're dead those two, dead." This assumption had been so vital to his tactical dispositions that he had no intention of allowing it to be discredited. "Get out of my sight and learn some soldiering."

Mischa put his fists in his eyes and collapsed at Viktor's feet, howling.

Volkov strode off to his mapwagon muttering to himself: "Next thing they'll be sending us girls."

"Mischenka," said the mulemaster after a while. "Where's the grog?"

The boy looked blank then understood. "Back of the driving box," he said, jumping up.

"Good lad."

Mischa skipped over to his wagon, suddenly happy, and returned before the mulemaster had time to fill his pipe. In the act of driving a wooden handspike into one of the little barrels of spirit he had brought, Mischa caught sight of something on the trackway. He stopped what he was doing and crossed himself vigorously with the spigot. "Christ and all His angels protect us."

Viktor went on filling his pipe. "Something up, boy?"

The liquor began to leak from the half-tapped barrel. "It's him," babbled Mischa. "It's him, and him with him."

"Now what kind of Russian is that?" said Viktor without looking up from his pipe. "The kind ghosts make you talk?"

"It *is* him."

"I know."

"You're not looking . . ."

"No need. I can smell him."

Proceeding downwind of the leading figure on the track was a sweet, ammoniac smell compounded on the breeze with the heady scent of alcohol coming from the partly-spiked barrel.

The mulemaster groaned. "That sod Myelnikov, pickled in camphor. Nothing can kill him. Immortal as a toad in a bottle. Here, lad," he said to Mischa. "First things first. Finish the job in hand." He kicked the spike and the vodka began to flow. As he lay on the earth drinking from the gash in the barrel, Viktor looked to the horizon.

Behind Myelnikov was a taller man.

"How's this?" asked Myelnikov, unharnessing the rifles before slumping onto the warm grass. His companion halted. The corporal stretched luxuriously and answered his own question. "Do me, at any rate. No harm in a breather."

The clearing was an oval hummock set at a slope fringed by poplars commanding a view of the distant house. From the top Valerian could see the river, green in the sun.

Myelnikov worked his jaws heavily, damning the pain in his back teeth. Dotted beneath the poplars was a half-circle of deserted beehives. "Thought I was blind, did you, lad?" he called out.

The tall slim figure shaded its eyes and turned away. The corporal dragged his rifle up by the beadsight and arranged it across his knees so that the barrel pointed slantwise on a line with Valerian's chest. With the butt he stove in the plait straw dome of the nearest hive which crumbled inwards covering its base of ashlar stone with the shells of dead worker bees. "Rotten buggering blind." When still no reply came he replenished the cartridge clip with spares from his top pocket.

Valerian slid down the hummock, hands raised in mock surrender before squatting on the ashlar among the bee-bodies. Myelnikov slammed home the clip with a chuckle. "Mind you, I was in shooting trim yesterday. I could have shot off anybody's danglies just for whoopee. Think of it — never would have known we was *alte Kameraden* from times back. Don't know what stopped me, specially with you in that showboy flunkey's rig."

Feeling through the unfamiliar pockets of the captain's greatcoat Valerian spoke for the first time: "Not a cigarette anywhere."

"Aw," said Myelnikov. "Now ain't that inconsiderate. An untidy man, though, my captain. Here," he grunted. "Have a lifesaver." In his outstretched hand were three stubby cheroots. Before taking one, Valerian sniffed them all from end to end.

"Well, don't I get an answer — why was you done up like a turkey pheasant?" The corporal's tone was bantering, and he left Valerian to smoke down a third of his cheroot, but his query was real and demanded satisfaction. The boy was tricky, deep. Myelnikov knew him of old.

"A diversionary tactic," said Valerian. "To confuse the other side. We might have been able to buy time in an attack."

"Don't bloody tic-tactic me," shouted the corporal. "That was regular Imperial get-up. Whose side are you on?"

Valerian threw out his arms and made as if to come closer, even embrace, but evidently thinking better of it, he sat back, flicking ash into the muss of bees. "There are no sides left to take, Pavlushka, and I am completely at your mercy."

In spite of his toothache this preposterous claim brought a grin to Myelnikov's lips. "You leave out that philo-sophic stop-me-gob and stick to facts. No *sides*? You can't take in an old shirker like me with that high-blown parley. I'll have you know," said the corporal thrumming his rectangular finger-ends on the catchplate of his rifle, "that as of now in this great land of ours there's more sides to be on than weevils in a sheep's arse." With bits of shrunken honey-comb and biscuits from his belt he quickly assembled a three-dimensional map on the ashlar slab, while Valerian continued to smoke impassively. "Here's your Germans south-west from us at Byelgorod and still moving before my captain lost contact with Kharkov this spring. Right wing manoeuvring so." Myelnikov coursed a line through the debris of bees' legs with a wetted finger. "Left bank of the Volga, and outflying squadrons moving out east. Ahead is my mates at a belting retreat, last heard of at Grushevka, here, Livensk here, then Varvarovka." From each spot indicated by a clump of dead honey cells the corporal trailed a line of biscuit crumbs away into the interior. "God help them too, they'll need every particle. Bastard Cossacks south-east on the rampage and the up and up, according to information received from one greasy trooper captured in March. So that's the bloody squeeze-box we're in." He concluded this part of his exposition by crushing together his fists along a north-west, south-east diagonal represented by his arms. "And that's not half of it, *parin*, we got Czechs with Russian officers east of Saratov commandeering the railroad, Poles skedaddling from the front into Little Russia where there's Whites and our lot fighting them, each other and, sometimes, the Germans. Now we're meat on a skewer, Valerian Isayevich, between the fat and the gristle, like you've always been."

Having been well served for intelligence by his lieutenants, little of this was new to Valerian. The very existence of his strange community had depended on such chaos. There had been brushes with so-called authorities but the focus of power changed so rapidly that the combination of his diplomacy, a long winter, the isolation of the Laskorin estates and, above all, his unhesitating deployment of force, had so far preserved him. But now he recognised that behind the thousand-mile-long skirmishing which Myelnikov had made graphic by sweeps of his arm, wheeled two masses of manoeuvre about to engage in a titanic struggle.

"Then it is as I always knew," said the boy. "Every man's hand is against us and you, Pavlushka, can destroy me without firing a single shot."

Yes, Corporal Myelnikov could do that, simply by handing him over to the sergeant at base HQ where they knew a thing or two about transmogrifying anarchist bastards who thought copping out of the world was some kind of superior lark. "That set-up there" — he brought his fist down on the beeswax comb which in his tableau had represented the Laskorin house — "wasn't ever a threat to anyone except those you chucked out to get it going. We knew about it, we tolerated it and we're waiting, *now*, for you to throw in your hand with us."

He remembered the boy from Lutsk, from Baranovichi, Yutrena Gorn, the Bukhovina, XX Guards, III Caucasian, the Grenadiers; no use trying to put the wind up him, he didn't know what fear was then and wouldn't now. Myelnikov mustered his resources. It was subtlety or bust, persuasion the only way. "I should have realised, of course. No major I ever met would have pulled his shot for a woman when he'd got that murdering bald vicar in the nick of his aim. A marvellous testimonial, that – even a thought to spare for the bleeding pony. You'll have to try better than that next time you impersonate an officer, boy."

His capacity for astuteness exhausted, the corporal fell to burnishing the trigger-guard of his rifle, and awaited the outcome. Valerian stared at the ground. Stabs of light issued through the leaves paling the grass stalks. Quietly, Myelnikov cursed. It was all go and no natter, like reading the Bible to a horse. And all the while, a quarter of an hour's sprint to the west, Volkov was camped out beside the maze with an understrength squad falling about, trying to get them ship-shape for a frontal assault on a bloody solid four-square mansion packed with an unknown quantity of well-fed, well-armed Anarcho-Christian-Communist fanatics. Christ.

"That's the stuff. Give it a good mulling, lad, review your options."

Encourage first, then let fly – the turnkey's approach. If the dwarf-lad was to be believed, Valerian was Jesus-in-the-desert already. Turfed him out, hadn't they, the chosen, after trying to nail him up for fornication and whatnot? But take him to the sergeant under close arrest and Volkov wouldn't have the brains not to shoot him for a stray. He'd only realise afterwards that, handled right, the boy was a gift from on high: Valerian knew every twig in that nest of God-croppers over the way. He was unexpended, walking intelligence, and had to be kept healthy. Would Volkov see it?

Undermanned, with no gift for command, the sergeant was in trouble himself. There might even be a welcome if Corporal Myelnikov brought home the goods.

Another burst and the lad should unwaver. "Enough of this shagging about. I want the solid stuff. Which way are you jumping? According to my information you've been choking on the soulfarming lately and gone straight off into common criminality. Our captain was wrong about your being his pal, wasn't he? I saw his face when we told him bye-bye. Made a mistake, hadn't he? Not pleasant to share his last moments with a thumping mutineer who'd slit officers' throats out of sheer buggeration when we collapsed in '17. And I tell you this, Valerian Isayevich, there's no place left for you to go and your life's not worth a Prussian's fart. Who wants you?"

"You do."

This was said so coolly that the corporal's hollow tooth seemed to bite on its own nerve, and he gave a howl of exasperation. He was overbidding his hand. The ploy must look as obvious as a dick in a nosegay. Myelnikov needed Valerian because Volkov needed allies, not prisoners. Time enough for the hangman when they'd taken the house. "We'll see about that," he said when the pain allowed him to open his mouth. Although Valerian was smiling now, kindly enquiring about his health, Myelnikov was going to give him one last squirt before abandoning diplomacy. "Friends won't be no good. My captain's as good as laid out, your woman's gone out of her brains and that bloody dwarf's a conniving little liar. As I reckon it, the best plan is to turn you over to Volkov with an account of how you shot our CO who was trying to stop you leading a mass break-out from that house. I know how to talk to sergeants. I can make it sound like Moses said it. Believe me, son, you're shite-high in the refuse. Consult your tripes before I run you in." As if to confirm that this would be the probable way forward he tightened the buckles on Valerian's carbine sling and tested it for play.

The boy hunched and raked the grass with his long fingers. "I no longer please her. My people have tried to destroy us both. Why should I throw in my lot with you?"

Myelnikov could not believe his luck. Movement at last. "Get your own back?" he suggested. It would have been enough for him, and, at one time, more than enough for this broken-down boy whom once he had idolised for his unnerving simplicity of heart, but Valerian had moved on since those days when two and two added up nice and easy. He'd messed himself, thinking too hard. "Remember Dvinsk when the running started and we was stuck at the tip of the salient with nothing at our backs? Half a battery and all of us whacked. Finished. Good for nothing. And what did you say? Back to the boghole. And we hopped it like heroes, firing that old Putilov all the way home."

"Those days are gone."

Force of recollection stirred Myelnikov. "Don't you believe yourself, Valerian Isayevich. They're sweet life itself to you and me." He shifted his back-pack and got to his feet. "Leave it to me. The story's going to be what I mistook it for. As far as Volkov needs to know you're still Kabalyevskii, Martin, the renegade major, people's friend. The bugger's at his wit's end to scrape up some kind of belligerent class to lead his troops up to the front door. Let him re-commission you. No other way out, boy."

Valerian raised his head, a flush spreading under the downy stubble on his cheeks. "Our other comrades – what happened to them?"

Myelnikov inspected him curiously. Fine swinging shoulders, wrestler's chest, thickset; a lovely-bodied lad who lived as clean as a suckling, couldn't drink, said his prayers, never swore. From village seminary to Divisional prize-shot. A mascot whose simple presence made every man in his battalion feel secure. They loved him, they still did. "Here and there. Alyosha the canary-fancier – remember? Filip? Andrushka the loader . . ." Myelnikov went through a roll-call of survivors: from Masuria, Courland, the Galician ravines. "And Viktor, I forgot Viktor, he's still on his pins. There's a point, I'll only need to tip him the wink and the others won't split, but with the sergeant you'll have to do it by feel. He's the New Model Man, the worst, a ripe pisswater stoat . . ."

All the way to the camp Corporal Myelnikov felt uneasy. He might talk soft about Viktor and that lot but, notwithstanding his apparent success at turning the boy his way, he didn't take himself in. Orders had never been his taste of spit-and-polish – the captain would have spoken to that – and the prospect of being biddable to Valerian Isayevich put the breeze right between his legs. One minute kisses, humping his baggage next. Trouble was, you never could calculate that breed of charmer.

It was full sun but the corporal shivered when he caught up and stood side by side with Valerian, looking down on one of the outer ramparts of the maze. Blokes dotted about, bare to the waist, tubbing themselves, with no proper guard set; the smoke from half a dozen cooking fires blacking the sky for all to see.

What would the captain have done?

38

She was weeping all over the captain, covering his hands and face with kisses. He was almost as embarrassed as Yasha. "Steady on, old thing," he said. "I'm not quite dead yet."

Ever since Valerian and Myelnikov had disappeared over the hill to test out their theatricals on Sergeant Volkov, Loulou had been flaunting her hysterics. Her schoolgirl howls were old hat to Yasha. He raised an eyebrow at the captain and pursed his lips. "Smoke?"

The tobacco tin had nearly run out but there was enough for a last gasper. Over Loulou's head the captain frowned back and nodded.

They had more in common than any lady and gentleman, right at the end, Spats and the dwarf, even if it was only a vice. To avoid close quarters with the hunched and twisted body Yasha passed over the lit cigarette to Loulou who placed it between the captain's lips. He supposed he'd seen worse but this man bore suffering like some people wore hair shirts. You knew so well what must be going on underneath that you longed for the relief of a curse or even a scream; but characters like this one probably spent their lives getting prepared for the last farewell. Not for the first time Yasha blessed the upbringing which had dissuaded him from morbid joys. "Look on the bright side," Ma used to say. Much good it did her, but Yasha approved of the attitude.

"You ought to have done me in," he said wryly. "Before I got you into this mess."

From his half-lying, half-sitting position at the tree-trunk the captain tried to smile. The effort clearly hurt him, for the twitch zigzagged up his cheek and he winced. But the voice was there, weaker but still drawly: "The biter bit – eh, Mr Kiteflier? I shouldn't have put the wind up you so conscientiously."

"My fault," said the boy. "Lies come easy when life is cheap."

Loulou bid for attention. "What is to become of me?" she wailed. Neither man nor boy felt that an answer was required. After a little while she struck up again: "I wish to die. To die here with Aleksei. For me, life is over . . ."

"God's teeth," murmured the captain, and laid back his head.

Yasha bristled. "Talk sense, woman. There isn't even a hatpin between the three of us. Corporal light-fingers snitched all the side-arms for his foray with that other light of your life."

"An uncompassionate soul, my Myelnikov," said the captain. "But a good shot."

"That makes two of them," said Yasha. "Practice makes perfect." He could not bring himself to call Valerian by name. The man destroyed everything he touched.

Loulou resumed her sobs and chafed the captain's cold hands. Most poignant it would have been had Yasha lit upon the twosome in a forest glade, chit-chatting between caresses. A proper sylvan tableau. But when the blood ran real and the lines were unprompted – "I did not realise until today," says the female lead, "how much I cared for you" – he wanted to jump on stage and kick the melodrama out of her. "Our past, Loulou dear, is perfect and untouchable." And out of him. He, at least, ought to know better. For too long Yasha had been an onlooker without a speaking part, stiff with tedium, stuffed with the cake-talk of their honeyed childhoods, the fresh-laundered doddle of their adolescent pangs and flirtations. Not a single thing had ever happened in their paper-moon lives that Yasha had not prayed on his knees for to pop out of their sky into his squalid little gob. Now they'd been quicksanded they wouldn't even wriggle, but waved bye-bye as if tomorrow were stopping with them.

Loulou had got round to her husband when pain stretched the captain's mouth. He smiled beyond her to the boy, who interpreted: the man had something to say which was not for the woman's ears. The *grafinya* was playing gooseberry.

"Natalya Igoryevna," said Yasha respectfully. "Could you leave us for a few moments while I attend to the captain? I'll call you when we're done."

She had been a nurse; she thought she understood; she went without a word.

It was a beautiful day.

"Here, Kiteflier," said the captain when Loulou was out of sight. "The left inner pocket."

Yasha slid his hand beneath the tunic and drew out two flaking cheroots.

"Now the other side."

The boy stuck both cheroots in his mouth and did as he was told.

"Webley pocket automatic," whispered the captain.

Yasha inspected the infant pistol in silence, placed it on the grass, lit the two cheroots and passed one over. His stomach rumbled. Something nasty was about to be shaken out of the captain's brains.

"Take Natalya Igoryevna to the tree hide." At the end of each sentence the dying man sucked hard on his cheroot: "Emergency rations there." Suck, puff. "Weapons, ammunition." The end of the cheroot was wet and bitten. "Get out before . . ." Yasha waited. "Before the balloon goes up."

Literally?

"West. By night. West, west. Disguise her."

Inwardly Yasha completed the advice. *As a bloke.* The same old bloody story.

The cheroot was a stub before he replied: "That's crazy. The woman's not my responsibility."

The captain spat out a mash of tobacco leaf and talked confidingly in feverish staccato. "Valerian will take up arms . . . With Volkov . . . Against his own people . . . Kill, kill, kill . . . She abandoned him . . . No one left . . . Volkov, the same . . . Perfect executioner finds his mate . . . *Verstehst du, Zwerg?*"

Der Zwerg hat gut verstanden.

The understanding dwarf would be baby-lady-sitting. Possibly for ever. Why the hell should he? Could he, though, actually abandon her? After all his trouble, and her trouble, and *his* trouble? His guts rumbled like an empty churn. Valerian was an assassin already. Teamed up with this Volkov he'd be a mobile firing squad. And all Yasha had was dwarf-issue – a lady's reticule pop-gun.

"Stick to Myelnikov," went on the captain, more fluent after a moment's remission. "He's an independent animal and he likes you. He'll hunt with the hunted, not with the pack. Volkov's new type of man has sickened him."

"And Volkov and Valerian?"

"Love at first sight, Mr Kiteflier. A marriage made in heaven."

Through a ventilation slit in the canvas hood of the map wagon Sergeant Volkov squinted out against the mid-morning sun.

At the last elbow of the beetling path was a short man in a balaclava bawling down to the troops.

The sergeant ground his teeth. That approach was supposed to be enfiladed. Where was the machine-gun detail he'd sent up to dig in? Bastard – kipping, bet your life. No use shouting from here, they hadn't even spotted the intruder on top of them although he was bursting his lungs.

Suddenly another man, tall, in a glinting dress cap, leapt from the trackside ditch, grabbed at the balaclava man from behind and fired off two bursts from the automatic weapon still strapped to his companion's side before taking the downslope at a run.

Balaclava-head stumbled, then joined in the charge. "You dozy . . . dozy . . . buggers . . ."

Troops sprang up like brigands at the finale of some savage opera, ragged, filthy, a few completely naked, and swarmed up the rise, screeching obscenities, to mob the leading man. As they wheeled him round in the sun, his cap fell off.

The sergeant reached for his pistol.

The corporal saluted with brass-hat vigour. A knot of idlers began to take an interest, coming closer. Volkov tried to soothe himself: *At all times calm self-possession is the attribute of a man in command.* He took out his notebook. *That's more like it.* "Now, give me the exact whereabouts of your officer."

Derision loosened the ranks of bystanders who were already in the know. Whispers circulated at Volkov's back. An expression of pained surmise shadowed Myelnikov's face. "At this moment, Sergeant?"

"At this *precise* moment."

The corporal rolled his eyes skywards. Muffled squawks passed along the line. "Having his last particulars taken, *starshina*, I should think, judging by his state of health when last sighted."

Volkov consulted his pocket watch and noted the time down in his book. "And who took him prisoner?"

"Prisoner?" said Myelnikov, addressing his comrades as much as Volkov. "Did I say anything about prisoners?"

"Ain't you got it yet, Sarge?" said Viktor. "Captain's snuffed it."

Stepping back one pace the corporal clapped Valerian on the shoulder. "And this here's his replacement, *starshina* — comes highly recommended by his honour the captain himself — Major Kabalyev-skii, Martin Aleksandrovich. Introduction effected previous to his honour's regrettable picking off by rebels in the woods."

Someone gave a whistle and a party of four troopers on fire-duty came clanking up with their buckets. Soon the onlookers would be swelling to a crowd.

In the brilliant morning light Volkov could see his own reflection in the stranger's eyes. Haggard and suddenly afraid, he put away his notebook with extra deliberation. "I'll deal with this, Corporal. Send those men about their duties."

There was a shuffling as the troops stood off without waiting for the command, then re-formed a little way away.

Volkov's immediate instinct was to buy time. But confrontation could be a risky business with old sweats breathing down your neck, aching for slip-ups. Take the steam out, make it genial.

Having come to his decision, the sergeant moved nearer and

fingered the right lapel of Valerian's greatcoat. Officers' weight, the right stuff, but that proved nothing. Could have robbed it off the corpse – if the captain *was* dead. And who in his right mind would take Myelnikov's word for anything? Looked the part, though, must be six foot or more. Broad, held himself well. All the attributes.

"Extraordinarily young for a major." The remark was well judged: slightly flattering, uninquisitive, but taken up as Volkov intended, as a challenge.

The men fell silent, interpreting Volkov's fitness for any future struggle from his present effect on the boy. Moments elapsed before Valerian spoke: "Field rank."

This was a matter subject to regulations, procedures, the proper channels. Volkov came into his own: "Where made up?"

Valerian told him, fluently, plausibly, the story he had elaborated on his trek to the camp.

"When?"

It fitted, it could just have been possible, units right, postings, the casualties. Volkov listened, planting a question now and again which ought to have stopped an impostor, but the boy held up, gazing back with a calm, unappraising look which betrayed no fear, no antagonism, no friendliness, but which removed from the sergeant all intimacy with the young man; the look on officers' faces, the rebuff, the pre-emptive turn-away like you were a nag trying to rub flanks with a post-horse.

Volkov hated him for that; for being adept under scrutiny, sure of himself, undegraded; for everything the sergeant knew himself not to be. But Volkov was not stupid, his time would come; until it did he knew from deep experience what was to be expected of him.

A second assault on the house had to be mounted before the enemy dug themselves deeper in. The captain had botched the first so that if this scum of loungers couldn't be got pulling together, they'd be thrown onto the defensive without enough supplies to sustain a holding action for more than a couple of days. After that, the only route out would be face-down in the river. He could goad these men, insult them, wheedle and incite them, but with him they would always be out of heart. After the last fiasco Volkov was pretty sure they were on the turn, prepared to run any officer through, whatever the standard he rallied them under, if next time they had to fall to and do it all over again.

Then let the major-lad take up his commission. He was bogus, a liar probably, shell-shock crazy to boot, but he had sway over the men – and not only this rubbish, for the sergeant himself had almost quailed.

Then let him be released among them, this Barabbas.

Without turning, Volkov retreated to the regulation distance for addressing an officer, ground his heels in the dust and saluted with all the snap of old Army deference. If he had been hypnotised by the stranger Sergeant Volkov could not have given deeper satisfaction by his simple performance. The men had willed his subjection, and triumphed in his becoming part of their own.

The boy accepted him as tribute, extending a hand in welcome, like the host at a party effusively singling out the least prepossessing of guests. "At ease, Sergeant, that'll do for the present. We'll have a word by and by."

It was mealtime. The soldiers began to disperse, straggling off in twos and threes.

"That man!"

Valerian's shout was so violent that several wheeled round involuntarily and began to dress a line.

"Sergeant, take his name and report to me an hour before sunset."

Volkov strutted out beyond the clearing to where the man lay on his back in the cow-parsley smoking a cheroot.

"A pleasure," said the sergeant, producing his notebook. "I've quite taken to our young officer already. Now then, that man — name?"

"Bleeding Jesus, Sarge, you know my name, you know my mother's name, you even know the names of the frigging birds round here . . ."

"Spell it out."

"For God's sake, you wouldn't credit it for stinking ingratitude . . . M-y-e-l-n-i-k-o-v."

"*Hunyadi Janos*," came a whisper. "Bitters. A splash of *Khoosh* . . ."

"He's had it," said Yasha, now convinced that the captain was a hopeless case.

Loulou had done her best with his wounds. In spite of her tourniquet the triangular gash in his thigh had opened again, filling up with brilliantly scarlet blood which gave little jumps in time with his heart-beat. "Arterial," she had said. "See how the blood leaps."

They had cut away the lower half of the captain's tunic and tamped the hole in his abdomen with the side panels of Loulou's wedding frock steeped in river water and the phial of boroglyceride filched from the body of the unit's only field ambulance man. But the stain was black, and spreading.

"*Hunyadi . . . Khoosh . . . Salutaris*," repeated the captain.

Yasha looked from him to Loulou, scared and uncomprehending. "What's he mean?"

"He is thirsty," she said. "He is remembering."

She did not care to explain what she knew: that the captain was almost as far from them both as he would ever be; back in childhood asking for a taste of the exotic mineral waters which in his youth, as in hers, always stood cooling in a glass bucket on a table under the trees at August luncheon parties. Yasha would never understand.

"He can't drink," said the boy. "He got it in the belly."

She took Yasha's cap as a dipper and went barefoot to the stream. Yasha held his breath and leaned over the body. Pink spume frothed at the captain's underlip. Christ, he was a goner. They'd got him in the soft parts, everywhere.

Suddenly, in the most ordinary way, the way you'd think a man in his state could never do anything again, the captain opened his eyes, recognised him and cleared his throat. "Now she's out of the way, Mr Kiteflier, I've got a favour to ask." Even the voice was characteristic – lackadaisical, serene.

"Sure thing, Cap," said the boy.

"Where's the pocket pistol?"

Yasha pulled the little Webley out of his boot and presented it on the palm of his hand.

"Loaded?"

Yasha checked. "All in order."

"Cock it."

Yasha did so.

"Safety catch on?" It was. "Then, my tiny coadjutor, place the gun in my right hand and curl my finger round the trigger."

All this and he could hardly keep his eyelids up, never mind his arm. He was a wreck. A limbless talk-box. Take no notice. But it was no good: while Yasha could face up to the dead, the nearly-dead foxed him completely. You wanted them to say something that sounded daft – like how they felt. But it was useless asking; and embarrassing too, to feel that they knew this and kept mum in that rather grand, superior way.

The pistol wobbled in his outstretched hand. "Talk sense, Captain," he said, weakly.

"Under the ear, man," ordered the voice.

In the whole of his life no one had ever called Yasha "man". Suddenly he felt close to the captain, but indecently close, being called upon to perform a service too intimate for the nature of their association. In desperation he had been turned to, and Yasha could not cope with the change. Ask a woman, ask Myelnikov but for Christ's sake leave me out. He wondered how he'd got so fancily squeamish: this weird bugger would have poleaxed him once, no question. Now he was asking for it himself. Let him have it, why don't you? You got him in this mess in the first place.

"I can't," said Yasha. It was true. He was a screaming washout. Books were one thing, but looking into real tough-guy eyes before blowing them out made the bile reach up your craw. Worse than this, the captain was humble, and the books never prepared you for that. No siree, out of the question. Much more and he'd be crying like a baby.

The dying man swore quietly, energetically, and then began to taunt: "Call yourself a man . . ."

"I never said that – you did . . ."

The captain licked away froth. "*She*'s got more between her legs . . ."

Oh God, what the hell was that woman doing – bunching up a floral tribute?

"I wish I'd put you down for the mongrel you are." The captain glimmered cheese-yellow, and the strings of his neck looked chickeny. "Said you were dependable, but half-breeds always rat. Steal our women. Poison wells . . ." As unexpectedly as he had begun to speak, the captain fell silent, his eyes wide open. Yasha hoped with all his heart that the man had died, but with a splutter he started up again on the queer names: "*Buffalo Lithia . . . Rosbach . . . Apollinaris, Alkaline acidulated . . .*"

"Fair enough," said the boy croaky-voiced. "Tell me again – where do you want it?"

Not a squeak. Yasha was grateful. He'd made his offer but not been called upon. Perhaps the captain would – how did it go? – quietly pass on, pass over. Always sounded like sleeping it off. He could sneak away, tell Natalya Igoryevna that her excellency had breathed his last and then just forget about it. Except he might not have and he'd wake in his agony and there'd be nobody there, or worse still – the wrong people would (he thought of those women and their hayforks). This captain had had everything: honour, trust, a kind of innocence, belief. Why should he be made to think differently at the end? It was too late to teach him anything about the real world. *As it was in the beginning is now . . .*

Yasha tossed up the pistol and twirled it by the trigger guard: too risky with those ladies' bullets. They'd come out the other side, neat as ninepence, and leave him lingering. And just one would have to do the job – he knew that he'd never be able to fire again. Then he spotted the rifle half-concealed under the captain's left leg and which Myelnikov had overlooked. He put out his small hands to the captain's long fingers which were tight round the barrel, and gradually loosened their grip. He slowly withdrew the weapon, estimating the angle necessary to keep the butt steady with the muzzle propped under the captain's left ear. Carefully, he dismantled the bayonet. The captain's hands dropped onto the bandages over his stomach. Yasha would have to do it himself.

If only it were dark, if only it weren't summer. This was lifeless winter-night's work. What would the woman say? Did she have a duty to anyone – Valerian, Martin, her husband or the captain? To this man whose laying-out he had been left to do? Already dead or dying, all her men.

Yasha knew his duty, knew it as he felt for the captain's finger and pressed it round the trigger. The man had to look good; look good for the sake of the woman, so she'd believe what Yasha knew to be true – that the captain was *treu und stark* and would have done it himself. Damn the world and women for what they brought you to.

Before he did it, he kissed the captain's lips, felt for the watch and lock of hair and took them from the top pocket of the tunic. With them were some white cards and he took those too. The man's eyes were still open, but he saw nothing.

Yasha knelt. *Proshchai*, forgive me, farewell, bye-bye, here goes. The feel of his finger was rough.

The gun went off much sooner than he had expected.

By late afternoon when the secret of the new commander's true identity was widespread among the men, Volkov was still in the dark. He could have said that he was just too busy carrying out the stream of orders which issued from the commandeered map wagon where Valerian sat stripped to the undershirt, poring over the welter of charts and papers accumulated over weeks by the sergeant and his dead captain. But Volkov was an honest man who permitted himself no delusions where business was concerned. Hierarchy of command was the very structure of life, and he was more than happy to fulfil its obligations now that responsibility had been lifted from his shoulders. And the major-boy recognised that; whoever he was he had the sense to assert his powers; unlike the captain who had never respected the limitations of the men placed beneath him. So Volkov made no enquiries and did his duty pointedly.

The men responded likewise. Fires were doused, equipment refurbished, damage made good. It was a long day. At dusk Valerian conferred with his sergeant on the fire-step of a slit trench out from the encampment in the maze. There, in full view of the great house, the plan of attack was disclosed.

Had he not been such a hard-bitten man of affairs Volkov might have been overwhelmed, at this point, by the confidence reposed in his discretion. Not only that, but his judgement was actually sought, he was listened to, taken into account. That this trust was genuine, he had no doubt: the sergeant was shrewd enough to recognise that the boy admitted him to such confidences expressly in order to distinguish him from the rank-and-file subordinates who, at this moment, were concentrating in the centre of the maze on the orders of Volkov himself to be addressed by their new commander. But it was heady, this complicity; emotional. One could thrive with a man who enclosed you within its atmosphere. Only they had knowledge; only they could direct.

Volkov had once been in love; the memory was sufficiently fresh to summon up that strange feeling of repulsion mixed with an uncontrollable desire to please which then had delighted and humiliated him. This present closeness had to be similarly fought. If the boy did the work, so much the better. If he died young in doing it, all well and good. If he wanted Volkov's help, then he should have it.

For a man who was master of himself, like the sergeant, reality was very simple: the future was the future of him and his kind exclusively; to secure it he would utilise any success. He enjoyed watching them, the smart ones, devising strategies, only to come to grief in their own victories. The boy was a saviour, no one could quarrel with that; his dispositions classical; the house would fall. Volkov and he would see to that. Tomorrow they would ride knee to knee at the corruptible world.

39

Next day Yefim buried his wife at first light. Schmidt read the lesson. Afterwards, he took Yefim's hands in his, and kissed him on the lips, tender as a woman.

There were no other mourners. Across a greeny eastern horizon the sun rose from glimmer to fire raising a cool wind which smelled of the sea and engulfed the empty paddock where Masha's shallow grave bulged under garlands.

Left alone, Yefim turned full-face to the light and howled.

This was the only ceremony permitted that day. The other dead, five or more at the last count, would have to remain where they fell, at their posts overrun the night before last. Vissarion, in anticipation of a final desperate assault from the enemy, had ordered a withdrawal from the outer lines to more defensible positions close to the house.

For an hour after dawn the four surviving lieutenants discussed strategy on the steps of the west front by the river. Not one knew when or where the attack would come. The day before, Schmidt had led a mounted detachment to reconnoitre the approaches along the village road to the north-east where the first machine-gun unit had been ambushed in the night action, but had fought its way back to the stables. The armourer had since reported the weapon serviceable but he was urgently low on ammunition – the women kept bringing up the wrong calibre from the cellar store – could something be done? Yesterday Schmidt had been glad to leave the unanswerable problems to Vissarion and canter through the heat haze, inspecting ditches for abandoned armaments firm in the belief that the enemy was re-grouping, and for him at least there would be nothing more disturbing than an occasional pot-shot from the woods. As it happened there was not even that, only a sound of cheering from the direction of the maze, preceded by distant automatic fire.

Makar and Osip had stayed behind, Osip to keep observation from the eastern salon which overlooked the park. With its upward slope to the ha-ha and terrace his was the easiest ground to defend; for which he thanked God, because his troops were largely undisciplined women who were slow with their weapons and kept crowding in to stare at his hideously injured ear. As the day wore on he took increasingly to the Laskorin champagne, much to the contempt of Vissarion who was posted with a dozen fit men below the south-facing library, the only commander untouched by the deaths of Titus and Solomon and the only one to have guessed that the enemy, whoever they might be, would never rest until they'd tickled every last garrisoneer out of this madhouse and stamped him into the dust.

Noon came and now the silence of the enemy was unbroken.

Schmidt took advantage of the lull to spruce himself up at the zinc-lined horse-trough in the cobbled yard. "Licking their wounds," he declared vigorously towelling his ears. "I told you last night. They'll need more than a day to retrench after that bleeding. Out of ammunition, too, I wouldn't wonder. Ten to one they've taken too many casualties to chance another throw. All we need do is keep them pinned down until dusk and they'll pull out during the night."

Osip had left the salon and come up from the distant landing stage on foot. In the rough and tumble undergrowth of old Mitya Laskorin's devastated fire zone the heat was intense. The lieutenant unwound his bandana and swilled his face in the trough. His wound re-opened and began to bleed. "Fools," he said.

Confident that the worst was over, Schmidt was inclined to humour Osip who was probably lightheaded from loss of blood. That, and the drink. "Who's a fool?"

"Fools," repeated Osip in a wandering monotone, brandishing a retractable telescope at the house, park and river. "Fools are fools are Russians who shoot other Russians. Their own kind, my comrades, what did they bring my Titus and Solomon to — those officer-priests, those jailbirds?"

Schmidt buckled down his cartridge pouches, passing over this reference to Valerian. "We made no prisoners of men under arms, Osip Nikolayevich, so how can you be so sure there's even one true Russian man among the enemy? We can't tell, not for definite."

"Who else but our own kind would have come to punish us for our conduct?"

Or would have sought to save us, or spare us, or damn us. Only our own.

Schmidt's sole desire at this time was to deflect ruinous passions. He crossed himself twice. "Well, there's a doom-laden croak, if ever I heard one. What is it you want, Osip Nik — surrender? Because that's what it would be if we listened to you, and no mistake." He glanced round the empty courtyard. A few hours ago, troops would have been here listening, might even have acted because however stringently led, they'd been rattled already by Valerian's murders, let alone his defection. Talk to them of fate, and there could be a mutiny.

"Don't you come that with me, *brat*," muttered Osip after once again plunging his head into the blood-streaked water. "No bastard coward-talks me. Who saw them off, night before last – you or me? This time you think they'll run without a fight, do you, Hermann? Think they're packing their traps? Here." He slid out the telescope to its fullest extent before passing it across the trough. "Take a look up river – whose side is that on now, ours or theirs, or maybe its own?"

Schmidt plied the glass from bank to river uncomfortable in the knowledge that he knew exactly what to look for. The deceased Fedya had thought it an omen. The old women had prayed against it, thinking it was live. Now, nine miles to the north-west it was threading sluggishly out of the narrows, piling its bulk against the cross-stream of the broadening river. If Osip had been boy or *ba-bushka*, information might have sufficed: a gun in a boat: to be precise, a 210-mm. howitzer, the first Schmidt had seen since the Bosphorus bombardment in 1916, and an infamously unreliable piece. But Osip knew more about such weapons than Schmidt himself, and wanted the fact of the motive, not the fact of the thing.

Out of ignorance, the German aired his knowledge: "She's nothing new. We've tracked her sailing for a day and a half, and she's moved slower than a bug on treacle. Know what I think, Osip Nik? She's coming to take them off as soon as it's dark. Big enough, too. You could seat half a battalion under her welts . . ."

Osip had spotted figures round the gun-mountings. How many? Two? Perhaps three.

"Well, there you are," said Schmidt. "They couldn't bring it to bear, not that bulk, and even if they could . . ."

He was right, Osip agreed. For manual loading they needed a party of six, at least. Still . . . *Still*. The reservation, once stated, came into its own, and while Schmidt brooded, Osip took back the glass.

Over-stimulated and fatigued after night-fighting and a sleepless day, he could not separate the effect of heat-wobble from the slight rock of the pontoon as she slid into midstream behind the tow. Then he saw again what he thought he had seen earlier from the north-facing window on the first floor: a movement which he had gone down to the landing stage to verify with the platoon on the jetty. "What does Vissarion say?" he asked.

Before Schmidt could answer there was a whistle from the direction of the stable clock tower and Becky came racing across the cobbles in a commotion of skirts and high heels.

"Hey, leave off, you," she panted when Osip swung her by the bows of her quilted satin bed-jacket and sat her down on the lip of the trough. "I got a message."

"It'll wait." Osip kept his eye on the German who appeared too stunned to speak. "Well, Hermann, *Kamerad*, you're not the leading man nowadays, but what's our orders?"

"Him?" crowed Becky jabbing a finger into the water. "He's no good. Gets scared."

"Don't he just," said Osip grimly. "What say we all sit in a row right here and chew our nails, Hermann?"

Out of sheer and sudden nervousness Schmidt twice pulled the focus of the telescope, then tried a third time.

Becky giggled and picked white hairs curling over the neck of Osip's blouse. "It's the women that run things, *dyadya* Osip. I'm under orders from Katya. Want to know what she says?"

Osip knew his women. Battle discipline, impending death, the loss of Valerian, nothing would quench them. If necessary they'd harness themselves to the gun-train. Better a girl than this cringer. "For the last time, Hermann, old soldier . . ."

Without a word Schmidt broke the brass tube across his knee and threw the wreckage into the trough.

"Well, would you credit that for bloody infernal cheek?" said the girl. "Nerve of it. If I was a man I'd do 'im for that. Do them the lot, I would. Except you, of course, *dyadya*, if you give me a gun."

All the women and every boy of Becky's age had been allotted some kind of weapon and placed on battle alert but the girls had been segregated to a makeshift surgery where they sat with grannies amongst the iodine bottles, bandage rolls and buckets of orange disinfectant. "Now if you was to give me one, I might let you . . ."

Schmidt shook his fists at the sky and screamed: "Shut your sloven little whore-meat slash before I kill you, girl!"

Becky burst into a peal of high, derisive giggles: "Oo-er, hark at his nibs. I can keep my legs together for you any time, Mr Jerusalem, no bother, specially now I'm saved."

"There shall be no salvation for child-strumpets."

"That's all he knows," said Becky fondly, turning to Osip who held her round the waist. "You men never listen, that's your trouble. It's all over, Katya says; there's a horseman coming up the carriage road waving a white flag."

* * *

Before hoisting Igor astride the saddle-blanket of his mule, Sergeant Volkov had allowed him half a mess-tin of vodka. They could spare that, he assured the Cossack, in view of the emergency.

In spite of its split hoof the mule was too underfed to play up and almost as tired as the man. The new officer whom almost everybody except Igor seemed to know, had told him what to say but the Cossack had forgotten to ask for proper directions so he felt stupid hobbling along on the lame mule past the kitchen garden looking for a way in while on the terrace a lot of old women called him such dirty names he couldn't help blushing.

Eventually he found himself on what had once been a gravelled drive leading to a sort of entrance block guarded by stone lions. Two men, one bald with a beard, the other very tall, emerged from the porter's cubby-hole inside the portico. Both men were flanked by two sturdy fellows in blue leggings and all four were armed with pre-war Austrian rifles. The mule stopped of its own accord.

"Looking for someone?" said Schmidt.

The Cossack felt the tremble in his mule's right foreleg as he shifted on her back to waggle the strip of grey tent sheet hooked to the end of his bayonet. "Who's in command here?"

"That'll be me, soldier," said Vissarion.

Relieved by this easy fulfilment of the first part of his task, Igor felt more cheerful. "That's a stroke of luck then because my old hinny's nearly done up. Wasn't my idea, this," he called across to the bodyguard in rankers' camaraderie. "Our sergeant's got ambitions too. He wants to save lives by a *process of negot-iation*, he says."

The men in blue leggings only stared.

"A humane NCO," said Schmidt amiably. "Now, isn't that nice?"

The mule craned down to lick its sore leg, almost unseating the rider.

"And you've come like a brave lad to state his terms for him?"

"That's right," said the Cossack, hauling on his mount's neck, unable to look directly into Schmidt's eyes. "I can't remember exactly but you know the sort of thing: call it a day now and he'll go easy on you later in the Name of the People."

"Surrender?" said Vissarion.

"I can't say he said the word. Compromise, he said, honourable compromise."

The shorter of the two guards, a red-faced youth with an unkempt beard, stepped out of line. After rooting around in his cartridge belt he brought out a little round loaf which he broke in two giving one half to the mule, the other to Igor. The Cossack wrenched off a big piece of the week-old bread and popped it into his mouth before stuffing the remainder down his boot-top. The mule's hide rippled at her neck as she crushed up her share. "You're Russian," said the guard. "All Russians are on the same side."

"We was, boy," said Igor. "But progress is progress and times change. I could tell them back there that you're as simple as me, lads after my own heart, not the re-act-ionary scum that Sergeant Volkov has you down for, but look at it his way – fortifying a manor house against the tide of history is a crime against the people . . ." Such a concept was actually incomprehensible to Igor but the new young officer had insisted upon his getting it by heart and he repeated it now like a slogan. He didn't understand either why the major was so mad keen to smash up this fine big house and the poor souls in it, but Igor didn't really mind so long as there'd be pickings and women and the killing was from the winning side.

"Go back," said the youth, pleating a fold of loose skin at the mule's throat. "Tell your comrades to leave us in peace. There's been enough death."

"Consider it done," said Igor. Better and better. The new officer had said they might turn awkward if he didn't play it right, and he ought to know having been their prisoner, but judging by this lad they must be soft in the head. "Now just hand over your weapons and place yourselves under orders."

The guard stood back and caressed the stock of his rifle.

"It's all right, you'll see," urged Igor.

Schmidt was still smiling. "Whose orders?"

Several fresh-faced lads drifted out of the house and sat on the portico steps looking casual. Their armaments were first-class. Unprepared for an audience Igor stiffened his legs alongside the mule's belly and rubbed his left knee to get the circulation going. "A good question," he said at last. "But I'm just the arms and legs that's stuck onto the spine and goes no further."

The steps were filling up. Igor counted heads rapidly. Christ. There could be a regiment in there, all sleek and armed and well fed. "Our sergeant has his officer, but who orders who is a bit unsettled for the moment."

"Then you'd be better connecting yourselves up to the numbskull who sent you on this fool's errand than pretending to take free men in charge," said Schmidt with a sidelong glance at his troops.

By now even Igor sensed the reality of the situation and fell back on the third point of his instructions. "If that's how you want it," he shouted. "You can all go to buggery together because I've got news for you, mates. We're no amateur outfit playing at soldiers; we lay our plans against information received."

"And what would that be?" said Vissarion.

"You've no reserves, you're out of supplies, we've blown your mines and you've lost two of your best commanders."

Igor had been led to believe that these items would be a knock-out, but neither the German nor Vissarion gave any sign of yielding.

"Is that all?" said Schmidt.

Rubbing the sleep from his eyes the Cossack pondered at the blank sky. "Except for the house. We know all about that, inside and out." This ought to have been the ace but somehow he felt he was throwing it away. "Floor by floor," he added pointlessly, before devoting his attention to the mule which was becoming restive.

"Traitors," bawled a lean old man in a slouch hat and waistcoat.

"Very helpful," responded Igor matching shout for shout. "I'd go in for a bit of co-operation at your age instead of staggering around waiting for your stick-legs to get broke by our case-shot. I tell you, Dad, there's a time for everyone and yours is ticking as loud as a monastery clock."

For a few moments they exchanged insults before Schmidt intervened. "Can't you see what he's doing, Gerasim? He knows nothing, they sent him with nothing so he's making it up."

The calm lie exasperated Igor. "Me? Think I've got the brains to invent it? There's this woman back at ours. Some of her tales'd give you a fit. Here," he called to Gerasim over Schmidt's head. "Want to hear what his lot's got up to when you was oiling your wick in a dream?"

Gerasim did not, but there were enough who did for the Cossack to launch willy-nilly into some of the stories related by the white-armed, fat Polly for whom he had a great lust.

"That red whore was mad," said Vissarion equably. "We cast her out for filthiness."

Igor's prim-mouthed girl was velvety-dark, so there were obviously other easy women on the loose. The sooner him and his mates ran into them the better. "God's truth, your honour, you may have done righter than you thought."

For the first time, Schmidt, who up to now had managed to control his attacks of panic, lost his composure. The hinny snorted when he gripped her nose by the bridle. "Your business is done, brigand. Tell your sergeant or officer or whatever puff-cock struts on your back that I'm not a vindictive man but I'll take a righteous delight in stretching his neck alongside the woman's when my moment comes."

Igor loosened the stirrup girth on the mule's sore flank before giving a gentle heel-tap to her ribs. "You can count on me to do the necessary," he said with a grin. "I can guarantee that our Major Kabalyevskii will be tickled pink at the joke."

Schmidt laid a hand between the hinny's ears. "Now there's a grand old Russian name. And to think I took your leader for a genius of the future without a quartering to his escutcheon. Now you're telling me you're at the beck and call of the old kind as soon as they change cap-badges."

Taken unawares, Igor was embarrassed. A year ago his battalion had lynched their brigadier. Under discipline once more he felt guilty and resentful at its reimposition, but if this bald man was right, he'd feel even more of a fool knowing that blokes like he'd helped to murder now had the hanging of him, too.

"Get out of it, rubbish," he roared at Schmidt's men, who sprang from the steps to pack round his mule. "He's a man like anyone else. Decent, too . . ."

"Underneath! . . ." "When you get to know him!" ". . . If you say 'sir' . . ."

The catcalls and sarcasm flew thick and fast as Igor struggled to lollop his mule into a ragged three-legged stride. "Heathen bastards!" he hollered back from between the stone lions. "We'll burn you out, see if we don't!"

Mischa peered into the blackness which seemed to squash back restricting his very breath. The passage stank of bone-glue and all about him was the cluck and gurgle of seeping water. When his haversack caught on the pebble-shale of the roof the sound grated with ear-splitting violence, and he wriggled back waiting for some light from ahead where the officer was squeezing himself through the dark.

After his parents died no one remembered Mischa's real age but when war came the village elders put him up for service as a well-grown lad and the authorities took him without question – such were the times. Mischa hated that almost as much as he hated the Army. He was convinced that there had been a terrible mistake, and his sense of injustice erupted in nightmares for which his fellow-recruits beat him. The cure had not worked, the black hole in which he found himself now, too terrified even to crawl, was worse than any dream.

When the officer was near he was so killingly lovely that Mischa would do anything to keep him near, but now he was out of reach up ahead, clearing a sandfall. The boy bemoaned his own youthfulness, ready to scream if anything live crept out of the walls to touch his bare flesh, and hated his officer for popping up from nowhere with a promise to save them all from death, and getting young lads like Mischa to hurl themselves into any fantastic operation, just to be at their new major's side.

For what seemed an age he sucked the edge of his wrist, choking down a scream, until the call came: "Give a hand here!"

At the instant of command Mischa's body responded, as if independently squirming him up until his head bumped on the major's boots and he was able to pass the hand-axe and trowel from his leg-pockets, completely restored by the warmth and feel of his officer, a brave lad once more who had ventured to break through no matter how many armed men and women hid in the cellars, waiting to shoot him dead.

But as so often happened, his anticipation was crueller than the fact of events and he was disappointed to find that nobody and nothing awaited him except a sudden glow where the tunnel broadened out to a sort of chamber with a shored roof under which both he and the major could relax to full height.

"So far, so good," said Valerian, swinging round his kerosene lamp.

Mischa could have wept for the humiliation of his previous fears. "I've been in action, you know. I was all ready."

"Of course you were. I know how you felt," said the officer. "That's why I picked you."

To Mischa the words were as understanding as a touch of hands and he brightened at this further evidence of the major's insight. "Sounds silly," he confided. "But I don't like the dark either, never did."

Valerian was no longer listening. Mischa followed him through a brick arch to an expanse so vastly black beyond the cast of the tiny lamp that he would have collapsed to his knees if the officer had not turned him from the impenetrable shadow, given a chuckle, and set the lamp down on what looked like an oversized trunk. A couple of twists and the wick blazed forth. Mischa corrected his mistake: the trunk was a crate, still padlocked, one of many. Hundreds, perhaps, racked up everywhere. He thought of the field mortuary at Gorlice before realising something was wrong.

"When we started in," he began slowly. "You forgot the stick-torch in my pack. And I couldn't get at it. So you didn't need a light."

The major yawned and stretched. His shadow divided along the grain of the boarded walls like an over-lifesize cross.

"You must trust this place," whispered Mischa. "You've been here before."

For a moment Valerian stared at Mischa as if the boy were at fault for having deduced such an obvious truth. "Before, yes. Many times," he said. "But this is the last."

Accepting his officer's foresight with simple belief, Mischa contrasted it with the sloppiness of the people in the house: "Fancy leaving a lamp, though, it could have got knocked over and started a fire. That's the trouble with some folk, no sense of detail."

Valerian meanwhile had hacked away the padlocks from several of the crates and thrown back the lids.

"These all the types?" the boy asked, almost brusquely now the time had come for him to assert his technical flair.

When the major nodded, Mischa began to unpack his kit. Opening the haversack he took out a roll of lintless broadcloth which he carefully spread over the hardpacked earth. While Valerian watched, fascinated at the touch of the boy's thick fingers on the metallic sheen of the nose-case fuse, Mischa counted aloud as one by one he unhoused the mechanisms of the timing device and arranged them in order along the left-hand edge of the cloth.

"How long?" asked the boy.

Valerian stared at the frustum, top-plate, creep spring, winding wheel and all the other clockwork components which twinkled in the lamp like the insides of a transparent wrist-watch. Once he himself had worked as unerringly; now he felt the tremor in his hands which had remained with him since that morning at Lemberg when he stopped back the detent prematurely on an exactly similar shell fuse and one hundred and fifty pounds of amatol had detonated in the barrel. "Minutes," he said.

"Minutes?" The boy held the brass drive-chain into the light. "This little set-up only counts in seconds, your honour – twenty-two, thirty, forty-five, sixty – one minute maximum."

Failure to calculate. Child's play. And I failed and shall fail.

"Then overwind the watch train."

Complacent in his expertise Mischa smiled up at his officer and chinked the little gear wheels together in the palms of his hands. "Has to be German, hasn't it, sir? So can't be done. Foolproof, that's the trouble with the best munitions. I always prefer something cruder myself, something native."

The boy went from crate to crate, nosing down at the packing like a terrier trained to sniff out composition powder and percussion pellets. "Impact . . . Time and Impact . . . Graze . . . You could prime a number one siege battery with this class of armings." A few moments' work and he had assessed the contents of all but the last crate. "Ah," he said. "Now this is more up our street – trench-mortar delays."

To Valerian they appeared indistinguishable from the fuses of the unflighted bombs with which he had destroyed Anton's convoy a year ago, but the boy explained that depending on the fill of acid these could be pre-set for one hour, two, three – anything up to two days ahead. Mischa was proud of his strange mastery: "Or in sequence with a few minutes' gap, just to make sure in case some are dud."

"An hour to the first, an hour's all I need," said Valerian. "Then do that. Set them all."

In the long silence that followed Valerian could only watch as Mischa crouched over the task like a child winding a top. Light danced on the walls brilliant with the flash of salts eating at the crumbly brick. This was the final operation. For the present he had killed enough. Igor's mission had ended in predictable failure but a way had to be found which was neither victory nor surrender, and there must be no more death.

"Mischa, are you never afraid?"

The boy turned, rounding his orangey eyes into the unblinking stare of a rodent surprised by the light. "Nearly all the time, your honour – you must have noticed that – except at my work," he murmured, twisting back cautiously to resume his dismantling. "What the sergeant calls the mistress of a one-legged beggar – consolation for inadequacy."

Mischa's nightmares before battles were insufferable to his company who would have killed him long ago but for his wizardly gift. Volkov, the most experienced of men, trusted him uninstinctively, on the evidence. While the boy worked, everyone near felt himself to be in a state of grace; security was perfect, and faith took on meaning.

"Is he a harsh man, this sergeant of yours?"

"Fair. When occasion warrants, and that's pleasant while it lasts – like the work."

In the fate of the boy Valerian could foresee his own. Once conflict ended they would be thrust back to the edge of the nightmare from which they both had emerged into action.

Mischa did not speak any more until the last fuse was primed. "One," he said, mopping the excess acid from the pinhole inlet before reviewing the completed line of cones in reverse order. "One – five, one – ten, one – fifteen . . ."

Valerian nodded. Five chances, each irreversible. "Send the signal to your sergeant immediately. By now he will have embarked and he must know what has been done here. Remember, I am relying on you."

By mid-morning the night breeze had livened to strong gusts from the north which caught the pontoon broadside on. Although she sat low in the water from the weight of the artillery piece rigged below her waterline the old grain-lighter had swung out from the line of her tow-launch and was now skewed midstream presenting stern and bow to opposite sides of the river.

As browny wavelets slushed through the gunwales Sergeant Volkov sat astride the arm of a crane projecting over the rudder, and began to feel sick. "Signal him again," he shouted back to another figure crouched under the gun-caissons, struggling with the hand-pump. A sudden pitch of the stern brought Volkov within feel of the scummy emerald and yellow stain blurting from the sluice. "Don't flag the bugger, shoot at him," he roared against the wind.

Corporal Myelnikov abandoned the pump and clambered across the slithering anchor-chain and under-deck tackle to the base of the crane. "Want me to lay one across his bows, Sergeant?" he called up. "Or is it *Captain*, now we're tossing and pitching?"

"Do something, man, before he rides us out of the channel into the shoals . . ."

Before Volkov could finish the wind veered with a buffeting smack which jolted his head upwards against the top drive-pulley of the crane, and for a while he was silent, keeping observation on the stranded tow-launch and spitting blood onto the waves. Myelnikov knew that there was nothing to be done until Viktor could get up steam to pull them round, and resigned himself to a drenching. He'd been here before so he ought to know the ropes.

Until a couple of months past he'd taken his turn as a deck soldier helping to nudge this flat tub down from the north where his captain had requisitioned it off a couple of corn merchants from Byelitz who were planning to unload the contents onto the Viennese bread-market after the Ukrainian peace-treaty. Bastards. Last get-rich idea they'd ever had.

"Give him a chance, Sarge, he's having to stoke and steer the little tart singlehanded."

It wasn't Viktor's fault; it wasn't even Volkov's fault, for once: the trouble was *Barbara*.

Myelnikov hated her, bloody great sow, every knob and buffer of the useless hump of her stuck amidships, sullen as buggery, with the shell up her breech that took four men and a cradle to load.

White smoke flooded from the launch's tall stack, the bow hawser lifted for a few seconds dripping weed, then disappeared again. Another yard of logs and Viktor might coax enough pull out of his day-trip puff-puff. But she was still underpowered for the beast at her tail.

Volkov became alarmed at the volume of smoke. "You can't do that," he screamed from his perch. "The man's a brute – she's not one of his mules. Pile in any more and he'll rupture her tubes."

The launch reversed, coming so close that both men could hear the clank of her pistons, idled for a moment, then slouched back on her stern as Viktor let her popping engine rip. Myelnikov prayed never again to have his nostrils tainted by the bilge-stink, wet rust and sour grease inseparable from naval machinery. There was a jolt as the hawser tightened to its full stretch, and in one gentle sweep the lighter began to come round at the head. Myelnikov watched the sky cant across the stubby barrel of the 210-mm. howitzer and cursed his luck. After coming into range the orders were to stand off midstream and at a pre-determined signal open fire east to landward. What it really meant amounted to this: a corporal who knew as much about bastard heavy short mortars as the hairs on the next man's arse, was deputed by his sergeant who knew even less, to drop a two-hundred-and-sixty-five-pound shell, spot on. One go only. No chance, that weight, of getting another up her. Myelnikov gloomed at the toothed arcs on the howitzer's elevating gear, wishing her back in the field barbette they'd dug her out of on the banks of the San.

The sergeant had deeper misgivings. The entire operation, which had been thrashed out with the young officer the day before, was critical as to time: a co-ordinated attack from land and water required almost perfect synchrony unless the enemy was to seize the initiative and attack before the offensives were combined. Every minute lost in swinging round the lighter had brought the prospect of being defeated in detail closer and closer. Although the lighter couldn't be hit by the old seventy-seven which was the only artillery piece the other side had, at this rate it could take her another two hours of slow going to close into range. By that time his troops in the maze, already outnumbered and exhausted from the previous onslaught, would be getting the pasting of their lives. What then? There was the real plan, of course: even if the timing got dicky or *Barbara* didn't do her stuff, the major was still going to blow the house himself.

Volkov rode up his cuff to inspect the heavy watch on his white wrist, then scanned the left bank. There was the house, looking as permanent as the woods and water. Something stank about this business. It all seemed so plausible how he explained it, but the new major had been too keen with his offer to do the dirty work. As his doubts hardened, the sergeant became more imperious: he was committed, no good spreading unease in a crisis. "Tally ho!" he roared clenching both fists at the wake of the steamer. "Full speed ahead!"

Over the thrug of the engines Viktor heard nothing but eyed Volkov's reflection in the glass pressure dial. The pompous twat was pretending to be friendly, but he wanted you to know he was in charge. He knew the type only too well: a death-in-the-aid-ofexpediency bugger; a bugger who'd go to the bottom clutching the rule book he went by.

Huddled under the lee of the pontoon's starboard, Corporal Myelnikov waved his superior into a dry place beside him. "Listen, Sergeant, I've been thinking."

"I'm glad you had the time," said Volkov. "Be a good lad and keep it to yourself. I've got the figuring to do."

For a short while there was silence as the sergeant made calculations with the aid of his notebook and pocket compass.

"That's no good," said Myelnikov, poking a finger at the inked triangulations festooning Volkov's digits. "You might as well shovel shit into an oven. They'll pip us. It's too late for sums. You're not the only one who can work out where we are and how far there's to go. They'll be doing that, back at the landing jetty, and once they clock the time gap, they'll do a clean sweep of our lads before this tin of slops gets *Babs* a grapple."

In Volkov's judgement this assessment was perfectly just; their only hope was in the enemy's greater incompetence; but he had no intention of being outranked by the corporal's common sense. "That contingency has already been taken into account," he said, clipping papers together. "I would advise you not to countenance defeatism."

"Aw, scrub that kind of talk, Sergeant." Myelnikov seemed almost to be pleading. "I shouldn't have listened any more than you should."

"To what?"

"To him, Sarge, for Christ's sake, to your frigging contingency major."

For a second or two, fear contracted Volkov's stomach. His reservations about the officer seemed about to be confirmed, but the sergeant was too wily a political animal not to have been prepared, even for that. After all, contingencies were his line. "I think I can detect the qualities of a man well enough, Corporal Myelnikov – or do you mean to impugn my judgement of character?"

"Im-pugn is it? Give me half a chance and I'd im-fucking-pugn his scut on a lance-pole." As Myelnikov became more excited, Volkov breathed deeply, masterfully. He was right. He'd been right all along.

"His name's not Kabalyevskii . . . ."

Right.

"Where d'you think he came from – out of the sky to save us from sin?"

Out of the sky, out of the house. Now I know what I thought I knew and planned for accordingly.

"He's a bleeding little waster who took everybody in, my captain

384

along with the best. And he's never going to mine that temple of his,"
went on Myelnikov. "No more than he'll wait till we drift up like
scum on the stew, because by then he'll have skipped with his saints
after doing in our boys. What got into you, Sarge, falling for it?"

Volkov bore the corporal's skimble-skamble in contented heart. If
you were wrong, always admit it, but when you were right – keep
them guessing. "Do you remember the soldier's oath, Corporal Myelnikov?"

"Which one?"

"The only one, man: *Before- the- face- of- the- working- class- of-
the- Soviet- Socialist- Republic- and- of- the- entire- world- I- promise-
to- follow- the- calling- of- the- warrior- of- the- workers'- and-
peasants'- Red- Army- in- all- honour- to- study- military- science-
conscientiously- and- to- preserve- as- I- would- the- apple- of- my-
eye- the- People's- and- Army's- possessions- from- deterioration- or-
spoliation.* Understand what that means, Corporal?"

"Bits here and there, *starshina*," said Myelnikov, mystified at
Volkov's total lack of reaction to his betrayal of Valerian.

"Exactly, so you'd best be leaving the intellectual side of soldiery
to me."

After a choppy run of a mile, the wind diminished to a breeze as they
entered the mouth of a wasp-waisted channel between stretches of
high, dense forest. In this dangerously narrow sleeve of water the
corporal strained his ears beyond the quietened chug of the launch
for the slish of fire and following plink of small-arms' shot on the
lighter's plates. They had no armour to pierce. One burst of a
duck gun would do for this piss-tank however intellectual she was
navigated.

What a match! Volkov who fancied his chances versus Valerian
who thought he was God. They were shorn goats being hurdled to
the slaughterman behind Viktor in line ahead, all because Sergeant
Write-it-down thought he was flasher on the uptake than that
swagger-eyed boy Viktor used to call Angel who had them then where
he had them now – pecking at his fingertips like a gilded priest.

Twenty minutes into the channel with only an occasional slurp and
thump from the driftwood coursed down by spring freshets, the
lighter barrelled cheerfully onwards, apparently immune. Myelnikov
eased himself up, careful not to disturb the sergeant who was napping
on one of *Barbara*'s wickerwork mats, and began to prowl around
the grey hulk of the howitzer.

She was a sea-cow all right, shrugged back on her cradle, snout
speckled with field camouflage and spume. Three tons of steel blubber

and knobs. Infantrymen weren't supposed to know the secrets of girls like her, but Myelnikov had picked up a bit during the transport, helping to bed her down on the sandwich of mats and steel plates through which she was bolted to the cellular iron boxes filled with earth that had been spanned across the bottom of the lighter.

"Needs firmness," the artillery NCO had said when they tightened her up. "For the shock of her recoil."

The corporal spun the handwheel of the elevator traction until it engaged, and traversed the barrel half a degree east. Her hydraulics felt smooth as a pup. Inside she must be intact.

He knew what they were waiting for, but there were no requirements for a direct hit. Bring her to bear at maximum elevation and even a fall-short would terrify the wits out of the most hardened troops. He'd seen it under night-time bombardment, dug in up to his neck, when a mistime burst a mile high in brisance more livid than the splitting of suns. Poor sods – you might even be sorry if you believed they could be sorry for you. Myelnikov caressed the sealed breech of the howitzer with investigative fingers. "Fuck the imagination, *Baba*, point is, how do we do you, old girl?" He and Volkov knew the drill – they'd seen it enough times – they could set her up – trouble was, they didn't know what to expect once she fired. If she fired. Or blew in the breech. Or at the muzzle. All they knew was that with an old gun, her barrel bored out and relined to a smaller calibre, you could expect temperament, and one blow-back would do for her and them all.

Then, at last, he saw the signal, Mischa's Verey flare miles away over the eastern woods. The boy had got through: Valerian had kept his word and the house would blow.

It was time to wake the sergeant.

Makar watched the towboat clear the head of the channel. Above the river, the sky was a warm grey. If it hadn't been for the troops behind him, strung out round the landing stage and dug into the scrub by the riverside façade of the house, he might have enjoyed this morning blow along the finger of the jetty over the slap and crick-crack of waves.

Another life and he could have been a dawn traveller anticipating the docking of his pleasure steamer at a deserted wharf.

The pontoon inched on blackly like a sea-going slug, making, what – two knots, three knots? Against the denuded foreshores of this neck of the river it was hard to judge her progress, but one thing was plain – the gun was in traction, as Osip had guessed, every curve of the bank bringing a compensating response in the traversing gear that maintained her angle of fire relative to Makar's own position.

He'd said nothing to the men. They thought they were fireproof squeezed between the ribs of the wood piers under his boots, reckoning on a volley or two to bust her seams as the old pontoon glided past. There was no salvation in the truth, not for them or their hoppoes back at the west wing tucked into the niches of the rusticated façade, who thought they'd decoyed this great duck all for themselves.

"A mixed lot," Hermann had said when the allocations were made. This meant the boys and all the old men, while the German took off north with the spanking hard-biters to where he judged the big hit would first come. Boys were plucky, and Makar had seen grandfathers stand their ground, but once this river-bitch boomed they'd think it was the voice of God. Trouble was they'd already been blooded in the inconclusive night skirmishes two days before and fancied themselves for heroes.

Leave them at ease. There'd be no defence except scattering, once the howitzer found her range. But where could they go? Let them cling together and die before they realised what battle was, let alone war. With worse troops Makar could have hoped for justice on the complacent, the cowardly, the perfectly assured who'd stick a neighbour through the throat because he had three horses, but this was the sort who couldn't begin to comprehend evil; too young and too old not to feel at peace with God and themselves. Let them be.

To his right the orange nimbus of a muzzle-flash tinted the summer foliage, and the timbers of the jetty quivered from the rambling ground shock as the old seventy-seven opened up at fifteen thousand yards. With a sweep of his arm Makar described the shell's parabola: and came thumb down on the spot, approximately two miles short and a thousand yards wide, where it creamed into fluff on the placid river.

Cursing his imperfect longsight, Sergeant Volkov found a foothold on the cradle of the gun, steadied himself against the air recuperator, and donned his spectacles. Across the flat expanse of water another boom from the seventy-seven was already dwindling on the breeze. The fuzz on the left bank of the river sharpened into tiny figures clustering at the rear of an uncouth field-piece that had seen better days; behind the breech loader the lines of the house stood hard and compact against a wall of cloud.

The efficiency of his lenses gave the sergeant a touch of omnipotence: all for show, the business with the seventy-seven, you could see that; old men and kids being ordered to make a gesture. They must know how useless it was.

Afterwards, Myelnikov remembered that it came with the sun, but when the sun came he had felt nothing except an unaccustomed warmth at the small of his back which made him turn to Volkov as if the sergeant himself were the source. And Volkov saw him do that, and leant out from the cradle, beginning an order: "Take her a . . ."

Then he stared.

Perhaps he knew what was happening, because Volkov kept on staring as if there were something to see that wouldn't let itself be seen no matter how hard you stared.

"Take her a . . ."

Abeam, abaft, a walk, a cake, a word, anything to keep him with her, and me and us together always and again?

God almighty, the bugger held on so tight you thought he must be nailed to the buffers, never going to drop. And when he did it was a feet-first progress, stiff as he stood, never a crumple.

The glasses were his downfall. Obvious, when you thought about it. That sudden rift in the cloud setting him agleam was enough; two blips, a dit-dot flash, talking sunshine telegraphese to the lone sniper. A longshot but a dilly, took from behind, probably, off one of the fire-watch towers that dotted the high woods at the outlet of the channel.

In the sump Myelnikov kept his head down out of respect for optical sights, cursing the gnats.

Above the crackle of rifle fire from the bank came the thump of the seventy-seven. The fall of shell was too aimless to do harm but at each explosion the pontoon bucked slightly from the wash. He had counted three when the engine of the steam pinnace stuttered and went into a humping cough which chimed in with the swish of an incoming round from the field-piece. The bow hawser slackened then whipped back with a jolt which threw Myelnikov onto his back. As he struggled to pick himself up in the bilgewater, the wake of the shell-burst clopped the lighter amidships. A suck and a roll this time combined with a pull on the bows to produce a shudder which Myelnikov felt down his spine. High up on the gun Sergeant Volkov's body wavered then began to slide. In the momentum of the fall Myelnikov discerned his fate. His luck was totally up, for in the direct line of the sergeant's drop was the projecting trigger-limb of *Barbara*'s breech.

Down it goes and up she comes and the colour is red.

When the blast hit him Myelnikov was already between water and air, caught as he jumped from the lighter's rudder-end. The gun made her motion effectually, hurling the monstrous shell from the highest point of elevation to bob like a dolphin in the thin air miles above, while down below she passed the entire forty-three inches of her recoil through mats, plates, earth-packed caissons and the rust-eaten bottom of the listing pontoon.

Out on the jetty, under an open sky, Makar did not feel the least bit afraid. As an experienced gunner he knew what to expect from the attitude of the howitzer's snub barrel: she was shooting high for a plunging chop on the house, half a mile or so behind his position.

Before the noise was the flame, and the split-second between them was distracted by the might of that final moment before the barrage opened, just as he remembered from his first experience, years before, of heavy fire.

Then he had felt no anticipation, but was simply bewildered at the intense reality of the objects around him. Someone, he remembered, was filling a galvanised tub from a kerosene can and the water glistened in the sun, nearly blinding him. A man with his arm in a splint sat in a bomb crater greasing his rifle with bacon fat. Even as the shell sought them out with a noise like a canvas sheet the size of a forest ripping itself down from hem to hem, before grounding in an express-train rumble that shook the brain in his skull, Makar had not been afraid because he could not believe that which he had so vividly perceived would never re-emerge from the swirl of ochre vapour blotting land and sky.

When the grove was obliterated in a cloud of shell-splinters Makar rejoiced. And because he could not tell how many men lay mutilated or dead there, or know that the outer walls of Valerian's quarters and the whole of the governess's cornerside sitting-room on the ground floor had been blown clean away, his joy was impregnable. The howitzer had toppled itself with that one last vaunt, yet the house had remained.

So long as the house withstood, so should they.

40

Had Sergeant Volkov been granted respite as brief as the moment which the bullet took to pass behind his eyes, he would have accomplished a remarkable feat of gunnery. But left helpless against the yaw of the lighter, *Barbara* laid herself off by that fraction of an arc which, when uncorrected, ensured that the shell deviated south-west and dropped a thousand yards wide.

In the sycamore grove, slashing with his bayonet at overhanging branches while his two companions, little more than children, wrestled in the dust, Yefim felt it coming. There was barely enough time for apprehension to become awe, then a fear too momentary to be elicited in movement or cry; but sufficient to know the weight of crushed air, solid and impenetrable as the segments of a column, piling before the nose cone, into his chest. There was that, and the scream of jamming train brakes in a tube which seemed to be stoppered by his head.

A quarter of a mile away the last remounts, seven mares and a yearling, which had been grazing in the riverside paddock by the cobbled courtyard on the west façade were killed instantly by the blast. On the other side of the house the long windows of the grand salon fell inwards, decapitating a plaster shepherdess in the *basso-relievo* frieze above the double doors.

According to plan, the four Krupp field guns concealed in the lakeside scrub immediately took up the bombardment with high-explosive rounds.

When the tall casements of the salon disintegrated from the shock of the howitzer shell's detonation, Osip was on his knees, his back to the blast, rifling the bottom drawers of a silvered-limewood desk which stood by the doors at the inner wall. The wine which he had already drunk combined with the single-mindedness of his search for more, rendered him doubly fortunate for he was relaxed at the moment of impact as well as protected by the outdrawn flap of the desk. Hazy from blast, with no idea what was happening, he stayed where he was.

From the terrace below, screams rose up between the thudding of the fifteen-pounders at the waterside, and his first thought was for his women, strung out behind the stone balustrade, horribly exposed to the fire. He was kicking his way out backwards through the smashed glass when a couple of elderly women, one with a bandaged arm, staggered in through the double doors, unaware of his presence, and began loudly to praise God for their escape. As he emerged, both rounded on him at once: it was all his fault, he was their man, why had he not foreseen this? The house was falling about their ears while he hid under the furniture. What was he going to do?

Osip tried to shout them down with confused, contradictory orders, but the thump of the guns started up again in concentrated salvoes which seemed to creep nearer with every burst. He leapt to the sill of the nearest empty window. The noise stopped, and he could hear the drone of the old women's voices. Below, the flagstones of the terrace were deserted, and far out on the fringes of the park black smoke was spiralling eccentrically into the tree-tops.

The brief time of quiet was sufficient to clear Osip's head. From the drift and hang of the smoke he was able to deduce the situation. The house itself was not under direct attack. At any rate, not yet, for judging by the smoke, shell was bursting way off, off by a mile or more, still in direct line but being laid back by the gunners, not in error but for some purpose which he could not grasp. While he pondered the reason for this, orangey spurts freckled the tourmaline expanse of the lake, and to the north-east where the park merged into wilderness, a rubble of branches and dirt boomed up in a vertical cone which shuddered the house to its foundations.

Why not open the range and crack on to the very threshold? There was nothing to prevent it. With the seventy-seven down at the river they had no reply, and the people now streaming back across the park knew that, and must be expecting the shrapnel rounds to spray among them every minute, and yet they came on unscathed, not believing their luck or God or their star. It was a queer do, this. Someone wasn't serious; someone, concluded Osip, was having them on.

Voices came from behind him calling for help. Katya stood by the open double doors, sallow with pain, leaning back on the push of Dunya's hands against her spine, trying to relieve the ache from her unborn child. "Harder, harder, Dunyasha, darling. I think my time has come."

A remission. Then again came the spindletop screech of four

small-calibre shells whistling almost in unison on their depressed trajectory between the stand of great elms by the lake. Blood began to dribble from Osip's ear and the discrete trickling of it suddenly perplexed him, and he tore wildly at the bandage, throwing it to the floor where he stamped on it, childishly, without thought for anyone or anything, except the relief of being rid of a maddening irritation, and able to hear freely unimpeded for the first time that day.

Suddenly the doors were flung wide to their hinges buffeting Katya right and left as a horde of small children forced a passage into the room. The pregnant girl was carried forward in the crush, spun round and finally collapsed with a scream a few yards from Osip's feet.

"To hell with this," he bawled, his shout drowning in the enormous hubbub of gunfire and squeals. He stood in their midst, fending them off, as child after child fought its way to him, terrified, weeping and looking to him, the only man present, for protection. Having come to a decision, Osip cleared a space for himself by brutal use of his elbows, snatched up his Chauchat carbine, stuffed its two remaining magazines under his blouse, and continuing to beat off the children, began to hustle a way through to the parkside of the great salon.

Becky caught at his spurs when he reached the open casement. The shelling had lifted and in Osip's good ear her voice was piercing: "Off already, *dyadya*? Without a bye-bye?" She hung on as Osip stretched out to peer down at the flagstones. "My, you've a long way to go."

He heard her, and heeded. The drop could break his back. "Only reconnoitring, *dushichka*," he said very loudly and flexed his strong legs sufficiently high for the girl to scramble onto the sill where she nestled to him, cub-like, taking in his whisper: "Two saddle horses fresh as water, a mile off, just under the scarp . . ."

Katya had managed to clamber upright, saw him and came butting through the scum. "Swine," she called helplessly. "Where d'you think you're going?"

Becky fumbled beneath her skirts unlooping a coil of plaited telegraph wire one end of which she fed to Osip who slid it under the bottom casement bar.

"I'll kill you for this," screamed Katya, lurching on the slithery broken glass. "I'll kill you, I'll kill you."

With the barrel of his Chauchat Osip twisted the knot around the bar then hacked the wire under his right boot testing it for strength. Katya was almost within a handgrasp when a three-year-old boy clutching a wooden doll bowled into her side and she tripped, slashing her knees on the glass. "Coward! Filthy deserter!"

"Brought it on yourselves, woman. You had the choosing," Osip shouted back, Becky in his arms. "A man who deserts has a fool for a commander. Try your luck with Vissarion."

Becky clung on, rapturous, kicking out with her ankle-boots against the flat pillar as Osip swarmed her down to the cool, bare slabs of the terrace where the triumph of her final screech dipped away under the vigour of renewed close-order fire from the battery by the lake.

Vissarion strode into the salon cradling an infant in each arm. Katya went for him claw-handed. "Oh, what's the use, what's the use, you're too late. Osip has betrayed us. What's the use of men, what's the use . . . ?"

"You mean you let him, you silly bitch. Why d'you think I gave you a gun – to play games with? You should have shot him. That's what you would have done, isn't it, little man?" he chuckled to the child mewling at his chest. "Shot him dead."

"I dropped it. What do you expect from a woman in my condition? And I'm sure my time . . ."

The gaunt lieutenant placed one of the children in her arms and set the older on the floor where it uncurled from sleep, gave a racking cough, then crawled over to *babushka* Marya who had begun to sweep the mess of broken glass as if it had been flour spilled in her own kitchen. "Calm down, girl," he said, kicking the shards towards the old woman's handbroom. "Osip was only a Cossack and Cossacks always rat. Bring me water."

Katya could find only the wine which Osip had left under the desk. Vissarion drank deeply, then bellowed at the children who fell quiet, more fearful at the sound of this huge man's anger than the crash of shells which continued to scream in from the lake. "You, woman, yes, you," he called to old Marya who stopped sweeping to follow the direction of his gaze to the stock of ammunition-boxes piled in the furthest corner of the salon. "See those, dearie? Right. Then you can start sorting through them. What are you looking for? .315 calibre, Gran, that's what you want to dig out. What if it's not there? If it's not there, *dusha moya*, none of *us* will be for much longer, and that's the God's truth."

"Are we in trouble?" said Katya.

The lieutenant prodded the swell of her belly with the neck of his empty bottle. "Worse than you, Katyushka, some of us, or soon will be." The smile was tender. "We may be standing on an arsenal, darling, but, *prilyest*, nothing fits. Matching up our guns to munitions is all at cross purposes, like trying to feed tigers with grass. Here." He drew from his belt the companion piece to Katya's lost single-shot pistol. "Join the old dears on their wild-goose chase; you might have more luck than I've had getting things together."

As the girl's fingers closed round the butt, a wild shout went up from the doors: "Out of the way, you blasted kids, the wounded's coming up, make room there! Who's in command?" And the first survivor of the rout on the hill staggered to his knees on the threshold, almost dropping the youth of seventeen whom he had carried across his shoulders the entire length of the park.

To the troops in the maze the chief virtue of Valerian's plan of attack was its consideration for them. Given the nature of the ground, they were not to move against the defenders of the house except under heavy artillery cover; and even with the assurance of that, they were not to advance to close-quarters. It would be enough, he had promised, if they could hold off at a distance any sortie which the fall of the howitzer shell at the enemy's rear might provoke. Moreover, they could feel doubly secure in the knowledge that before any sally could be mounted, the house itself would probably be destroyed by Mischa's mining of the cellar.

Respectful of their commander's skill in sparing them the kind of casualties suffered during their disastrous night foray, Valerian's troops deployed confidently before Schmidt's emplacements to the north from where, so they had been briefed, the strongest resistance could be expected.

The terrain was well-chosen for defence. A quarter of a mile forward from the north front of the house a man-made hillock ran parallel to the extent of their line, blocking access to the great portico, and providing an artificial vantage point from which their position could be overseen. Built for the Laskorin children years before as a toboggan run, the slope was gentle, but capable of being murderously enfiladed by two machine-guns for which Schmidt, in the winter, had ordered pits to be dug.

Carrying out Valerian's instructions, the troops in the maze threw up an earth breastwork opposite the rise and, without replying to the sporadic fire from the third machine-gun entrenched on the crest, awaited the onset of the big guns. From the west front of the house spoil thrown up by the howitzer shot high in the air, but the burst was out of sight of the men on the hill, and the shock too far back to cause much damage. No panic ensued, only a quickening flip-flop of bullets along the breastwork as the two wing machine-guns traversed to co-ordinate fire with the Hotchkiss at the crown of the rise.

From his observation post at the rear of the pit, Schmidt looked back to the house. Apart from a corner of the north-west wing which had slithered into rubble by the cobbled courtyard, the main structure had somehow stood up to the blast, but once the range was determined closer placing was only a matter of time, and with that would come the final débâcle.

Needing to think, he ordered his men to break off the action, and was flagging the same message to the outlying crews, when the yowl of an incoming shell from the lakeside battery struck him momentarily dumb. The base of the hill took the impact, loose ground quaking under the gun-tripod which canted forward on two legs, fouling the breech with soil.

Hadzhii's gunners adjusted sights and put down another group of four slap under the lip of the second machine-gun emplacement, slewed, and did the same on the left. Every man on the ridge believed that he was about to die. And although Schmidt was a seasoned campaigner, the truth of the situation did not occur to him until the barrage had lifted and shells passed harmlessly overhead, to find niches deep in the rear along the confines of the park. But by then it was too late to communicate reality to his men, and they behaved, as Valerian had calculated they would, wildly, unreasoningly, incapable of thought, exhausting their last stock of ammunition against the troops entrenched below in four to five minutes of almost continuous fire.

Afterwards, when the soldiers rose from their entrenchments to charge up the unguarded hill, Schmidt's first gunner walked down to meet them, his hands in the air, calling on the rest to follow. Schmidt shot him dead as he walked. And this was enough for the rest who rallied under his threats and made off down the far slope of the mound towards the house without a glance for their commander who followed behind, at a heavy trot, brandishing his carbine.

High above the great central stairway the glass was damaged but the dome had remained intact.

Out of the swelter of the park Schmidt found comfort in the blue-tinged light of the vestibule. His men had gone, obedient to Vissarion's commands, but the German lingered behind dreamily, recovering, cooled by the marble and the empty space which seemed to draw him inwards to its quiet.

A shadow slid into motion: a pale figure resolving itself against the diffuse light; tall, crop-haired, in an ill-fitting soldier's blouse. As the man's stride lengthened bringing him almost within conversational distance, Schmidt gradually discerned the gold of the head beneath the flax-violet, gridelin haze filtering in through the fractured glass. Heavy brows, those acid eyes, the steadfast mouth. It was him. The whore had razored him down to the look of a beardless Christ, and Valerian seemed gentler with his short hair, almost vulgarly pretty.

By the closed double doors leading to the old salon he willed the boy to come to him.

"Hermann. I hoped you might have been killed."

Safe within the core of the house Schmidt felt no panic. Here he could be calm once more, as calm as the presence of this unpredictable creature, alone and vulnerable in the heart of his enemy's camp. "No, Master, as you see, here I stand, awaiting you."

"I have come to offer you safe-keeping, old comrade. In less than an hour this house will be a ruin."

Schmidt smiled at the familiar insolence. "You, making the offers, as always. Well, I've done with acceptances and you have nothing left to give. Save yourself, if you can."

"The soldiers have welcomed me," said Valerian.

The hem of Schmidt's robe fluttered at the polished calves of his boots. "That may be, but how can they trust you after what has been done to us here? Trust cannot survive this."

The west wing had gone entirely, so they said, and smoke was seeping along the gallery, although no fire had as yet taken hold. The doors to the main apartments were shut tight against it and through the heavy mahogany panels he could hear the cries of children.

"Fetch out my people, Hermann. Gather them together here."

"Then what will you and your soldiers do to this place?"

"Fulfil our bargain in mutuality, Hermann. I pledged them this house for my life – only when they knew those fuses were set would they follow me. And they shall have their performance, but my people were never part of the contract."

There must be more to it than that. Schmidt did not believe that any real soldier would have trusted the boy. "You came too late, and to the wrong man. Vissarion is our leader now, and he's too much of a fool to trust to God Himself. He'd rather see this house blaze than submit to your words again. He'll kill you first, then anyone who'd listened."

Valerian's answering smile was helpless, undisputing, seeking direction. If Vissarion were now confronting the appeal in that face, would he remain firm?

"Get away from here while there is still time." As he said this Schmidt realised that he had been preparing for quite a different final act: a swift rending clash without words, in which the boy would crumple beneath him, succumbing to age and experience. But instead he had been provoked into concession. The fight was unfair. Valerian knew him too well, knew he was different because he believed, but had doubts, loved unwisely, but had depth to his heart; stupidly passionate, ambitious only to follow, never to lead.

"How can I leave you?" said the boy, coming closer. "Where I go you shall always be with me."

It was then that the German saw Valerian was unarmed. "Once you betrayed me and will again."

"Never," said Valerian. "Those who turned against me betrayed you." He advanced a further step. "The world has come between us, you and I."

Rain gusted through the shattered rotunda onto the stairs and the uncovered floor. The distant guns growled.

"The woman came between us, Master, not the world."

Valerian watched over his adversary with that same remote concern which Schmidt had seen in his eyes when he had come from the woman. "The woman was of the world and has returned to it."

Schmidt wondered at the absence of regret in the face before him. He did not want to know what had become of Natalya Igoryevna. She had once deeply humiliated him; and the memory of that, together with the consequences of her liaison with the boy, were still fresh enough for him to derive nothing more than a faint satisfaction from the knowledge that Valerian had finally lost her after the more terrible loss of himself to house, community, fellows and friends. "Go to Vissarion yourself if you care so much for the people here. Why ask me? I owe them nothing. They betrayed me just as you did." Knowing that finally he would give way and detesting the impulse of his own weakness, Schmidt stubbornly postponed the moment of concession, waiting for the boy to ease the bitter ache at his coming surrender, put things right between them as they had been in the times before the woman. But when Valerian gave nothing, Schmidt realised that he had never known him, that here he was not merely confronting the novelty of the boy's changed appearance, but a reversal of feeling putting him away from former allegiances as surely as the woman had sheared the flow of his hair.

It was almost piteous to watch him; an inglorious apparition of his former self; defenceless, a target waiting to be hit. There was something lost from that face, something which the disciple wanted to banish before the memory of it caused them both irretrievable pain. And what would it take? One cold act of will to acquit him of sorrow.

The sear-catch of his carbine under his thumb, Schmidt counted: at three, at five, at ten?

The boy noticed the movement of hand and lips, smiled, turned away and sat down on the bare step of the stairway, presenting his back. "You're a good man, Hermann, but you never had much common sense."

The flat condescension of the words and actions would have provoked an unimpassioned man, but to one of Schmidt's temperament it formed the perfect rebuff. "Damn you to hell, boy," shouted the German, uncluttering himself from the carbine to send it spinning across the floor. "Why can't you fight me?"

Back from the unturned head came the unwavering voice, sweet with humour: "At dawn? With old Laskorin's pistols? Or *épée* – is that how your fancy runs? Come on, old fellow, you're no *bréteur*, and neither am I. There's no time left, Hermann. And nothing to fight for. If I die so do our people, because the battle is already lost, don't you see?"

Disarmed and speechless, Schmidt allowed himself to be walked slowly round the great circular hall beneath the rotunda while Valerian tended him with soft, pressing encouragements. And the more the young man brought his elder's spirit to life by the revival of the dream which they had once held in common, the stronger the sense he had of himself as a participant in his own play, continually surprised at the power of his own words, but grown so accustomed to voice them that there came a time of detachment between speech and effect during which he could observe himself and his companion playing out their roles.

It had always been a place of death, this house. Twice he had been driven out. This time he would go, willingly, choose his companions, leaving the malignants and drifters to go to smash in the ruin of it; he would be strong again, he would lead; and once more his faithful would prance for him, as the soldiers had, out of fear and the uncertainty of love.

As he let his boyish fingers trail under the man's chin he knew when and how it would be achieved.

"Vissarion may not listen," said Schmidt hesitating at the foot of the grand stairway."

"Vissarion will listen because he has no choice. Because the people have the choice, and they have not forgotten me, and they will listen."

In the middle of the salon children were playing spillikins with Spitz rifle bullets, and while Katya moved amongst them in a soft leather apron clutching her unloaded pistol, they squabbled over their game, ignoring the groans of a stocky young man who lay along the inner wall bleeding from a flesh wound to his throat.

"Less of your row, boy," Vissarion was shouting as the guards allowed Schmidt to squeeze through the narrow gap between the

double doors. "What sort of example are you giving these young-
sters?"

After his one-to-one encounter with Valerian in the desolate stair-
well, Schmidt warmed to the queer cosiness reigning in this last
stronghold of the house where children could still feel secure. "Hard
words, Vissarion," he said with a smile, turning to observe the dozen
or so other wounded who sat in a quiet and unmoving huddle at a
distance from the young man.

"Hard times make hard men or kills them in the process," replied
the lieutenant draping a heavy machine-gun belt across his shoulders
before buckling on his long old-fashioned pistol. "Now, have you
come to be useful or is it a spell of nursing-duty with young Katya
you want posting to? All the same to me, or to them." He nodded
towards the injured and the children. "We've all got the measure of
you now, after this morning's little shebang."

Instead of rising to the taunt, Schmidt beckoned over the smaller
of the two guards on the door, a portly ex-grenadier in nankeen
breeches whose daily task throughout the winter had been to fire off
occasional bursts from the machine-guns at the park entrance in order
to prevent the coolant solidifying in the frost. "Here, man, you know
a thing or two about feed-wheels." The German whipped the cartridge
belt ends from the tuck of Vissarion's breeches. "Where does this
pretty necklace belong?"

The old soldier flicked his thumb-nail at the webbing of the belt.
"I already told him," he said, cocking the slant of his brimless forage
cap first at the questioner, then at the commander. "But he ain't no
end of a listener, especially when he's schmickered."

The man's tone was unruly, overweening; since dawn he had been
watching Vissarion become drunker by the hour. "See that?" he
asked Schmidt, pointing to a couple of splintered ammunition boxes
atop the heap of cooking pots and wicker baskets of clothes stacked
in the near left corner of the room. "He did that smash-up from sheer
aggravation because they had this rubbish in them." He slid a hand
under the belt and felt the weight of metal individually amassed in
the two hundred and fifty pouches. "Rubbish," he repeated. "Maxim
– right belt, wrong cal. It's all like that, either one or the other, never
both. He knows."

The final words came in a shout which the children, still absorbed
in their game, took up as a chant: "He knows . . . He knows . . ."
as the grenadier resumed his post by the door.

Schmidt slung the useless cartridge belt over their heads onto the
heap where Katya caught it and began unscrambling the bullets one
by one. "We got some talking to do, old fellow." The German made

himself comfortable on the baize top of Vissarion's desk, his spur points jabbing at the bottles stowed away in the kneehole. He consulted his fat steel watch. "And by my reckoning there's between forty and forty-five minutes left to do it in."

At the lull in the shelling induced by Valerian's signal both men had moved to a part of the room furthest away from the grenadier and his companion, and were conversing in low voices under the sill of the last rank of blown-out windows. The park was silent now except for a pitter of raindrops on the terrace.

"I need to think," said Vissarion when Valerian's offer had been outlined to him. "And to think I need to drink. Katyushka, fetch me a bottle."

But Katya went on stubbornly trying to force each cartridge in turn into the undersize breech of her pistol, spitting on one, polishing another, never losing patience.

"Get a hold on yourself, man," hissed Schmidt. "Folk are looking up to you for acting not thinking. Philosophy was never your style." Then on and on came the foxy, ingratiating buzz of subdued eloquence: "The only way . . . The only solution . . . an end . . . life renewed . . ." *Salvation, salvation, salvation.*

Vissarion turned on his tormentor, hood-eyed. "Running away, you mean? Giving in – like you did with these fellows here?" he said. "They know about you and so do I after they told us what happened up there, on the ridge." He gestured towards the silent wounded. "Me? I'd have buried you alive in one of those pits." The lieutenant knew the battle was lost; he also recognised a scapegoat when he saw one and rejoiced in this opportunity for humbling Valerian's former second-in-command.

Schmidt bore it abjectly, would have had his own head served upon a dish if necessary in order to accomplish his end; for Valerian had told him that a people deprived of victory would demand a sacrifice, and he must be prepared to offer himself. Only temporarily, of course, that went without saying. Once the people were out of the house Valerian would resume charge and praise and blame would be allotted according to his, not Vissarion's, judgement. So the German held under the lieutenant's railing until Katya, overcome with pity at his meekness, pushed Vissarion aside. "We will come with you, Hermann, the children and I. We, too, have suffered enough. Take this." And she thrust her pistol under Schmidt's bandolier. "Let me be the first to disarm myself."

* * *

"I know you won't believe it," said Polly. "But I'm finding all this rather sublime."

Had there been leisure and space for his pursuit of this opulent creature, Igor would have pretended to understand what she meant, and agreed. For the moment, however, he stared away incuriously at the crowding sky.

Lying prone between Igor and Polly, the huntsman ignored his wife and eased himself closer to the Cossack: "What's supposed to happen next?"

Having been ordered not to divulge the major's plan to these civilian ex-prisoners, Igor remained silent. Besides, since the defenders streaming across the park had now disappeared into the house, unscathed, he was in the dark himself.

"That artillery of yours," Belyakov persisted. "It's laying back, falling short. Nothing's being hit. Who's the clown in charge?"

The man's wife might have a twat for a husband, but he was a twat who knew about gunnery. Holding off was part of the plan, too. Igor began to feel harassed and, in order to maintain belief in the job in hand, he reviewed Major Kabalyevskii's scheme, step-by-step, testing for blunders. Flop number one: the shell from the river had missed by a mile. Trust Volkov to muck it. The fat house still squatted there like a toad on a shovel. Still, a bomb from below was as good as one from above, and he knew Mischa had primed the place, underground, to go up at a touch, and like the major, he believed Mischa had done it and trusted him when he sent up the signal-flare.

At this point, calculated Igor, the hero should be standing on a table haranguing the mob, but having failed once himself to make them see reason, the Cossack was sceptical over this side of things. If he'd been asked to quote odds he would have balanced the near-certain fact of the house-people being almost out of ammunition against the eloquence of his commander, and come out with a slight bias in favour of the major sweeping all before him. But religious folk were dicky, and time was passing.

"Keep mum, girlie," he whispered to Polly. "You're not out of the wood yet."

"Poppycock," said the girl. "They've given in. Look down there. It's quite deserted. I knew that would happen once my brother took charge."

From the moment Valerian had made his dramatic appearance at the camp with Corporal Myelnikov, Polly had conscientiously re-affirmed the nature of their relationship; and, as the new major took charge of the men, he also commanded the girl's reminiscence, leading her to fabricate pleasing little childhood stories of nursery campaigns with toy soldiers in which her brother invariably took the victory. As a break in the tedium of waiting for the attack on the house to begin, these tales were indulgently received by Igor and anyone else who cared to listen. And she was not wholly a liar, for the dead Petya and Valerian had united in her imagination to become a single emblem of glory, resurrected and created anew as the splendid major. The source of this confusion was now as lost in Polly's fantasies as the real Kabalyevskii whom she had met once or twice before the war and judged to be as dull as his watercolours.

"Call him 'brother' once more, woman, and I'll kill you," whispered Belyakov loud enough for the Cossack to overhear. Polly felt safe, that was what the incestuous burble signified: her brother, her house, his sister, his house. Valerian was willing her to him in some magical, treacherous way. That was why she had refused pointblank to stay behind and nothing he said could prevent her coming with the main assault group.

There and then Belyakov swore that if a chance came he'd kill them both.

The distant gunfire ceased and the light rain began to ease. A tall young man appeared on the top step of the portico waving what looked like a giant's shirt, white and gold with touches of crimson, which the huntsman recognised as the same ciclatoun chasuble Valerian had worn on that ill-fated summer's day of double-weddings.

Polly let go in a yell: "Yoo-hoo, over here, darling, wait for me!" And lurched into a run towards Igor's Major Kabalyevskii, meeting up, on the way, with two separate parties of troops who had thrown down their weapons and were lumbering across the wild garden in back-packs and waterproof capes dripping with rain.

Igor muttered something.

"Cease-fire?" asked the huntsman.

"Hell-fire, more like. Quarter of an hour, even less, and that heap is supposed to be going up like a hot gasbag." He was damned if secrecy mattered any more, not now that the major had come up front. "I'd lay ten to one it won't – that mad Mischa kid's a bit of an amateur, know what I mean? – But don't you think you ought to be down there in case she gets scorched?"

Before Polly reached the portico Valerian had gone back inside and an old woman wandered out of the house, her long staff tapping on the stones.

"Who d'you mean?"

"Your wife, I mean, who else?" said the Cossack. "She is your wife, I take it?"

"She's my wife."

"Thought so. Nice bit of snibley, your missis. I wouldn't mind . . ."

Three more women, fat and elderly, hobbled out and were helped down the steps by a couple of boys while around them a great gang of other children carrying rattan suitcases, boxes and baskets, poured onto the brick-dust gravel of the carriage-way. One small girl tripped on the last step dropping a big round bundle which rolled open on the verge to reveal a number of queer-shaped hats. A tall blonde woman caught Igor's eye but he quickly discounted her: pregnant. And armed, for Christ's sake, with a trooper's rifle that she was hugging to her apron. Married, too, if that was her husband coming behind, the high scraggy one with a baby howling under his arm. Amidst the milling stream of figures was Major K as skippy as a lamb, floating the whitey-gold article on a raffia string to catch the warm up-current above the house where it soon billowed out like a glinty dragon-kite.

"They kept their guns." Belyakov was watching the people from the house. "Don't tell me you surrendered to *them* – they were losing . . ."

Igor laughed. "Our side handed over its weapons like good 'uns, in a gesture of peace and goodwill, but don't bother yourself, there ain't a single round in any of them."

"Where's the wounded?" continued the huntsman. "I don't see any stretcher-cases. There's bound to be wounded. Where's the wounded, eh boy?"

Igor had been relying on the unobservance of the huntsman in the light of his wife's desertion, but the fellow was turning out to be a bloody shrewd, undomesticated freelance prick. "That's confidential matters," he snapped. "Orders. In any case, we can't even provide for ourselves, never mind cripples who're going to die anyway."

"His orders?"

Igor nodded.

"But he said they were his people," began Belyakov. "All of them . . ."

The Cossack grabbed him by the throat of his blouse.

"Listen to me, scab, I'm losing my brotherly love for you, and that's a fact. While we're alone I'll say this, and say it once and final. Where I've been the last few years, I've been ordered to do things and see things that no decent man ought to be made to do or see. Our old captain, the Kingdom be his, was an idle sod who couldn't stand trouble, so he let his NCO have his head, and Volkov's a man of mean conscience, a fanatic. His usual orders were to massacre the inhabitants of houses like this, and we did, down to females and kids.

I wouldn't insult myself to justify it. It was necessary. We're cavalry, we had to have freedom of movement, and no hangers-on. Now this new commander of ours, he's got no more call to be pally with the people in that house than Sergeant Volkov had. Kept him prisoner, tried to kill him, kill his wife, and you and yours, didn't they, but there he is, showing mercy, making allowances like a saint at bleeding heaven's gate, so he's got to be better, hasn't he?" yelled Igor, tears running down his face. "Tell me he has, you bastard, tell me, tell me that waiting for him hasn't been a fucking great waste of the best of my life."

Half a mile down from the house, Valerian stood in the rutted wheelway of the carriage-drive conferring with the company quarter-master. Between them was a tripod set under a walnut-veneered box which, a few moments before, the NCO could be seen bearing up to the rendezvous on outstretched arms.

At a blast from Valerian's trench-whistle, he tented the back part of the box under a fustian blanket before veiling his head and shoulders with the overhang. Apparently dissatisfied with the drop of the material, Valerian twitched off the cloth and relaid it across box and crouching man with a turn of his wrist. Again he blew on the whistle; there was a sizzly flash followed by a pop and the quartermaster emerged holding aloft a rectangular glass plate which Valerian placed in the empty black dressing-case at his feet. Another blast and the procedure was repeated at least a dozen more times.

Flat on his back at the wayside Belyakov made the mistake of expressing surprise; why a house, he wanted to know, and not people; surely the people ought to come before buildings when last-minute photography was done?

"Will you never achieve a sense of decorum?" asked his petulant wife. "Can't you see, he is recording images of the irreplaceable before it disappears forever. Those creatures you call people," she went on, mouthing at the onlookers who were taking a great interest in the actions of the photographer, "those creatures reproduce like beasts. What do he or I care for animals who can –" and here she used a word which Belyakov was astonished to hear from her lips – "themselves into being, *ad infinitum*, every nine months?"

All around the speechless Belyakov objects of Polly's contempt suddenly began to take cover, pulling children into the hollows of the roadside with the help of the soldiers. Polly refused to budge, and started to argue with the shy young trooper who was trying to herd all the able-bodied, childless women into a single group before leading them off to safer ground beyond the end of the drive-way. With a

shrug the youth abandoned her to the care of her husband who
recoiled from the very sight of his wife, drew his knees up to his chin,
and rested, trying to still the throbbing in his head. He couldn't even
work up the spirit to look out for himself. If she wouldn't take cover
it was all the same to him. He was too tired to care, too sick. There
was nowhere to hide, not in the end, so let them both be buried there
and then, above ground, under a storm of leaping bric-à-brac from
the old family home.

The thought appeased him. One last crack and rumble and he
would be forever peaceable and unapprehensive, so roll on, fucking,
strutting, strolling roll on, make it good and big and final, roll me
over, cover me; one day, some time, soon, now, whenever it comes
let it catch you napping. The familiar repetitive obscenities of his
soldier's prayer numbed the passage of time. His head drooped,
following the whole of his body into the comfortable suspension of
waking trance.

The hard snigger of a young girl brought him back. The women
had gone, the children and most of the troops. Yet the sun had come
through, and for a moment that appeared to him as an inexplicable
fact of nature about which he ought to be very annoyed, but as he
withdrew from his daze he saw the house, too, was still there, and
the annoyance was overtaken by his sense of melancholy fury at
having been somehow bamboozled.

Polly was seated in the shade of a wide beech-tree beyond the
further edge of the drive, plaiting a grass-chain and flirting with Igor.
Belyakov was too far away to hear what was said but he stiffened at
the highness of her voice which exulted over the Cossack in earnest,
rather bullying explanation; from the toss of her head and flutter of
fingers at the neck of her blouse, he saw that she was on her dignity.
Valerian stood over them, taking no part, his back to the house.
Everyone, including the four soldiers squatting at Valerian's feet, was
looking away from Belyakov into the fine afternoon haze beyond the
photographer's tripod.

Stumbling down a little col between two high coppices of spruce
came the crowblack figure of Schmidt in his priest's robe.

The appearance of the German heralded a further outbreak of photography: this time longer, and exclusively personal, each image
posed and overseen by Valerian who constantly interrupted the
quartermaster with orders to stop, to wait, to retake until every detail
of stance, gesture and expression was perfectly formulated. For the
best part of an hour exposure followed exposure, each contrived with
that same finicky orderliness which had once marked the composition

of his paintings; and as with them the effect was oddly primitive in its high melodramatic tone. One picture showed him and Vissarion stood face to face, looking deep into each other's eyes, emblematic of their armistice, while the little posse of troops held their rifles at the trail and gazed out to a far horizon depleted of foes. All was peace and accord and victorious high spirits. Headgear was swapped, and much fun was had with hats from the bundle. At the end of the session Vissarion led his men off into the soldiers' camp in the maze where a meal was being prepared.

Only Schmidt kept aside, brooding in the clear sunlight, feeling more and more nervous and foolish at his exclusion from the mime. When Valerian chose to notice him it was with an invitation which the German took up with obvious pleasure, and he made his way across the trackway to where Belyakov lounged in the grass. "The master wants us in his mummers' tale," he smiled. "The three of us together. A reconciliation."

Reluctantly the huntsman got to his feet, trying to recall the last time he had exchanged a civil word with Schmidt whom he had long since discounted as a normal human being, let alone a comrade-in-arms, but his present situation was so highly dangerous that soon he might want an ally. Valerian, in this busy, exalted mood, could turn like yesterday's milk, so if he wanted to top off his epic with pictures it was safer to go along with the farce.

"Just look at you," murmured Polly when he had crossed to the group round the camera and was standing aimlessly side by side with the German in front of the perspiring quartermaster. "Do you always have to behave like a lout? You're filthy. It's so degrading." And Belyakov made no resistance as his wife combed back his hair between her fingers, brushed away the grass stalks from his beard and dabbed the red dust off his brow with the edge of her sleeve.

Valerian arranged them against the backdrop of the house leaving a narrow space on the left between himself and the German around whose shoulder he had carefully placed Belyakov's right arm.

The photographer was already under his hood awaiting the command, when the boy leant sideways. "This is high style, Hermann," he confided. "Quite the old days, but I seem to have mislaid my pistol. Be a good fellow and lend me yours. I must look the part, after all – don't you agree?"

Schmidt did, and did so, honoured at the request.

"*Now*," said Valerian through his smile.

There was no blood, no wound to be seen, and although he was holding him in close embrace, Belyakov felt no shock in Schmidt's body as Katya's tiny bullet punctured the space between the German's fourth and fifth rib, passing on through his heart to lodge, fully spent, against the silver fleurets of the elaborate buckle which secured the end straps of his bandolier.

"There's a thing," said Igor, when they laid out the corpse on the battered grass verge. "Belted the right way round he could have been laughing. A man ignores the proprieties of dress, as our old Sergeant Volkov used to say, at his peril." Between his finger and thumb the lead ball of the cartridge looked clean and unlethal, its only flaw a dent on one side which glistened in the sun.

Until then, in spite of the report which he had perceived simultaneously with the camera flash, Belyakov had not understood how Schmidt died. When he slumped, almost keeling over the huntsman, he had thought only how fat the man was, how stupid to have been running like that in the heat. And this impression had lasted through attempts to rouse him.

Valerian stood apart from the group round the body, the skirts of his long stockman's oiled coat flapping in the breeze. He had broken the pistol at the breech, and whistling softly all the while, was coaxing out the little rimfire shell with a blade of shrapnel.

"You arrogant young bastard," shouted Belyakov. "Stop fiddling. You've killed a man here already with your slap-happy way with guns. Chuck that target-plinker away before there's another accident."

Igor looked up. "This is war," he said sententiously. "Accidents happen in war."

Everyone near accepted the naturalness of this explanation, including the quartermaster who scrutinised his camera for possible blemishes. Instead of discarding the pistol, Valerian snapped it shut on the unextracted shell and tucked the barrel down the back of his belt before sauntering over to where the men knelt to their work of stripping Schmidt down to the skin. Meditatively he prodded the corpse with the toe of his boot as if expecting it to move, until one of the troopers, taking this as a signal of their lack of seemliness, felt round for the black camera-cloth and covered up Schmidt's lower parts. While Valerian stood so close above them, they broke off the task and slid back on their heels to accept the strong cigarettes which the quartermaster handed round in his canteen.

"Igor," said Valerian. "Tell me what you think. Was this an accident?"

This time Igor did not look up. Across his head Valerian was staring directly into the eyes of the huntsman. The Cossack's answer came unspontaneous; the answer to a question which had already been asked, decided and ought not to be revived. "Yes," he said. "As your honour knows. It has to be so."

"That miserable devil loved you," said Belyakov to Valerian.

"Bosh," exclaimed Polly. "The man was a menace. If you hadn't been such a soulful Christian you would have killed him yourself when you had the chance, but now the milk's spilt, it's a family matter and nobody else's business."

He looked at his wife without seeing her and remembered that bright morning on the Stochod road when Valerian had shot the officer. "By God, Valerian Isayevich, I should have left you to rot years ago. I ought to have known you by this time," he said. "Do it to him, do it to us – no one is safe from now on." And Belyakov continued to remember Major Alekseyev, and Major Alekseyev's widow. "Where is she then, your woman?" Once, twice, he had saved her life. Her third time might have come and gone. "Where have you hidden her?"

The soldiers have hidden her, knelt in the ditch to cover her body against what they had done. He waited, sure that this was true. He had seen it done, the boy had done it before. Afterwards he was always the same – calm, impassive, severe.

Polly tamped the crown of a bowler over the crush of her hair. "Well, I never, my dear, so *that's* our little worry, is it? Don't you trouble yourself about that madam; I'm perfectly sure Natalya Igoryevna is making herself comfortable somewhere, without any thought for the likes of you."

Follow him, little wife, follow him, and in the night they will come for you, too.

"Shut your stupid mouth, woman," Valerian shouted. "You understand nothing." Almost imploringly he held out his arms to Belyakov. "I did my best to protect her, Vlady. I tried, you know that, but she was wilful, refused me, would not take care . . ." As Valerian continued to berate himself in this wild reversal of mood, Belyakov drove home his intuition.

"You mean she's dead, don't you, boy, and you know more, you know who killed her, only it's hard, isn't it, to get that out – you know, though, you know, don't you . . . ?"

It took a while for the implication to register with Polly. "Oh no, that can't be . . . Not my brother, he couldn't have, he loved her." She stood up to put the question direct. "You did, didn't you?"

Valerian scuffed his boot down Schmidt's naked side. "Look no further," he said.

Belyakov's anger blazed out in a roar which made Polly quake, expelling all the guilt for his knowledge, so long suppressed, of the circumstances of the husband's murder and the man who had committed it; knowledge which had always so shamed him in Natalya Igoryevna's presence. "You blasted scheming liar, Valerian Isayevich. That pathetic fawner couldn't have killed any woman, never mind the one you'd taken to wife. He was soft, man, too soft, a feeler, and that did for him, didn't it? A touch was all he ever wanted, a quick rub up from master or mistress. That's all. No, not him, not him. You killed her, didn't you, *brat*, like you killed her first man? Once you drew the line at women, but it took a woman, a wilful woman, hard, a woman like her, to rob you of your last little scruple. Women, children, innocent or guilty, they're all one and the same to you now."

Igor leapt up. "Here, this isn't right, I'm not taking bollocks from a runty civilian." Before Valerian could restrain him he had spreadeagled Belyakov on the ground. "You learn some discipline, Blabberlips," he grunted, reversing the rifle between their bodies."Or this won't be the last smack your mauling gob gets from me." And he brought up the butt-end of the stock twice into the huntsman's jaw, and would have gone on oblivious to Polly's squeals and his officer's commands, until his comrades dragged him off, still protesting: "Well, he got what was coming, stupid bastard, didn't listen like his honour told him – never harmed the female, risked his life for her, but when she'd gone he had to get even. Makes sense to me. What more does a bloke want?" he asked Apollonya Dmitryevna. "Isn't that right, missis?"

Later that day Polly was at the far end of Volkov's map-wagon stooping over a wide basin, naked to the waist. When Valerian entered she turned without covering herself, and let fall the sponge.

"Sister," he said. "What is to be done with your man?"

"He was no man to me, brother, so why do you ask?"

"Because he saved you. As once he saved me."

"Then he has fulfilled his existence, my dear." She seated herself on Volkov's camp-stool and smoothed back the damp hair at her temples. "So what further use can he have?"

Valerian crouched down before her, resting his chin between her knees. In the early evening shadow his eyes seemed a vivider, gentian-ella blue. Polly eased him closer by playful stabs under the curls at the nape of his neck.

"He's been frightfully rude, you know, and not just to me. Some of the men wanted to beat him. Murder might have been done, but it's no good trying to reason with such brutes because they took no notice when I said he had his good side underneath all that spite . . ."

For a while the soft voice flittered on, quieter and quieter, making sense only as accompaniment to the dance of her fingers on the line of his upturned mouth, feeling open the lips with her strong unvarnished nails. Clasped in this queer embrace the boy's gorse-flower hair mellowed to olive against the dusk of her underskirt imbued with the citrus tang of sweat and a characteristic *odor di femina*. The voice came on, remorselessly, warm, urging: "Let us make up to him for what he has lost, poor Vlady. It was not his mistake, he cannot be blamed. Give him two horses, his gun and provisions and allow him to go. He has the skills to live."

Valerian smiled up, fronting the press of Polly's rose-mallow breasts, with no thought other than that of justice and the pleasure of this companionability with his sister's body. *Flesh of one flesh.* "Would you like that?"

Beneath his gaze Polly felt herself uncontract and the silverworm tingle made her jut at his face. "You know I would." She could not understand why the boy withheld his beautiful mouth.

"Would he like that?"

"Oh, he would, he would, I know he would." The whisper was guttural now, almost a sob; her touch harsher, straining.

"Are you my sister?"

"Whose else am I? Yes . . ."

"Are you his wife?"

Under this relentless cross-questioning Polly began to doubt her choice of moment. Perhaps the transition had been too brusque, perhaps he was tired. Perhaps, God forbid, he was shocked. "Only in name."

"Only in name?" said Valerian. "You forget, my love, that I united you in marriage."

Polly stiffened in distaste. "But that was make-believe, surely, only a game?"

"For you, apparently, but then, poor Vlady was never a match for your sophistication."

"Oh God," cried Polly, pushing him away. "How horribly mean. Are a few silly words recited over my head going to bind me forever to that vile-tempered creature who couldn't even . . . ?"

"Sacramentally," said Valerian. "So you must go with him as a sister, if not as a wife."

"I shall stay with you. With you I shall be both. Let me stay."

"I have known that all along." The boy got to his feet. "That is why you should go."

Polly could not believe him, not now, after they had touched and he was so near, and had confessed to her effect. "It's that cat Loulou, isn't it? She was frightfully bossy, you know, it wouldn't have worked with a man like you." True sisterly tenderness could be enough now that Loulou was gone. "Hardship never was her *forte*, she was much too spoiled and vain to have stuck with you. Believe me, my dear, I grew up with her."

Apparently unmoved but in no hurry to leave, Valerian was mooching among the heap of charts and notebooks which Polly had swept off Volkov's table in order to make room for her basin. Now and again he extricated an article of her clothing, handing it back without a word until Polly had accumulated a large bundle. She resisted his implied request to cover herself by rolling the clothes into a tight ball in her lap and pummelling them like a washerwoman. "That rubbish could be valuable," she said, stretching out a toe to point at Volkov's papers. "Gosh, he was thorough. There are lists and lists. The things he knew about people! Even us – especially you, of course, that goes without saying, but there's miles of stuff about quite ordinary individuals. Very useful to weed out malcontents because now you'll need to do that, won't you? I mean, after you were betrayed and everything?"

Although she had not read Volkov's files she had guessed correctly at their contents; and not surprisingly, since a lot of the material about members of the community had come from her. "I could be quite good at that sort of thing."

Anything, anything, I would do anything for you, to others for you, with others for you, to you, with you . . .

Valerian seized the basin, held it still for a moment before tipping a stream of orange-scented water onto Sergeant Volkov's laboriously-assembled memoranda. "Where *we* are going," he said, carefully replacing the empty container next to Polly's soap, "we shall do our own book-keeping."

Alone afterwards in the wagon, Polly stripped herself naked and posed, until dusk had long become dark, in front of the wide fragment of pier-glass at which Sergeant Volkov had been accustomed to shave. Each segment of her body reflected back in the mirror seemed to add up to a triumph of nature so flawless that she would have wished there and then to present it whole to Valerian. But the time would come, she had only to wait. Meanwhile she must formulate her demands, as the sergeant used to say: she simply *must* have some new clothes.

In the late twilight a lone boy on a horse came at a walk down the old carriage road. The boy was weeping and very dirty.

From a long way off Valerian recognised them both. "Mischa," he called out. "Where did you find him?"

At the sound of Valerian's voice Mischa reined in the horse which was stretching its neck towards his master, and broke into sobs. "I'd shoot me, if I was you," he howled at a distance. "I deserve it, being sorry's no good. I'm useless, I've always been useless."

"Accept it, Mischa; the house will outlive us all." There was a sombre finality in Valerian's words which made the boy shiver, and he slid down from Emir's broad grey back, rubbing his eyes on his sleeve.

"I suppose you must be right. Does that mean you're not angry with me?"

Valerian only laid his hand on the boy's head and smiled. "Your friend – what's his name – he was your friend, wasn't he? – Viktor. Yes, Viktor, he made it back to camp over an hour ago."

Having seen the howitzer founder Mischa had watched helplessly while the tiny steam pinnace was dragged into the tailrace of the sinking lighter, and had given the mulemaster up for dead. He let go with a whoop of joy.

"Nearly drowned and a little concussed, but recognisably your man," Valerian went on. "No sign of sergeant or corporal, though. Such good chaps, too. A pity, a pity."

There was no trace of regret in Valerian's voice as he sprang onto Emir's back and rode away. Yet although neither Myelnikov nor Volkov was a seemly object for grief, Valerian was now more than ever preoccupied with the dead, and spent the remaining hours of daylight threading through the ruined park with a burial party, marking out on the endpapers of one of Sergeant Volkov's used notebooks the positions of the makeshift graves which his sappers dug. Some bodies could not be found; many were unidentifiable; and only he knew where lay the bodies of the captain and Natalya Igoryevna. This information he kept to himself. At dusk he returned to the camp but the work went on all that night under lanterns.

When the engineers trooped back exhausted in the early morning Valerian was asleep. The clatter of their spades woke him and he lay for a long while thinking about Mischa; and wished he could have shouted back before the turning of the road cut him off from view, that the failure hadn't been Mischa's but his own in not telling the child, face to face, that it was not acid he had used in the fuse-cones but holy water from the phial Valerian had taken from the priest he had murdered the day before Natalya Igoryevna's arrival at the house.

VI

PAVEL

Midsummer Day 1918

41

They had taken turns to keep watch. Yasha's fifth spell came in daytime but sleep was hard to resist. All sounds of battle had long ago ceased and now there seemed nothing to listen or look out for, so while Loulou slept below, he leafed through the captain's papers in the tree hide, searching for something to read. After a while, the tight upright handwriting began to hurt his eyes; in any case the subject matter – appreciation reports full of technicalities and graphs – was too boring to keep him awake. Then he remembered the cards which had lain untouched in his belt pouch since the captain died.

They were print sure enough, mostly Gothic and Roman, embossed on brilliant white card. Slowly Yasha fixed them with map-pins one above the other along the central bole of the hide. Same size, same feel, same colour, but different wording each time: Jäger, Cornelius, Overweg, Janisch, Schultz, Senff–Pilsach. The jobs they had, these guys: adjutant to a lieutenant-general, hydraulic engineer, secretary to the Oberberghauptmann of Bautzen, flax merchant, even a confectioner from Thuringia and a select florist; addresses in Rouen, Karlsbad, Budapest and Sydney, New South Wales, Australia. Friends? Business associates? A careless first glance would leave that impression, but taken all together the cards had a standard quality which intrigued Yasha: as if they were some kind of issue, like boots or rounds of ammunition.

Two-thirds a trade directory, the rest a roll-call of European nobility. Rempen, I. F., Dealer in fine wheat. That was Russian. So was aide-de-camp to General Zveryev, Ritter von Kreis; and Ballet, manufacturer of chocolate. What had the languid old fox been up to? Then it occurred to Yasha that he had never known the captain by name, not his own, only by the one Loulou in her distraction had stuck on him. And that gave the key to his game: normally the captain would have made his own presentation and backed it up with the gilt-edged pasteboard of one of these identities. Bearing, manner, accent, nerve – he had all the doings to pull off a creditable performance as secretary to the provincial governor or an expert in imported agricultural plant. Played right, these cards could have dodged him from Little Russia to Le Havre with nobody the wiser to who he really was and what he did.

Rain was pattering on the leaves overhead as Yasha searched the run of cards for a suitable alias. Two could play at that game. Humperdinck. God, that'd be like wearing a bell round your neck. Nitschmann? Nebe-Pflugstädt? No point in going any further, they were all suitable, all dwarf-sounding names. No, that wasn't the problem. He stood on tiptoe and stretched out his neck. Not a chance – a dwarf needed more than a name to lengthen his legs.

A cool one, my captain, quite capable of setting out on a stroll two or three thousand miles long, just as his many brethren were probably doing at this very moment. Some hopes for Rubin, alias *Zwerg*.

Besides, there was the woman.

Two days he'd been with her after they'd tidied up the remains of the captain. On the path to the hide she was quiet and submissive, even when he lost the way. Brooding. With that, and the noises, his first night had been bad. She slept like a baby, twelve hours, but in the restive dark of the forest he thought he heard footfalls; and once, he could have sworn, someone whispered her name.

The sun came up with rain clouds while she was still uneasily dreaming, calling out in her sleep, and he had covered her with the shalloon bags that Myelnikov used to store his carbine magazines.

The howitzer shell came without warning. Literally out of the blue, sweeping a hot wind over the clearing and blanking out the sun. The field battery took up the signal, and thudded in rapid-fire, quickening the very roots of the trees. Too terrified to move, Loulou had burrowed her head into his jacket and they both sprawled in the open under the oak-apples plopping from shaken branches. At the outset he had swiftly deduced that they were way off the reach of fire, but when the bombardment stopped as suddenly as it had begun, he would not let her get up until the spat of heavy machine-guns signified that the infantry battle had begun.

In the late afternoon Loulou poked her head through the floor-trap of the hide, her face as moody as ever amidst its floppy nimbus of uncut curls. "You're doing no good here," she said. "Come down and help me with the man. He won't wake up."

"Be damned if I will. Thought you were a nurse, you've got bandages and iodine-stuff out of the captain's box so slap them on, why can't you?"

Now she was awake, his spell ought to have been up, but Yasha went back to his cards determined to keep going until the patient came to. He might have it in mind to massacre them both the minute his eyes opened. How much longer was the reptile going to sleep?

Myelnikov had barged in on them, more dead than alive, long after all sounds of battle had faded, and collapsed at Natalya Igoryevna's feet, eyes rolling. After she stripped off his sopping combat outfit, he looked like a drowned newt that couldn't seem to hear or even see them. Hoping against hope that the corporal was too far gone ever to recover, Yasha nevertheless helped to roll him up in the captain's horse blanket and stow him away as far as possible from the Madsen.

If death had obliged the impeccable captain to turn in his disguises perhaps the corporal would rise up to greet them as strangers. Yasha had liked the captain, even admired him, but he wasn't anyone the boy had ever known, so should the woman condemn herself because Valerian had similarly taken her in?

The cards flickered in the play of light through the slits of the hide.

It was cold. Yasha came out of a deep sleep, squealing from the vicious cramp in his legs. In the centre of the clearing Corporal Myelnikov looked up from the pile of sticks he was blowing into flame. "Told you about that before," he called cheerily. "Does a lad harm, galloping his maggot in the wide-open spaces."

The boy hobbled across, rubbing his calves. The turf was already hot at the bottom of a neat little trench the corporal had scooped in the sand. They took turns to bellow it up.

"What's going on?" bawled Yasha between puffs.

"A spot of homeliness, that's what." Myelnikov cupped his hands against the sparks which popped out haphazard from the tinder-dry brush.

"Bit risky, isn't it, I mean, with the smoke . . . ?" This remark, too, was shouted very loud.

"All right, sonny, all right, no need to kick up a dido. Ears is on the mend and the brain has never been more pristine. Ask her."

Myelnikov knew Natalya Igoryevna was there, behind them. Yasha turned. The tight ragged frock had been discarded in favour of a soldier's loose blouse and breeches. In her arms was a cylindrical silk bag which had once contained sticks of field-gun propellant. "Will this do, Pavel Aleksandrovich?"

"Put it down there," said Myelnikov without looking round. "Can't you see, I've got work to do." He resumed blowing alone, and clucked his tongue at the fire as if coaxing a pet animal.

Yasha watched her take out a tin, scrutinise it for damage before replacing it carefully in the bag, seemingly unaware or indifferent to his presence. Only when he moved into touching distance did she speak: "They have gone, Yashichka, while you slept. Pavel Aleksandrovich saw them go, every last one . . ."

The expressionless voice trailed away.

Yasha peered under the smoke from one to the other, mystified by the intimacy between her and the corporal. Her eyes were swollen from weeping. His face, which Yasha was inspecting for the first time deprived of balaclava and camouflage smears, was that of a still young-ish man; a face that, given time, nice things might happen to the owner of.

"How long have I been asleep?"

"Fifteen, sixteen hours."

A whole day and half a night. Plenty of time.

They drank sweet black tea and ate with their fingers from a communal dish of melted cheese and breadcrumbs which sat cooling on the grass by the side of Myelnikov's kettle. It was frugal but more than enough. Replete, they grew listless, except for Yasha whose curiosity had revived.

"What about him, then?"

Natalya Igoryevna looked so barnstorming tragic he left out the name but Myelnikov knew who she meant. "Search me," he said, stamping the heel of his boot on the rim of the trench until another dry sod fell into the flames.

"Dead, maybe?" There was always hope.

The corporal gave a shrug and looked away from Loulou into the heart of the fire. "Not so as you'd notice. Leastways, not when I last saw the bugger."

"Gone, though, you said?"

"Not me, Twinkle, I told you – ask her."

But Loulou had no story to tell, not of her own; so she told Myelnikov's and as he listened Yasha began to understand why the corporal refused to tell it himself at first.

After the lighter went down Myelnikov, who could hardly swim, had somehow dog-paddled ashore and wandered half-deaf and in a daze through the old fire zone, up to the house.

"He saw all of it," said Loulou. "All the terrible things that the shells did, but the most terrible thing was how the injured people were left to die while Valerian brought everyone out of the house as if no one else mattered."

"Devilish," murmured the corporal. "And the devil alone knows how he did it or why they let him. Out they came, your mates, to join mine, not one of them firing a shot."

Myelnikov had been unarmed, otherwise he might have let fly

418

with a winger himself, mesmerism or no mesmerism, regardless of consequences, but he must have passed out for a bit because next thing he remembered he was lying in a shell crater. Valerian was further off this time, the house people seemed to have disappeared, and the boy was alone except for some troopers from the maze who were scuffling on the ground over a body that got eventually slung into a cart and wheeled away. "A peep out of me and I would have been next on the list, specially when I ought to have gone to the bottom with old Volkov like he'd worked out we should when *Babs* did her bit. Perfect, that was, having us out of the way. He never meant to blow that house. I warned Volkov but it was too late by then, and he was a fool anway, too webbed up in his paperwork to reckon he could be thimble-rigged by a kid not much older than our wagon-boy."

Yasha shivered at the accuracy of the captain's prophecies. "So you beat it home, back to mother?"

Loulou blushed defensively. "Pavel Aleksandrovich has behaved most nobly, Yashichka. Why, hours before you woke he made another sally out into the park, although he felt most unwell. Tell him what you saw, Pavla."

Oh, yes, do, tell me what you saw, Pavlushka, you screaming piratical renegade, thiever of better men's women, tell me.

"Wagons, a string of them, moving south."

"So you see, my dear," said Loulou. "Valerian never made any attempt to search for us."

Yasha remembered the mysterious voice that first night, the calling of her name, the smash of branches round the hide, and he understood why she was lying. Eventually she'd come to believe that Valerian had abandoned her, so as to feel better at having abandoned him first. A girl's game she'd not yet grown out of. "My life, what a pair of big soft lasses you make," he said. "Hoodwinked by the Sacred Heart of Judas. Oughter be stitched in sackcloth, you two, back to back."

This last sparked off Myelnikov. "Hey, smouch, think I'm enjoying this? How'd you feel if some plush-bum had made a travesty of your best inclinations?"

That it wouldn't be the first or the last time.

"You watched us away from my captain, you saw her white-headed boy surrender his weapon and trot behind me down to the sergeant like a foundling nosing for tit?"

Something like that Yasha had seen.

Myelnikov flicked his right index finger back and forth magisterially. "Well? How'd you reckon you'd feel?"

Just as Yasha did each time he fell for their *schmus*. "You only got took in like everyone else. No need to make a song and dance out of it."

The corporal disagreed. His pride had been hurt. "*I'm* not everyone else. When your Ma was cutting bread on you, squidge, I was cutting barbed wire. You think I didn't know him properly – that's what she says too."

Loulou's cheeks glowed red from the fire and her humiliation.

"In this day and age," said Myelnikov portentously, "you don't often come across real love."

This was too much for Yasha who confronted Loulou directly: "When are you gonna give that old tune a rest? Since you and me first took to the road you've been rattling on about fancy-men." A shower of endearments had even come his way over there in that place. It was her tactic and she was plying it now like a veteran. While he'd been asleep she must have broken down in front of the corporal and confided all. You bet. Nothing less would have sweetened his pickle.

"Watch your mouth, you," said Myelnikov. "What do you know about feelings? She's been crying because he won't have her no more."

"And I suppose he's stuck under a bush somewhere howling his eyes out, vice versa?"

"Don't think he won't, neither. He'll have his regrets, no bones about it."

"Still think you know him, do you, can still read his mind?"

Myelnikov squeezed Loulou's knee. "Don't let him worry you, missie, it's lack of experience that makes him cynical. No man could lie easy after losing a lady such as you. I know, it happened to me."

"No more, Pavel Aleksandrovich," whispered Loulou, breaking the silence at last. "Please."

The glimmer of nostalgia died in Myelnikov's eyes. "Deserted me, in the end, anyway, my old woman. When I came back on first leave in '16 she'd pledged the house to the village store-keeper for forty roubles and took off with a Jew-pedlar. Demolished, I was. Cried like a kid. Once in a lifetime, that kind of feeling."

The irrelevance of this oppressed Yasha. By rights of long service he should have been the one comforting her, not this scadger. "Waste of time, that stuff. Look where it's landed the pair of you."

Loulou spoke again so quietly that he couldn't catch what she said but the corporal nodded morosely, pursing his lips round a non-existent cigarette. The captain had long since exhausted the supply of tobacco. "Don't mind me, missie. I'm only a sweatpig ex-combatant who's lost his bearings. I'll never serve again, not if I can help it, not after that smirking Lucy-boy ran me up my own touch-hole."

"Very noble," said Yasha. "So what are you going to take up? As far as I can see you're qualified for nothing except doing damage. In any case, you can't just cash yourself out of an army. They'll docket you for a criminal and hound you down if you skip."

Over the camp fire Myelnikov clinched with Yasha's contemptuous stare. "My, my, shag-face is trying to learn me a lesson."

"Well, it's true, isn't it? You're an outlaw, now, and we'll be in it too for harbouring you, and all because of that madman whose lies you swallowed."

"I'm no criminal," said Myelnikov. "I'm what I always was – a political. When I goes underground stay close and they'll have a job to pin anything on us. But that's beside the point, lad. Her and me, we've been wounded in the spirit. *Maimed.*" Proudly he repeated the word. "And it's better owning up to it than making up stories about yourself."

"Go on," scowled Yasha. "You're make-believe up to the eye-balls, just another bloody romancer."

Myelnikov paid no attention to him. "Take the lady here," he said. "This lady offered to a man the sum total of her existence, but the man she extends that devotion to is only a reprobate, a partial member of the human race. Now, I've spent my life in the service which is a similar dissembling beast, and like her I've given it enough. In a manner of speaking, in point of service to the evil ways of men, we're on the same footing, we've both had enough. But that doesn't mean we can't weep for our loss. Cry away, missie, then have a good nap and wake up a new woman. There's only three rules for this life: mistrust the authorities as much as the opposite sex, don't write things down, and never go to sea. I ought to know, I've done them all."

Natalya Igoryevna woke at the turn of day and lay on her side watching the night sky thin between the leaves. Almost midsummer. Last Midsummer Day, on the roof, she had woken with Yasha.

Me and my friend Pavlushka are playing with our soldiers.

Fragmentary, dry, a line from a book, a child's book, messages laid on the page like the pressed cornflowers, stiff and blue; that book, the Laskorin children's book. *We can put them all out in one go on my Daddy's big table.* Pavel, Pasha, Pavlushka, the new friend. Corporal Pavel Aleksandrovich Myelnikov, the new big friend. *We make up rules with a dice. If you throw a six you knock down one soldier.*

The book and the dice and the flowers and the table had blown into the fire of the soldiers and been consumed. *Kill all, kill dead.*

Petya had not had the luck of his bastard half-brother: six after six, the luck of the devil, the fey doom of legend in children's books. *They take ever such a long time to set up before you kill them.*

But Petya had not been beautiful. What, then, did he share with Valerian?

She still could not know if the cry she had uttered from the top of the ladder in scorn and despair, that cry which had prompted Masha and Matryona to try to finish her but which had led to their own deaths, was plain, simple truth. It was too early to tell. Already she was more desolate than Mademoiselle Brancas could have felt when she gave birth to Valerian; even more friendless. And this child, if it came to exist, Valerian's child, would it grow up to be a match for its father, or a throwback to the ugly doomed little boy, the half-uncle Petya? It would make no difference. The child's graceless formulae blundered in her head like errant bees: *Kill them all. It takes ever such a long time.* It always did.

Now Valerian again came to her only in dreams calling out in that old imperious way, but when she woke he had changed into Yasha who shouted that no one was there and told her to sleep. She knew that real sleep would not come until she was free of the blond boy: *Kill them, kill them all . . .*

Apprehensive at the prospect before them Yasha had argued for a respite of twenty-four hours in which to recuperate. Instead of reply Myelnikov packed up his Madsen and strapped the long box to the boy's back. Who knew when it might come in handy? If they had no use for the weapon themselves they could sell or barter it for safe passage; meanwhile Yasha could start by learning to love it.

Out in the park, stumbling under the heavy, awkward shape, he felt like a child carrying its cross.

Except for a flock of bunting crows circling the high parapets, the house appeared virtually the same as he remembered it from before the battle. On this side there were none of the gaping holes which the noise of the barrage had led him to expect. Taking Myelnikov's lead, Loulou skirted the gravel drive, leaving Yasha to make his way through a quagmire of wheel-rutted mud, shredded sacking and rags that marked out the turning circle of the cumbrous wagons in which Valerian had evacuated the remnants of his community. On an improvised billboard hanging from a trace-harness slung between two trees was a notice which she read aloud:

"'DANGER: HIGH EXPLOSIVE. DO NOT ENTER. STATE PROPERTY. LOOTERS WILL BE SHOT. BY ORDER. KABALYEVSKII, M.A.'"

After the name came his rank and the title of the unit he commanded.

"My God, he meant it," she murmured to Yasha. "He was deadly serious, even to becoming a new person."

The corporal moved her on with a gentle push. "No sense in loafing, then, is there? Best make tracks before the State has a fit of efficiency and sends out a search-party to squat on its proprietorial rights. Tomorrow we want to be on the far side of that river."

Yasha heaved up his burden and followed north.

At midday they arrived at the ford but the river was so swollen that the shallows were lost under turbulence and there was no chance of a safe-crossing. The woman and the boy were exhausted already, forlorn at the nature of the journey upon which they had embarked.

Myelnikov gazed over the waters, scrubbing his yellow teeth with a chewed end of twig. "Ten miles on there used to be a raft-ferry for transporting cattle. It may still be usable. We'll push on and see what's what."

Ah, Kostya, it was so long ago, Loulou intoned to herself. Why did you not kill me then? Aloud, she said: "Pavel Aleksandrovich, do we have to cross this river?"

"We do."

"Because we're going west, like the captain wanted," said Yasha.

"Poland? Are we really going to Poland? I have family in Poland, distant, but still family."

"Poland? I know Poland. You can keep it – and your family. I've had enough of both of them, like I've had enough of it here. Anywhere's better – except Poland. West," went on Yasha, after a sullen kick at the Madsen box. "Right to the water. Then I'll get a boat and sail to America. That's what I'll do. I'll get one from Holland, or from France, somewhere like that, and I'll go to America. They like people like me, Americans. I'll get there if I have to walk every step of the way."

Myelnikov spat out the twig pulp and tightened his belt. "All in good time," he said. "You can part the waters later, short-arse, but do us a miracle now and get stepping out under that tin."

Still dogging the course of the river they reached a run of larch copses at the northernmost tip of the estate where the old railway track steered off from the river. The bed of the line was still traceable under the grass, and Loulou recognised the ground which she and Yasha had traversed the year before.

"Last view," announced Myelnikov.

Loulou stared back. The house had hardly altered since that summer when she had caught her first glimpse of it between the trees. Valerian had said that the end would come in a rending of land and sky, but the house still perched there, crookedly, like a bird on the brink of sleep. With his passion for continuity Kostya had been a truer prophet. They had cut down his beloved trees but new ones would be rooted; Martin's beautiful railway had been scattered, but it would be relaid when Valerian–Kabalyevskii returned in a celluloid collar and buttoned-boots to issue commissarial edicts in the name of a new Kostya, a new Martin, as pure and formidable in his certainties as they had been.

"You know, I never seen the inside of that place," said Myelnikov.

"It was like a great ship. At Christmas they lit two thousand white and silver candles." And she wondered if one day soon he would also tell her what she did not know.

While they talked Yasha had dumped the box and was helping himself to the food in the provision sack.

"Hey, you!" shouted Myelnikov. "Go easy. Don't stuff it in. We've a hard march ahead with plenty of time for feeding. Ration yourself, boy, and feel the benefit."

"Yeah," said Yasha through a mouthful of cake. "Like they did with the Christmas candles? I don't want to be a kill-joy, Corporal, not when you're communing so nice with the lady, but all your sort ever got from her sort was a box of matches to light them up with."

For a while they rested and ate together before resuming their journey. By evening the trees were thickening into woods and the moon rose, but it was still light. Tomorrow the crossing, then forest, nearly all the way to the sea.

Note on Battles

Przemyśl (Russian: Peremyshl), Austrian fortress in Galicia (now south-east Poland) covering crossing of River San stormed by Russian South-West Army Group 5–8 October 1914.

Despite repeated onslaughts by infantry in which 73rd Crimean, 76th Kuban, and 75th Sevastopol regiments showed much valour, Russian attacks were beaten back by machine-gun and artillery fire from Austrian fortified emplacements. Commander of 19th Infantry Division wired Gen. Shcherbachev at Army HQ: "17.21 hrs 6 October: Assault in force ineffective without total destruction of enemy armoured artillery strongpoints by our own heavy artillery . . ." Since the main Russian armament consisted of 76-mm. light field pieces, with only a handful of 152-mm. howitzers, the request was a futile cry from the heart, and the armoured cupolas of the Austrian guns remained intact along with much of the perimeter barbed wire. Next day the attack was stood down.

Afterwards Gen. Brusilov admitted that although "artillery preparation could not be intensive or prolonged owing to the shortage of shells" he was convinced that the assault might have been carried by the outstanding courage of the Russian infantry. Such vaunts, however just, demonstrate the professional incompetence of the Russian High Command which continued to shift the blame for its failures until late 1917. (Quotations from Major General E. Z. Barsukov, *Artilleriya russkoy armii 1900–1917 gg.*, Moscow, 1948. Author's translation.)

Lemberg, Polish city (now L'vov, Western Ukraine, USSR).

After the failure of the assault Russian Third Army (Gen. Radko Dmitreyev) laid siege to Przemyśl which eventually fell to Eleventh Army (Gen. Selivanov) 22 March 1915. At the beginning of May the Germans under Mackensen drove the Army Group back on the San after breaking through the Russian line in Galicia, and brought up a siege-train of 420-mm. howitzers to Przemyśl easily reducing the forts which the Russians had failed to destroy the year before. By now in full retreat the Russian armies fell back towards Lemberg fighting a magnificent rearguard action in which III Caucasian particularly distinguished itself. Orderly withdrawal continued after ammunition was exhausted and all the heavy artillery lost. On 19 June Mackensen separated Third and Eleventh Armies (Gens. Lesh and Brusilov) confronting Brusilov at a fortified position west of Lemberg which the Russians held for three days while Third Army made for Lublin. It was his experience of these three days which came to haunt Valerian. At the end of June, after Brusilov had managed to extricate himself and retreat to the Upper Bug River, Russian losses were 400,000 prisoners and 300 guns. Mackensen was made up to field marshal after the 1915 battle.

Gen. Radko Dmitreyev and Gen. Russki, his predecessor in command of Third Army, were lynched by their troops in Pyatigorsk during the 1917 Revolution. A similar fate overtook Gen. Dukhonin, the last Imperial Army C-in-C. The happiest lot fell to Gen. Brusilov who became reconciled to the Soviets, remained a keen Moscow racegoer, managed the State studfarms, and died in bed in 1926.

Stochod, River in White Russia joining River Pripet about 100 km. north of Lutsk and 300 km. west of Kiev.

The Russians held a bridgehead on the Stochod at Tobol facing the German *Ostfront* line Riga–Carpathians (C-in-C Prince Leopold of Bavaria). On 4 April 1917 German troops captured the position by *coup de main* and the Russians deserted or surrendered without a fight. Concluding that the enemy before them was utterly demoralised by peace propaganda and war-weariness and might collapse along the whole extent of the front, German High Command pressed Gen. Dragomirov (Northern Army Group) for an immediate armistice which would have released troops for their hard-pressed armies on the Western Front. Dragomirov refused but local truces did break out spontaneously along the line. Although by July the Russians recovered sufficient spirit to resume hostilities, the failure of their last offensives ensured that the break-up of the Army would be final and total.